I0772608

STORMWAKER

SILVETTICA

Published by Silvettica 2023

Copyright © 2023 by Kevin Cox

This novel is entirely a work of fiction. The names, characters and incidents portrayed in it are the work of the author's imagination. Any resemblance to actual persons, living or dead, events or localities is entirely coincidental.

FIRST EDITION

http://www.authorkevincox.com/

STORMWAKER

BEWILDERNESS
BOOK FOUR

KEVIN COX

CHAPTER 1

AMBRIELLE HAD ALWAYS been drawn to the unknown, but this time felt different, as if the universe itself was calling out to her. She had always taken pride in being the one others turned to for help. It was gratifying to feel needed, to be an integral part of solving a problem. But lately, with all her focus on school, she had been left feeling more in need than needed.

When she'd told Gavian she would go to Isodonia with him, she couldn't help but wonder if he truly needed her. Though she supposed Gavian didn't exactly need her for this journey, he wanted her to come. He did want her to come with him, didn't he?

He hadn't exactly asked her to come along, and yet there was a look of excitement on his face when she expressed her desire to join him. It was hard to shake the feeling that she was imposing on his plans. Perhaps she shouldn't have demanded to go, but it had been so long since she had seen him. So long that she almost doubted he was real.

Rummaging through her old collection of plush animals, her hand brushed against something cool and metallic. Immediately, she knew what it was. The air seemed to crackle with newfound energy, as if the very walls themselves pulsed with anticipation. Lifting the silbrace Avo'Doria had given her, Ambrielle felt a rush of excitement wash over her.

Ambrielle quickly changed her clothes. Something about the

azure Elyravesian operations commander uniform made her feel strong. To add to it was her black- and red-striped raestrig skin cloak, a reminder of her skill in killing the wild beast in Anatharia. Maybe it was more luck than skill, but either way, it gave her a sense of power.

Her bedroom, which had become gray with monotony and routine, was now filled with a kaleidoscope of vibrant colors and shimmering light. It was as if the light outside her window beckoned her once again into the unknown, another chance for adventure. Still, something was missing.

She had looked everywhere but could not find them. Her boots made of leathery leaves of balcain, the largest trees in the universe as far as she knew, were not here. They had been handcrafted specifically for her by Corthian on Mekkinspire. She couldn't leave without them.

Returning to the hallway, she leaned against the doorframe of her little brother's room. Ryan and his friend Josh were too involved in the video game they were playing to notice her presence. He was notorious for borrowing her stuff without asking, especially something that looked like it came out of a fantasy movie.

Ambrielle walked into the room, moving clothes, books, and game accessories on the disorganized shelves. "Hey! Stop messing with my stuff!" he shouted from his sitting position on the floor.

As Ambrielle kneeled to peer under his bed, she asked, "Where are my boots, Ryan?"

"Get out of here! I don't have your boots!"

Standing up, Ambrielle strode in front of the TV, blocking his view. "I'm not leaving until you give me the boots." Ryan grumbled as he got up to open his closet. He handed the boots to her and went back to playing the game. At first, she thought he had damaged them but remembered the mekkadium heels had warped during her time in The Hollow, spreading over part of the sides of the boots.

Ambrielle sat behind Ryan and put her arm around him. "Even though you're a cute little thief, I might not see you tomorrow."

He scooted away from her. "Get out of my room."

Ambrielle got up and left the room. She stuck her head back in the doorway for one last look. "Thief."

"Weirdo," Ryan countered.

Heading toward her room, she heard footsteps behind her. She turned around as he wrapped his arms around her, giving her a quick hug before running back to his room. Ambrielle grinned, knowing he didn't want his friend Josh to see that.

"Tell Dad I'm going out," she shouted toward his room. "I'll be back the day after tomorrow . . . probably."

"You're going to be in trouble," he yelled back.

"No, I won't," Ambrielle said, as she sat on her bed, slipping the boots on over her socks. "I'm officially an adult now." She set her phone on the table beside the bed. It would be of no use where she was going. It would only worry her father more if he tried to call and she didn't answer.

Pushing the outside door closed, she paused before taking her hand off the knob. Something was eating at her. Had she forgotten something? No. It was something else. Something almost like dread, but not quite. As much as she wished to know the freedom of doing what she wanted without having to answer to anyone, she couldn't—at least not yet. Opening the door, she rushed to the counter by the refrigerator and grabbed a pen. After quickly writing a note to her dad, she signed it and stuck it under a magnet. Taking a deep breath, she closed the door and dashed through the yard into the pecan grove.

She found Gavian pacing around one of the old trees, breaking off pieces of fibrous green husk from a pecan.

"What kept you?" Gavian inquired as he put the pecan in his pouch.

Ambrielle stepped through the thick grass between the trees. "I wasn't gone that long."

As Ambrielle and Gavian emerged from the grove, the woods greeted them with a sense of peace and tranquility. The sound of rustling leaves filled the air, yellow and orange foliage raining down in the crisp autumn breeze. Swaying to the rhythm of seasonal change, the trees waved to her in recognition. This was Ambrielle's favorite time of year—a short but magical transition between the extremes of hot and cold. The world felt new and full of possibility. "Gavian," she said, and he brought his attention to her while they continued onto the small footpath through the woods. "You did want me to come with you, right?"

Everything seemed to fold back, revealing the dark and still fishing pond. "Of course I do," he said, as they stepped onto the creaky boards of the small pier. In that moment, the forest whispered a sigh of relief. She was glad he answered so definitively.

While they stood at the edge of the pier, Ambrielle smiled, holding the necklace her mother once gave her. As they leapt into the pond, a blur of voices passed by, and for a moment, she thought she would lose consciousness. Her hand found the familiar honeycomb patterns in the soft rock, and she noticed the blue light shining through the tunnel that led to one of the springs of Solsellion.

Ambrielle broke the surface of the water and watched Gavian climb onto the rocks along the edge of the spring. The gentle wind made the long red frond trees rustle against each other as she sat on the familiar stone. She squeezed her clothes, hoping to expedite the drying process. "Gavian," she called out, "how far is the spring that leads to Isodonia?"

"We never found that particular spring," Gavian stared through the trees, ready to move on. "We'll have to go to the Mogantum."

Ambrielle wiped away accumulated dust in the scratches on the stone that formed the words *Beware The Hollow*. "Mogantum?"

"That's what Avo'Doria named the citadel." Gavian took a gold object from his satchel.

Ambrielle moved beside him. "If we haven't cultivated life around its spring, does that mean Isodonia is still in danger?"

"That's what I'm afraid of." He put the golden silbrace on his wrist, and it closed around it. Red lights came on as it activated. "We've found some oases with dried up springs and no vegetation around them. We believe that, in order to drain the world associated with a particular oasis, living things have to be removed from the area."

"And you haven't found all the springs yet?" Ambrielle said.

Gavian turned toward her. "You'd understand if you had been here."

Ambrielle traced her foot across the sand, feeling a pang of guilt when she looked away. "Right. I guess I have a lot to catch up on."

He rubbed his hand on her arm as if recognizing her regret. "I didn't mean for it to come out that way. There are so many springs on this world. It's going to take a long time. Avo'Doria theorizes that there is one spring for every world in the universe containing some amount of organic energy."

"There is that much life in the universe? Wow!"

Gavian moved in closer. She could feel his warm breath on her forehead.

"Progress has been slowed. The Nulthereals have begun to defend certain territories. When we do find a new spring, we have to focus all our attention on it before we can move on," he said. "Otherwise, the Nulthereals will be able to move in."

"It's a good thing you finally remembered everything that happened on Isodonia; you know how to destroy them now."

"We need shadowstone." Gavian reached out to touch Ambrielle's golden-brown hair. "That's why Avo'Doria sent me to Isodonia. Hopefully the shadowstone that remained of the whidge and Nulthereals is still there."

She leaned her head back as he drew near, closing her eyes and anticipating a kiss, but it never came. Their time apart had been long enough that affection seemed awkward and unfamiliar. Maybe he was focused on the mission ahead. Once he found Darby and Dexius, there would be plenty of time for her and Gavian to get reacquainted. Regardless, her confidence in their relationship had taken a hit.

As they emerged from the forest, the sunbaked desert sand came into view, its bright and grainy texture contrasting with the cool shade of the trees they left behind. The dry air carried a faint scent of sagebrush and dust. Gavian led her down the slope of the first dune, the sand shifting beneath their feet as they made their way to a glowing red causeway nestled between two towers sparkling with tiny droplets of sunlight. When they stepped onto the path, Ambrielle felt the surface respond to their weight, digital waves rippling outward from their feet. The path carried them along faster than either of them could walk. This was one technology that she was glad they had brought from Elyravess.

They zoomed along the causeway over the dunes and the small rocky cliffs to the next oasis. Nearing the large citadel where the sentinels and drones had established the new capitol city, Gavian placed his right foot flat on the surface to stop his movement. Ambrielle did the same as he hopped off the causeway onto the sand. Two sentinels flew overhead, circling the area, and an enormous stone door parted from the structure and a sentinel in red armor walked out.

The sentinel came toward Ambrielle, the two in the skies landing on either side of her. All three of them bowed to her, their shadows stretched long in the near-setting sun. Unsure what to do, Ambrielle nodded to each of them. They stood when she did so, and the red one moved closer.

"Commander, you have returned," said the red sentinel. "I relinquish my charge to you."

"She's coming with me, Syra'Dosa," said Gavian. "On the mission to Isodonia."

"Commander?" Ambrielle said. "Me?"

Syra'Dosa turned to Ambrielle. "I would not advise the commander to expose herself to harm."

Ambrielle cleared her throat. "Well, I appreciate that, but if Gavian is going, then I am going too."

Syra'Dosa gave a quick bow of her head. "As you wish. Is there anything you require?"

"Where is Avo'Doria?" Ambrielle inquired, as her mind raced imagining the endless technology the sentinels on Elyravess possessed.

"Avo'Doria is on Elyravess," Syra'Dosa informed her. "She has duties there, just like I have mine."

"Ambrielle may need some extra energy pods for her silbrace," Gavian said.

"Certainly." Syra'Dosa opened a compartment in her shoulder and handed Ambrielle two glowing spheres. "Take mine."

"Oh, thank you." Ambrielle bowed her head in return, trying to hold all the pods in her arms.

"She needs something to carry them in too," said Gavian.

Syra'Dosa rocketed off through the wave-shaped archway of the citadel and quickly returned with a brown satchel. "I have learned that humans prefer flexibility in their storage compartments. Is this true for you as well?"

Ambrielle placed the two energy pods inside and strapped it over her shoulder. "This will do great, thank you."

Gavian seemed in a hurry as he turned, briskly walking toward the forest and the next spring. Ambrielle quickly caught up to him when they reached the first rows of apraeda trees, but Gavian's stride lengthened, and he outpaced her again.

It had only been a year, but seeing these trees again gave her a feeling of nostalgia. As Gavian rushed down a trail between the trees, Ambrielle picked a few of the low-hanging fruits. She took a bite. The taste carried her back to the Kavekkian city on Mekkinspire. It was amazing how tastes and smells could connect you back to an unexplainable feeling associated with something in the past.

Gavian was nearly out of sight as he hurried down the trail. Running to catch up, Ambrielle cut through a group of hovanoke trees. The trail darkened underneath the huge balcain trees where Gavian had stopped to wait for her. These were not as big as the ones on Anatharia, but they were probably still growing.

"Put some of these in your bag." Ambrielle handed him the apraedas.

He didn't reach out to take them. "Why are you picking fruit now? We don't have time for this."

"I couldn't wait." She continued holding the fruit toward him. "I haven't seen anything like this in so long. I don't want to waste them."

Gavian took the fruit and placed it in his satchel, strapping it down to secure the opening. They stopped at the edge of the spring. Ambrielle mentally prepared for the icy cold water.

He stood atop a cluster of jagged rocks facing the water. "See you on the other side," he said, before plunging into the crystal clear liquid and swimming toward the blue cave. Ambrielle took a deep breath and prepared to follow, but a wave of memories washed over her, flooding her mind with images of the past. It was here that she first met Sidaire and where she had once leapt into the spring to escape the oncoming Nulthereals. Through her journeys between worlds, Ambrielle had transformed from a timid soul into a bold adventurer. Standing here once again she didn't feel that same confidence she once possessed. Perhaps her quiet life on Earth had softened her.

The frigid water enveloped Ambrielle, stealing her breath for a moment before she pushed past the discomfort and dove deeper into the blue cave. The cavern loomed around her, its inky blackness becoming a sinister presence that seemed to lurk just out of sight. But the glimmering rays of blue light beckoned her forward, and she pressed on, her heart pounding with equal parts excitement and apprehension.

Emerging on the other side, she was met with the breathtaking beauty of Anatharia, the sun's rays illuminating every detail with a sparkling brilliance. Mekkinspire towered above her as she swam toward the three inlets in the shoreline to her left. Taunsin had told her these three inlets were part of a footprint of an enormous beast that was said to have lived long ago. She couldn't remember the name he'd called it now, but if it were real, Ambrielle would have been nothing more than an ant by comparison.

As she climbed out of the water, the scent of moist earth mixed with the tangy aroma of the lake. Gavian sat on a rock watching some of the alien wildlife gather at the lake to drink. The sound of the animals' excited chattering filled the air. A group of creatures with round, bloated bellies rolled down the slope toward the lake. They wobbled into the water, taking long gulps of the cool liquid. Using their long legs, the creatures rolled themselves back up the banks, their movements leaving deep impressions in the sand.

Ambrielle couldn't help but giggle watching them. "What are those?"

Gavian rubbed the whiskers on his chin. "I don't know. I don't remember ever seeing them." He stood and continued through the blue ferns around the side of the lake. The field had grown thick with bluish green grass. Without the Kavekkian bladestaves standing tall in the earth, it would appear as though no battle had ever occurred in this place.

Among the spears were groups of white crystals stacked together. She guessed the bladestaves and spears stood as markers for the fallen Kavekkians and Darterrans. Ambrielle glanced at Gavian just as he looked to her. Neither said anything, but she was sure he was thinking of the same thing: the loss of Taragris and Raegus when they fought against Medigrin's Darterran loyalists.

As they walked through the area where Raegus and Taragris had lost their lives, Ambrielle couldn't determine which graves belonged to them, but they had to be nearby. She looked up at the mountain, its side bearing the scars of the intense heat from the lykris that had melted and collapsed a portion of the plateau that once housed the market.

Ambrielle wanted to go and see Maetha again, but Gavian seemed anxious to get to Isodonia and find his friends. She would wait until they came through Anatharia on the way back.

Gavian headed toward the forest instead of the steps leading to the cave. "Why are you going this way?" Ambrielle wondered.

"It's the shortest way to the waterfall inside the cave. The Darterrans will be asleep, but they would hear us coming through the entrance."

Ambrielle nodded from her own experience. "You're right, they would."

They entered the forest. Rays of the light of the sun, Versoh, beamed between the blue and green leaves. Between the shadows of the enormous balcain trees, they returned to the spot where the Darterrans set their vecilators to absorb the energy of the sun. A hole in the rock went all the way down to one of the chambers in the cave. It led to where the Darterrans once kept the lykris next to the vault they'd tried so hard to open.

Ambrielle imagined the hole was meant to let sunlight in to energize the lykris so they could use it to burn into the material of the vault. The Kavekkians, who were afraid of the dark caves, hoped to learn more about the technology used by the ancients inside, but the Darterrans were never able to open it.

A loud bang startled Ambrielle as Gavian fired something from his silbrace at a nearby tree. He tugged at a glowing band that was now between his silbrace and the tree. "Hold on to me and don't let go," he said.

She wrapped her arms around his chest. "Are you sure this is safe?"

"Pretty sure." Gavian stepped to the edge of the hole. With the glowing wire taunt, he stepped in.

Ambrielle wrapped her legs around his to make sure she didn't fall. The silbrace made a winding sound, and they descended into the dark chamber. "Can my silbrace do this?"

"I don't think so." Gavian's feet touched the ground. "Avo'Doria made this one specifically for this mission."

Ambrielle loosened her hold on him and dropped to the ground. "What all does it have?"

"Besides the lylace I just used," Gavian said, pointing to a cylinder on top of his silbrace, "it has a lightblade and a lamp to see in the dark."

She looked down at her own silbrace. "I'm not even sure what all mine can do."

They both turned on their lamps, casting light into the dark chamber. The silvery waterfall cascaded through the rocks nearby, its mist enveloping Ambrielle's skin and collecting in tiny cold droplets. Gavian stepped forward, his eagerness to get to Isodonia obvious. Ambrielle's gaze wandered around the cavern as she recalled her previous explorations. In the beam of her silbrace, something on the ground caught her attention. Bright spots of orange scattered across the ground, invisible in the darkness but brilliantly reflective under the light.

Gavian turned as he stood in front of the waterfall. "Are you ready? Let's go together."

"Yes, just a second." Ambrielle traced the orange spots across the rocky surface. They led toward the side of the chamber ahead.

"Did you drop something?" Gavian turned around.

As she stepped toward the wall of the cave, she realized where the spots were coming from. "No, I just wanted to check something out." They led to the vault of the ancients. Ambrielle's heart quickened when she noticed something different about the vault, its shape.

"It's open!" Ambrielle shouted with excitement.

"Not so loud, you'll wake the Darterrans," Gavian said. "Are you coming or what?"

"Gavian, don't you see?" Ambrielle tried to slow her breathing. "The vault they could never crack is open!" She crept over to where the new opening had unfolded. There was a space big enough to walk into but not much more.

Gavian audibly exhaled. "Oh yes, that *is* interesting. It will give us something to do on the way back."

"Are you crazy? We can't leave without seeing what's inside!" Ambrielle nervously stepped into the opening of the vault. "It won't take long."

CHAPTER 2

With caution etched in every step, Ambrielle ventured into the vault, her heart pounding against the eerie silence that enveloped the space. As she crossed the threshold, a shiver raced down her spine, causing the fine hairs on the back of her neck to stand on end. The atmosphere within was heavy, burdened by the stagnant, musty air that seemed to cling to every surface.

The vault's darkness was punctuated by the beam of light from Ambrielle's silbrace, revealing a chilling sight—a row of containers resembling glass eggs. Each one lay empty, silent witnesses to forgotten stories. However, her gaze fixated on one particular vessel, its lid ajar, revealing a pool of dried orange liquid mirroring the dim light that danced upon its surface.

An unshakeable sense of intrusion washed over Ambrielle, as if she had stumbled upon secrets never meant for mortal eyes. Yet, fueled by curiosity and a touch of daring, she pressed forward. Her light, now a lifeline against the encroaching darkness, pierced through the shadows, revealing a hidden passage leading to a set of descending stairs. The descent awaited her, promising unknown depths and perhaps even more enigmatic revelations.

"Are you almost done?" Gavian's voice echoed in the cavern outside the vault. "We need to get going."

Ambrielle started down the stairs. "Almost."

At the bottom of the steps, the corridor ended at a wall of the impenetrable white material. If there was nothing down here, why have stairs? There had to be something beyond this wall. Feeling for any kind of release, she found a surface devoid of any discernable features.

She headed back up the stairs and toward the opening. Ambrielle gave Gavian a pat on the back as she passed by him, her fingers brushing over his clothing.

"Nothing inside?" he asked while Ambrielle quickened her pace, following the trail of orange drops.

"No," she answered. The trail led out of the vault toward the cavern outside.

"So, the Darterrans and Kavekkians spent all that time arguing about opening this thing, and there's nothing inside?"

Ambrielle followed the orange spots out of the vault and into the chamber.

"Where are you going?" Gavian called after her.

Ambrielle followed the trail into a hallway that was carved out of the rock. Long columns stood, decorating the path lit by torches that were mounted on each wall. "Whatever was in there was removed."

"Hold on, we can't go too far in these caves." Gavian started after her. "Medigrin and his followers are still here."

"I'll be quiet," she said, following the splatter of liquid toward the hall junction.

She heard Gavian's footsteps quicken behind her as he spoke. "I thought we were going to Isodonia. I want to find Darby and Dexius as soon as we can," he said, his tone short and curt.

Ambrielle glanced back at him and gave him a reassuring smile. "I know, Gav, but the vault hasn't been opened in thousands of years. There must be a reason that it happened now. It's like . . . we were supposed to find it."

"The only thing we are supposed to do is find shadowstone for Avo'Doria," Gavian said, his voice sharp and clipped. "But for me the priority is finding Darby and Dexius."

"We don't know what was in that vault," said Ambrielle as they came to the intersecting hallway. "Whatever it was, someone went to a lot of trouble to keep it from being opened. It could be dangerous. What if it's a threat to the caves and the mountain? Fegrin and Maetha are our friends too. If something were to happen to them . . . something that we could have warned them about . . ." Guided by the orange drops on the ground, she turned toward the path to the right.

"That way is a dead end," Gavian informed her.

Ambrielle continued ahead. "Well, *something* went this way."

The wall toward the end was not smooth like the rest of the hallway. It was thinner and rough, ending with thick roots and vines coming through the dirt.

"We can't go any further," Gavian said as he caught up. "Let's head back."

"There has to be something here." Ambrielle searched for more orange spots.

"Wait," he said, stepping toward the moss-covered stone. "This used to be a solid wall." Gavian traced his fingers along the rough stone, parting the vines.

Ambrielle pushed aside the twisted roots, forcing her way through the narrow gap behind them. Her pulse quickened when she caught a glimpse of a faint light up ahead. Gavian followed closely behind her after she ducked into the low space. The light grew gradually brighter as they crept closer. Ambrielle's back ached from leaning over, but she wasn't about to stop now. At last, they emerged into a new part of the forest, tucked away between two hills where the ground sloped gently downward. The sound of rushing water to their right suggested they were near the river that flowed through the ravine.

A huge black fowl leapt into the air, gliding off toward the canopy overhead. Ambrielle continued following the trail, sounds of owl-like birds surrounding them. It veered toward the left, leading them under the shadow of one of the great balcain trees.

With the forest darkening, she lost the trail. Backtracking with her light, she couldn't seem to find where it continued after a certain point. She hoped to pick it up again as she moved ahead. Ambrielle made sure Gavian was still behind her and weaved between a group of tall skinny trees. A distant roar made her pause.

"I don't think I've ever been in this part of the forest." Gavian stepped around the crisscrossing thicket. "Now that we are here, I suppose we may as well find out what is making this trail."

Ambrielle stared at the mossy ground between the tall ferns. "Help me look for more of those orange drops." The further she moved, the more difficulty she had navigating the tangled weeds and vines. "I can't seem to find the rest of the trail."

"You're going the wrong way," a male voice called from somewhere in the forest behind them.

Ambrielle and Gavian whirled around. Two small birds flew from their perches as they scanned the area. Ambrielle turned in all directions looking for the intruder. Gavian readied his silbrace, a metal piece lifting out and igniting, causing the blade to glow.

"I mean you no harm," said the unseen voice. "I came to offer my assistance."

"We're fine." Gavian turned to the new direction the voice came from. "We don't need any help."

"I know what you are looking for," it said. "I will help you find it. I only ask a simple favor in return."

Ambrielle moved toward the sound. "I don't even know what we are looking for. How do you?"

"Something passed through these woods recently. It was like nothing I have seen before," he said. "I believe that is what you seek."

"Ambrielle . . ." whispered Gavian with a bit of frustration in his voice. "I don't know if we should be doing any strange favors right now."

"I have seen you before," the stranger said to Ambrielle. "You walked with Maetha in the forest. It is a simple task, only to deliver a message."

Ambrielle perked up. "You know Maetha?"

"I do." The intruder walked out of the thicket. He was dressed in a cloak made of animal skins, thick fur around its shoulders. "Would you deliver my message?" He removed the hood. A Kavekkian, but not one she recognized.

"Who are you?" Ambrielle asked.

The Kavekkian stepped closer. "My name is Kidiru."

Gavian lowered his blade slightly. "Why can't *you* deliver the message?"

"I am no longer welcome on Mekkinspire," Kidiru said.

Ambrielle brushed a cluster of leaves from her view. "You were banished?"

"If the Kavekkians banished you, why should we trust you?" Gavian moved closer to Ambrielle.

Ambrielle turned to Gavian. "I was banished too, remember?"

"That was different," Gavian said.

The Kavekkian sat on an old, knotted root sticking up from the ground. "They banish anyone that doesn't keep to their strict rules."

"Why did they banish you?" Ambrielle stared intently at Kidiru.

The Kavekkian placed his hands together in front of him. "I was lightborn. Born on the first day of the new cycle. According to them, I was chosen by Versoh to study the artifacts of the ancients, to learn their wisdom, and to understand the nature of light and crystals. Most of my childhood was wasted working in the Vaesari citadel, listening to lectures in the courtyard. I was not made for that kind of life."

"Imagine every day looking out at the plains and forests of Anatharia and not being able to walk among their beauty. They wanted me to attend rituals and adhere to their restrictions, but I wanted to be free. I wanted to be a protector, to be out here among the wild. So, I refused my calling, and for that I was banished."

"That's not right," Ambrielle said. "You should've been able to choose to do what you enjoy."

Gavian extinguished the blade. "Sounds like Rethia."

"What did you want us to do exactly?" Ambrielle grabbed the limp end of a tree limb poking at her side.

Kidiru reached inside his cloak and pulled out something small and shiny. Gavian raised his silbrace slightly as Kidiru gave it to Ambrielle. In her hand were two crystals that fit together, a round violet crystal inside a larger crescent white crystal.

"It's beautiful." Ambrielle titled the crystals in her hand, admiring the way they glowed when they caught the sunlight.

"Give it only to Maetha's daughter, Aradel. Let no one else see it,"

Kidiru said. "When you give it to her, be mindful of her reaction. Every detail will be important."

Ambrielle continued to turn the crystals, their light reflecting off the nearby trees. "And then you will help us find what we are looking for?"

"That is my promise," said Kidiru.

Gavian turned to Ambrielle. "You're going to run errands for him now? We were supposed to go to Isodonia, remember?"

"Of course, we are," said Ambrielle. "I just want to see what was in that vault."

"You've already seen inside the vault," Gavian grumbled. "I don't know why you insisted on coming if you don't want to go."

"I insisted?" Ambrielle huffed. "I thought you were glad I came with you. If you want to go so bad, go ahead. I know the way back."

Gavian turned away from her, wiping his face and exhaling loudly. Ambrielle crossed her arms in front of her as tightly as she could, blowing a strand of hair out of her eyes. She didn't expect him to be mad at her for wanting to unravel this mystery. She thought he would be interested too. Maybe they didn't have as much in common as she'd thought. Finding him here had been too good to be real, she should have realized she couldn't be that fortunate.

Ambrielle played the last few moments again in her mind. She understood that he wanted to see his friends. It had been years since he last saw them, but why couldn't he wait a few minutes? Though, when they had been on Solsellion, she'd remembered her friends and her father and brother back on Earth and couldn't wait to get back and see them.

She should probably be more understanding, but at the same time she really wanted to know what came out of that vault. "Gavian." She tried to make her voice sound compassionate instead of frustrated. "I don't want to keep you from finding your friends, but I feel like this could be really important. I need to make sure it's not something that could bring harm to Lon Kavekkia. With the vault right next to the waterfall, we don't know that it won't affect Isodonia either."

Gavian twisted his lips. "I really am glad you are here. I was excited to show you places I had been on Isodonia and introduce you to Darby and Dexius. I just can't stop wondering if they are okay. If I'll ever see them again." A breeze rippled through the yellow hovanoke leaves, making shadows on his face.

"I understand if you want to go on without me," Ambrielle said. "We can meet up after this, and I will still visit your home world and meet your friends."

Gavian turned around for a moment, tapping his fingers underneath his shirt collar. "No," he said. "We need to stay together. This is important to you, just like Isodonia is important to me. If you can promise that, as soon as we find out what happened here, we will go to Isodonia, then I will wait."

Ambrielle looked up at him as he turned around. "Thank you, Gavian, I promise!"

CHAPTER 3

As Ambrielle and Gavian ascended the steps that led to the mountain path, a sense of anticipation mingled with the gentle breeze that caressed their faces. The path stretched before them, carved into the side of the ancient mountain. Black stone, glistening like scattered stardust, adorned the rugged terrain, reflecting the sun's radiant embrace.

"This is where we first met." Ambrielle's voice carried a soft lilt of nostalgia, her eyes sparkling with fond memories.

"I remember," Gavian said, responding with a tender touch, his hand finding its place on the small of her back. The contact offered reassurance, a subtle reminder of the connection they shared. For a brief moment, at least, she felt as though he was still interested in their relationship.

They passed by a doorway, and she recalled that it led to a large room hollowed out of the rock. Ambrielle ran toward it, peeking into the dark. Several sleeping Darterrans were inside, a few turning to stare at her, their fuzzy hair standing on end.

"Sorry," she muttered, and quickly moved away. They walked toward an opening between two tall columns of rock and entered the Darterran city at the first plateau. The trading post, which had been abandoned not that long ago, was now rebuilt with new wooden tables that lined the street.

They continued around the ledge to a set of steps that led them into a tunnel. When they came to the Kavekkian town circle, Ambrielle noticed the part of the entranceway that had collapsed from the damage Medigrin had done with the lykris.

Carefully stepping over a deep crack in the street, Ambrielle and Gavian made it to the busy commerce plateau. Some Kavekkians waited in line at the shops, while others stood in the middle talking. White beams ignited blue crystals that sent blue beams of light zigzagging around the city and into some of the dens, bringing their light inside.

Gavian followed as Ambrielle cut through the crowd, heading toward a gate at the far end. When she moved by the last row of tables, a familiar Kavekkian caught her attention. It was Corthian. His shoe shop had been moved to a different section, but the pleased expression on his face had hardly changed.

Ambrielle made her way over, around the line of Kavekkians waiting at his shop, and to the worktable in front of him. "Corthian!"

He blinked rapidly, stopping his work for a moment to glance toward her. "Ambrielle! Welcome dawn!"

"Welcome dawn." She leaned against the table.

Corthian moved around the worktable and looked down at her feet. "Still wearing the boots, I see!"

"Yes, I can never thank you enough," she said.

"Nonsense," Corthian said. "You more than paid for them." He kneeled, looking at where some of the mekkadium on the heels had melted and hardened on the shaft. "It looks like they are in need of a polish."

She raised her left foot and rubbed the rough texture. "Yeah, I messed them up a little, but they are still great."

"I can repair them," Corthian said. "Won't cost anything. I've heard you were quite the hero in the battle."

"Gavian did more than I." Ambrielle gestured toward Gavian. "He nearly died stopping the Darterrans' lykris."

Corthian turned to Gavian. "Is that so? Well done, my friend, we in Lon Kavekkia owe you a great debt."

Gavian looked a bit embarrassed as he spoke. "It was . . . a team effort."

"Are you going to finish my shoes or not?" said the customer waiting beside them at the table.

Corthian stood and moved behind the table. "Of course, of course, an artist needs a break every now and then."

"It was great seeing you again Corthian," Ambrielle said, moving out of the way.

Corthian waved and got back to work on the shoes. "Come back soon if you want those repairs!"

They passed through the gate and onto a winding set of steps. Further up the mountain they climbed, until they came to another plateau filled with holes and doorways carved into the rock. There were more blue beams crisscrossing into the openings.

Ambrielle spotted the one that looked most familiar, with the little window beside the door. She crept toward the window to peer inside.

Maetha and Taunsin both turned as Ambrielle leaned her head in the doorway. Maetha's rust-colored eyes gleamed with recognition. "Now there's a face I never thought I would see again. My dear Ambrielle, welcome dawn!"

"Welcome dawn, Maetha. How have you been?" Ambrielle stepped into the den instinctively but mentally berated herself for not waiting to be invited in.

Maetha got up from her seat and gave Ambrielle a hug. "I see Gavian found you. Why did you run off like that? Even with your note, we were still a bit worried."

Ambrielle swallowed hard. "I had some things at home that had to be worked out. I couldn't leave again without fixing them."

Maetha moved into her kitchen area while Taunsin sipped on a dark liquid in his cup. "I take it you fixed everything."

"Well, as much as could be fixed." As Ambrielle exhaled a breathy sigh, she caught the scent of woodsmoke from the nearby fire. The warmth emanating from the flames felt comforting against her skin, and the crackling of the logs added a soothing background noise.

"Sometimes that's the best you can hope for." Maetha grabbed a smoking pot from the fire. "Would you like some hot erommos juice?" The aroma from the pot wafted through the air, a sweet, spicy scent with a subtle tanginess.

"I don't know what that is, but I'll try some." Ambrielle stepped further into the room, allowing Gavian to come in behind her.

"Taunsin and I have begun a new tradition." Maetha filled two cups with steaming dark juice from the pot. "When Versoh reaches its highest point in the sky, we stop whatever we are doing and meet here for hot juice. Isn't that right, Taunsin?"

Taunsin muttered something audible but not understood, and Ambrielle leaned over to where he was sitting and gave him a hug as well. Maetha carried the two cups with her as she came out of the kitchen area. "Please, sit anywhere you like."

Ambrielle and Gavian each sat on one of the five chairs in the room. Ambrielle scooted onto the edge of the seat since the backs of the chairs were bent forward, not made for human comfort. Maetha handed her the warm cup. "It's important to take a break in the day. We chat about yesterday, tomorrow, and of course the old memories that we haven't yet forgotten."

"How have you been, Taunsin?" Ambrielle took a sip of the warm drink. It tasted odd, a little like root beer.

"I'm here, aren't I?" he said.

"Still the friendliest Kavekkian on Mekkinspire." Ambrielle grinned as she recalled the last time she had seen Taunsin. He had been carving a figurine out of wood. "Did you ever finish that figure you were carving?"

"Which one are you talking about?" Taunsin took a swallow of the drink. "I finish carvings all the time."

"That reminds me!" Maetha got up and moved toward the wall next to the short hallway. There was a wooden shelf with various knickknacks that Ambrielle couldn't identify. Maetha picked one up and brought it over to Ambrielle. "He finished this one not long ago."

Ambrielle took the object and examined it. A carved figure, a human, painted with dark yellow hair. It was wearing a white sundress with small pink flowers. "Is this . . . me?" The face was a bit boxy, and the nose was too pointed, but otherwise it kind of resembled her as much as a small wooden figurine could.

"It is." Maetha sat back down. "Pretty good for his first human figure, eh?"

Ambrielle's eyes drew up in excitement. "It's perfect."

"I would offer it to you," Maetha said, "but I would miss seeing it displayed on the ledge."

"Oh it's fine," said Ambrielle. "I'm pleased that you want it there, honored by both of you."

A low growl came from the back of the den. Gavian turned nervously toward the sound and rose from the chair.

"It's okay Blaez!" Maetha shouted toward the hallway. "He's beginning to lose his eyesight and has been a bit more defensive lately. I have to keep him shut up when I have visitors now."

"Poor thing," Ambrielle said.

"So, what brings you two to Mekkinspire?" Maetha glanced at both of them. "I know you well enough you didn't come only to talk with us elders."

"Well, we *were* going to Isodonia."

"We still are," Gavian interrupted.

Ambrielle glanced at him. "We're still going to Isodonia, but we found something in the Darterran caves."

"You went inside the caves?" Maetha leaned forward. "You know Medigrin and his pack are still there."

"Yes, we didn't run into them," said Ambrielle. "The important thing is the vault is open now."

"What vault?" Maetha's eyes widened. "The material that even the lykris couldn't break?"

"Yes," Ambrielle said. "It is open now, and something came out."

"Came out? How do you know?" Maetha wondered.

"There was some orange liquid that spilled inside and made a trail through the caves that led outside into the forest, but we lost the trail after that."

"Medigrin must have found a way to open it," Maetha said. "No telling what was in there. If it was something he can use against us, he will try to destroy Mekkinspire again."

"Something tells me it wasn't Medigrin, but either way I want to know what was taken out of there. We found someone that can find the trail again," Ambrielle said. "We need to speak to Aradel."

"Aradel?" Maetha set her cup on the wall divider behind her. "What do you need with her?"

Ambrielle looked over at Gavian. "We're supposed to deliver something to her."

"What is it?" Maetha asked.

"I was told to only show it to her," Ambrielle said.

Maetha stood. "If you want me to call my daughter from her duties, I need to know what this is about."

"It's a crystal," Gavian said. "Two crystals actually, fit together."

"Let me see it." Maetha moved toward her.

"We promised not to show it to anyone but her," Ambrielle said.

"Give it to me, Ambrielle," said Gavian. "I didn't make that promise."

Ambrielle hesitated, debating what to do. She reached into a pouch on her belt and handed the jewel to Gavian.

Maetha took it from Gavian, and her eyes immediately enlarged. "Do you realize what this is?" Maetha inspected it closer. "This violet crystal is amythite, the rarest in Anatharia. They use this as an amplifier inside the lykris. This is nearly enough that we could build another one. Where did you get this?"

Ambrielle moved her eyes around the room until Gavian answered for her. "From a Kavekkian named Kidiru."

"Kidiru." Maetha dropped back into her chair, still staring at the jewel. "I thought he would have moved on far away from here."

"He said he could track things in the forest," said Ambrielle. "He could help us find what came out of the vault."

"He probably could," Maetha said, "but we cannot give this to Aradel."

"Why not?" said Ambrielle.

"She must not know that he is near," Maetha said.

Ambrielle returned to the edge of her chair. "I don't understand."

"I will not let her throw away her life on a dream," said Maetha.

Ambrielle leaned toward Maetha. "A dream?"

"A foolish childhood dream," said Maetha. "One she does not need to be reminded of. She has outgrown it now and realized the importance of her calling to Lon Kavekkia."

"If she's outgrown it, then it doesn't matter, does it?" Ambrielle said. "Wouldn't she make the right choice?"

"I would hope so," said Maetha. "But I can't take that chance."

Taunsin coughed as he swallowed some of the hot drink. "There's a Kavekkian, you may know her," he said, "always telling everyone we shouldn't meddle in the affairs of others. 'It's all right to give advice,' she says, 'but you have to let them make their own mistakes.' She doesn't always follow her own words though, I'm afraid."

Maetha exhaled loudly, vocalizing her annoyance. "Taunsin, this is Aradel we're talking about," Maetha said. "I'm her mother. I can't let her throw away the life she has made for herself."

"She's left the den now," Taunsin said. "She's not under your protection anymore. She didn't become the head of the council by making stupid decisions. You brought her up right. Right enough to know that she can decide what is best for herself, and you can be proud of her for whatever she does."

"Why must you always turn my own words against me?" Maetha rested her forehead on her closed fist.

"Friends seem to do that in my experience," Gavian said. "The good ones anyway."

"We really need to know what was in that vault," Ambrielle said, "especially if it's dangerous."

Maetha leaned back in the chair, staring up at the rocky ceiling. "All right dear, we will go talk to Aradel." Maetha stood and handed the jewel back to Ambrielle.

✧

Gavian and Ambrielle waited by the Kavekkian statues in the courtyard on the highest plateau of the mountain. She noticed Gavian staring up at the decorative blue light beams as Maetha talked to the guards at the gate. One of the guards walked away between the rows of trees toward the mekkadium citadel.

Maetha waved them over. As they reached her, Aradel strode to the gate and opened it.

"I see the human has returned." Aradel closed the gate and turned around. "And brought another."

"You might show a little respect," Maetha said. "Ambrielle and Gavian both saved this city."

"Along with our Kavekkian protectors and citizens-turned-warriors, many died to save us," Aradel said. "Don't tell me they want to speak to the Vaesari again."

"No, just to you." Ambrielle stepped forward. "I was asked to deliver something to you." She pulled the jewel from the pouch on her belt and held it toward Aradel.

"What is this?" Aradel squinted as the crystals glowed brightly in the sun. She took the jewel, staring at it for a moment before her eyes became watery. A tear threatened to fall down her cheek, until she caught it, rubbing it away quickly with her hand. "He remembered . . ."

"How do you know who it is from?" Maetha queried.

Aradel wiped her eyes again. "He used to always say he was going to find some amythite, but instead of using it to amplify light beams, he was going to make me a jewel."

"What is this supposed to be?" said Maetha.

"The white durathyst is the crescent moon Pathea, and the smaller round violet amythite is Miraeda."

"And you're crying over a jewel of the two moons?" Maetha said.

"It's much more than that. Don't you see? I'm Miraeda to his Pathea," Aradel said. "The larger Pathea is in its crescent form holding Miraeda in his arms, embracing her, protecting her."

"I don't remember him ever giving you anything when he was here. Why would he give this to you now?"

"He never could find any amythite," Aradel said. "'A rare beauty can only be represented by the rarest, most beautiful crystal,' he'd said. He finally found one."

"I'm glad that's cleared up," said Maetha. "I guess we can get on with our day then. I'm sure you are very busy at the citadel."

"Where is Kidiru now?" Aradel asked "Is he around here somewhere?"

"He was in the forest last we saw him," Ambrielle said.

"Wait here." Aradel opened the gate. "I will be right back."

When she returned, she held a small black object out to Ambrielle. It had a simple wooden handle and a short black blade. The blade wasn't sharp or pointed, and it wasn't completely straight.

"Give this to Kidiru and tell him that life is often too complicated for a yes or no answer," Aradel said. "The only response I can give is this. There is much that needs work here, more important than he realizes, but if I ever feel like I can leave my station better than I found it, then maybe that day my heart will be ready to live among the wilds."

Maetha nodded either in approval or relief.

"I will tell him." Ambrielle took the small blade from her hand.

⌀

"Goodbye, Taunsin." Ambrielle kissed the top of his head as he remained in the chair at Maetha's den. She gave Maetha a hug. "Take care, Maetha, and keep him out of trouble."

"Before you go," Maetha said, scurrying off into another room and returning with a long-bladed staff made of mekkadium, "why don't you take this with you. You may need it."

Ambrielle's eyebrows raised. "I'm sure it means a lot to you. I can't take it from you."

"This one has never been used," said Maetha. "It has no sentimental value, take it."

"Okay then," said Ambrielle. "Thank you."

Maetha smiled. "Until the next dawn."

"Goodbye." Ambrielle waved.

"Well be with you both," said Gavian.

They began the trek down the mountain. Gavian's hand brushed hers as they walked side by side. Even in that brief moment, she felt the same electricity as before when their skin touched. It made her wonder if he still felt it too. After moving around the ravine into the forest, they found Kidiru waiting for them. Ambrielle told him of Aradel's reaction and her words. She handed him the small blade Aradel had given her.

Kidiru smiled when he took it from her hand. "I made this when we were very young. We decided that, when we were older, we were going to hunt the great weribo that rarely pass through Lon Kavekkia and bring back their giant horns."

"And that was the knife you planned to use?" Gavian grinned.

Kidiru chuckled. "We thought it was huge back then, perfect for hunting weribo." He turned to Ambrielle. "You held up your end of the trade, now it is my turn." Kidiru strode ahead through the trees, leading them back to the vine-covered tunnel between the two hills.

He moved on from there, expertly navigating the terrain, winding through the forest as if he knew exactly where to go. Ambrielle and Gavian followed, stepping into beams of sunlight that shone through gaps in the canopy overhead.

As they moved further into the forest, the air grew thick and humid, causing sweat to bead on her forehead. A thick carpet of decaying leaves and moss covered the forest floor, releasing a pungent earthy scent. The towering balcain trees blocked out the sunlight, casting eerie shadows that seemed to twist and weave around them.

Ambrielle's boots sunk into the soft, squelching mud as she leapt over a sodden ditch, evidence of water's occasional intrusion leaving behind twisted roots and debris. Despite the dimness, the forest was not completely devoid of light. Hundreds of bioluminescent mushrooms glowed in shades of orange and violet, casting an eerie radiance around them. They grew on rotting logs, thick hills of moss, and between the upright branches of old twisting trees.

As they pushed their way through the dense thicket, the woods seemed to come alive around them. The trees whispered secrets to one another, and the leaves rustled and danced in the breeze. The sun broke through the branches, casting dappled patterns of light on the forest floor. Kidiru urged them forward, his footsteps muffled by the soft underbrush. A chorus of songs filled the air when a flock of birds took flight, their wings beating the air with a rhythmic whooshing sound as they escaped to the tops of the trees. The network of vines and bushes gave way to a lush clearing filled with dark green ferns.

Ambrielle's breath caught in her throat as they emerged from the clearing to behold the breathtaking vista before them. The lake, with its shimmering aquamarine waters, seemed to stretch out endlessly before her eyes, reflecting the golden, green, and blue foliage of the valley that surrounded it. The foothills in the distance looked like a wall of emerald, standing guard over the tranquil waters. The small island in the center of the lake was a verdant oasis, a lush forest rising majestically from its heart.

"Have you ever seen anything like this?" Ambrielle turned to look at Gavian's face. He stared out at the lake, seemingly transfixed by its beauty. She couldn't help but felt a twinge of jealousy that he had never looked at her in that way before.

"The Darterrans never went this far that I know of." He brushed the hair out of his eyes as Ambrielle leaned on his shoulder.

"This is Lon Vellica." Kidiru gestured across the horizon. "There are only a few of us who inhabit this land, those who are not welcome on Mekkinspire. A society of the banished."

Kidiru led them down a small trail toward the banks of the water. Pointing toward two wooden kayak-type crafts, Kidiru looked back at Ambrielle. "One of the lukids has been missing, likely taken by the stranger you seek." The boats were made with two big logs attached together and sat in the wet sand at the edge of the lake. "For your kindness, you are welcome to take one of the lukids. I believe this stranger went to the island."

The three of them shoved the lukid into the water. Ambrielle and Gavian jumped on as it slid across the sand into deeper water. Kidiru gave them an extra push, while Gavian reached one of the seats hollowed into the log. He grabbed an oar and began propelling them further. Ambrielle took the other paddle and joined, feeling the coolness of the lake seep through the wooden shaft and into her palms. She tried timing her strokes with Gavian's to keep them moving straight.

The lukid moved surprisingly fast over the water. It was amazing how clear and calm the lake was. A few choppy waves greeted them, but the lukid sliced through them with ease. Moving further out, they could no longer see the rocky land at the bottom of the lake.

When they were halfway to the island, a long dark object passed underneath the boat. As more of it came by them, Ambrielle got a sense of just how big it was. An animal the size of a whale or larger swam quickly, churning the surface of the water when it moved by. It turned and swam back toward them. Ambrielle gripped tightly on the two logs beside them, nearly paralyzed. The thought of getting knocked into the water with that lake monster terrified her.

The creature was largest at the front, tapering into a thinner body to its sweeping tail fin at the back. Swimming with two large winglike flippers, it glided through the water with incredible speed.

"Keep paddling," Gavian told her, but she was too afraid of attracting the creature's attention. Once it moved out of sight, she paddled with renewed vigor, eager to get to land. Gavian had to speed up to keep the boat from turning toward his side.

The lukid hit the beach, and Ambrielle jumped out. Gavian tugged the wooden craft further onto the sand and sat beside her to rest. "What do you think you're going to find?"

"I don't know." Ambrielle tried to slow her breathing. "I'm beginning to get a little scared."

"I'm glad I'm not the only one." Gavian stood, surveying the thick forest ahead. Chirps, squeals, and screeches rang out through the trees. The small island was teeming with life. Hopefully it was only birds and nothing dangerous. Ambrielle looked back across the water to where they had come from. It was too far away to tell if Kidiru was still waiting for them or not.

Ambrielle wiped the sand from her clothes while Gavian headed toward the thicket. Catching up with him, she strapped the bladestaff around her back and ignited the laser in her silbrace. Cutting into the mass of vines and underbrush, she made her own trail.

"I was about to do that," he said, moving in behind her.

"Well, I did it first," Ambrielle teased as she continued to cut her way through the woods. They came to sparser area, and Ambrielle disengaged the laser. Leafy ferns covered the forest floor, and strange trees, bulbous at the base of their trunks and becoming skinny toward the top, were scattered around. They had no limbs but sprouted big pink and purple leaves, like a paper fan. She had never seen their like in Anatharia or anywhere else.

Passing through a row of tall flimsy reeds, Ambrielle found the orange liquid on one of the stalks. She swept them out of her way, searching for more drops on the ground. She found another and then another, following the spots of the dried orange substance. The forest grew quiet as she crept along the trail of spots until she found something. In a clearing between two hovanoke trees, a large vault stood. Smaller than the one in the caves, but it had the same white material and texture. Ambrielle suddenly stopped, unsure what to make of it.

CHAPTER 4

THE GLADE SEEMED to come alive with a haunting melody, its ethereal notes cutting through the stillness of the air. Five delicate tones followed by a momentary pause, and then the enchanting melody repeated, resonating from somewhere ahead. The sounds seemed to emanate from the very heart of the glade, beckoning Ambrielle with a mesmerizing allure.

As Ambrielle followed the alluring melody, her focus fixed on the vault that lay hidden within the glade, her senses heightened. However, so engrossed was she in her quest that her foot unexpectedly struck something hidden within the grass. A startled gasp escaped her lips as she stumbled, her heart pounding against her chest.

She glanced down, her eyes widening in both shock and apprehension. There, lying lifeless on the ground, lay the body of a humanoid creature. Its form was twisted and still, the aura of death hanging heavily in the air. Ambrielle drew back, a shiver coursing through her when she realized she had unwittingly stumbled upon a grisly sight—a corpse from another realm.

Gavian ran over to see what she was reacting to. He crouched beside the dead being. "It looks old."

As the musical tones continued to play, they seemed to be coming from the corpse itself. Ambrielle kneeled next to Gavian, wanting to find the source of the melody but not prepared to touch something dead. Ambrielle reached forward. Her hand grazed the soft material of its clothing. Ambrielle fell backward, recoiling in terror as something stirred beneath the veil of the dead being's clothing. It suddenly freed itself and flew into the air.

A small spherical object with four eyes hovered over them. The object emitted a blue light, running it over Ambrielle. It played the five-note melody again and lit up with blue and orange lights. "Thank you for answering my call," the object said with a mostly monotone voice that modulated for inflection. "I have not encountered your species before, but you would not have answered my call if you were not friends of the Cereveshians." Ambrielle looked at Gavian, who glanced back out of the corner of his eye. "There is an important need of you. The awakener has received the signal. Evidence of the Nulvarians' return has been discovered, which can only mean one thing: A seal has been opened." The orb floated over to the corpse. "The signal freed her from her stasis only recently, but unfortunately, before she could awaken the datascribe, she perished."

"What happened to her?" Ambrielle furrowed her brow. "How did she die?"

The orb fixed its attention back on the remains of the dead extraterrestrial. "Her body was in a state of advanced age. Her organs began to fail. Eventually her heart stopped beating."

"I'm sorry," said Ambrielle. "What do you need us to do?"

The orb moved to her at eye level. "Hold out your solex."

After a moment of confusion, Ambrielle realized it meant her silbrace. Ambrielle held her arm out to the orb, and it landed on the silbrace around her forearm with a flash of pale blue. Ambrielle felt a jolt when it seemed to connect.

"The siriant of your solex appears to be corrupted," the orb said.

"What does that mean?" Ambrielle asked.

"With your permission, I will need to rebuild it," said the orb.

She wasn't sure if it was a good idea or not, but she had come this far. Might as well keep going. "Okay, but don't damage anything."

The orb's lights blinked around its circumference. "This framework is odd. This will take some time to realign. How long have you had this solex?"

"It's actually a silbrace if that matters," said Ambrielle.

"I do not have anything in my records of silbrace, but the architecture is close enough." The orb whirred and whistled as its lights moved in various patterns. "Update complete. I am now bound to you. You may call me Wegin."

"Bound to me?" Ambrielle asked. "What do you mean?"

"I completed my former proprietor's final order. I appended the siriant of her solex to yours," said the orb. "I will follow your commands once her objective is completed."

Ambrielle glanced at Gavian, who was rubbing his forehead, likely growing frustrated that her excursion continued to expand. "What is the objective?"

"Your solex contains the unique siriant to unlock all Cereveshian akreums," said Wegin. "You must act as the awakener in her stead."

"Awakener?" Ambrielle said. "What do I need to do?"

The orb darted away, flying toward the vault. "Awaken the datascribe first. She knows all the locations of the hidden akreums."

"In there?" Ambrielle said.

Gavian sighed. "Why can't things like this happen when there is nothing else going on?"

As Ambrielle walked forward, her silbrace lit up. A tingling sensation traveled up her arm, and the lights blinked faster with each step toward the vault. When she reached one of the sides of the unbreakable material, her silbrace played the same five-note melody she'd heard before. The shape of the vault shifted, changing into an open structure like that they had seen inside the Darterran caverns.

An intense orange glow spilled out from the vault, casting an otherworldly hue over the entire area. Ambrielle's eyes were drawn to the egg-shaped glass container that sat in the center of the chamber, just like those she had found empty in the vault inside the caves. Unlike those, this container was filled with a pink, cloudy gas that swirled and shifted, obscuring whatever was inside. Ambrielle stepped back as the pod opened. The smoke cleared, revealing the form of a creature lying prone inside the container. Its body began to twitch and convulse, as if struggling to break free from the confines of its glass prison.

"You will need to assist her," said Wegin.

Ambrielle and Gavian rushed to her when she tried to move. They each took one of her arms, helping her out of the container. She set her feet on the ground, but they had to hold her up. After a few minutes, the being was able to able to stand on her own.

She had light orange skin, darker around her eyes and speckled with white dots. Her face appeared nearly human, but with a flatter brow and nose. The young woman's hair was blue, a slight part in the middle, two thick strands flowing over each side of her face, curled at the end. Part of the ends of her long hair was tapered around her neck in three separate folds, while the rest of it ran behind her shoulders. Behind each ear, the hair was shaped into wings intermingled with what appeared to be two of the static stylers used by the synthetics on Elyravess. A few other strands of hair seemed to flow independently of the rest.

The young alien woman choked when she drew a deep beath, her chest heaving with every cough. After a few moments, she calmed herself, and her breathing became normal. She climbed out of the chamber, holding on to the side of the formed doorway as she stepped onto the ferns and soft soil below.

"Are you the awakener?" the girl said, blinking her light blue eyes.

Ambrielle looked at Gavian, unsure how to respond. "I am Ambrielle. Are you the datascribe?"

"Yes, my name is Tetra'Novis." The girl's eyes scanned the forest behind them and then Ambrielle. "You are not Cereveshian. I did not expect the awakener to be alien. Your name seems familiar, but this place . . . it doesn't look anything like I remember." Tetra'Novis stepped past Ambrielle, limping her way toward the body of the dead Cereveshian woman behind them. After staring at the body for a moment, Tetra'Novis placed her hand over her chest, "She looks so old, how long has she been here?"

Wegin flew over to the dead woman. "She was the former awakener but perished three planetary rotations ago, but prior to that she had been alive for 3.7824 million revolutions."

"Million?" said the girl. "Convert to Cereveshian time."

"My answer was in Cereveshian revolutions," Wegin said.

Tetra'Novis clenched her eyes shut before opening them again. "Has it really been that long?"

Wegin hovered nearby. "Do you require an answer or is this a rhetorical question?"

Tetra'Novis turned to face Ambrielle. "So, I take it the Nulvarians have returned?"

"I'm afraid so," said Ambrielle. "Do you know how to stop them?"

Tetra'Novis arched her back with determination. "What level of infestation have they reached? Which galaxy are they in?"

"I don't really know," Ambrielle said.

"I've seen them on Isodonia," said Gavian. "If that helps."

"And they are also on Solsellion," Ambrielle said.

"So it has spread to at least two worlds," said Tetra'Novis. "We have a lot of work ahead, but first we need to honor this fallen one." She paused for a moment. "Do you know her final wishes?"

"She believed in the Afterglow," Wegin said. "She wished to be planted in soil among seeds of trees, shrubs, and ferns."

"Interesting." Tetra'Novis played with her dangling strands of blue hair. "She followed the Ureon's beliefs even though she never came with us to Averess. Please, if you could both dig. I don't yet have the strength."

"Dig here," said Wegin as he moved to an area not far away. "This should be the softest soil."

Ambrielle tried to use the bladestaff, but it wasn't an effective tool for much more than poking holes in the soil. She kneeled and used her laser, but it did little but scorch the dirt. Using her hands, she began clearing out some of the dirt. She glanced at Gavian, who was staring into the distance. "Are you going to help?"

"I'll be right back." He ran off through the forest the way they had come.

It surprised her, but surely, he wasn't going to leave the island without her. She went back to digging. Gavian came running back holding both of the oars from the boat. He dropped one of them at Ambrielle's feet and started using the other to dig into the soil. It wasn't as effective as a shovel, but it was far better than digging with her hands. The scent of damp earth filled her nostrils while they moved the soil. Gavian's heavy breathing and the sound of the oar hitting the ground added a rhythmic beat.

Tetra'Novis limped around the area, bringing back some hovanoke nuts as well as some seeds from the purple blossoms and placing them into the dirt at the bottom of the hole. They rolled the body of the woman into the grave. Ambrielle could feel the weight of the soil as she helped Gavian cover the body, the dirt clinging to her skin and clothes.

"I realized where I remember your name," said Tetra'Novis. "It was among those on the strange tablets we found."

Ambrielle felt a tingle on the skin of her arms. "The tablets of the ancients? Aren't *you* one of the ancients?"

"No, the ancients you speak of are the Ichtek. They once dwelt in the caverns of this world. We believe it was they who created the tablets, but we do not know why," said Tetra'Novis.

"Ichtek?" Ambrielle said. "Who are they?"

"Ichtek is the name of a Vyndarian sect that first uncovered the—" Wegin started.

"The data you contain is due to my studies. I will answer the questions," said Tetra'Novis to Wegin before turning back to Ambrielle. "The Ichtek are part of a reptilianoid species known as Vyndari. They are the oldest intelligent life we have found evidence of but are now nearly extinct," said the alien girl. "If nothing else, they are an enigma. Notably, their development of technology is minimal in comparison to other known races, yet their presence is pervasive throughout the cosmos. We encountered a few of them on this world during the war against the Nulvarians. They were obsessed with light, harnessing it with certain crystals. Other than that, we have only found ruins of their civilization. We think it was they who first uncovered the rifts. If the Nulvarians have indeed returned, it is probable that the seals on the rifts have been compromised and must be re-established."

"What kind of rifts are you talking about?" asked Gavian.

Tetra'Novis coughed as she started to speak but soon settled herself. "The Nulvarians used them to enter our universe. There are rifts on several worlds. We may not have even found them all, but the ones we found we sealed up, built the vaults around them."

Ambrielle's eyes lit up. "Is that what is behind the wall? In the cave there was a big vault with stairs going down, and the hallway just ends."

"Good, at least the one here is still sealed," said Tetra'Novis. "It sounds like we need to close the ones on Isodonia and Solsellion. If we are fortunate, those are the only two that were opened."

"So, the Ichtek," said Ambrielle, "why did they put names on tablets?"

"We know very little about the motivation of the Ichtek," stated Tetra'Novis. "Unfortunately, we were forced to kill many of them as they were aiding the Nulvarians."

"Aiding them?" said Ambrielle. "Why would they do that?"

"The Shadows must have controlled them," Gavian said.

"If that is the case, they are especially vulnerable to the Nulvarians' control," said Tetra'Novis.

"But the Nulvarians want to destroy this universe," said Ambrielle. "Why would any species want to help them?"

"As we have traveled the vast reaches of the cosmos, we have come across numerous sentient beings. However, we have observed that all of them exhibit some degree of illogical thinking in their beliefs and actions." Tetra'Novis sucked in a raspy breath. "In the event of the Nulvarians' resurgence, it is imperative that you activate the remaining members of our society. This device"—she extended a small, round object, slightly smaller than a golf ball, with delicate, shimmering filaments beneath its surface—"when inserted into your datamus, will aid in the identification and location of all necessary individuals."

"Wait." Ambrielle offered the object back to Tetra'Novis. "I don't have a datamus."

"May I examine your solex?" Tetra'Novis requested.

Ambrielle raised her arm toward the alien girl, allowing her to inspect it.

"Fascinating," Tetra'Novis observed. "It appears yours does not possess one."

Gavian nodded toward the buried Cereveshian. "What about hers?"

"It would not be functional for your physiology," Tetra'Novis clarified. "It is specifically attuned to the genetic code of its proprietor. Does your starcraft not possess a similar mechanism?"

"We don't have a starcraft either," said Ambrielle.

"You took on the task of an awakener, yet you possess no starcraft?" Tetra'Novis queried with surprise. "How do you intend to traverse the seven galaxies and activate the remaining members of our society?"

Ambrielle raised her hands to her hips. "I didn't ask to be an awakener. I was only trying to help."

The alien girl played with one of the longs strands of blue hair that curled near her chin. "How did you reach Solsellion and Isodonia if you have no starcraft?"

"Through the spring," said Gavian.

"I don't understand," Tetra'Novis said.

"On Solsellion," Ambrielle said. "The springs that connect to other worlds."

Tetra'Novis's gaze shifted to the grass at their feet as she absently traced her lower lip with her finger. "I do not recall such information, but my solex is able to read the data. If this spring can transport us to the appropriate planets, we can proceed with the awakening."

"Why do you need an awakener exactly?" Gavian gestured toward the grave of the dead Cereveshian. "If *she* woke up, why couldn't you and everyone else?"

"She was among the select individuals who remained in this universe. Once they reached a certain age, they would enter a dormant state for preservation," Tetra'Novis explained. "The majority of our population transcended to a higher realm. Our physical forms persist in this universe, but our consciousnesses resides in Averess."

"What woke her up then?" Gavian asked.

"It was a signal," the extraterrestrial girl stated. "In the event that the Nulvarians had again breached this universe, the signal would have been transmitted to her in order to activate the remainder of our society."

"Why didn't you just make the signal wake all of you?" said Gavian.

"Excessive automation can be perilous," Tetra'Novis remarked as she began coughing again. "It can be compromised or infiltrated. The whereabouts of our physical forms must be kept concealed. There were once many designated awakeners, who initially did not want to make the journey to Averess, but after the data began coming in, they couldn't resist."

"You must be the ones who made the sentinels on Elyravess," Ambrielle said. "The founders?"

"Ah yes, Elyravess. It was a picturesque planet prior to the arrival of the Shadows." The extraterrestrial girl closed her eyes, as if in deep recollection. "You are correct. We did become known as the founders. We were the apex civilization, the sole beings capable of traversing intergalactic space and sharing our knowledge with other worlds. Though we were diligent in allowing them to evolve along their own trajectories, you are, or will become, our progeny." Tetra'Novis cleared her throat. "Before our transcendence, we deployed many automatons to explore the universe and discover worlds not yet populated by intelligent life. They were to document these worlds and assist those civilizations that had developed to the point of reaching these worlds. The automatons were programmed to activate the awakeners if the presence of Nulvarians was detected."

Ambrielle glanced at Gavian and then back at Tetra'Novis. "We need to get to Isodonia. What are you asking us to do?"

"We must hurry," Tetra'Novis urged, her voice strained. "The Nulvarians will not wait for us to be ready. We must gather our warriors and prepare for battle. Go and awaken those who have defeated the Shadows before. Wegin, guide them to the temple. I will rest and join you as soon as I am able." She lay back on the log, her breathing shallow and labored.

"Received," said Wegin.

"You sure you will be okay here alone?" said Gavian.

"Indeed," Tetra'Novis said with a serene expression. "My physical form may require some time to recuperate, but it is nothing that will impede our progress."

Gavian and Ambrielle strode through the forest as they followed Wegin to the shore where they had left the lukid. The air was thick with otherworldly noises, a symphony of clicks, chirps, and buzzes. Ambrielle imagined there were alien insects and frogs hidden all around them. With a running start, they shoved the boat off into deeper water and climbed on.

As the boat glided away from the shore, they steered around the island, heading toward the unexplored land on the other side of the lake. The cool water lapped against the sides of the lukid creating a gentle rocking motion. Ambrielle's eyes darted back and forth across the water searching for any sign of movement. The surface of the water was calm, but she knew the lake monster could appear at any moment, its massive form rising from the depths. After all that digging, paddling through the water was beginning to tire her arms, but she endured it until they made it to land.

A thick forest of red and light blue trees awaited them. Gavian cut through the foliage with the laser blade on his silbrace until they came across an old statue. Its details mostly worn away from weather and time, it seemed to be wearing a long-hooded robe and had a strangely shaped head.

A mound of growth comprised mostly of maroon-colored ivy stood between the old, gnarled trees ahead. Peeking through the foliage was a surface of smoothed stone. It was stained with dark streaks of grime collected in the apertures between the stone blocks. Slashing through the vines revealed the corners of an open doorway.

After working to clear the opening, Gavian and Ambrielle switched their silbraces to light the dark interior. Thick webbing strung across the small tunnel of the entranceway. The webs layered as far as they could see in the light.

"I'll light it, you cut," Gavian said, as he moved to allow Ambrielle to slip past him.

"No way." Ambrielle took a few steps back. "Most insects I don't mind, but spiders . . . I don't deal with spiders."

"But you are the awakener," Gavian joked. "You have to go."

Ambrielle gritted her teeth. "If I have to be the awakener, you can be the trailblazer."

"Wegin, what about you?" said Gavian.

"I'm afraid I am not equipped to clean this space," Wegin said. "I have been designed for analysis and information."

Gavian took another look into the dark tunnel, scratching the back of his head. "All right." He turned off the light and ignited the laser again, burning through the web as he moved forward. The webs were like strands of cotton, parting easily to the heat, but there were so many that strands still clung to everything. Frustrated with the slow progress, Gavian found it easier to pull the webs down with his hands, but it ended up getting wrapped all over him. He went back to the laser, burning a square cutout to walk through the tunnel.

He turned the light back. "I think I found the end, come on through."

"You have to clear all of those webs," said Ambrielle.

"That's the best I can do with this stuff." Gavian brushed something off his shoulder and shrieked. He came running through the tunnel toward

Ambrielle. When he made it outside, there were large red spiders crawling on his back. Ambrielle's hands twitched when she saw them.

"Get them off me!" Gavian slapped the back of his jacket with his hand. The spiders were about the size of tarantulas, but these had claws on their front two legs like crabs. Ambrielle removed one of her boots. While trying to keep her hands as far away from the spiders as possible, she slung the boot across Gavian's back, raking the spiders off.

"I guess you don't like spiders either." Ambrielle grinned.

Gavian removed the jacket, making sure they were gone. "I don't like anything crawling on me." He put the jacket back on, tugging it tight against his back, and stepped back into the tunnel.

"Shall I scan the area for any other potential threats, Ambrielle?" Wegin asked.

"Please do," said Ambrielle as she stood in the entryway.

Wegin entered the interior, scanning while he moved around. "There are approximately 461 of these small creatures, mostly under large rocks and in the upper corners of the room. You should be safe if you avoid these areas."

"It may have been better not knowing." Ambrielle tried to switch her mindset to remembering that she was much bigger than the spiders. She pictured herself confidently walking through the tunnel, unconcerned with any spiders that appeared. Bowing her shoulders and taking a deep breath, she reminded herself that she had faced far more dangerous creatures than these.

Ambrielle stepped into the dark tunnel, walking as fast as she could. Holding her arms close to her body, she kept going until she ran into something ahead of her. Gavian grunted as she knocked him forward.

"Sorry," Ambrielle whispered but continued nudging him forward.

Ambrielle's silbrace began to flash when they came into a wide-open space with a high ceiling. Stepping down into the ankle-deep water of the main floor area, she felt the coolness of the water seep through her boots and over her toes. The water made a soft sloshing sound with each step as they passed several raised structures made from the familiar white material. The smaller akreums lined the perimeter with a few in the middle of the room.

Wegin moved to one of the vaults. "Some of these akreums are empty, but most of them contain life-forms. This is one you could open."

Reaching to touch the surface, Ambrielle played the melody in her mind. Her silbrace started playing it too. The vault began to transform, reconfiguring its shape to allow access to the egg-shaped glass container inside. There appeared to be the body of a male Cereveshian inside the clouds of gas. As the clear shield faded and the clouds of gas inside dispersed, his long straight spikey hair became visible. He wore clothing with shiny white plates of armor.

Gavian and Ambrielle stepped back when he sat up from the chamber. The Cereveshian struggled to crack open his eyelids. Rubbing his face, he began blinking rapidly. He drew in a deep breath and immediately began coughing. Ambrielle stepped forward, hesitantly reaching toward him, unsure if she should help or not.

The Cereveshian glared at them. "I hope there is a good reason for pulling me back into this world."

CHAPTER 5

AMBRIELLE ASSISTED GAVIAN as they moved with careful urgency, offering their support to the Cereveshian emerging from the chamber. Wobbling on unsteady legs, the Cereveshian stepped onto the platform, raising Ambrielle's concern.

"Tetra'Novis told us to wake you." Ambrielle wondered why he appeared angry.

"If that is true, where is she?" The Cereveshian turned his attention to Gavian.

"On the island across the lake." Gavian planted his feet as if anticipating an attack. "She didn't have the strength to get here."

The Cereveshian's round blue eyes moved back to Ambrielle. "So, you are the awakener, I presume."

"I suppose I am," said Ambrielle. "The Nulvarians have returned, and we need your help to fight them back and seal the rifts."

The Cereveshian's face twisted in pain when he straightened his back. "This vessel was never intended for such prolonged stasis. My strength has diminished. I no longer have the capability to engage in combat."

"So that's it? We went through all this for nothing?" Gavian said loud enough to echo in the room. "You are just going to let them destroy the universe? How are we supposed to defeat them?"

"Even in our prime, total elimination was unattainable." The Cereveshian warrior faced Gavian. "We sealed the breaches to hinder their infinite reinforcements and neutralized those present in the universe."

Something splashed into the water, startling them when they moved toward the source of the sound. Water flowed from somewhere in the ceiling, dropping into the water on the lower floor. Gavian tugged at his jacket. "We've destroyed some of the Nulthereals, but—"

The Cereveshian's shoulders shook as he laughed silently. "Nulthereals pale in comparison to our previous conflict—" He inhaled deeply, and a cunning grin spread across his face, like he was relishing a memory. "The most epic battle I ever bore witness to, the defeat of Versepirath on these very plains. I am Dracos'Arkon. My name is scribed in every nexus across the seven galaxies of the Sederine Cluster."

Gavian leaned in, intrigued. "What's Versepirath?"

"It sounds familiar." Ambrielle wandered the pathways of her brain trying to recall where she had heard the name.

Dracos'Arkon snorted, turning away from them. "Versepirath was a Nulvarian parasitic creature called a Primevus that crossed the rift prior to our arrival. It concealed itself and subsisted on the life force of its hosts, increasing in size while it absorbed sufficient energy to maintain existence."

"How did you destroy it?" Gavian's voice again echoed through the chamber.

"We battled it for days, employing all available resources, until one method proved effective." The corner of Dracos'Arkon's lips curled. "Sound."

"Sound?" Gavian jerked his head back. "How would sound destroy it?"

"Wait"—Ambrielle tapped her finger on her bottom lip—"is Versepirath the creature that made the giant footprint in the river?"

Dracos'Arkon rubbed his forehead as if it was beginning to hurt. "We lured it to the great river and eradicated it there. Nulvarians use life energy to shield their aethrum forms from the physical universe. Certain sound frequencies disrupt that energy, but caution must be exercised. Interaction between matter and aethrum leads to mutual annihilation, causing an irreparable tear. If you interfere with that shield, proximity to water is imperative. Water has the ability to bond with aethrum, neutralizing it and transforming it into a form that can coexist with matter."

"So Taunsin was right"—Ambrielle became excited—"it really *is* a footprint!"

"Versepirath had no legs," Dracos'Arkon said. "The only marks it left in stone were from its tentacles that extracted energy from the soil and vegetation."

"What did it look like?" said Ambrielle.

"Like something that does not belong in this universe, eldritch and ominous." Adjusting his balance, Dracos'Arkon leaned against the vault. "If it still stands, you should visit Lon Kavekkia. When Versepirath crumbled, its largest fragment plunged into the riverbed, leaving a pillar of black stone. The Ichtek named it Mekkinspire."

Ambrielle's eyes grew large. "Wait . . . you're saying Mekkinspire is a piece of Versepirath?"

"You've seen it." Dracos'Arkon's breath quickened. "Yes, it was that massive."

Gavian rubbed the whiskers on his chin. "So mekkadium and shadowstone are the same thing. I thought they looked similar."

Ambrielle removed her mekkadium bladestaff for another look, inspecting its iridescent sheen. This new revelation made her nervous to touch it. There was a faint, almost imperceptible vibration that tingled her fingertips when she held the cold, smooth material. "Is it safe to be around? Maetha and the Kavekkians are living on Mekkinspire. They have no idea that it's the remains of a creature from The Hollow." Ambrielle's focus on the world around her faded as she contemplated what that might mean.

Coughing, Dracos'Arkon bent forward. Patting his chest with his fist for a moment, he recovered and breathed steadily again. "I never imagined anyone residing there; it would be a challenging ascent. Nonetheless, it should not present any danger."

Gavian stared intently. "What about these sound frequencies? What do we need for that?"

Dracos'Arkon stifled a cough. "We integrated sonic weapons into our solex, based on the geowaves utilized in mining. I'd offer you my solex, but it wouldn't function for you. A Cereveshian craftsman is required to make one. Tetra'Novis should have information on the whereabouts of a craftsman. If not, there should be plenty you can wake on Cerevesh."

The idea of going to the home planet of the founders sounded exciting to Ambrielle, but she had no idea which spring could take them there, and she had promised Gavian. "First we have to get to Isodonia, there have been Nulthereals there."

Wegin floated between them. "If you need sound, I can generate more than voice. I'm sure my scream would scare them away. Would you like to hear it?"

"I'd rather not, Wegin," Ambrielle said.

"If you are going to Isodonia, there are mining colonies there," said Dracos'Arkon. "Miners used tools with sound technology as well. Perhaps they would be a viable alternative."

"I don't remember any mining colonies," said Gavian.

"The priority is locating the rift and closing it," Dracos'Arkon said. "But, where Nulthereals exist, a creature like Versepirath is likely nearby. Even after the rift is sealed, someone must eliminate it before it's too late. If ignored, it can expand enough to devour the world."

"How do we seal the rift?" Ambrielle asked.

"Plastra will be necessary. The same material the akreums are made from," said Dracos'Arkon. "Once you locate the rift, the Cereveshians in stasis nearby can provide assistance."

"We killed the Blight Whidge in Isodonia," Gavian boasted. "Would that be the kind of creature you're talking about?"

Dracos'Arkon shook his head no. "As per our understanding, a whidge serves merely as a subordinate to a Primevus. The whidge harnesses vital essence from organic life to allow a Primevus to manifest their full power into the universe. Expanding the essence is necessary to accommodate the growth of the Nulvarians. They cannot tolerate direct contact with it. Nevertheless, the elimination of a whidge would inevitably impede their advancement."

"Was Versepirath one of the Gaith?" Gavian asked.

"Versepirath was a scion of one of the Gaith," said Dracos'Arkon. "The scion of Vazerinaz the Unyielding to be precise."

Ambrielle tapped her lip with her index finger as she tried to imagine what any of the Gaith even looked like. "So Versepirath was like a son or daughter of the Gaith?"

"Consider Vazerinaz a vast ocean," said Dracos'Arkon. "If you were to dip a small container into that ocean, fill it, and bring it to shore, Versepirath would be that part of the ocean filling the container."

Ambrielle began to contemplate how immeasurable the vastness of the Gaith must be. "I see now why defeating them is not an option."

"If there is a Primevus on Isodonia, where would we find it?" Gavian scratched the stubble on his face.

"It could be anywhere," Dracos'Arkon replied gruffly. "Depending on its size, it could be in a cave, a hidden crevice, anywhere suitable for concealment." He winced as he began to cough violently, doubling over in pain. "I should be the one leading the battle and sealing the rift, but I must return to the chamber," he said, looking at the blood on his hand. "The toll of time is finally catching up with this body. My spirit needs enough strength for another battle ahead. For my consciousness will have to journey back through the Savage Dark to return to Averess."

Ambrielle had so many questions, but now a new one had emerged. "The Savage Dark?"

"I'm afraid the amount of data you require exceeds the time I have available. The Savage Dark is nothing you will ever have to worry about," Dracos'Arkon lay in the glass chamber bed. "Our fates rest in your hands, my comrades. If this universe falls, our bodies fall with it." He raised his hand in salute as the glass egg closed and filled with pink gas.

"Wasn't Tetra'Novis supposed to meet us here?" Gavian said when they left the temple.

Tetra'Novis had thought she would get her strength back, but after everything Dracos'Arkon had said, Ambrielle was skeptical. "We need to help her back into the chamber."

Ambrielle's mind raced to process everything they had learned, while they made their way out of the temple and back through the forest to the lake. From there, they took the boat across the lake to the island. After cutting their way through the thicket, they found their original trail, following it back to the vault.

It remained open, gleaming in the bright sunlight of Versoh through gaps in the trees. "Tetra'Novis!" Ambrielle called out. Tetra'Novis lay in the black dirt not far from the vault. Ambrielle's heart dropped as she hurried over to her. Tetra'Novis appeared to be sleeping, but something seemed wrong. Gavian shook her arm, trying to wake her up, but it was no use. Her body, which had been preserved in the stasis chamber for over three million years, had finally succumbed to age.

"Wegin, do you think she would want to be buried the same way?" Ambrielle asked.

"It is difficult to say," said Wegin. "It is unlikely anyone would be offended with this kind of burial."

"What about the information she had?" said Gavian. "About all the akreums."

"I don't know if we should wake any more of them," Ambrielle said.

"We're going to need to find some way to seal the rift," said Gavian. "How are we going to do that without asking them?"

"I guess you have a point," Ambrielle said.

Wegin's lights started to blink rapidly. "I should be able to interface with her solex and access the data she intended for you."

Approaching Tetra'Novis's lifeless body, Wegin activated a beam of light that connected with her solex. "Solisphere acquired."

Curious, Ambrielle spoke up, "What exactly is a solisphere?"

Wegin responded, "A solisphere is a comprehensive three-dimensional map of the topography of all the planets the Cereveshians have explored. These in particular have their akreum locations marked."

Ambrielle and Gavian used the oars to dig a second hole beside the other Cereveshian. Before covering her with soil, they placed hovanoke nuts around her as Tetra'Novis had done for the other. Ambrielle took solace in that she was now at rest but also hoped there was an Afterglow, whatever that may be, and that she would find her way to it. "I wish we had put her back into the vault before we left."

Gavian rubbed Ambrielle's shoulders while she stood looking at the mound of dirt. "We did what she asked us to do."

"I guess we did." Ambrielle turned toward the forest the way they'd come. Her thoughts became cloudy and muddled. "It just feels like . . . I don't know . . . like we could have done more. We should have helped her back into the chamber before we left."

"We didn't know what was going to happen," Gavian said. "We could only work with what we knew at the time."

Ambrielle voiced a familiar sentiment while they climbed into the boat. "I suppose everything happens for a reason." This philosophy had become a guiding principle for her, especially after her mother's death. It was the only way she could rationalize the unfairness of life. The events of her previous encounters with the Shadows had only reinforced this belief, solidifying it in her mind.

The cool evening breeze sent shivers down Ambrielle's spine as it whispered through the trees beyond the shore ahead. Twinkling in the darkening sky, the first stars of night appeared, casting their soft light over the water's surface. When they approached the beach, the sound of the waves gently lapping against the sand grew louder. The crunch of the boat's hull coming to a rest against the sand jolted her.

The faint scent of woodsmoke mixed with the briny smell of the lake filled the air when they passed the nearby village. There was no sign of Kidiru. He'd probably grown tired of waiting, if he'd intended to wait at all.

As they entered the woods, making their way toward the entrance of the secret passageway into the caves, Ambrielle couldn't shake off the eerie feeling that enveloped the forest at night. Every step they took on the brittle leaves that crackled underfoot seemed to amplify the stillness of the night, making her feel like an intruder in this world of darkness and shadow.

Their steps were soon joined by nocturnal creatures calling to each other through the woods. Haunting trills and uncanny shrieks followed them as they came to the glen where the dark tunnel was nestled between two small hills. Gavian held the vines out of the way, allowing Ambrielle to enter the tunnel.

As they emerged from the tunnel into the carved stone of the Darterrans' hallways, footsteps and voices echoed nearby. Ambrielle and Gavian crouched in the shadows by the wall, keeping out of the glows of torchlight.

Two Darterrans walked past, one noticeably larger than the other. Gavian's eyes widened when they both recognized him. It was Medigrin, the gral of the Darterran pack who opposed the Kavekkians. He carried a silver mallet, spinning it in his webbed hand as he walked.

"I don't care about the danger," Medigrin growled. "Keep digging."

"As you ask, my gral," said the other. "I only bring it up as a precaution."

Ambrielle and Gavian waited until they could no longer hear the Darterrans' steps and quickly moved into the vault chamber. Moving past the vault, Ambrielle's silbrace lights began flashing again. She stepped toward Gavian, who was standing in front of the waterfall.

"You ready this time?" Gavian could barely hide his excitement. Droplets of water gathered on his skin as he inched closer.

Ambrielle met his blue eyes, making sure the bladestaff was secure around her shoulder. "Ready."

Without further hesitation he stepped into the wall of water, vanishing completely. Ambrielle opened her pouch. "Wegin, I'm going to have to put you in here for a minute, okay?"

"Received," said Wegin, floating into the open bag. Ambrielle closed the cover and walked into the spraying mist.

CHAPTER 6

Sheets of water rushed over her when Ambrielle stepped through the falls. She found herself in a tunnel of moving mirrors made of gushing liquid. Her reflection flashed in the same way a strobe light would.

A throng of voices filled her mind, rushing toward her like a storm. Ambrielle began running through the tunnel, picking up speed as their words took shape. She refused to focus on them, clouding her mind with random thoughts and dashing out of the dark and into a bright light.

Gavian caught her by the arm before Ambrielle could run off the boulder into the water at full speed. She grabbed him, catching her breath, the adrenaline still racing through her. The rushing water flowed into a large pool from the mountain towering above them.

"You heard the voices?" Gavian shifted his feet, grabbing ahold of something sticking out of the rock, steadying them both on the slippery surface.

Ambrielle nodded, glancing at the white and gold obelisk that Gavian was holding onto. "Is that—"

Gavian's head tilted, following the path of her gaze. "My sword! Just where I left it!" He stepped off the boulder into the shallow pool. Gripping the handle, he strained until the blade came loose from the rock. He held the black, wooden hilt, lifting the white metal blade with gold edges. The end of the sword was broken and coated with crystalized mekkadium from the Blight Whidge he and Malidora had fought a few years before. Sliding the flat part of the blade across the legs of his pants, he wiped the mud and moss from its surface.

"So that's the rokensword," Ambrielle said, as he held it out for her to see. The rokenstone encased in the handle was black with violet sparkles inside. "It looks powerful."

Gavian extended his hand and helped her ease into the shallow pool. She waded through the flowing water until Gavian slowed near the edge of a pit lined with black stone. It was filled with water, taking on the endless current from the waterfall. "This is where we killed the Blight Whidge, where its dark blood spilled onto the ground. The hole kept growing until it reached the lake."

"I guess that's why Dracos'Arkon said not to disrupt their energy without being close to water." Ambrielle followed Gavian, who trudged around the water's edge. Her satchel started moving, and Wegin suddenly flew out. "I do not like the dark."

"Sorry Wegin." Ambrielle reclosed the covering on the satchel.

Wegin flew back and forth between them. "This appears to be a different planet. I will begin analysis."

"You brought that thing with you?" Gavian said, a large spray of steam erupting from a geyser ahead.

"Of course, I did." Ambrielle could feel the heat emanating from the steam coming up from the rock as they circled safely around it. "He may come in handy."

Wegin hovered over Ambrielle's shoulder. "This is Isodonia."

"Yes, very handy . . ." Gavian said sarcastically. The geyser hissed behind them, leaving the pungent smell of sulfur lingering in the air.

"Known for its vast array of unique crystals, Isodonia is home to one of the largest mining colonies in the known universe. It is also rich in useful metals like isorite, lakra, and silgen."

Gavian let out a sigh.

"I'm afraid that is all the data I possess about this world, but I will acquire more while we are here," said Wegin.

They moved away from the mountain, traveling across a road of hard clay. Eventually they came to a walled city. A mixture of stone and wood, the walls seemed hastily built, certainly without aesthetics in mind. "This is Grenova, but I don't remember the walls being this high before."

Ambrielle stood next to him. "Sometimes memories aren't perfect and change the way we perceive something."

Gavian moved along the wall. "There should be a gate right here. He examined the boards, attempting to look through any crack he could find. "It used to be open to outsiders for trade." He squinted as he tried looking through the space. "There were people of all kinds coming in and out of here."

"You have changed a lot in the four years since you were away," Ambrielle said. "I suppose it's natural for some parts of the world to change too."

"I suppose." Gavian pressed his lips together. He kept looking at the walls in dismay.

Ambrielle moved up beside him. "Where I live, things are always changing. There may be a store in one area, and a year later, there's a different store there. Everything changes."

Gavian rubbed the whiskers on his chin. "Something just doesn't feel right about this."

"When we find Darby and Dexius we can ask them," Ambrielle suggested. "Which way is Strakenbridge?"

Gavian faced away from the walled city, staring at the horizon. "Let's see. Muloken is down this road that way," Gavian pointed into the distance. "The brook nearby could lead us to Strakenbridge, but that wouldn't be the most direct way." He moved his arm toward the right. "That should be about it. Let's go this way."

"That seems very scientific," Ambrielle said sarcastically.

Gavian looked back. "If it's not exactly right, it will take us close to it."

"I thought you had a bad sense of direction." Ambrielle grinned. "Maybe we should go the opposite way."

Gavian took a deep breath in. "It can't be the opposite . . ." He exhaled. "I'm going this way. You can criticize me all you want if I'm wrong."

"I'm teasing, Gavian," Ambrielle said. "We're out here together, on your home world. This should be fun."

He forced a grin. "Yeah, you're right. I guess I'm a little on edge."

"I understand. I get nervous seeing friends again after a long time," Ambrielle said. "Lead on. I will go wherever you wish to go."

Gavian started out, leaving the dirt path that led to Grenova and heading into the grassy plains. The bendy, tall grass gave way to a terrain of ridges formed in dried hardened mud. Pools of water collected in the ridged channels, providing a resource for small, scaly creatures that zipped in and out of cracks and crevices in the rock.

"What are we going to do for food?" Ambrielle said. "I'm getting hungry."

Gavian paused for a moment and then continued. "We'll find something along the way."

The stormy sky churned above them while they trudged over the rugged ground. Climbing a small hill, Ambrielle noticed a red crystal protruding through the rock. She wandered over to take a closer look, and Gavian slowed his pace while walking ahead.

It was a rough-edged stone with a few naturally polished facets. The smooth surface gave it an icy look. Ambrielle tried to break part of it from the rock, but it was too strong. She aimed the silbrace toward it, intent on cutting through the base. It would make a nice souvenir to bring home.

How long must it have been here, forming from pressure and time? Starting as an irregular, rough-textured stone, nature had shaped it, painfully wearing down its rough exterior into a beautiful sheen. It was able to become this because it had been left to the toils of this world. The world allowed light and temperature to work their magic with its chemical composition. What might it become in fifty years? A hundred? Ambrielle took one last look at the red crystal and moved on. She decided not to interfere in whatever destiny had in mind for it.

Quickening her steps, she caught up with Gavian heading toward a line of trees. The land sloped downward as they neared the edge of the woods. With the dense clouds keeping out a portion of the sunlight, the shade of the trees made it all the darker. Ambrielle turned on the silbrace's lamp because she didn't want to step near anything that could bite. The dim sunlight ahead seemed bright by contrast, peeking through the sparse row of trees ahead.

A body of still water, too wide to cross, lay before them. Beyond it were rows of sturdy-looking houses, oddly hexagonal in shape. Ambrielle hated to admit it to Gavian, but she was already growing tired. Even though it was daytime here, they had spent all day and into the night in Anatharia. It was likely late on Earth as well. Either way, her body's time clock was telling her it was time to rest. If this town was welcoming to strangers, it sure would be nice to be able to sleep someplace cozy.

"What town is that?" she said, as Gavian walked along the side of the water.

He weaved his way through short green trees and scattered bushes. "That's what I'm trying to find out."

Shuffling through damp leaves, they came to a place where the water ended. A small road in the middle of the woods led into the town. The buildings and houses were all assembled in a circle around a large pond in the middle. Old clothing lay discarded along the dirt path. Two wheels, made of wood and big enough to fit a wagon, sat broken near what appeared to be an old inn. They neared the structure.

Only silence greeted them as they moved onto a path that circled the pond. Ambrielle slowed, unsure if the residents would welcome strangers. Gavian approached one of the buildings, moving to a boarded-up window to peer inside.

He shook his head and continued past a stack of logs speckled with dirt licked up by a recent rain. Ambrielle wandered between the houses to a small garden. "Hello!" she called out, leaning down near the leafy plants that grew in the soil. Their produce was picked clean.

Ambrielle spotted a grove of small trees behind one of the houses. It looked like someone had picked most of it, but there were a few round yellow fruits still hanging from the trees. The fruit was slightly firm to the touch when she snapped it off the tree. She bit into the fibrous texture; it had a tangy, sour taste, as though it had not yet ripened. Still, it would be something to fill her empty stomach.

Gavian's lightblade cut through the boards covering the door to the house, while she gathered as much fruit as she could carry. She rushed toward the house as Gavian opened the door. The interior was furnished, with other decorations still in place. A melted candle sat in the middle of a square table with five chairs around it. Quilts were draped over a wooden couch in front of a large blue and gray rug on the floor.

"What do you think, Wegin?" Ambrielle asked, as Gavian pulled a chair out from the table.

Wegin floated around the room and then down the hallway. Ambrielle sat beside Gavian, letting the fruit roll onto the table surface. He took one, inspecting it in his hand for a moment before taking a bite.

"I do not detect any intelligent life forms," said Wegin, zooming beside Ambrielle.

Gavian paused munching on the piece of fruit. "Hear that? It doesn't think you're intelligent."

"He's smart enough to know we already know we are here." Ambrielle smirked.

"Affirmative. Your presence was pre-established and thus was excluded from my analysis," Wegin said. "There are currently 1,098 life forms inside, which include 164 species of insect and 1 species of mammal."

Ambrielle felt her chest tighten. "Hold on, let's go to one of the other houses."

"The other houses would only have slightly higher or lower numbers," Wegin said. "They are all in generally the same state of maintenance as this one. Moreover, these numbers are not even abnormal. They are in the normal range."

"Are you serious? Okay, never report the number of bugs again." She took another bite of the fruit, trying to put her mind on something else. "What do you think happened here? Why would everyone leave this place?"

Gavian swallowed before speaking. "I don't know, but it's beginning to worry me. The buildings are in good condition though. It's nothing like the condition of Muloken or Samavere when the Nulthereals attacked."

"They didn't leave in too big of a hurry." Ambrielle sucked out some of the watery juice spilling from the fruit in her hand. "They took the time to barricade the windows and doors."

Gavian's eyes wandered around the room. "Yeah, doesn't make much sense."

"We should check the rest of the house and see if we can find a clue." Ambrielle liked the idea of solving a mystery, but Gavian sat quietly, finishing off the piece of fruit. She peeked through a slit in the boarded window. The other houses across from them were quiet and calm. A road trailed off from the center of town through the woods that surrounded them. Part of the pond was in view, reflecting the cloudy sky beginning to grow dark with the setting of the sun.

Gavian finished another bite and got up from the table. "Oh, you're waiting for me?"

"I thought you would be more familiar with the houses on Isodonia," Ambrielle said, though in truth she was a bit nervous about walking into the end of the dark hallway alone. Wegin may not have found anything, but she was unsure how infallible his information was. She turned on her light.

"Waiting for the next request," said Wegin, as he hovered over Ambrielle's shoulder.

The three of them entered a room with a big shelf filled with old books of stitched-together parchment. There could be interesting information here, but it would take hours, if not days, to go through. The other two rooms were bedrooms. One contained two small beds with clothes stacked on top of them. Three carved wooden figures of swordsmen stood on a shelf beside one of the beds.

In the other room was a large bed. Someone had taken time to make it up perfectly before leaving. A barely used candle was set on a table beside the bed. Something didn't seem quite right. Even though there were signs that someone lived here, its state gave the appearance of a set piece more than a real house.

Ambrielle looked around to make sure no one was there, and then she opened one of the drawers. A few pairs of trousers with patches sewn into them were in the first drawer. Another contained necklaces and rings mainly, set with sparkling gemstones. They had an old style to them that was not common on Earth. It would be nice to keep one to take back. She picked up one of the rings and tried it on. It was too big for her ring finger, but she didn't have to wear it. She could start a collection of things she found on other planets.

She rubbed her bottom lip, imagining showing it to her friends. No one would have anything like this. Ambrielle set the ring back inside the drawer. It was fun to dream about, but she couldn't take it. The people that owned the house would probably be coming back eventually.

Gavian seemed interested in one of the shelves, picking up different pieces and setting them back down. They appeared to be claws from an animal, not just the nails but the fingers along with them. The upright claws made creepy shadows against the back of the shelf when Gavian's light moved over it. She knew people who had animal heads mounted on their walls as trophies, so perhaps it wasn't that unusual. It struck her as eerie, nonetheless.

A rush of air outside made Ambrielle jump, a whooshing sound followed by a quick screech. Gavian moved to the window, and Ambrielle came up beside him. They peeked through the cracks between the boards as a hollow clomping approached outside. A dark-cloaked man riding on a four-legged creature strode around the pond in the center of town. The creature was tall, with a muscular body like that of a horse but had a long neck that tapered to its head. It had a short snout and a bulbed forehead with two small horns protruding from each side of the top of its head. Its long legs extended outward, bending at its knees and ending with hooves. A short snakelike tail swayed behind it while it came to a stop.

The rider dismounted, pulling a silver sword from beneath his robes as he ambled toward a house not far from them. The sword's hilt was oddly curved and appeared glassy like a green crystal. His black robes shifted like silhouettes against moonlight. Something seemed unnaturally imposing about him. The tall figure made his way to the door, searching for any separation he could find to glance through before moving to the next building. Even with the boards covering the opening, Ambrielle felt exposed and ducked below the window. "Who is that?"

"How should I know?" Gavian leaned away from the wall, looking down at her.

"I require more data about this planet to answer questions such as this and—" said Wegin.

"Wegin, shut up!" Ambrielle said. "Please."

Ambrielle and Gavian stared at each other for a moment, listening to each other's breath.

"What do you think he's doing?" Ambrielle whispered, time seeming to slow. Every moment that passed felt like a lifetime.

Gavian's eyes darted around the room. "Why do you always ask me things I have no way of knowing?"

"Well, it's your planet," Ambrielle sharply whispered. "I thought you might know something about it."

"Pardon me, I didn't realize I was a tour guide," said Gavian, sitting on the floor.

Ambrielle could hear her heart beating inside her. If the front door opened right now, she feared her body wouldn't be able to take the stress. She couldn't resist any longer. Ambrielle rose up and peered through the crack between the boards. The rider was at the house beside them, scraping his sword against the walls as he moved along the outside. Diving below the window, Ambrielle tried to calm her breath. "Maybe you should find out what he wants," she said, glancing down, realizing her hands were shaking.

Gavian slid toward the bed. "Are you crazy? I'm pretty sure he's not here to borrow a cube of sugar. There are too many strange things going on around here. Whoever he is, I would rather he not know we are here."

The anticipation of hearing the door open suddenly was too much. She looked through the window again, watching the cloaked man slowly move toward the house they were in. He moved toward the window of the living area. Inside the black hood, he wore a silver mask. The mask was inhuman, sloped toward the chin in a long triangle shape, almost like a beak pointing down instead of out. The hollow eyeholes had an evil slant.

Moving away from the window, the man stood in front of the door. Ambrielle realized he was looking at the boards they had cut through to get inside. The door sprung open, and Gavian and Ambrielle both scurried behind the bed.

The long whoosh and short screech sounded again when the dark figure stepped into the main room. The robed man continued to walk about the room, and the wood creaked with each heavy step. Ambrielle's heart raced as she readied her silbrace.

The clunking footsteps came closer. He was coming down the hall, scraping his sword along the walls along the way. He entered the other bedroom, dragging the metallic spike across the walls. The whooshing sound rose again while the unknown figure entered the last room. At this distance, it sounded like a deep shivering inhalation, followed by a short screeching exhale.

Ambrielle slid under the bed as much as she could without making a sound. She grabbed onto Gavian for comfort and to stop from shaking. He reached out, finding her hand and holding it tight. The metallic scuffing against the walls stopped.

The heavy footsteps started again, this time moving further away. The front door opened and then clapped against the frame when it closed. Gavian and Ambrielle crawled to the window. In the quiet gloom, the cloaked man placed the silver weapon back into one of the bags on the creature's saddle before climbing on and riding off down the road he'd come in on.

Gavian and Ambrielle stared out the window in silence. He glanced at her from the corner of his eye, and she turned away from the window toward him. "Was that a whidge?"

"No," he replied, moving from his knees into a sitting position on the floor. "The whidge, even in human form, radiated darkness. That was someone in black clothing."

Ambrielle moved to the bed, sitting on the edge. "Are you sure? There was something . . . off about him. He was wearing a mask over his face."

"I wonder if that is why the people left." Gavian leaned his sword against the wall and sat on the bed beside her.

"Do you think it has something to do with closing up Grenova?" Ambrielle wondered.

Gavian's eyes continued to dart around the room. He didn't respond but seemed to be pondering the question.

She leaned back, propping herself on her hands and burrowing them into the soft quilt. "I'm tired. I need sleep, but I don't know if I can stay here now."

"We'll be fine." Gavian rested his hand on top of hers. "Whoever it was is gone now. Whatever they were looking for, they didn't find it here."

"I hope you're right." Ambrielle grabbed hold of his hand. "It's getting dark in here."

Gavian stood and ignited the blade from his silbrace. The room glowed in its red light as he leaned over the bedside table. Picking up the candle, he brought it into the beam enough that it lit the wick. He set the glowing candle back onto the table and climbed into the bed.

Ambrielle smiled, pulled down the quilt, and slid underneath. "Good night, Gavian."

He smiled back in the flickering candlelight and he got into the bed beside her. "Good night."

She felt his heart beating with his chest rested against her back. It was comforting knowing someone was here with her in the dark. Someone she trusted.

CHAPTER 7

R ED HUES BURNED through the gaps in the boards covering the window as Ambrielle climbed out of bed. Gavian remained asleep, and she chose not to wake him. Creeping into the hallway, she remained on her guard in case the black-cloaked man had returned.

Scanning each room on her way, she moved into the living area and peeked outside. A blue bird flew onto a branch of one of the trees behind the houses. Three low chirps stood out from the other singing and chattering of wildlife near the town. These were quite different from the high-pitched songs of the birds on Earth or even Anatharia. The blue bird flew away as a gray bird darted toward it and settled on the same branch once the blue one had left. Perching on the limb of a taller tree, the blue bird resumed its song. A moment later, it moved again when the gray bird flew toward it.

Ambrielle watched them continue to play this game through the trees of the nearby woods until she lost sight of them. Sitting at the table, she took a bite of one of the fruits she had gathered the day before. Her thoughts wandered to Earth where her brother and father might be waking up, getting ready for breakfast. Her dad would be frying strips of bacon as he always did, her brother, Ryan, asking him when it was going to be ready. Though the time difference between the worlds made it unlikely it was morning there, she chose to imagine them all eating break-fast at the same time.

The image of them together made her happy. She had learned from her mother's absence not to take anything for granted. Is this really where she should be right now? So far away from her family, on a distant planet, somewhere out in the universe. Suddenly, being here felt a bit wrong. No matter where she was, it seemed some kind of doubt would seep in. This was likely nothing more than stress and anxiety. If she focused on whatever the next step was, she would feel right again.

Ambrielle heard footsteps coming down the hall. Gavian stumbled into the room, looking as though he was half asleep. His face seemed to brighten when he saw her at the table. Pulling up a chair next to her, he sat and took a bite of the fruit. "I hope you got enough sleep. I want to get to Strakenbridge by nightfall."

"I hope you can keep up with me then." Ambrielle tried to fix the mess of thick hair bunched up on top of his head.

Gavian shook his head, moving from her reach as he finished up the last bite of fruit. When they moved outside, Ambrielle ran over to the fruit trees and gathered what was left to place in her bag. They set off up the road that led through the small, wooded area, passing by a long block of wood nailed to two posts. Both turned to read the sign at the entrance of the town. *Avendal* it said. Moving on into the wide-open wilderness, they crossed over a series of small hills, through tall grass and golden meadows filled with flowers.

"What are those?" Ambrielle leaned toward a cluster of flowers where two flying creatures flapped their wings around them. They were like large butterflies with triangular tail wings and two slanted wings on each side of their bodies. Their wings were teal with light brown tips and black patterns that resembled a stained glass window.

Gavian's feet swished through the grass on his way over. "Flitterlyns, we had those on Rethia too."

"I wonder how they get all the way up the mountain." She held out her finger, hoping one of them would rest on it.

"You know, if you really want one to land on your finger, you should try being a little less intimidating with that bladestaff," Gavian teased.

Ambrielle rolled her eyes. "Very funny. I'm sure everyone is just trembling with fear at the sight of me."

Gavian chuckled. "I'm sure they are. But in all seriousness, I guess we could both use some practice with our fighting skills."

Ambrielle nodded in agreement. "I feel like I'm a bit uncoordinated with this thing sometimes."

Gavian smiled. "We'll get there. After all, you are wearing the fur of that raestrig you killed."

A breath of excitement, pride, and fear filled her when she thought about that day. She appreciated that Gavian recognized that she brought some value to this mission. "Thanks. It was mostly luck."

"I'm not exactly a master swordsman," said Gavian. "I guess everyone needs a bit of luck starting out."

Ambrielle grinned. "Yeah, but you're still better than me."

Gavian shook his head. "Not by much. But one day we'll be good enough to take on anything."

She laughed, turning her attention back to the flitterlyns. "Do you think some of them just came into existence up there or did they fly all the way up the mountain to start a flitterlyn colony?" Ambrielle gave up on them alighting on her finger and stood up. "Or maybe something else brought them there."

Wegin rotated as if looking at the flitterlyns with his different sensors. "Many insects are capable of flying at high altitudes, including some butterflies. They may have flown up the mountain over time, or they could have been carried up by winds or other natural forces. However, more research is required to determine more about this particular species."

"See, Wegin *is* handy," Ambrielle said. She inspected a cluster of flowers growing among the wispy grass.

"What are you talking about?" Gavian turned around and walked ahead. "Let's not talk about Rethia. I despise that place."

"It wasn't all bad." Ambrielle reached down and picked one of the yellow wildflowers. "Rethia will always be home. It made you what you are today."

"Living there taught me nothing," said Gavian. "Nothing good anyway."

"Adversity is a powerful teacher." Ambrielle twirled the stem of the flower between her fingers while she followed. "Steel doesn't become a sword without fire. It must be shaped, tempered, sharpened into the weapon it is meant to be."

Gavian stopped and turned to face her. "What I am now, it is despite Rethia, not because of it."

"But that is because of its leaders, not its people," said Ambrielle. "You still have good memories there."

Gavian glanced back as he strode ahead. "It was all a lie. I don't know if there is anywhere I can really call home. There's no place that offers true comfort because there is no one I can trust."

"Not even *me*?" Ambrielle felt her chest begin to cave in.

"You haven't done anything to make me not trust you, but neither had anyone else until they did. I am comfortable with you, isn't that enough for now?" he said. "Trust is a process, right?"

Ambrielle brushed her golden-brown hair out of her eyes. "Well, I trust *you*."

"How can you trust me already? Maybe we have different definitions of trust, but it takes time." Gavian glanced ahead. "When you left Solsellion, I didn't know if you were ever coming back."

Her throat felt constricted, making it harder to breathe. She reached for the jewel on the necklace her mother had given her, trying to calm her nerves. "You said you understood. I'd planned on coming right back until I realized my mother had died."

"I do understand," said Gavian. "Like I said, it's just going to—"

Rustling in the grass on the other side of the hill gave them pause. Ambrielle readied her bladestaff, and Gavian raised his sword. With no place to hide in the open field, they braced themselves for whatever was about to come over the rise.

A strange four-legged creature with yellow-green skin moved down the hill toward them, carrying a walking stick. Everyone startled when they saw each other. The creature wore a brown hat and leathery boots on each foot. Two bags were draped over its body, hanging on each side of it. "You are heading in the wrong direction," he said. "Don't you know that?"

Ambrielle relaxed after hearing its friendly tone. "What direction should we be headed?"

"Any other direction," he replied.

Ambrielle looked at Gavian. "What is that?" she whispered.

"A Breghobbin," he replied.

"Is he safe?" she asked.

Gavian nodded his head then turned to address the Breghobbin. "And why is that?"

"If you keep heading that way, you'll be going straight into the war." The Breghobbin pointed his stick toward the horizon behind him.

"War? What war?" Gavian gave his sword a spin, bringing it back into position pointing at the ground.

The Breghobbin reached into one of the pockets of the bags draped over his back. "The Gurrians. They've been razing city after city. Every day they get closer to Strakenbridge."

Gavian stuck his blade into the ground. "That's where we're headed."

"We have friends in Strakenbridge," Ambrielle said.

The Breghobbin's sharp teeth crunched as he chewed on something he had pulled from his bag. "It is doubtful your friends would still be there. Those of us who can't fight the giants are leaving."

"Who are the Gurrians?" Gavian leaned on the hilt of his sword as the purple light of the rokenstone reflected on his face.

"They are giants from the cold north." The Breghobbin spit something into the weeds beside him. "They've united with the Grundians to destroy Nalacea, slaughtering everyone in their path."

"Why would they kill everyone? Don't they need other races to do their work for them?"

"Nothing about it makes sense," said the Breghobbin. "The world has gone crazy."

Gavian shuffled his feet in the tall weeds. "Where is everyone heading to?"

"The Gulflands, as far away from the giants as possible."

Grabbing the hilt with both hands, Gavian rested his chin on top of them. "If they have left, I don't know that I'll ever find them again."

"We'll find them, Gavian." Ambrielle set her hand on his shoulder.

"Don't stay around here long." The Breghobbin continued chewing the small crunchy pieces. "There are Grundians in these lands as well. They are pushing toward Strakenbridge on both sides."

The wind blew across the grassy hillside in waves. The skirt of Ambrielle's blue outfit rippled in the gust. "What's stopping them from heading south once they are done with Strakenbridge?"

"Strakenbridge is well defended. We can only hope they will prevail," said the Breghobbin. "If they don't, at least they will reduce the giants' numbers."

Ambrielle pointed the bladestaff toward the distant horizon. "Well, maybe if everyone stayed to fight, you could stop them at Strakenbridge."

The Breghobbin stopped chewing. "I'm not a soldier," he said. "I would have trouble walking on two feet to hold a sword. I can't fight giants. Those who are capable are staying, and I wish them well. Most of the shopkeepers and craftsmen like me would not be any use in this war."

Gavian pulled the sword out of the ground. "Soldiers will need craftsmen."

"I stayed as long as I could," said the Breghobbin. "Too many others have left. I can no longer afford to buy the materials I need. There's no way to make a living there anymore. You would be better off to join me."

Gavian turned toward the rows of hills behind the Breghobbin, causing the breeze to lift the hair on his forehead. "Thank you, but that is our mission," Gavian spoke with conviction. "We're not turning back now."

"It's his destiny," Ambrielle teased.

"You will need fate on your side if you are going there." The Breghobbin leaned on his walking stick and began walking past them. "Some must see for themselves to understand when they have been given wisdom. I hope your journey does not end before the lesson is learned."

Ambrielle watched the Breghobbin move down the hill. "I think he just told us we are stubborn and stupid."

Gavian ran the rest of the way to the hilltop. "I never said it was my destiny."

"It was just the way you said it,"—Ambrielle grinned—"'We're not turning back now,' all heroic sounding. We're heading into a war to find your friends, in the heart of the storm, sounds like destiny to me."

He flashed a hint of a smile but appeared to hold it back. "I wish life did work that way."

They stood at the edge of a small cliff with three forests lying ahead of them. There were two smaller wooded areas to their right and a wide forest to their left. A stream curved through the glen between the hills, disappearing into the trees.

Heading down the slope, Gavian walked toward the stream. Ambrielle watched for a moment and then followed him to the edge of the water. Filling a container with the water from the slow-moving brook, Gavian brought it to his mouth and took a drink.

"Is that water safe?" Ambrielle raised her brow as she watched him gulp it down.

Gavian filled up the container again. "Seems fine to me."

Wegin swooped to the flowing surface of the stream, dipping some of his sensors into the water. "It appears to be safe for all life forms to consume."

Ambrielle took a drink and handed the container back to him. Gavian placed the container back into his satchel. "So you believe that thing?"

"Well, he can analyze bacteria better than we can. It's best to make sure," Ambrielle said, walking with Gavian beside the stream toward the forest.

Gavian swung his blade, cutting a path through the thicket as he entered the woods. "I walked across this land for close to a year without needing synthetics to tell me what to do. Worrying about everything all the time . . . it can take the fun out of it."

"Out of what?" Ambrielle stepped onto the path he was making, keeping a safe distance from his sword.

The blade made a white streak when Gavian slashed through the underbrush. "Living. If you worry too much about dying or getting hurt, you may survive longer, but are you living? How can you discover new things without taking a risk?"

"I take risks." Ambrielle stepped over a group of yellow wildflowers. "You can't rush into everything without knowledge, but some things you do have to learn for yourself. My mom used to tell me not to be afraid to make mistakes, that failure is the path to success."

Gavian propped himself up on his sword, wiping the sweat from his forehead. "That's what Lirah used to tell me." He picked up his sword and went back to chopping through the reeds.

"Do you miss her?" Ambrielle allowed the thought to slip out before she realized it.

"It would be nice to see her on occasion, I suppose." Gavian swung down on a looping vine crossing his path.

Ambrielle swallowed, trying to bring moisture to her throat. "Do you plan to see her while you are here?"

"It would be too risky going back to Rethia," Gavian said.

Ambrielle kicked through a tangle of vines. "But otherwise, you would go and see her."

Gavian lowered his sword as he came to a stop. "What are you getting at exactly? Lirah and I practically grew up together. She was the only friend I had for most of my life. I had feelings for her once, but that is over. Now that I've had time to think about everything, I think it was for the best. I don't think we were suited for each other."

Ambrielle's cheeks burned. "I'm glad everything worked out the way it did too. Everything happens for a reason."

"You keep saying that." He began walking further into the forest. "What do you mean?"

"Well, I mean that things have a way of working out for the best in the end," she said. "If we could see the timeline of our whole lives, we would understand that even the worst things are leading us to what we need."

Gavian hacked at a vine that was giving him particular difficulty. "It doesn't always work out like that though. There are plenty of things that go wrong, as much as you need them to be right."

Ambrielle slid the chain of her necklace back and forth. "When my mother passed away, it felt like the whole universe was against me. My friends stopped talking to me. I got behind in school. I think I actually invited it because I wanted people to notice what I was going through. I didn't want to go to them as if I needed them. I was supposed to be too strong for that."

"From what you told me, it wasn't like anyone intervened." He continued to chop into the thick but limp vine. "You had to do a lot of work to get things in order again. Life is chaos. The universe doesn't care if you live or die. It's neutral, indifferent. It's up to us to try to bring the chaos around us into order."

"The universe has laws, systems. It's not all chaos," said Ambrielle. "Sometimes things in our life break, but it happens so we can grow and overcome when we need it most. Like I said before about steel being tempered."

"So, anyone who dies does so to help other people grow?" said Gavian.

Ambrielle collected her thoughts. "Everything in this universe has a beginning and an end. Everything dies, but not without purpose. I don't think my mother died for no reason. I don't know what that reason is yet, and I may never know. But I know I have matured and grown because of it. If I could have her back, I would gladly take it over any personal growth, but I think there is something greater than us out there in the universe. It probably doesn't see death the same way we do. It knows what we need better than we do ourselves.

"The universe must want me dead then." The vine whipped through the bushes when Gavian's blade went through. "It has tried to kill me a few times."

"But you're still here." Ambrielle brushed the reeds away as they pressed ahead.

"Maybe for now but . . ." Gavian's voice trailed off suddenly, and he quickly placed his sword underneath his belt, moving to shield her eyes from the sight ahead.

Oblivious to Gavian's gesture, Ambrielle stepped around beside him. The lifeless forms of several individuals lay scattered on the ground, forming a somber heap amidst a cluster of small cabins. Gavian ventured further into the diffused sunlight, his gaze fixated on the motionless figures strewn across the grass. Men, women, and even children all lay still, their bodies bearing visible wounds to their chests and abdomens. The air was heavy with an eerie silence, broken only by the faint rustle of leaves and the weight of their somber breaths.

Ambrielle turned away from the sight. "Who would do something like this?"

"This does not appear natural," said Wegin, hovering over the bodies. "I can only surmise that they were murdered, but allow me to gather more information to do a full analysis." Wegin scanned the corpses with a light beam, one after the other.

Gavian and Ambrielle moved on, passing by a large stone with the name *Ferinoke* chiseled into it. They moved into a clearing, walking between rows of wooden cabins. The clearing ended ahead, leading to more thick woods.

As they approached the forest's edge, the rustling of the trees sent shivers down Ambrielle's spine. Her heart pounded when a horde of giants burst through the thick foliage and emerged into the sunlit clearing. The colossal beings towered over them, standing ten to twelve feet tall, with large bellies and massive arms that displayed their strength.

With a surge of adrenaline, Gavian and Ambrielle swiftly changed course, darting back into the shelter of the dense woods. Despite their seemingly slow motions, the giants closed on them with astonishing speed, their massive strides devouring the distance.

A towering giant's hand closed around Ambrielle, lifting her off the ground. Upside-down, she dangled helplessly. The giant scrutinized her with curiosity and amusement. The giants swarmed Gavian when he reached for his sword, seizing him in the same manner. Gavian's sword slipped from his belt, crashing to the ground below.

"Add them to the pile!" said one of the giants.

Another one stepped forward. "We need kips for the mines. Take them to Grungal!"

"Ogolameth wants us to kill the kips," said the first one.

The giant carrying Ambrielle joined in the debate. "Ogolameth said to kill everyone that lived in this town, and we already did. These kips are ours. I say we take them to Grungal."

"Ogolameth needs more dead. Kill them both!" the first one said again.

"You touch her, you die!" Gavian shouted, the metallic hum of the lightblade in his silbrace activated. The blade of light pierced the big, meaty hand of the giant holding him. A cry of guttural pain came from the giant, and he dropped Gavian to the ground. Wisps of smoke curled from the seared wound on the Grundian's hand, accompanied by a faint aroma of charred flesh.

"Gavian!" Ambrielle cried out, as the giant raised his huge fist to pound Gavian into the dirt. The fourth giant came over and picked Gavian up off the ground, pinning his arms against his body. "Wait!" said the giant. "I know this one!"

"How do you know this kip?" said the wounded giant.

The fourth giant knocked the other on the head with his fist. "Look at him! It's Gadunk!" He shoved Gavian closer to their faces so they could get a good look.

"It *is* Gadunk!" said one of them, squinting.

"We've been looking for you, Gadunk," said the giant holding Ambrielle. "You thought you could leave Grunda?"

"He let all the kips out!" said the third one.

The one holding Ambrielle looked him over. "What should we do with him?"

The wounded Grundian snarled. "We should pluck his limbs."

"No," said the one holding Gavian. "We take him to Grunch!"

"Grunch been looking for Gadunk," said the third. "He will reward us."

The Grundian shook Gavian, spilling the blanket and water container from his satchel. After he saw that the lightblade was not coming off, he pulled a cluster of vines out of one of the trees and wrapped it around Gavian, trapping his silbrace against his body where he couldn't use it. "Take the other kip to Grungal."

The first and second Grundians swiftly ensnared Ambrielle with thick, coiling vines, immobilizing her when they tightened their hold. Ambrielle struggled against the constraints. The rough texture of the vines scraped against her skin. She kicked her legs and writhed in the giant's grasp, trying desperately to catch a glimpse of Gavian. "Gavian, I'll find you!"

"Ambrielle!" Gavian's shout was muffled as he twisted and turned in the giant's hands and they moved in the opposite direction.

She watched the Grundians carry him off until they disappeared into the dense foliage.

CHAPTER 8

DRENCHED IN PERSPIRATION, Gavian found himself helplessly ensnared within the colossal grip of the Grundian. The passing hours blurred together, and his consciousness teetered on the precipice of exhaustion while they traversed the untamed wilderness. The thunderous footfalls of the Grundians reverberated through the air, shaking the very ground beneath them. One of the giants bore a striking resemblance to Grack, a Grundian that Gavian recalled from his time in Grunda.

Finally, the procession came to a halt, settling into an impromptu camp for the night. Gavian's heart sank when he realized his captors had created a makeshift pit, a cruel crevasse hewn into the unforgiving rock. It was to be his prison, a place of confinement from which he could not escape. No matter how desperately he tried, his leaps fell short of breaching the precipice, leaving him trapped within its unforgiving depths.

Defeated, Gavian slumped against the rocky walls of his subterranean confinement, seeking respite in the meager comfort they offered. Weariness consumed him, urging him toward the edge of sleep, even in this desolate pit.

&

With the arrival of dawn's gentle light, the relentless hands of Grack plucked Gavian from the depths of his rocky prison.

Resuming their arduous journey across the vast plains of Isodonia, Gavian's mind raced, torn between the dire need to escape this plight and his unwavering concern for Ambrielle. The knowledge that she was being forcibly taken to a place known as Grungal gnawed at his thoughts. In the clutches of the Grundians, she would be subjected to laborious tasks, undoubtedly serving as their unwilling pawn. Yet, he found a glimmer of solace in the belief that she might survive the ordeal.

Regrettably, the same could not be said for Gavian. His prospects appeared grim, for he knew all too well the unimaginable strength wielded by the likes of Grunch. A death at the hands of such a behemoth would be an agonizing fate, a prospect he could ill afford to accept. Survival hinged on his ability to break free from this inescapable web of captivity. He steeled his resolve, the weight of impending doom only fueling his determination to concoct a plan, to seize the slimmest chance at freedom that awaited him in the darkest corners of his mind.

Gavian was suddenly dropped into the dirt, and several Grundians crowded in, surrounding him to have a look. "I found Gadunk!" said Grack.

"It *is* Gadunk," said a Grundian that Gavian knew as Plop.

As Gavian mustered his strength, he sat upright, determined to survey his confining surroundings. He was encircled by imposing walls of fallen, majestic tree trunks atop rugged rock, his vision obstructed by their towering presence. A pile of large rocks sat in the middle of the perimeter. To his right, remnants of a once-roaring bonfire lingered, its charred wood still emanating the faint scent of smoke. Amidst the gloom, a glimmer caught his weary gaze, beckoning him from the far corner of the enclosure. A pointed stone, radiant with a mesmerizing shade of green, seemed untouched by the weariness that surrounded him.

"We finally got him!" another giant said.

"I had to fetch water for weeks when you let the kips out!" Plop roared at him, covering the side of his face in spit.

Griz towered over him, his hulking form blotting out the sunlight. Gavian grimaced, using the sleeve of his torn shirt to wipe away the thick, viscous saliva that had landed on his face. The pungent odor of Plop's breath lingered in the air, assaulting his senses.

"I had to catch more tregs, and then I had to feed them!" Griz's deep voice boomed through the air.

Glug, a burly giant with a gruff voice, spoke up, his words laden with a mix of frustration and obligation. "I had to tend the crops!" he grumbled, his massive hands fidgeting as if still occupied with his agricultural duties.

"Let's see how far we can throw him," Plop suggested, a wicked grin spreading across his face.

Glug stepped forward, a devious glimmer in his eyes. "Let's see how far we can kick him."

Drin, a towering brute with a gravelly voice, joined in the sadistic banter. "We should see who can stomp him the flattest!" he bellowed.

The Grundians cheered with each proposition, their voices blending into a cacophony of excitement and anticipation. But their boisterous revelry abruptly ceased when thunderous footsteps approached, shaking the ground beneath them. The giants turned their attention away from Gavian, their expressions shifting from malicious glee to caution.

"You betrayed us, Gadunk," Grunch said, the ground shaking when he pounded the tree trunk he used as a club into the dirt beside Gavian. "And now you will suffer." With Grunch's weapon nearing, Gavian was reminded of the sticky remains caked between the gnarled roots on the end of it. He picked Gavian off the ground. Grunch was a giant among giants. Formidable and intimidating even to the biggest Grundian.

The other Grundians gathered around him, yelling and cheering. "What are you going to do with him, Grunch?"

Grunch tugged at the matted hairs on his chin, then lifted his club off the ground. A devious smile split across his face as he handed Gavian over to Grack. "Toss him into the air! I want to see how far I can smash him with my club."

The Grundians laughed and cheered while Grack prepared to throw Gavian. Struggling to get his hand free of the vines, Gavian tried to think of anything that might help him survive this. Was there a way to lessen the blow? Could he get his silbrace lightblade in a position to hit anything other than himself?

He was tossed up into the air, slowly turning over like a log. He flung back his shoulders and neck, pitching backward, and then stiffened his muscles to speed up his fall. Turbulence ripped through the air as Grunch swung and missed. The cheers died down when Gavian hit the ground hard. It took him a moment before he was able to catch his breath again.

Plop grabbed him and threw him toward Grunch. The cheering rose, and this time Gavian rolled hard when he left the fingertips of the Grundian, hoping it would mess with Grunch's timing. Another loud whoosh went over him. Grunch had missed again.

"We should kick him instead," Drin said.

Grunch swung his club at Drin, knocking him across the dirt into one of the walls. "This is my game! I'll get him on this one." Drin lay motionless on the ground.

Gavian struggled to move. If he could get the blade in position to attack the Grundian before he tossed him into the air, maybe he would have a chance.

"Grunch!" said one of the giants. "The stone!"

As dusk approached, the pointed stone glowed with a green light from within. Black, rotten vines and moss surrounded the stone. It looked familiar, like the stone in the dark forest deep in the swamp.

"Do not touch Gadunk until I get back." Grunch hurried toward the stone, sitting in front of it on his knees. He put his hands against the stone as he stared into it. The glowing light reflected on his face, and he seemed to be in a trance.

Grack kept Gavian pinned to the dirt with his foot, and the other Grundians went back to talking and taunting each other, some laughing. One of them punched Glug, and they started fighting. This should've been the best moment to escape, but Grack's foot was putting enough pressure on him that he could barely move. The more he wiggled around, the more weight the Grundian put on him.

Long shadows and orange streaks through the clouds marked the setting of the sun. Animals barked from the distant woods. A whistle rose from the horizon, growing louder. Another joined it, and then many more as something struck Grack. He lifted his foot off Gavian, pulling an arrow out of his thick hide. Swarms of arrows rained down on them, hitting the ground around him. Gavian rolled over and found a spot to use the giant as cover. After the initial shock, the Grundians ran to the stack of boulders in the corner of the walled area.

Grack bounded toward the rock pile, hurling the large stones toward the trees where the arrows were coming from. Gavian continued working to get his arms free of the vines. He rolled to one of the arrows stuck in the ground. After sliding along the dirt to where he could grab it with his hand, he pried the arrow out. He tried to turn the sharp arrowhead toward the vines. It wasn't working.

Another volley of arrows came from the trees, aimed at the approaching giants outside the perimeter. Most of the arrows either ricocheted or only barely penetrated the tough skin of the Grundians. One of the Grundians, however, was felled after being pummeled by so many arrows that a few of them plunged deep. The unseen archers seemed to split up, with the next salvo coming from multiple directions. Gavian tried to keep under the shadows of the tall Grundians while the arrows flew.

A group of lancers rushed from the tree line, charging the Grundians who were closing in on the archers' position. Glug underestimated the threat and was skewered by a lance. The other charging soldiers weren't so lucky, with the Grundians swinging fists and feet and knocking them away with deadly blows.

Grunch moved away from the stone, dazed at first but soon realizing what was happening. He pulled out an arrow that had lodged in his chest and grabbed his club. Stepping into the battle, Grunch used his tree club, swinging it in wide arcs. He decimated the lancers.

Gavian continued trying to free himself, rolling over when a huge furry creature came charging at him. As if the Grundians and the flying arrows weren't enough, a wild beast's jaws were now bearing down on him, and he had no way to defend himself. The beast grabbed him in its teeth and began dragging him across the clay.

Grunch leapt over the wall to attack the archers, while the furry beast carried Gavian through the opening in the logs and into the forest. A group of archers surrounded Grunch, most of them focusing all they had on him as he whaled away at them, breaking trees in his way. The beast carried Gavian toward a group of archers and dropped him onto the leaf-covered ground.

One of the archers cut through his bindings. Gavian nodded at the man and ignited the lightblade on his hand. Three Grundians pummeled soldiers from behind, dwindling their numbers and forcing them to flee. One of the Grundians grabbed a rock from the ground, and Gavian drove the lightblade into the lower back of the giant. The Grundian stumbled, reaching for the cauterized wound. The bowmen focused their fire on the wounded Grundian, who fell to the ground decorated in arrows.

Grunch continued his rampage, killing soldiers while he smashed into the trees where some of the archers were positioned. Although most of the archers scattered for cover, one with long auburn hair underneath a dark red hood dashed into the clearing Grunch had bored into the forest. Grunch swung his club toward her, smashing it into the ground. While Grunch ripped the weapon from the turf to raise it again, the red archer fired on the run, loading arrow after arrow, shooting at Grunch. Most of the shots bounced off, and the ones that stuck did little damage.

Grunch turned, following the red archer, as she zigzagged around him. With Grunch's back now exposed to the bowmen, they fired another volley, landing several shots in his skin. Grunch became furious, smacking a soldier with his club while keeping his gaze on the red archer.

With Grunch momentarily distracted, Gavian seized the opportunity. In a brisk motion, he lunged forward, his lightblade slicing through the air with precision. When the blade made contact with the back of Grunch's massive leg a sizzling sound filled the air, accompanied by the acrid scent of burning flesh. Smoke billowed from the searing wound, mingling with the forest air.

Before Gavian could strike again, Grunch reacted with a sudden, forceful kick. His huge foot connected with the ground, causing clumps of dirt and loose stones to be propelled into the air. The projectiles pelted Gavian, the gritty texture of earth grazing his skin and the sharp edges of stones stinging upon impact. The assault momentarily disoriented him, his vision obscured by a cloud of dust and debris.

Grunch leapt forward, his forceful landing shaking the surrounding trees and sending leaves fluttering to the ground. The impact left in the dirt displayed his intent to crush anything in his path. The red archer gracefully evaded Grunch's assault, and a dance of survival unfolded. The contrast between the immense size and power of the giant and the agile, swift movements of the archer created a mesmerizing spectacle. Each leap, tumble, and evasive maneuver showcased the grace and finesse of the red archer.

Grunch repeatedly stomped the ground, creating more thunderous impact craters. With lightning reflexes, the red archer sprang into action, executing a series of acrobatic hurdles and springs to evade the devastating blows. Meanwhile, a group of archers unleashed a barrage of arrows upon the smaller Grundians, diverting their attention, while Grunch, the imposing figure among them, focused his relentless assault on the red archer.

With the red archer fueling his rage, Grunch continued his unwavering onslaught, rapidly pounding the surrounding area with his colossal club. The red archer, however, displayed incredible agility, deftly weaving around the bone-shattering strikes. Grunch's stamina waned with exhaustion setting in, while the archer expertly exploited every opportunity to remain just out of his reach.

With a swift motion, the archer managed to gain some distance, quickly turning around and unleashing a deadly arrow toward Grunch. The arrow soared through the air with blinding speed, leaving a trail of brilliance in its wake. The arrow found its mark, striking Grunch squarely in the forehead.

In an instant, Grunch froze, his gigantic frame quivering as he dropped his massive club to the ground. Smoke billowed from his charred and blackened head where the arrow remained. The ground itself quaked under the weight of Grunch's lifeless body, the earth trembling with the impact of his colossal fall.

Gavian worked his way through the incoming soldiers. Ahead of him, Plop and Grack leapt into the fray, causing them to scatter. Gavian swept his blade across Grack's side, diving between Plop's feet before he could retaliate. The angered Grack shoved Plop to the ground to get to Gavian. The soldiers went after Plop, quickly dispatching him with a barrage of arrows. Grack snatched Gavian off the ground, trapping him in his giant hand.

An evil grin spread across Grack's face as he began squeezing Gavian. He turned his back toward the arrows and kicked away some of the lancers closing in. It was getting harder to breathe, so Gavian pressed his feet against the Grundian's huge palm, struggling to escape the grip. Pushing himself up, he found a pocket in the giant's hand where he could move his silbrace arm enough.

Gavian burned through the Grundian's fingers with the lightblade. Grack immediately loosened his grip, and Gavian jumped from the Grundian's hand. He blasted the giant in the face, cutting into his neck and chest. The Grundian fell to the grass below.

Cheering sounded across the battlefield while a few soldiers ran toward the archer in the red hood. They raised her above their shoulders, and she lifted her arm in triumph. Gavian slowly eased to his feet, straightening his legs to make sure he could still stand. He dusted himself off, doing an inventory of the cuts and scrapes, but didn't find anything too serious.

"Tav'rian!" a voice called out. Gavian turned toward the group of cheering soldiers. He must have been hearing things. "Tav'rian!" He thought he heard it again. The archer in red signaled emphatically as the soldiers returned her to the ground. She charged toward Gavian. Uncertain of her intent, Gavian braced himself. The archer wrapped her arms around him, holding him tight. Gavian awkwardly put an arm around the archer, who had obviously mistaken him for someone else. Perhaps sensing his hesitation, the red archer withdrew. Facing him, she removed her hood. Gavian couldn't help but stare at the sight of the beautiful young woman with long auburn locks and braided strands. She looked up at him with big brown eyes.

"Darby?" The thought rolled out of Gavian's mouth before his brain had settled on a conclusion. "Is it really you?"

"We thought you were dead!" She buried her face in his shoulder again.

This time Gavian hugged her with no hesitation. "How . . . You look so different . . ."

Darby giggled, "It's been a while."

"That was you that killed Grunch?" Gavian was flabbergasted.

Darby stepped back, brushing the hair away from her eyes. "With one of my rokenhead arrows! Dexius has been teaching me how to use a bow, so I made those rokenstones you left us into arrowheads."

"Way to show 'em fillers can fight too!" one of the soldiers shouted when he walked by.

As the soldiers continued their jubilant celebrations around them, Gavian stole a quick glance beyond where Darby stood. The scene was filled with exuberance and relief. Beads of sweat dotted Darby's forehead, and she absentmindedly wiped them away with the back of her hand.

"Darby, you're amazing," Gavian uttered, his voice filled with admiration. "Where is Dexius?"

Darby's expression softened, her eyes meeting Gavian's. "Dexius is with the Storm Brigade," she replied, her voice tinged with a hint of melancholy.

"You're fighting in this war?" he asked, his tone a blend of curiosity and worry.

Darby nodded her head no. "Dexius is, but he made me promise I wouldn't join," she admitted. "He says I'm not ready yet."

Gavian's gaze returned to the smoldering remains of Grunch's massive body sprawled across the dirt. "Looks like you're fighting to me."

"Fillers unite!" shouted a woman.

"I'm on the scout team," she explained, her lips pressing together in a straight line. "We stumbled on this Grundian camp during our reconnaissance, and on our way back to report it, we ran into Inferno Brigade."

"I can't believe you killed Grunch," Gavian mumbled. "I hate the thought of you being in danger, but I guess they need people like you."

She pressed her lips together. "I can't believe it either. I'm not supposed to engage, but he was slaughtering my team. I still had two rokenhead arrows left, I had to do something."

"Darby, I have to get to Grungal," Gavian's voice grew urgent. "Can you tell me where it is?"

"Grungal?" Darby put her bow into its sling to carry on her back. "I've never heard of it. But we haven't found many Grundian hideouts."

"They took Ambrielle, and I have to find her!" said Gavian, while some of the soldiers ran by to assess those who had fallen in battle. "They said they were going to Grungal."

"Who is Ambrielle?" Darby adjusted the straps on her shoulder. "And how long ago was this?"

Gavian's face softened when he spoke of Ambrielle, his voice tinged with both affection and concern. "Ambrielle is . . . She's everything to me," he confessed, his gaze drifting momentarily into the distance. "It was about . . . maybe a day ago when they took her."

"Where were you when she was taken?" Darby reached out and placed a hand on Gavian's arm, her touch a gentle reassurance.

Gavian furrowed his brows, trying to recall the details. "A small town in the woods, I think it was called—"

"Flumpy!" Darby called out as a big furry beast ran toward them. It was the animal that had grabbed Gavian in its jaws and carried him into the forest. Gavian started to back away while Darby gave the beast a big hug. It stood looking at Gavian, wagging its tongue while Darby stroked its light brown fur.

"You're petting that thing?" Gavian said, with the beast staring at him. "It tried to eat me earlier."

"Flumpy wouldn't eat you," Darby said, making faces at the animal. "She's a rescue vorren."

Gavian stepped back when some of the fallen soldiers were dragged across the grass in front of them. "A what?"

"A vorren," Darby said. "There's a bunch of them in Duris Canyon, but they like it out here too. Don't you Flumpy?"

One of the archers approached, crouching beside the beast Darby was calling Flumpy. Darby glanced over at the archer, who was wearing a dark green and black cloak and hood. "You should give Flumpy a hug for rescuing you," she giggled.

"Aye," said the archer. "She does love hugs."

"Bradwyn, this is my friend Tav'rian," Darby said. Even after all this time, she still called him Tav'rian instead of Tavarian. It was strange hearing that old name again, but she was not aware of the one he went by now.

"Actually, I go by Gavian now," he informed them.

"Gavian?" Darby wore a look of confusion, while the husky archer extended his hand.

"Good to meet ya," said Bradwyn, shaking Gavian's hand. "Our little Darby won us fillers some respect today!"

"Fillers?" Gavian questioned, raising an eyebrow.

"That's what they call us," Bradwyn explained. "Strakenbridge and a few other major cities formed an alliance against the Gruns. They needed more troops, so they accepted volunteers. Some of us came from smaller towns without our own military. The seasoned soldiers started calling us fillers because we lack their extensive training. They don't view us as capable fighters."

"So, it's meant to be derogatory?" Gavian inquired.

"Aye, mostly," Bradwyn acknowledged. "I can appreciate that we don't have their level of experience, but that doesn't make us worthless."

"Yeah, that doesn't sit right," Gavian agreed.

"I saw you take down a couple of Gruns yourself, you joining the Inferno?" Bradwyn asked.

"I'm not sure," Gavian replied thoughtfully. "I didn't come here with the intention of fighting in a war. Right now, I have to find someone."

"What town did you say it was Tav?" Darby inquired, apparently forgetting his new name.

"Ferinoke," said Gavian.

"Grundians were in Ferinoke?" Bradwyn said. "I hope the people there made it out in time."

"I'm afraid there were many dead when we got there," said Gavian.

"That's a real shame," Bradwyn said. "Terrible shame. If all these towns had trusted each other before this happened, more of them may have banded together to join us instead of running away."

"He said it was about a day ago," Darby said to Bradwyn.

"Aye, if we can get there while the scent is still fresh, it could lead us to another Grundian hideout," said Bradwyn.

"Then we could help Tav'rian find his friend!" Darby said. "Stay right here, I'm going to tell Captain Holkson!"

Gavian watched Darby run over to a group of soldiers. Flumpy bumped against his leg, nearly knocking him down.

"She's wanting a pat," Bradwyn suggested.

Gavian hesitantly put his hand on the thick-haired back of the beast. A middle-aged man with graying hair and a thick mustache eyed Darby while she spoke with wild arm gestures. The man called to another. Darby watched them talk.

As Darby started back, the second man came walking with her. He appeared to be older than most of the soldiers and wore a brown coat with a rust-colored tunic underneath. His posture exuded a sense of confidence that few had. "I'm Captain Holkson," he said, reaching out to shake Gavian's hand. "I hear you may be able to lead us to a Grun hideout," he said.

"They were heading to a place called Grungal," Gavian said. "They were taking my friend there."

"There are many caves in this region, a lot of mines as well," Holkson said. "Too many to search them all. If you can lead us to one, it would be a great help."

"I can show you the spot in Ferinoke where they took us," Gavian said.

Captain Holkson popped a small stick into his mouth and started chewing on it. "There ain't many folks around these parts like you, who are willing to step up and lend a hand. If you're inclined to join Inferno, we'd be glad to have you. Just remember to follow orders," he said, his words accompanied by a firm nod.

"Thank you, sir," said Gavian. "Right now, my only concern is finding Ambrielle."

Holkson walked past Gavian, striding purposefully into the midst of the soldiers. His voice carried across the field as he bellowed, "Inferno Brigade! No more time for rest. It's time to pay our respects to those who've fallen in the service of this alliance." He pointed toward a distant mound on one side of the forest, his gaze unwavering. "Archers, start digging graves on that ridge. Swordmasters and lancers, you'll handle the hauling. Let's move with efficiency, people. We need to be on our way well before dark. And remember, no markings on the graves. We don't want that wraith to find them."

Gavian stepped toward Darby. "What wraith?"

"There's been stories about a demon in black who steals the souls of the dead," said Darby. "We've found shriveled bodies turned into stone. Don't even have the smell of rotting flesh."

"There was a man in black robes and a silver mask that came through Avendal," Gavian said. "Fortunately, he didn't find us."

"Do you think it's the Blight Whidge?" said Darby.

"We destroyed the Blight Whidge," said Gavian, "Malidora and I."

"What happened?" Darby said. "Where is Malidora now?"

"One of the Nulthereals swallowed her," Gavian said.

"Like my brother," Darby said. "Why didn't you come to us in Strakenbridge? Have the Grundians been holding you all this time?"

"I fell into some kind of portal to another world," said Gavian. "I couldn't even remember who I was until recently. I came back here to find you and Dex."

Darby's lips poked out as her eyelids closed. "I would have stuck with the Grundian story."

"I'm serious," Gavian said. "That's where I met Ambrielle. The same thing happened to her."

One of the soldiers handed Darby a shovel. "You can help dig with us archers," Darby said, handing it to Gavian. "The sooner we get done, the sooner we can find your friend."

CHAPTER 9

AMBRIELLE WAS THROWN into the dark cage just before the solid wooden gate slid shut and the latch outside slammed into position. Torchlight danced through the gaps in the walls surrounding the cage. The wooden structure had no ceiling, but the fence posts were too high to climb over. The sky was replaced with the rough textures of dark stone.

Somewhere along the way, Ambrielle had lost the bladestaff, but she still had her silbrace. What were they going to do with her? What did they plan to do with Gavian? Whatever happened, she couldn't resign herself to this cage. She had to escape somehow to help Gavian.

What had happened to Wegin when the giants took them? She could really use his assistance right now. He could still be in the town of Ferinoke, waiting for them to return.

A rustling sound in the corner of the enclosure startled her. Ambrielle backed against the wall, afraid to glimpse into the unknown but equally afraid not to. Mustering some semblance of courage, she slowly crept toward the unseen noises.

When she moved toward the corner, something scurried past her toward the other side of the pen. The small, blue-skinned creature's chest heaved as it breathed rapidly. Ambrielle realized it must be frightened of her as well. She sat on the rocky floor against the wall, setting her palms in her lap.

"I'm not going to hurt you," she said, trying to sound as non-threatening as possible. The creature glanced at her for a moment before hiding its face in its hands. Metallic clanking rang out in arrhythmic patterns throughout the cavern while Ambrielle stretched out her legs. "My name is Ambrielle." She turned away from the creature, looking at her silbrace. She could use its laser to easily escape this enclosure, but she had to be sure she could get away. Once the Grundians realized she had it, they would likely remove it in the most brutal way possible. Ambrielle turned back toward the creature. "How long have you been here?"

The blue creature's long pointed ears raised, and its small black eyes moved back to her.

"Do you know where we are?" she asked. Its ears drooped as it shied away. Perhaps it couldn't speak, but there was an understanding in its eyes.

"This is a mine," said a young boy, sliding forward out of the shadows and revealing himself to Ambrielle.

The boy looked to be about ten years old. He seemed surprisingly calm, considering the situation they were in. When Ambrielle's eyes adjusted to the dark, she could tell there were two others leaning against the side of the cage, possibly sleeping. "Why did they bring us here?" she whispered, trying not to disturb those who were sleeping.

"To work for them," said the boy, the torchlight dancing on his face. "They're looking for nyxite."

Ambrielle scanned the rocky walls that surrounded them. The veins of minerals glinted faintly in the dim light. "What do they do with that?" Ambrielle wondered.

The boy shrugged slightly. "I'm not sure," he said. "I haven't been here that long."

The air in the mine felt heavy, the metallic scent of the ore mingling with the dampness that permeated the underground chamber. "I'm Ambrielle," she said, her voice a fragile whisper against the sounds of hammers beating on solid rock. "What's your name?"

"Thomin," he replied with a small smile, as if appreciating the momentary respite from their dire circumstances.

Curiosity getting the better of her, Ambrielle pressed on. "How did you get here?"

Thomin's voice grew somber. "We were heading to the Gulflands," he said. "There wasn't enough to eat. My father said it was because of the war."

"Is the rest of your family here too?" Ambrielle asked.

"I got lost in the woods," Thomin admitted. "Part of the convoy got stuck because they couldn't fit through the trees. I went down to the stream while they cut some trees down, but when I came back, I couldn't find anyone."

"That must have been scary," said Ambrielle. "Maybe when you get out of here, you can continue to the Gulflands and find everyone."

"I don't think we're ever getting out of here," said Thomin.

A flame bobbed in the dark outside the cage. Someone moved toward them. The latch was raised, and the gate flung open. A large hand grabbed the blue creature, and it squealed as it was removed from the cage. The gate slammed shut, and Ambrielle watched the Grundian carry the blue creature off into the shadows.

When the gate opened again, a giant's hand grabbed Ambrielle by the legs, dragging her out of the enclosure into the open cavern. She squirmed in the strength of its grip, and the Grundian carried her through the cave toward the sounds of asynchronous metallic clanging.

In the glow of the torches, several creatures and humans swung pick-axes, chipping away at the rock along the side of the chamber. One of the Grundians marched back and forth among the miners, flexing a steel chain in his hands. The Grundian dropped her onto a hard ledge slightly above the cavern floor.

"Get up!" shouted the Grundian, brandishing his chain. She stood between a human and the blue creature from the cage. Both were hammering into the stone, a mixture of clay and loose dirt in the sides of the cave. Ambrielle grabbed a pickaxe lying in the dust and joined them, while the Grundian with the chain turned and walked back by the line of workers. The wooden handle was rough with prickly splinters, but she soon found a spot worn smooth by its previous users.

Using the heavy pickaxe with both hands, she banged it against the rock. The rock she hit had no give at all, making the pickaxe bounce back.

Her hands went painfully numb from the vibrations. She watched the others for a moment, hoping to learn the best technique fast. The blue creature held the hammer near the top, not taking big swings but focusing like it was hammering a nail. Ambrielle mimicked the movement, and the rock began to slowly crack under her steady tapping.

The stone crumbled, spilling dust and gravel down the side of the wall into a steel mesh grating beneath the ledge. The grating was covered with larger bits of rock, some of which were silver tinged with red. The giant walked behind them, swinging the folded chain into his palm. Ambrielle sped up her movements with his approach, hitting the rock wall as fast as she could.

The Grundian guard turned and walked back down the line. Ambrielle rested while his back was turned. The blue creature glanced at her as she stopped working.

The Grundians at the forge looked at each other, until one of them spoke, "These workers are slow! We need more metal."

"Whip those kips into shape!" said one of the Grundians. "Splat, get those kips moving!"

Hearing his name, the Grundian holding the chain turned his head. He swung the chain at one of the humans mining at the other end of the line. "Work faster!" The blow knocked the human off his feet, and he rolled off the ledge onto the steel grate.

Ambrielle began to work faster, afraid she could be next. The Grundians by the forge glanced at each other. "Splat, stop beating the kips," one said. "You're slowing everything down." One of the Grundian women raked the collected pieces in the grate toward a container. After the container was filled, another Grundian dumped it out into the forge. There had to be rock and dirt along with bits of metal. One of the Grundian blacksmiths worked on a mold of cooling material, hammering it into shape.

After working for hours, weariness set in, and Ambrielle could barely lift the heavy axe above her waist. Finally, the Grundians rounded them all up and carried them back to the cage. Ambrielle was thrust back inside, and the gate slammed shut. Two other giants opened a second cage of workers and pulled them out for the next shift.

Her muscles felt stretched as she rubbed her arms. Thomin, the older humans, and the blue creature all had their eyes closed, either already asleep or resting, and did not want to be disturbed. Ambrielle lay against the sturdy wooden bars, maybe she should get some rest too.

After she dozed for a short while, the bouncing light of a moving flame awakened her. The biggest Grundian she had seen so far lit one of the darkened areas of the cave, and then he climbed toward a stone outcropping. A shiny gray crystallized stone stood upright in front of him, the flame causing every facet to sparkle. The giant kneeled in front of the strange stone, placing both hands on its surface.

His face glowed with a green light that seemed to be coming from within the large crystal. Staring into the stone, he appeared to be in a trance. A few of the other Grundians nearby continued to work, smelting and hammering the metal into form, indifferent to the Grundian at the stone.

Ambrielle continued watching the Grundian's head sway back and forth as he looked at the crystal stone. What was he doing? He seemed to be experiencing something, but what? After a few moments, the Grundian stood and ambled down the ramp toward the forge. He called the others to him and spoke. As much as Ambrielle strained to hear what was said, she could not make anything out.

Wiping the hair that hung over her face, Ambrielle caught the blue creature looking at her from the other side of the pen. It quickly looked away when their eyes met and scuffled into the corner. She leaned on the sides of the cage, trying to find a comfortable position to rest after the long day. Blisters burned on her hand where the handle of the pickaxe had rubbed her skin raw. As best she could, she ignored the discomforts, trying to ease her mind into sleep.

✦

She woke with pain in her shoulder, after having fallen asleep in this unnatural position. The blue creature and the humans seemed to be having better luck, since they were all fast asleep. Ambrielle stood to stretch her neck. She couldn't be sure how much time had passed but guessed it had only been a couple of hours.

The metallic pings from the hammering of the rock persisted since the other shift was still at work. Ambrielle froze when a growling rose from the cavern outside the cage. She relaxed when she realized it was one of the Grundians snoring. Other than the snoring and hammering, the cave was silent, no chatting among the giants. Perhaps they were all asleep too.

Igniting the laser on her silbrace, Ambrielle quietly began to cut through the wooden bars of the enclosure. She cut at an angle on one end and the opposite angle on the other, hoping it would make it easier to put the bar back into place and hold. Unsure whether she would be able to escape the cave, she at least wanted to see how she might get out.

After cutting one of the bars, she tested the space and was able to squeeze through with a bit of work. She grabbed the wooden bar and forced it back into place, well enough to not be noticed without inspecting it closely. Quietly as she could, Ambrielle crept past the workers. Staying out of the light of the torches as much as possible, she felt a steady flow of cool air. It seemed to be coming from a tunnel past the mining wall.

Ambrielle paused, waiting for the guard. Unlike Splat, this one carried a chain around his neck, holding on to each end. He turned around, walking behind the line of prisoners while they chipped away at the stone walls. She moved into the tunnel, using the sides to guide her in the low light.

The rushing sound of water ahead of her grew louder with each step forward. She crept toward a faint blue light. It gave her a familiar sensation, like following the blue glow inside the spring. Or the blue vortex that used to flash into her mind, which she had used to escape The Hollow.

The tunnel came to an end, opening to the cool night air and flowing waters. She stood at the edge of a wide river. The currents were swift, distorting the reflection of the blue moon behind the dense clouds. She rubbed the chill from her arms as she stared across the water, helplessly hoping Gavian was still alive. If he somehow got away, how would he ever find her here?

Stepping across the uneven terrain, Ambrielle navigated her way over rough rocks, feeling their jagged edges under her boots. The sound of her footsteps echoed in the desolate landscape, blending with the distant rustle of the wind. She reached a small sandy beach, and the texture of the smooth grains shifted beneath her feet, offering a momentary respite from the harshness of the rocky surroundings.

The air carried the scent of burning wood, mingling with the aroma of cooked meat. Several Grundians huddled around an orange campfire, some sleeping, others cooking near the blaze. Ambrielle turned and dashed back to the entrance of the cave. To escape, she would have to cross the river. The current was too strong to swim. A boat or some kind of floating device would be necessary.

Ambrielle treaded back through the tunnel toward the mining area, crouching away from the light when the guard faced her direction. She caught a glimpse of the large, pointed crystal that the big Grundian had stared into. As the guard moved along, she hurried toward the cages.

One of the sleeping Grundians near the forge stirred. He stood and stretched his massive arms. Ambrielle hid in the shadows, waiting for him to turn away. The guard was nearing the end of the row of miners and would be coming back this way soon. He would see her in the light of his torch, unless she found another place to hide, but the woken Grundian continued staring toward the mine.

At the end of the row of workers, Ambrielle spotted Thomin digging into the rock. They had changed shifts. With no other choice, Ambrielle ran up to the ledge. She grabbed a pickaxe out of the grate just before the guard turned and started hammering it into the rock.

"Where were you?" asked one of the women. "You're going to get us killed!"

Ambrielle shied away from her, still working away at the rock. "I'm trying to help us get out of here."

"I don't know what kind of game you are playing, but you need to fall in line," the woman snapped. "They'll punish all of us if you try to escape."

The mere sound of the woman's voice grated on Ambrielle's nerves. If only she would just shut up, everything would be fine.

"Just keep working," one of the men interjected. "Don't worry about her."

"You saw what happened last time, Luken. They will kill us." The irritating woman turned her attention back to Ambrielle. "Go climb into the other cage! Don't take us down with you!"

The woman's prominent, pointed nose and the deep lines of condescension etched across her face only served to irritate Ambrielle further.

"You're going to get yourself killed if you don't keep digging, Thakia," Luken said. "You're only causing more trouble."

Ambrielle decided to ignore the woman's rants and focus on the work. Thakia's words gave her a new perspective. If the Grundians would punish the whole shift because of her actions, she couldn't leave unless they all could escape.

Stretching her shoulders, Ambrielle went back to banging into the rock with the sharp end of the pickaxe. The Grundians around the forge were all awake now, working on more metal objects.

"What are they doing with this ore exactly?" Ambrielle whispered once the guard moved away.

Thakia's rhythmic clangs stopped for a moment. "Be quiet, troublemaker."

"Metals," said the man to her left. "They're looking for just about any kind of metal."

The guard turned around, walking behind the row of workers. The hammering sounds quickened in tempo as he moved by. Once the giant was out of range, Ambrielle rested. "What do they do with all this metal?"

"They are going to beat you if you don't keep quiet," said Thakia. "You've been warned."

Thakia's voice motivated Ambrielle to swing her pickaxe with even greater force, creating a cacophony of noise in an attempt to drown out the sound of their voices.

"I've heard they sometimes eat it," said Luken.

"Eat metal?" Ambrielle continued to clang her hammer on the rocks.

"Some kind of ritual," Luken said. "They think it makes them stronger."

"They cover wounds with it too," said Thakia.

The man glanced at Thakia with a grin. "Strength is everything to Grundians. A wound is a sign of weakness, and the only way to cure weakness is with strength."

"Must be why they've got metal for brains," Thakia snickered.

The guard made his turn and strode toward them. Thakia hammered away at the rock while the giant snarled on his way by. Pebbles and dust fell on them as the cave shook. Ambrielle turned to find the biggest Grundian stepping toward the forge. She wanted to tell Thakia to be quiet, feeding her words back to her, but she didn't feel like making the effort.

"Three more days" one of the Grundians said to the others. "Get as much out of them as you can."

The other giants beat their fists against their chests, grunting something resembling a cheer, while the big Grundian headed past the mines into the tunnel that led to the outside.

Ambrielle wasn't sure what he meant, but it bothered her. What was happening in three days? She went back to hitting the stone with her pick but couldn't focus. Thomin was to her left, swinging as hard as he could at the rock in front of him, while Luken and Thakia took turns hitting the same stone.

Thomin's small frame trembled as he struck the stubborn rock wall with his pick, his efforts yielding little progress. Ambrielle noticed his face was flushed with frustration and fatigue; he seemed to be fighting back tears of exhaustion.

Keeping an eye on the Grundian overseer, Ambrielle put down her pick and gently placed a hand on his shoulder. "They are not watching you right now. Take a moment to catch your breath."

Thomin wiped the sweat from his brow, his small hands gripping the pick tightly. "I'm going to get in trouble," he said. "It's no use. This rock won't budge. It doesn't even look like I've done any work." He let out a weary breath. "My father says I need to be strong to help protect the family, but I can't even break this stupid rock."

Ambrielle crouched down to Thomin's level. "You are stronger than you think, but strength is more than just muscle. It's also about endurance and perseverance. In some cases, it's finding the right strategy."

Thomin looked up at Ambrielle, his eyes searching for answers. "What do you mean?"

Ambrielle smiled when the words came to her. "Sometimes, instead of attacking a problem head-on, we need to find the weak points. Look for cracks or fissures in the rock, that's where we can make a difference."

As the overseer started back their way, Ambrielle resumed hammering at the stone in front of her. She watched Thomin study the rock in front of him, testing other areas around it with his pickaxe. He directed his strikes to a new spot.

A crack began to form in the stone. With each precise hit, the crack widened and began to crumble. Thomin's eyes widened in amazement.

"You did it!" Ambrielle pumped her fist, and Thomin beamed with pride.

When Ambrielle and the other workers began to tire out, the Grundians brought the other shift in to continue what they had started. Exhausted, Ambrielle quickly fell asleep leaning against the side of the cage.

"Ambrielle," a voice called out to her, rousing her from her slumber. She groggily stirred, her eyelids parting slightly while she struggled to regain full consciousness.

"Please confirm identity," the voice persisted, urging her to respond.

"Huh?" Ambrielle muttered, her mind still clouded with drowsiness. However, the sound of her own name managed to penetrate the haze, prompting her to pay closer attention.

"Ambrielle," the voice repeated, its tone filled with familiarity.

This time, she managed to wake enough to fully open her eyes, blinking repeatedly to bring the world into focus. As her vision cleared, she noticed a floating orb outside the wooden cage, its presence both surprising and comforting.

"Wegin?" Ambrielle's gaze fixed on the orb. Her voice was laced with astonishment. "How did you find me?"

"I have been following you ever since you were taken," Wegin explained, his robotic voice resonating.

"Wegin, lower your voice," Ambrielle interrupted, glancing anxiously at the slumbering figures around her.

"Apologies." Wegin complied, lowering his voice to a soft hum. "Though I couldn't catch up in time, I managed to extract residue from the grass and soil, isolating the genetic code of your attackers. After filtering out irrelevant data, I focused on tracking anything my sensors could detect of you in my memory banks."

Ambrielle couldn't help but feel a surge of gratitude toward the robotic assistant. She knew Wegin's logical and analytical nature, but his unwavering commitment to her safety touched her in ways she hadn't expected. "Thank you Wegin, you're a great assistant."

Wegin's lights blinked with simulated acknowledgement. "I am programmed to prioritize your well-being, Ambrielle. Your safety is of utmost importance. I am pleased to have found you, as I did not enjoy our time apart. Would you like me to use my cutting device to open the cage?"

Ambrielle shook her head, determination gleaming in her eyes. "I can do that myself. What I truly need is a way to navigate past the Grundians near the cave entrance. How did you get past them?"

"Stealth mode," Wegin replied, his color fading into the dark background until he was nearly invisible. "Does your silbrace have that capability?"

"I don't think so," Ambrielle replied, trying to imagine herself turning invisible with her silbrace, but nothing happened. "Nope."

"You really should have it installed," Wegin suggested in a matter-of-fact robotic tone. "It's quite useful."

"Thanks. I'll keep that in mind," Ambrielle said, a hint of sarcasm in her voice. "So, what would be the best way for me to get by the Grundians out there?"

"The Grundians were smart enough to sleep on different schedules," Wegin informed Ambrielle. "If you wait for a moment when those awake are preoccupied, there is a chance you could get by them."

Just then, someone stirred inside the cage, breaking their conversation. "Ambrielle?" Thomin mumbled, his voice filled with sleep. "Who are you talking to?"

"No one, Thomin," Ambrielle replied, offering a reassuring smile. "Get some rest." She shifted further away from the others in the cage while Wegin hovered close by. "We need to find a way to get everyone in this cage out of here. And hopefully, we can also free the occupants of the other cage."

"That significantly lowers the odds of success," Wegin remarked, calculating the potential risks.

"Well, it's important. We can't leave them here," Ambrielle insisted. "Can you cause some kind of distraction to draw their attention away?"

"It would need to be something that keeps them occupied for several minutes," Wegin analyzed the situation. "I will work on a solution," Wegin affirmed, his floating form hovering closer to the wooden bars. "But first, please attach this tracking sticker to your skin, enabling me to pinpoint your location at all times."

Grabbing the item that emerged from one of Wegin's slots, Ambrielle swiftly complied. "In the meantime, I'll try to come up with a plan. When you find something that will work, come back to me." She placed the small adhesive sticker on her arm. "Hurry, Wegin," she urged, her voice laced with a mix of anticipation and worry. "I have to get out of here so we can find Gavian!"

I N THE TRANQUIL morning air, the tall grass swayed gently in the wind. As the dampened sunlight peeked through the foliage, a glimmer of gold caught Gavian's eye, a small beacon of hope amidst the somber surroundings. His weary face transformed in an instant, excitement and relief flooding his features. "My sword!" he exclaimed, his voice infused with a renewed sense of purpose.

Darby emerged from the trees and approached him. Her eyes widened when she recognized the distinctive weapon. "Is that the rokensword?"

Gavian nodded, spinning the blade skillfully and testing its weight and balance. "I was afraid I had lost it again." A sense of pride filled his voice.

Folding her hands together across her chest, Darby gazed at the sword. "It would have been a shame if you hadn't found it." The wind tousled the unbraided parts of her hair as she stepped toward the trees. "I'll call the captain over."

When she returned, Captain Holkson and several other soldiers pressed their way into the clearing.

"This is where she was when they took Ambrielle," Gavian said, extending his hand to indicate the spot.

Captain Holkson wrinkled his nose, removing the small stick from his mouth. "This place smells of death."

"There were several bodies piled up over there." Gavian pointed behind one of the wooden cabins to where he and Ambrielle had first entered the town.

Bradwyn guided Flumpy into the vicinity, the creature's keen senses actively at work. The furry animal began sniffing the grass while nudging against Gavian's leg.

"She wants you to pet her," Darby informed him.

A hint of hesitation flickered in Gavian's eyes, but he mustered up the courage to give Flumpy a few quick pats on the back of her head.

"There are some Grundian tracks here, leading in various directions," Bradwyn interjected, drawing their attention to the ground.

Gavian waved in the direction he'd seen them carrying Ambrielle. "Best I could tell, they were taking her that way."

Captain Holkson took charge, striding toward the cabin at the front. "We need to give these people a proper burial."

The soldiers followed him, with Darby not far behind. As much as Gavian hated to see the dead residents again or to smell the rotting odor, he hurried to catch up with Darby.

Circling the pile of bodies, Holkson placed his arms behind his back. The soldiers unpacked their shovels again and started digging. Gavian moved alongside Darby, grabbing one of the tools to help.

"Seems like we spend most of our time digging graves," quipped one of the lancers.

Bradwyn brought Flumpy around the cabin but took a step back when he saw the bodies. Once the first hole was ready, a couple of the soldiers prepared to move one of the corpses.

A long hissing sound came from somewhere nearby, followed by a quick shriek. Holkson and the others stopped all motion, as if they had turned to stone. After a brief moment, they all darted out of the clearing and into the thicket, heading in the opposite direction from where the sound had come from.

Darby's urgent grip on Gavian's arm conveyed a sense of imminent danger, so he relented and moved with her into the woods. The noise sounded eerily familiar, but the most unnerving part was the stark fear etched on their faces. Crouching behind the cover of trees and dense bushes, they waited.

Peeking through the foliage, Gavian watched a figure cloaked in black stride past the cabins toward the pile of corpses. The sun glinted off his silver mask as he made his way out of the shadows of the buildings and into the open light. It was the same man Gavian and Ambrielle had encountered in Avendal. Pulling aside his robe, the man drew his blade. Silver steel reflected the light, but there was something strange about the sword. A ghostly illumination radiated from the hilt, pale green in color.

The cloaked being approached the bodies of the dead, readying his sword. With his blade hovering above them, the dark figure pulled a small ring under the sword's cross guard, and a scintillating smoke began to rise from the corpses, swirling like ethereal tendrils. The smoke entwined and danced in the air, drawn toward the silver blade. When it made contact, the once-faint green glow in the hilt surged with an intense brilliance.

The energy force, the life essence of the deceased, became the sustenance for the insatiable hunger of the sword. While the vibrant energy was consumed, a profound change befell the bodies of the fallen. Their once-solid forms seemed to undergo a metamorphosis, akin to the petrification of wood.

Their flesh took on a stony texture as the life drained out of it. The contours of their faces and limbs sharpened, as if chiseled from stone. Their eye sockets now appeared hollow, devoid of any remnants of life or emotion.

Holkson and the others remained deathly still while they peeked through the trees. When were they going to attack? Though there was something that seemed almost supernatural about this fiend, he was still only one man.

A shivering hiss ending with an abrupt howl sounded while the hooded figure uncovered his sheath. The sword was returned to his side, and he closed his long robe around it. He left as quickly as he had entered, vanishing into the shadow of the trees. Darby and the others stared at the spot where he was last seen.

After a few moments, they crept out into the clearing, their nerves frayed and twitchy while they surveyed the transformed corpses. The sunken, deformed faces with hollow eye sockets and gaping, toothless mouths gave them a horrific, ghoulish appearance.

Darby took Gavian's right hand in hers. "That was the wraith."

Gavian leaned toward her ear and whispered, "Even these guys fear him?"

Moving away from the group, Darby began walking into the forest ahead. She glanced back at Gavian before continuing, as if beckoning him to follow. Pushing back the long, slender ends of the branches, Gavian met her outside the hearing range of the soldiers.

She spoke in a low voice, "There have been stories. Some say the wraith is immortal. A group of soldiers claimed to have surrounded the wraith and were unable to hurt him while he killed three of them before they fled. He can take the essence of the living and the recent dead."

"What do you mean by essence exactly?" Gavian said.

Darby's eyes moved away from him. "Their soul, their energy, whatever you want to call it. It looked like white smoke with sparkles in it."

"So, they are afraid of that happening to them? If there's a soul, wouldn't it leave the body after death?"

"It's not literally their soul I don't think, but I'm not sure what it is." Darby inhaled deeply.

"Move out!" yelled the captain. The soldiers marched out of the wooded area to where they had tied up their riding creatures. Some climbed onto their backs, while others got into two shippies being pulled by docimares.

The docimares stood tall and robust, their muscular frames adorned with a lustrous coat of light brown fur. With large, docile eyes that gazed upon the world with gentle curiosity, they grazed upon the grasslands, their antlered heads bent low. Natural formations of armor plates adorned their backs, blending seamlessly with their supple fur. Gavian followed Darby onto one of the shippies, and before long they were heading away from Ferinoke into the open wilderness.

Without the road, the ride was rough. Gavian had to keep a good grip on the side of the shippy to avoid being tossed out. Darby glanced at him a few times while they rode, but he couldn't think of anything to say. His head was swimming with images of Ambrielle and what she might be going through. Maybe he should never have agreed to let her come with him.

"I don't think I've ever seen you look so worried," said Darby as everyone was thrown sideways when the wheel bumped over a rock. "Who is this girl, Ambrielle?"

Gavian breathed in slowly, gathering his thoughts. "I met her on Anatharia. I just don't want anything to happen to her."

"So, she's pretty important to you then? More than a friend?" Darby raised her eyebrows.

Gavian glanced at a young woman with metal armor and Bradwyn, who was combing Flumpy's hair. He would prefer not to talk about this in front of two strangers, but he didn't want to seem scared by not answering either. "I care about her. We've been through a lot, but—"

"Tav'rian likes a girl!" Darby interjected with a mischievous giggle.

Bradwyn joined in, his laughter filling the air while he continued his gentle grooming of Flumpy.

Gavian felt his cheeks grow warm, and he rubbed the side of his face, attempting to maintain composure. "Well . . . Yes, that's true."

"This is great news!" Darby exclaimed, a smile lighting up her face. "I'm happy you found someone new."

"You were so quiet the last time we saw each other," said Gavian, as the wheels of the shippy slowed while traversing a soft, muddy patch of land. "It's strange to see you so talkative."

Darby tilted her head thoughtfully. "Really? Well, around here, everyone always says I'm the quiet one."

A playful grin spread across Bradwyn's face. "Oh, she's definitely quiet. She usually talks to Flumpy more than any of us, that is until you arrived on the scene," he said, casting a teasing glance at Darby.

"I just hope we can find Ambrielle soon," Gavian said, "before it's too late."

"We will find her," Darby reassured him, firmly placing her hand on his shoulder. "I just know it."

"I wish I could believe that," Gavian said, as the shippy came to a stop. The captain and two other soldiers climbed down from their docimares.

"We need to get Gavian a sheath for his sword," Darby announced to Bradwyn and the young woman beside him.

"No doubt about it," they heard one of the soldiers say while they stared at the mud. "That's a Grundian footprint."

Captain Holkson walked toward the back of the formation and rested his elbow on the shippy. "How old?"

"Looks fresh to me, sir," said the soldier. "No more than few days."

"Good, we're on their trail," Holkson said, slapping the side of the shippy cart as he left.

Soon they were moving, but it wasn't long before the column halted again. Gavian and Darby strained to see what everyone was looking at. The captain lifted something from the dirt. Recognizing the object immediately, Gavian leapt out of the cart, running toward the captain.

"That's her bladestaff!" Gavian shouted.

Captain Holkson inspected the weapon and handed it to one of the soldiers.

"Please. May I hold onto it?" Gavian said.

The captain eyed Gavian for a moment and then took it back from the soldier. He passed it to Gavian. "Keep it in the shippy for now. If we need it, I expect you to hand it to someone who can use it."

Gavian nodded and took the bladestaff back to the shippy, and the small column started moving again. They moved through a meadow filled with flowers and red crystal formations. On either side of them were lush, thick forests. Darby marveled at the big orange and white flowers as they passed by.

"How did you and Ambrielle first meet?" Darby's attention went back to Gavian.

"We met on Anatharia," said Gavian. "I guess we were the only two people there, but there was more than that. It was like, as soon as I saw her eyes, we connected."

"Have you kissed her yet?"

Gavian looked away when he felt heat spreading over his face. "I'm not sure I should be talking to you about this."

"Why not?" said Darby. "I'm not a kid anymore you know."

"Why do you want to know all this?" Gavian eyed the other soldiers around them. "Being in this group is probably a bad influence on you."

"You sound like Dexius." Darby rolled her eyes. "I only ask so I can help."

"You have experience with this?" Gavian asked.

"No. I haven't even been courted yet," said Darby. "Dex is rather—I think he's scared everyone away. Or maybe I'm just ugly."

"You're not ugly, that's for sure." Gavian was underselling her beauty, but it would feel weird to tell her that.

"Aw, thanks, Tav!" She cradled his arm with both hands. The wheels of the shippy began to grind into hard gravel, and the soft grassy plains thinned out. A boiling gray mist moved briskly across the silver quilted sky. The scattered light of the sun fell low in the western sky. As much as Gavian was pleased to see Darby again, it was tainted by the absence of Ambrielle.

"You should have seen Dexius"—Darby snickered—"at the Sylvermist Festival last season. I shouldn't laugh, but he's always so sure of himself, I can't help it."

Her laugh was infectious. Gavian chuckled without even knowing what was funny. "What happened?"

"Though he denies it, I think it was his first time dancing with a girl," Darby giggled again. "He nearly ruined the eldken dance. Kept tripping over his own feet trying to keep up with the girl. He fell down twice, bumped into one couple, and nearly made both of them fall into the fountain."

Gavian laughed, though he imagined himself doing the same thing if he tried to dance. "Girls expect you to dance?"

"I think so. That's what couples always do after the workday. The taverns have a big dance outside every night of the bright moon."

A sense of dread passed over him. No one had ever heard of dancing in Rethia, but he had seen people dancing in Strakenbridge. Though it was interesting to watch, he had no idea how they knew what to do. What if Ambrielle ever wanted to dance? What would he do then?

Darby must have read the uneasiness on his face. "I've never danced with anyone either, but I learned some of the steps. I could show you if you like."

"You go to the taverns?" Gavian grew concerned Darby was becoming like Malidora. They both lived through tragic events at an early age.

"I don't go inside," she said. "But I like to watch the bright moon dance every month, and the Sylvermist Festival is fun. When it gets dark, they have a big dance around one of the fountains. Then there's the Solaria Festival, that's always fun too."

"That's a lot of festivals," Gavian said.

"It seems like such a long time ago." Darby looked away to the grassy plains while they rode. "There hasn't been anything like that lately." They bounced as the shippy hit a rough patch of terrain. Darby steadied herself. "You never answered my question, Tav."

Gavian glanced out at the blue patch of clouds that covered the moon. "As I told you, I don't go by Tavarian anymore. It's Gavian now."

"Gavian?" Darby blinked, a hint of confusion crossing her face. "Why Gavian?"

Taking a moment to gather his thoughts, Gavian responded, "Tavarian died the day I left Rethia. That name is best left buried."

Darby looked at him as if trying to read his mind. "We all change, Tav. It doesn't mean you have to forget who you were. I'm not the same person I was when you left, but those experiences are still part of me."

Gavian couldn't help but hear Darby's words in Ambrielle's voice. Thinking of her made his chest feel tight and empty. He bit his lip, the frustration of being without her beginning to swell inside him. Why had he told Ambrielle that he didn't completely trust her? He did trust her, but he didn't want to admit it so freely after he had been betrayed by the leaders of Rethia, by Lirah, and by Medigrin while Gavian lived in the Darterran caverns. It made him feel like he was supposed to withhold trust; otherwise he was a fool. He brought his focus back to Darby, hoping to keep her from reading the emotion on his face.

"It's a name I was given in Rethia," said Gavian. "I never felt comfortable there. Even though I wanted to be part of something, the community. I never was. I want to forget that part of my life completely. I want to build a new life that counts for something, that matters."

She brushed her hand through the messy waves of his hair. "That's how I felt about Muloken when it was under the Shadows' influence. When they blamed my mother for all the food in the garden dying. After she was killed, and no one would help me bury her and they left her in the house to rot. I wanted to wipe the whole town away. I wanted them all dead . . ."

Gavian searched the others' faces, worried what they were going to think of her. "Darby—"

"Bradwyn came from Muloken, like I did. He knows what the Shadows have done. Vilura came from Heralga," Darby gestured toward the woman sitting across from them. "One of the first towns attacked by the Grundians. We're fillers," she said. "We have to stick together. We've become each other's confidants. In this war, you've got to have pillars to lean on. Otherwise, you won't last very long." Bradwyn and Vilura nodded their heads in agreement, and Darby continued, "What I was trying to say is that the Nulthereals used those feelings. The same way they did with the people in Muloken. I'm no better than them. I may not have acted on it, but I would have. I found some of the refugees of Muloken in Strakenbridge, and many of them couldn't look at me. I reminded them of the worst part of themselves. But I forgave them, just as I asked for their forgiveness." Darby pressed her lips together, taking a moment before she spoke again. "Now when we see each other, we smile. Because we remind each other of the best part of ourselves."

"You're saying that we're no better than a city that murders students to solve their resource problem?" Gavian said.

"We all have darkness, flaws, whatever you want to call it," she said. "If you choose to hide from it, you deprive yourself from overcoming it and growing."

Gavian drew in a deep breath. What must go on inside Darby's head? Where did this wisdom come from? As much as it seemed contrary to everything that helped him cope with the betrayals in Rethia, her words cut true. "I've been going by Gavian for four or five years now. It's part of who I am too."

"Then I will call you Gavian," Darby said, "But it's going to feel really weird."

The grassy plains were gone now, and they rode over pebbles and hard clay. Approaching some large pools of rainwater collected in gulfs and fissures, the column stopped as Vilura and some of the soldiers climbed off their mounts to fill their flasks. Bradwyn jumped down and walked Flumpy to the edge of one of the pools for a drink. Though Gavian knew he should add some water to his own flask, he was anxious to get moving. He watched Vilura talking to one of the swordmasters, who handed something to her.

One of the soldiers signaled the others to come look at something on the ground, probably more Grundian tracks. Gavian tapped his fingers on one of the metal frames holding the wooden shippy together. Vilura returned to the cart, handing Gavian a worn sheath he could strap on his back.

"Thanks!" he told her, drawing the sword from his belt and putting it into the sheath then strapping it on. The soldiers returned to their mounts, and the column started moving again. Changing direction, the column curved further to the north.

After traveling across the rocky wilderness for a while, Gavian drifted in and out of sleep. He was suddenly awakened when the shippy splashed through a narrow brook winding between two small, grassy hills. "This area looks familiar."

"I think we are close to Grunda," Darby said, as they climbed up the hill. The shippy was knocked around from one side to the other on the uneven ground. Piles of large stones and tall wisps of grass stretched out ahead of them. Small red crystals dotted the landscape.

They rocked back and forth across the sparse vegetation with little to see. Eventually, they came to a cluster of trees with one that was enormous, standing out among the rest. One of its branches was split, hanging on by a thread, and the other end lay against the ground. Tall reeds and thick bushes slowed the docimares and other animals.

The sun had passed the top of the sky on its way toward the horizon when they came to the Vallohal River. It was a part of the river that Gavian had never seen before. Further down the shoreline was a round hill with smoke coming up behind it.

The column came to a stop, and Darby, Bradwyn, Flumpy, and Vilura jumped off the cart. Gavian hurried behind them as many of the soldiers grouped into formation. A few riders stayed back, keeping the docimares steady while the rest of them crept through the tall reeds.

As they drew closer, Gavian could see a Grundian on the hill sitting on top of a huge stack of boulders. He faced the river and had not noticed them yet.

"Who's our best marksman?" Holkson called out.

A woman strode forward. She appeared to be Grenovan, with curved horns on either side of her head. "That would be me, sir. What do you need?"

Gavian eyed Darby. "She's better than you?"

"Definitely. Korasi is almost as good a marksman as Dexius," said Darby.

"You looked pretty amazing against Grunch," said Gavian.

"Aye, that she did. What she lacks in marksmanship, she makes up for with agility and speed," Bradwyn said. "There are few archers who can move like her."

Darby smiled coyly and turned to Gavian. "Dexius says I should have been a swordmaster, but I wanted to learn the bow."

Gavian surveyed the walls, looking for a gate or any kind of weakness. He glanced back to the hill and the Grundian sitting on the boulders. He looked back at the wall again.

"Take down that lookout, I need an arrow in his neck on the first shot," Holkson said. "Get as close as you need without being seen. As soon as the lookout is down, we take the hill."

Korasi moved cautiously through the reeds while the Grundian continued watching the river. When she got closer, she kneeled and took an arrow from her quiver. When she drew back the string, the Grundian turned around. He roared, alerting other giants that were obscured from view behind the hill. Korasi's arrow grazed his cheek as several other giants stormed toward them.

With the giant on the hill no longer important, Korasi aimed at the closest giant heading toward them. A volley of arrows swarmed toward the charging Grundians. Vilura and the other lancers took position in front of the others, pointing their long spears forward. Korasi launched her arrow, bringing one of the giants down.

Darby fired into the incoming crowd, and Gavian pointed toward the hill. Darby swiveled toward the giant, who was holding one of the boulders from the stack with both hands, ready to throw it at the brigade. Her arrow hit the Grundian in the chest. The giant stumbled, dropping the large stone, which landed on top of him, causing both the Grundian and the boulder to roll down the hill.

The Grundians hit the row of lancers, and some of the giants were impaled on their spears. The rest of them swung clubs and hammers, sending the lancers sprawling. With the world around him in chaos, Gavian was unsure what to do. He wasn't part of this brigade and had no idea how they maneuvered, but he did not want to stay here and watch while everyone around him was hurt or killed.

He powered on the sword, the lightning inside the rokenstones beginning to vibrate the blade, making it appear as a blur. It became lighter in his hand. While the lancers regrouped to hold back the Grundian attack, Gavian rushed left, hoping to outflank the giants.

He decided a hit and run attack was the best strategy. Attack one and move out of range. After a volley of arrows whipped overhead, Gavian moved into attack range. Before he could use the sword, one of the Grundians raised his hammer to attack him. The giant's backswing gave Gavian enough time to leap out of the way before the hammer crashed down.

Gavian's sword vibrated through the air, its weight featherlight. He brought it down as hard as he could into the side of the Grundian. With a brilliant flash of light and a clap of thunder, the giant was brought to the ground. Before the other Grundians could turn to see what happened, twisting bolts of light arched from the smoldering giant, halting another four of them mid stride. They tipped forward almost simultaneously, crashing into the dirt. With one swing, Gavian had taken out five Grundians.

The lancers kept the remaining Grundians at bay, while the archers pelted them with arrows and the swordmasters slashed at them from behind. Gavian stood back, afraid the rokenstone-fueled blade would end up hurting the soldiers if he attacked again. Darby, Korasi, Bradwyn, and the other archers continued their barrage until the last Grundian had fallen.

"Where did you get that sword?" Vilura stared at the blade in Gavian's hand.

Gavian began feeling uncomfortable, aware of the many eyes on him and the sword. He glanced at the rokenstone at the crest of the hilt as strands of energy still glimmered within. "I found it abandoned and reforged the blade."

Captain Holkson moved toward him. "No sense in a filler having it.

Give that weapon to one of the swordmasters and we might be able to turn the tide in this war."

"That is no mere weapon," said Vilura. "It is Stormwaker!"

"There she goes again." Bradwyn shook his head. "You know good and well Stormwaker isn't real. There's no magical weapon that can save us from the Grundians. It is on us to be courageous and smart, the willing defenders of this land. Only we can show the fearful that this fight can be won."

"Whatever it is," said Holkson, "we can use it."

"How does this weapon work?" One of the swordmasters stepped forward. "Let me wield it, and I will use it to its fullest potential."

Captain Holkson saluted the swordmaster, crossing his arm over his chest. "Yes, lend it to Hilvan. He is one of our best."

Gavian hesitantly lifted the sword, pointing to the black stone that gleamed with purple and white energy under its surface.

"Wait—A rokenstone?" Hilvan took a step back. "What is it with you fillers and rokenstones? You and Darby can keep them. They may kill Grundians, but sooner or later they will also kill you."

Gavian considered explaining how the hilt was made to insulate his hand from the lightning but decided it likely wouldn't change his mind. Besides, Gavian preferred not to give up the sword anyway.

"We may fall in battle one day," said the captain, "but it would be a waste to die to a rokenstone."

Gavian and Darby walked behind the hill while the others searched the Grundian camp. One prisoner had been found among them, but it was not Ambrielle. The Grundians had used this man as a butcher and cook. The soldiers led the man to one of the carts, taking some of the cured meats he had prepared for the Grundians' next meal.

"I don't know how we'll ever find Ambrielle," said Gavian, as he and Darby climbed onto the shippy.

"The trail leads further on," Darby said, the convoy starting to move again. "This was just the first hideout we came to."

CHAPTER II

AMBRIELLE SHIFTED UNCOMFORTABLY, trying to ignore the stench of the Grundians' meal as they sloppily dropped bits of meat and bones on the cavern floor. The sound of their chewing and grunting filled the air, making her cover her ears in an attempt to drown it out. She stared at the strange green crystal she had observed one of the giants peering into. What did he see?

Suddenly, a crash of thunder sounded from outside the cave, causing the giants to stop for a moment. They looked at each other, unsure of the source of the noise. The sound of the thunder mixed with the clanging of the miners' picks and hammers, echoing through the chamber while the other shift continued digging.

Sitting in the corner of the cage, Thomin broke the silence he had maintained until now. "Must be storming outside," he said, his voice barely audible over the Grundians' clamor.

With Luken, Thakia, and the other humans in the cage fast asleep, Ambrielle moved over next to the boy. "It will be okay. The storm won't hurt us in here."

"I know," he said, his wide eyes not leaving the giants' direction. Thomin shifted his position, resting his head on his bent knees. His eyes remained wide open, unable to relax.

The Grundians went back to eating again. Ambrielle tried to instead focus on the echoes of the miners at work. She wondered how Gavian was faring through the storm. She had to believe he was still alive. Thomin rested his head on his bent knees, wide awake.

"Can't sleep?" Ambrielle whispered, trying to avoid drawing any unwanted attention and leaning her face against the wooden crossbars. It was an obvious question, but she hoped it would get him to talk and maybe forget about everything around them.

He shook his head, no.

"Where did you live before your family decided to leave?" Ambrielle asked, noticing one of his shoes was coming apart and the lace that was holding it together had come untied.

"Delancin," he said, as he made a loop in the lace string. "Everyone left. We planned to go to Lamesca. I've never been there before, have you?"

"No, I haven't," Ambrielle said, looking at the boy with sympathy. "What have you heard about it?"

Thomin worked to get the string through the loop with his fingers. "All I know is that it's in the Gulflands."

Ambrielle rubbed the back of his shoulders. "I'm sure your family is coming back for you."

"I don't know how they will find me in here." Thomin hung his head, struggling to get the string through the loop.

Sliding in front of him, Ambrielle took one end of the string and made a new loop, holding it while he pulled the other end through. "The forest you got lost in, do you remember where it is?"

Wrapping the string around the loop, Thomin pulled it tight. "It's called Elderglen, it's one of the biggest forests in Isodonia."

"Maybe when you get out of here, you can go back to Elderglen, and they will find you there." Ambrielle sat back against the cage.

"I don't want to go back," Thomin's eyes grew distant. "There was something bad in those woods."

Ambrielle rested her hand on his shoulder. "What do you mean?"

"I don't know," said Thomin. "But I heard it walking. It made these screaming sounds."

Ambrielle's mind immediately went back to the dark-cloaked being that had stalked her and Gavian in the small, abandoned town of Ferinoke. Her heart dropped when she thought about Gavian. If only she could find something that would distract the Grundians outside long enough to get away. What was taking Wegin so long?

The splashing of water echoed through the tunnel that led to the outside, while the sounds of voices grew louder, permeating the mine. Abandoning their food, the Grundians hurriedly seized hammers, clubs, and loose rocks, prepared to confront whatever was heading toward them.

Arrows whistled through the air, their sharp tunes harmonizing with the thunderous hoofbeats of charging animals. Thomin grabbed the wooden crossbars, pressing his face against the gaps to witness the unfolding battle. It was the distraction Ambrielle needed. Powering her silbrace, she cut through the thick wood with ease. With the bars still smoldering, Ambrielle pushed on them until they teetered over, scraping against the uneven stone floor.

"Let's go," she whispered to Thomin. Luken, Thakia, and the others began to wake up to the chaos around them, and Ambrielle and Thomin crawled through the open space. Holding Thomin's hand, she guided him toward the back wall of the cave, as far away from the fighting as she could get.

"Stay right here," Ambrielle commanded Thomin, her voice cutting through the chaos as a group of waking Grundians surged past them to reinforce the left flank. Taking a deep breath, she tried to summon the courage to do whatever needed to be done to survive this. Seizing the opportunity, Ambrielle propelled herself from the side wall, her body a blur of motion, laser emanating from her silbrace. With precision, she directed the searing beam toward one of the giants hurtling past.

The intense light scorched deep into the thick skin of the Grundian, piercing his ribs with seething energy. Ambrielle swiftly tumbled away, evading the retaliatory strike of the towering creature, his massive fist whipping through the air where she'd once stood. Struggling to maintain his balance, the wounded Grundian raised his hand again, ready to unleash a second assault, but the damage inflicted proved too grave. The resounding thud reverberated throughout the cavernous den when the hulking figure crashed heavily onto the rugged floor.

A hail of arrows hurtled toward Ambrielle with the force of a tempestuous wind. Quickly reacting, she sought refuge behind the towering forms of the giants, their massive bodies providing temporary cover. However, her respite proved short-lived.

As the giants succumbed to the relentless barrage of projectiles, Ambrielle propelled herself sideways, narrowly evading the impending catastrophe. The giants plummeted to the ground with bone-shaking impacts, their backs impaled by the multitude of arrows that rained down upon them.

Ambrielle glanced to where she had left Thomin. Her heart pounded with dread when she realized he was gone. Fear gripped her, and she desperately scanned the dark cave through the chaos. "Thomin!" she cried out. The clash of weapons and the cacophony of battle drowned out her calls, making it even more challenging to locate him.

She darted through the mayhem, her eyes searching every nook and cranny, her voice strained as she shouted his name. Time seemed to stretch while Ambrielle's frantic search intensified. Her gaze darted from one skirmish to another, her heart sinking with each passing moment. Then, in a fleeting glimpse, she spotted a small figure crouched behind a stone near the forge. Relief washed over her.

Arrows whizzed dangerously close to Thomin's sheltered position, clubs collided with bone-jarring force, and blades glinted in the dim light, threatening everyone around her. The danger was imminent, and Ambrielle knew she had to act swiftly. Ignoring the looming perils that surrounded her, she sprinted toward the forge.

A Grundian charged forward with thunderous footsteps, his path on a collision course with Thomin. Ambrielle's muscles tensed while she closed the distance. Everything seemed to move in slow motion as she extended her arm, silbrace ablaze with focused energy. With a rapid and precise swing, she lashed her laser across the giant's back, a searing mark etching across his thick skin.

As the laser's intense heat scorched through the Grundian's flesh, his momentum wavered. It was all Ambrielle needed. She seized Thomin's arm, her grip unyielding, and pulled him away from the encroaching danger. The ground trembled when the enraged Grundian turned, his fists swinging in a wild arc, fueled by fury and the desire for vengeance.

Ambrielle stood in front of Thomin, aiming her laser as far as it would reach when the giant approached. He raised his enormous fist, and then a look of pain contorted his face as a lancer's spear pierced his chest. The force of his fall cracked the long spear. The lancer emerged from the shadows, revealed when the fallen Grundian hit the floor. His lance remained lodged in the creature's body, impaling the giant through the very wound in his back that Ambrielle had inflicted.

The cavern air grew heavy with the acrid scent of sweat and dust. With each fallen Grundian, the cave became quieter, the space once filled with the tumult of combat now surrendering to a somber stillness. After the last Grundian fell, one of the soldiers strode into the center of the cave. "You have been liberated by the Storm Brigade! If you wish to take the fight to the Gruns, we have need of you!"

Silence enveloped the cavern, the only sound the collective breaths of the survivors.

"I want to join!" Thomin ran over from the side of the cavern.

The soldier turned toward the direction of the voice, narrowing his eyes as he saw the boy. "You're too young to fight, son. Where is your family?"

"I lost them," Thomin said. "But I can fight."

"You have more courage than most of the people in this land, kid," the soldier said. "We can't allow you fight, but we may have some work for you if you can follow orders."

"I can do that!" said Thomin.

"All right, take any useful items we can carry and let's move out!" yelled the soldier, who appeared to be the leader of the group, prompting the others to scatter through the mines searching for anything of value.

One of the swordsmen removed his helmet and began walking toward Ambrielle. "Are you okay?" he asked, as she stood staring at the strange green crystal in the higher reaches of the chamber.

Ambrielle blinked out of her stupor to focus on the soldier. "I think so."

He was young with bronze-colored skin and strange hair, white and black, patterned like zebra stripes.

"I'm Nemeris. Do you wish to join the brigade or do you plan to leave for the Gulflands?" the swordsman said.

Ambrielle glanced at him, his golden eyes looking right back at her. "I can't join right now," she said. "I need to find Gavian first. He was captured by Grundians, and I don't know where they took him."

"We are searching for Grundian hideouts in this region," Nemeris said. "Come with us, and there's a good chance we will find him soon."

"Ambrielle!" said a strange voice.

She turned to see Wegin flying over the cavern floor toward her. "Wegin!"

The swordsman gazed back, and Wegin came to a rest, hovering over Ambrielle's left shoulder. "Does that thing belong to you?"

"Was the distraction sufficient?" Wegin asked, as he flew close to her.

Ambrielle wrapped her arms around Wegin. He tried rotating in her hold, not seeming to like being constrained. "Definitely sufficient," she said. After a moment, he seemed to settle down and allowed her embrace. "Though it might have been better if the fighting had stayed outside of the cave."

"What sort of creature is it?" said Nemeris.

"He's a robot, I guess you could say," Ambrielle said. "I found him only recently."

"I'm a synthetic drone assistant," corrected Wegin.

"Whatever it is, it led us straight to this place," said Nemeris. "We likely wouldn't have found it otherwise."

"Good job, Wegin," said Ambrielle.

Wegin rotated happily in place.

"Do you think it could find other Grundian hideouts?" Nemeris asked, while the soldiers gathered scraps of metal from around the Grundians' forge.

"I have data of their genetic code," Wegin said. "I can take samples and find traces of them from several years ago. Covering a wide area systematically, we will eventually find them. The real question is how long it would take to find them."

"The sooner the better," Ambrielle said. Thakia waved to her while she ushered Thomin toward the exit tunnel.

"I should also inform you that, according to Tetra'Novis's data, there is an akreum nearby," Wegin said.

Ambrielle's eyes lit up. "Where?"

"It looks like it could be part of this cave system. Wegin zoomed around the forge, lighting a path that led further down into the cavern. "It's not one that Tetra'Novis marked to be awakened, but—"

"Dracos'Arkon said that miners used sonic devices to dig," said Ambrielle. "This is exactly what we need!"

"Where are you going?" Nemeris called out, as Ambrielle hurried behind Wegin.

"Thank you for everything. I'll catch up with you later," she said. "There's one more thing I need to do first."

"I can help," Nemeris said.

"Thanks, but I better do this myself," said Ambrielle. Her eyes diverted to Wegin, who flew through a crevice between two great boulders.

Nemeris trotted after her. "May I ask why?"

Ambrielle let out an exasperated breath. "If you're going to come, don't ask me to explain what you're about to see."

She walked through the crevice into another open chamber. It was filled with crystals that sparkled in Wegin's light. In the middle of the area, a huge crystal pillar stood. It had a green tint, much like the one she had seen the Grundian look into. At the base of the crystal was black mold covering the rocks of the cavern floor. Ambrielle's heart skipped a beat when she noticed the skeletal remains of a Grundian not far from the crystal.

Beyond the pillar was the white material of an akreum that had been partially excavated. Several broken pickaxes and hammers lay scattered on the ground. The Grundians had apparently tried to open the akreum but, like everyone else, were not able to break through the material.

Playing the melody in her head caused her silbrace to sound it audibly, echoing through the cavern. Dust scattered while the akreum changed shape, instantly accommodating an opening for them to enter. Nemeris stared ahead, saying nothing as Ambrielle stepped inside the vault. Shelves with various crystals and rocks filled the interior. Machine parts and what appeared to be robotic arms were scattered about the floor. One of the egg-shaped stasis chambers, like those she had encountered before, stood at the back wall. Ambrielle approached, and the opaque gas began to clear, revealing the Cereveshian inside as he began to wake up. After he took a deep breath, his body tightened, and he began coughing.

The Cereveshian was shaking when he opened the container and slid out. Ambrielle tried to catch him, but he fell to the floor. He grabbed her arm, holding tight. "Strange. Everything is so . . . solid here." Glancing up at her, he released his hold and moved onto his hands and knees. "Why did you wake me?"

"The Nulvarians have returned," Ambrielle said, as Wegin floated behind her.

The man breathed in, slowly and deliberately. "But I'm not a warrior," he said. "I am Azel'Deris, the geologist. Why would you choose me?"

"The seal around the rift is broken," she said. "I was hoping you knew how it could be resealed."

"If you are truly the awakener"—rubbing his eyes, the Cereveshian shook his head—"shouldn't you be more prepared? I'm afraid I don't have any plastra here, which is what you need to contain the rift."

"Well, where could I find some?" Ambrielle inquired.

"Did you not hear me?" said Azel'Deris. "I study rocks. I had nothing to do with containing the rifts. You awakened the wrong person."

"I thought Cereveshians knew everything," said Ambrielle. "Weren't you called the founders? The beings that ascended beyond this universe to a greater calling."

With some difficulty, the Cereveshian moved into a sitting position on the smooth floor of the akreum. "That's what many said about us, the other races." He drew in a long breath. "I suppose we encouraged it and then became convinced." His eyes stared past Ambrielle, Wegin, and Nemeris. "Being back here again, in this physical space, I wonder if it was all really worth it."

"What do you mean?" Ambrielle asked. "If what was worth it?"

"Our desire for more data," said the geologist. "Sometimes I wonder if we did more harm than good."

"What kind of harm did you do?" Ambrielle asked.

The Cereveshian's eyes met hers for a moment before wandering away. "With any new advancement, there is a price to be paid. Whenever one thing is gained, another is lost. We never weighed the consequences. Always moving ahead, more data, more knowledge. Perhaps there are some things not meant to be known."

"Like what?" Ambrielle wondered.

"You ask too many questions." Azel'Deris furrowed his brow as he stared off toward the darkness in the entryway. "Now that I am here, I am beginning to see things in a new light. Leaving this universe behind and seeking more data in the realm of Averess . . . we lost our way. We didn't bring this knowledge back to the universe for anyone's benefit. We never wanted to leave Averess. Things were so much easier there, without the life and death cycle, without having to consume living things to survive. It was an entire realm of new data."

"Can you at least tell me where the rift is?" Ambrielle asked.

"I do not know," said Azel'Deris. "This information was not given to everyone. They were determined to be dangerous before I had a chance to study any of them."

"Dracos'Arkon mentioned that the Gaith always send a Primevus through the rifts to each world they want to conquer. Do you know where it might be on this world?"

"I know nothing of this universe in this present time," the Cereveshian said. "Why didn't you get Dracos'Arkon to find it?"

"He went back to Averess," said Ambrielle.

"Either way, you came to the wrong place," said Azel'Deris. "Unless data on rock formations or tectonic plates is what you need, I can't help you."

"Fate seems to have brought us here," Ambrielle said. "There must be something you can tell me."

"Fate?" said the Cereveshian. "The Everance is much more complex than that."

"He is correct," said Wegin. "None of the akreums on this planet are marked for awakening."

"Yes, but there were mines . . ." Ambrielle started. "The sonic weapons! Do you have any sonic weapons here?"

"I don't remember any sonic weapons," said the Cereveshian. "I have a geowave in my solex that can use sonic waves to break rock, but this one is locked to my genetic code."

Ambrielle wrinkled her nose. She thought she was on the right track that started when she found the vault opened. "Thanks anyway. We'll help you get back into the chamber so you can return to Averess."

"I'm not going back," said Azel'Deris. "Not yet."

"But you have to," said Ambrielle. "Your body is too old to survive."

"Please help me leave the akreum," he said. "I wish to see the crystals again."

Ambrielle turned to find Nemeris standing in the opening. "Help me take him out into the cave."

Nemeris hurried over and grabbed the Cereveshian's left arm while Ambrielle took his right. The geologist tried to take steps while they moved him, but it was mostly them dragging him across the floor onto the rocky ground in the cavern chamber.

The geologist raised his arm toward the cavern wall, his solex making a dim violet light. With no beam extending out of the solex, Ambrielle began to wonder if its power had drained. Then she saw it; the crystals on the wall across from them began glowing. As the Cereveshian aimed his hand around the chamber, the area came alive with the light of the crystals. Blue, violet, red, and yellow, the crystals sparkled in many colors.

"Still as magical as ever," said the Cereveshian in a raspy voice, the colors of light reflecting on his skin and shimmering with each hue.

It was a beautiful sight to behold, a kaleidoscope of colors forming triangular patterns of soft light all over the chamber.

The Cereveshian opened his mouth to speak but stopped. Sudden urgency gripped the Cereveshian as his eyes widened, his gaze fixated on something unseen. His mouth opened to speak, but he hesitated, his attention drawn to a strange presence within the chamber, the large crystal pulsating with a vibrant green glow. Its gentle hum filled the space. "I don't recall there being a nyalith in here." His breathing began to sound labored.

"Do you want us to get you back into the chamber now?" Ambrielle's concern deepened, her hand gently reaching out to the Cereveshian's arm.

The man's eyes bulged with realization, as if a sense of urgency overcame him. He started coughing violently, his frail body shaking. "The automatons!"

Ambrielle patiently waited for him to elaborate, her eyes narrowing in confusion.

Amidst his coughing spell, the Cereveshian managed to gasp out his words. "Automatons," he rasped, his voice strained, "they . . . the mining . . . pulse attachments . . . geowaves." He took a ragged breath, his gaze pleading with Ambrielle. "If you bring me some of the parts inside the akreum . . ."

After a moment, Ambrielle remembered the parts on the akreum floor. She dashed into the vault with Wegin following, searching the scattered robotic arms and other machinery on the floor. The Cereveshians had automatons that did the actual mining, and those automatons had their own attachments: geowaves. But unlike the Cereveshians, the automatons didn't have genetic codes to exclude others from using the technology, like the solexes and silbraces did. Ambrielle picked up as many parts as she could carry and set them down in front of the Cereveshian geologist.

Between hacking coughs, Azel'Deris rummaged through the parts until he picked out a metal slab, his hands trembling with effort. "This is it! One of the geowave attachments!" he exclaimed, his voice strained yet determined.

Ambrielle eyed the flat, square piece suspiciously. How could this small object be anything that could break rock with sonic waves? More than that, how could it defeat a being like Versepirath?

"This is its compact form," explained Azel'Deris, his voice a mere whisper amidst his coughs. "The automatons had a mechanism in their arms that would open and close it, you'll just have to find a way to open it."

Ambrielle's gaze shifted from the Cereveshian to the mysterious metal square, contemplating its enigmatic nature. "You don't know how to open it?" she questioned, her curiosity coupled with a touch of frustration.

"I never had a reason to use the automaton attachments," Azel'Deris said, his breathing ragged. "But I trust in your resourcefulness. You will figure it out."

"Wegin?" Ambrielle called out.

"I have never been utilized as a miner," Wegin replied.

"But shouldn't you have access to some massive network of data or something?" Ambrielle said.

"I apologize, but there is no nexus on this planet to connect to," Wegin responded.

"I wish Gavian were here," Ambrielle lamented, as she thought of his penchant for understanding mechanical objects. "He would be able to figure it out."

The geologist closed his eyes. A sense of dread crept over Ambrielle, and she feared the worst, knowing his condition was deteriorating rapidly. "We need to get you back in the chamber!"

"I don't think I can make it," he said, his voice barely audible.

"I'm sorry!" Ambrielle shouted. "I'm sorry for waking you!"

He looked at Ambrielle for a moment. "You have nothing to be sorry for," the geologist wheezed, his voice fading with each word. "I should be the one apologizing to you . . ." He struggled, seemingly unable to complete the sentence, his strength waning. His face went slack, his eyes half-open.

"To me?" Ambrielle said, her voice trembling with a mix of confusion and grief. "For what?" Her words hung heavy in the air, echoing in the silence of the chamber. She waited, her heart aching. "For what!" she exclaimed, her voice filled with frustration and longing. Tears welled up in her eyes, and she hastily wiped them away, trying to regain composure. She didn't understand her own emotions. Why was this affecting her so much when she didn't know him?

The Cereveshian's eyes popped open as he had another coughing attack. "For not being more helpful."

Nemeris pulled the Cereveshian up, and Ambrielle assisted, bringing him to his feet. Though he had a hard time holding up his own weight, they were able to get him back to the chamber and rest him inside.

"I can't face the Savage Dark," the Cereveshian mumbled, his voice barely audible. The glass egg started to close around him. "Keep to the path . . . Keep to the path . . ." he repeated to himself, his words growing fainter while the glass sealed shut, locking him inside. A soft pink gas began to fill the chamber, surrounding him in an ethereal mist.

Nemeris released a noticeable sigh, his breath carrying a bit of intrigue. "I've never seen anyone like him. He must have been from a faraway land."

"Far away and long ago," Ambrielle replied, a melancholy tone to her voice.

Nemeris leaned closer, his curiosity piqued. "So, his kind enters a state of hibernation, I presume?"

"Something like that," said Ambrielle, a somber expression crossing her face.

The pulsing glow of the nearby nyalith grabbed Ambrielle's attention. She remembered seeing the one in the other chamber, one of Grundians holding onto it while he had peered inside. Ambrielle walked closer to the crystal, wanting to know what the Grundian had seen within.

CHAPTER 12

GAVIAN HELD ONE end of the tarp as Bradwyn grabbed the other. Tucking it around themselves to help shelter them all from the falling rain. The Grundian tracks they followed were being washed away. The patter of rain intensified, playing a rhythmic beat on the canvas that covered them. Someone at the front of the column yelled something, but Gavian couldn't make out the words.

The shippy veered away from the river. Gavian lifted the tarp, bringing his head out from under it. "We're not leaving, are we? We need to follow the river."

The cart driver peeled his tunic away from his shoulders with one hand. "Heading toward better turf. The banks are getting muddy."

Doubt crept into Gavian's mind while he rode alongside Darby and the other members of Inferno Brigade. The thought of embarking out on his own, unburdened by the collective decisions and compromises of the group, whispered enticingly to him. Perhaps, he mused, venturing forth solo would grant him more agility and autonomy in his search for Ambrielle. He could move swiftly, making decisions solely based on his instincts and judgment.

But now that he had found Darby, how could he leave her again? Especially considering how much she was trying to help him find Ambrielle. Traveling alone might grant him more flexibility, but it would also deprive him of the brigade's diverse skills and long-range transportation.

Gavian settled back under the tarp, glancing at Vilura and Bradwyn in the seats across from him. Darby leaned against his shoulder for a moment before suddenly moving away. "Oh, you're wet!"

Thunder rumbled in the distance, vibrating through the ground and resonating with the shippy beneath their feet. The air crackled with electricity, making him worry that the rokenstone in his sword, or even the arrowheads that Darby had left, might attract lightning to them. Darby seemed unconcerned, scratching Flumpy's back with the heels of her boots. She knew more about rokenstones than anyone he had encountered. If she wasn't worried, he shouldn't be either.

Vilura's black hair dangled over her face as she slumped in the seat. Her eyes were hidden from view, robbing him of knowing whether or not she was awake. Gavian leaned over, attempting to gain a vantage point where he could tell.

"What?" she said, straightening herself into her seat. "What are you staring at?"

Startled, Gavian turned away. "Nothing, sorry."

"You want to say something, say it." She brushed the hair away from her eyes as the wind roared, fighting with the tarp.

Gavian's fingers found the wet side of his jacket, trying to dry it with his sleeve. "What was that you were saying about the sword, Stormwaker?"

"We were having a nice, quiet ride," Bradwyn said, "and you had to get her started on that again."

Vilura playfully punched Bradwyn in the side and then turned back to Gavian. "What do you want to know?"

"Anything," Gavian said. "What is the myth you were talking about?"

"All right then," Vilura leaned back, rubbing her palms together. "Where should we start."

"Sounds like we're getting the long version," said Bradwyn.

Vilura stuck her tongue out at him and continued, "Well, the myth, as Bradwyn calls it, is that, many centuries ago, this land was conquered by a powerful being named Malhannon."

Thunder rumbled in the distance, shaking the ground, and the shippy vibrated beneath them.

"He enslaved many of our ancestors. He worked some to death and killed many more for sport." Vilura pulled the tarp further over her as the wind changed direction. Darby leaned in close, seemingly interested in the story. Bradwyn continued rubbing the fur under Flumpy's ears, rustling the tarp that hung over them.

"Malhannon fought with the ferocity of wild animals, with tooth and claw. He was far too fast to face at close range," said Vilura. "They only thing he feared was the anger of the clouds and the power they wielded."

"He took control of the land, city by city. Nothing could stop him," she said. "There was little hope left in the world in those days. Many thought it was the end of our kind. But the watching clouds of the skies had not forsaken us."

"Really laying it on thick, aren't you?" said Bradwyn, tucking his arms in close to his body.

"If you don't like hearing my stories, why bother listening?" she said.

"I can't even hear the thoughts in my head with you droning on," said Bradwyn. "Get back to it, so you can finish."

Vilura waved her hand in his face. "Anyway, the clouds did not approve of what Malhannon had done," she said, "disrupting the balance of the land they had been watching over since the first dawn. The clouds grew dark and angry, sending a torrent of winds and lightning to scour the land. They succeeded in wounding Malhannon. But he hid in the caves deep underground until the storm weakened."

"I seem to remember this being more interesting the way you told it before," Bradwyn said.

Vilura glared at him for a moment before facing Gavian again. "The clouds knew they had to find a way to reach him before he recovered. They gathered their power to send all their might into the stone of the world, though it didn't destroy them. Their power awakened the materials in the stone. Fusing metals with their force, the clouds forged a blade that could reach Malhannon in his lair. Stormwaker was born."

Darby leaned in toward Vilura, as if to hear her better over the pounding of the rain.

After a short pause, Vilura started again. "With such a powerful weapon, the clouds needed someone to wield it who would not use it for their own gain. So, they created it in a way that only those deemed worthy could touch the blade and live."

"That part never really made sense to me," said Bradwyn. "How was that supposed to work exactly?"

"That's the part you have trouble with?" Darby joked.

Bradwyn's shoulders bounced up and down while he laughed silently. "That among other things."

Vilura eyed both of them. "You two may not care, but Gavian asked to hear it, so if you could save the comments, I'm almost done." She took a deep breath and then resumed, "Where was I? Oh yes, so no one would come forward to test their worth and take the blade. There were none sure enough in themselves to risk death. One day, a humble craftsman named Grendon Thett decided he could inspire the others if he tried to take the blade, saying that death was a risk he would gladly take if there was but a chance to save the people. When he grabbed the sword, the clouds knew his willingness to sacrifice for his people and proclaimed him worthy to wield the blade. Grendon Thett entered their domain. Wielding Stormwaker, he brought the power of the clouds into Malhannon's lair, slaying him once and for all. After saving his people, he offered Stormwaker back to the clouds until a time when it would be needed again."

"That is actually an interesting story, though I doubt its historical accuracy," said Darby.

Gavian slowly nodded his head. "I have to say, it does sound like a myth."

"It probably is," Vilura said. "But I still love the story."

Gavian tapped the hilt of his sword where it had settled between two seats, a bit disappointed. "I thought you meant this sword really could be a legendary weapon."

"It does sort of meet the description though," Vilura said. "And it's fun to think about."

Darby turned to Gavian. "You could make it legendary."

The shippy began to slow and came to a stop. "The other shippy fell into a hole and broke an axle! We're stuck for a bit!" someone shouted from the column ahead. The shippy driver turned toward the edge of the woods, pressing through a tight space between the clawing tree limbs. Some of the soldiers in front of them were using axes to chop down a tree that was in their path. Once they were able to get the shippy and other vehicles free of the woods, Holkson called everyone to go back through the trees on foot and help the other shippy that needed repairs.

Flumpy shook her fur dry as they climbed down, getting most of them wet in the process. They found the other shippy lying slanted in a black, syrupy substance. It seemed to be all around this area. The black ooze dripped from the rotting trees and their bark and wood, as if they were in the process of melting. Gavian had seen areas like this before. Malidora named one of them Blightwood. It was like every living cell had been drained out of this section of the forest.

They detached the shippy from the docimare's straps, with several soldiers tugging on the animal's harness. Then, they attempted to lead it away from the muck. Gavian helped carry boxes of cargo off the shippy to make it lighter and easier to lift. While someone handed him a crate of rations, a glimmer further into the blighted forest caught his eye. A faint green glow emanated from a stone standing upright in the middle of the rotting vegetation. He had seen the same kind of stone years ago in the Galurigan Swamp.

The cargo was nearly unloaded when he set down the crate. Meandering his way toward the stone, Gavian remembered Grunch sitting in front of a stone exactly like it in the Grundian camp. Gavian rubbed the stubble on his chin. Years ago, when he gazed into the stone in the swamp, it felt weird, like his consciousness left his body. He had seen Solsellion, though he hadn't known it at the time. What would Grunch have seen in the stone?

Careful not to get his trousers in the black gunk, he crouched in front of the stone. The green glow began to pulse as he drew closer. Taking hold with both hands, Gavian stared deep into its shiny facets. Bending and twisting, his mind scattered, stretching out in all directions, faster and faster toward something at a great distance. Rushing through an entangled labyrinth, he felt out of control. Effervescence coursed through veins and stems of the stone, interconnections upon interconnections. Suddenly coming to a stop, his mind seemed to collapse and then reassemble itself.

A familiar being in black robes, wearing a hood over a silver mask, walked through a wild forest. Pillars of stone stood among the blossoming trees. The man continued until he crossed over into a circle of darkness. Gavian peered into the nyalith, seeing rotting black melted stumps, a more advanced state of blight than the one his physical body stood in now.

The man pulled back his robes and drew a silver sword from its sheath. It was the same black-robed man Gavian and Ambrielle had seen in Ferinoke.

A voice from above tore through the silence, "I trust you have come with an offering, ripe with the life essence I desire."

The man in the black robes kneeled. "Indeed, I have."

Floating above the trees was something that should not exist in this, or any, world. An eldritch monstrosity, as black as void, but surrounded by a bright shimmering shell. Its shape quivered and pulsed while it gazed at the black-hooded man with its two sets of three red eyes, each of different size. It was covered in tendrils, all in different stages of growth. The largest were encased with bright veins wrapping around them, and they writhed into the ground.

"Your obedience is commendable, Pythus. You are a credit to the Ichtek," the monster said. "Present to me the essence you have collected so we may assess our progress."

The man it called Pythus turned the sword, pointing the strange hilt of the sword in the direction of the voice. A white smokey substance reflected in his silver mask while it flowed out of the base of the sword. The entity seemed to breathe in the essence as it streamed into a disk of energy surrounding the area.

"Excellent, your efforts have augmented my power in this domain. I can now make my way toward Tildenhal. However, I still require a greater influx of energy to truly manifest. In the meantime, I have become aware of another settlement that dares to remain within our reach. Their defiance will only hasten this world's demise. The Grundians shall deal with them, and after they have been eradicated, you will bring their essence to me."

Pythus stood, bowing his head. "It will be done."

Gavian's focus waned when he felt another connection pulling at him through the gossamer strands of the vast network. Twisting through its veins, he arrived in another space. Another presence was near. In a dark chamber, barely lit by rippling torches, this presence peered into a similar stone.

His mind pressed forward to get a better look. A girl with long, dark blonde hair peered into the stone, her eyes the color of rich mahogany, and freckles on her cheeks. She searched across the infinite void among the billions and billions of intersecting pathways and saw him gazing at her as she gazed back at him.

"Ambrielle?"

CHAPTER 13

A S THE NYALITH stone glowed green from within, Ambrielle's mind began to twist into a long tunnel. Her consciousness stretched through time and space until she felt something. Another soul was present here, staring back at her across the void.

Ambrielle's spirit resonated with soothing warmth, relief, and happiness welling up inside her. She tried to contain it long enough to get the words out. "Gavian! You've alive!" He appeared to be outdoors, but the trees around him were dark as night. She felt the connection between them beginning to slip away. Focusing on his face, she tried to hold on as long as she could.

"Where are you?" his voice echoed, like waves washing over her.

Before she could answer, she was torn away, falling into the flow of energy that traveled in all directions. Lost in the interconnecting swarm, she was tugged toward another convergence. Her mind began to anchor to it.

"I summon three fists of the Grundian hordes, Twick, Grunch, Rugrug, for I have need of you," said a low, thick voice that reverberated through the ether. A vision of a massive horror hovering over the trees of a dark forest filled Ambrielle's mind. Its shapeless form heaved, as it seemed to drain life from the forest around with huge tendrils that burrowed into the soil. "The rest of you, return to your stations. I have no further use for you at this moment." A silence persisted for a moment, and then new surges of energy materialized among the endless pathways.

"We are here, great Ogolameth," said one of the Grundians across the void.

"You have done well. Many have fallen to your might. I am aware that some have fled toward the south, but we shall attend to them in due time. However, there is one city that has eluded your grasp. It is perched on a towering mountain, yet there is no path to reach it. I shall plant its location within your mind. Find a way to ascend by any means necessary. Spare no one. The horde with the highest body count shall be granted sovereignty over the mountain as a reward."

"The mountain will be ours!" said a Grundian voice.

"No! It will be ours!" said another.

"Grunch," said Ogolameth, "I have yet to hear from you. It would be unwise to defy me."

Ambrielle felt an unsettling gaze coming nearer, peering through the fibrous tangle, toward her mind.

"Open your mind to me," Ogolameth said, as the bright layer around him began to scintillate. "I can see there are three of you here."

Ambrielle felt tendrils snaking around her mind, attempting to penetrate her consciousness. One of them began pushing its way through, but she jolted free of the connection, falling backward onto the surrounding stone.

Wegin rushed toward her. "Ambrielle! May I be of assistance?

Nemeris came over to help her up. "Are you okay?"

She rested her forehead in her palm; objects began to solidify. The flickering torches animated the grooves and crevasses in the rock around them. "Yeah, I'm good."

"You saw something in the stone." Nemeris helped Ambrielle to her feet. "What was it?"

Attempting to comb her hair back into place with her fingers, she glanced back at the stone. "I saw Gavian. He's still alive!" Her eyes traced the cavern floor. "There was something else."

"Tell me." Nemeris placed his hand gently onto her arm.

Ambrielle's eyes moved between Nemeris and the floor. "Something about the Grundians." She struggled to gather her scattered thoughts, her voice trembling when she spoke. "They were being directed by a commanding force ordering them to attack a city and wipe out everyone."

"What city?" Nemeris leaned closer. "Did you catch its name?"

Ambrielle hesitated, her brows furrowing in concentration. "It was a city atop a mountain."

Nemeris frowned, his confusion evident. "There are no cities on the mountains."

"It must be Rethia!" Ambrielle exclaimed, her eyes widening with realization and urgency.

Nemeris raised an eyebrow, his curiosity piqued. "Rethia? I must confess, I've never heard of such a place," he admitted, his voice tinged with intrigue. "Are you certain about its existence?"

"It's somewhere toward the south I think," Ambrielle said. "We need to find Gavian! He knows where it is." She turned to Wegin. "Wegin, do you think you could find more crystals like this one? They are called nyaliths. Maybe that will lead you to Gavian. Will you see if you can find him?"

"Instructions received," said Wegin, as he flew off toward the cave opening.

Ambrielle returned to the stone, peering inside once again. The surface remained solid; the glow that was inside before did not return. "I can't see anything now." She stood, brushing the hair back from her face. "I just wish I knew where to look," she said. "I don't even know where to start."

"We'll be leaving soon," Nemeris said. "Why don't you come with us, and we'll figure this out."

Ambrielle followed Nemeris toward the pale light at the end of the tunnel. They came out of the cavern at the river. Stepping along the wet stones at the edge, Ambrielle made her way onto the rain-soaked weeds and grass. A chorus of birds sang a haunting song from the tops of the sparse trees. Soldiers rummaged through the fur and leather clothing of dead Grundians. A black iron kettle hung over the smoking remains of a bonfire. A few of the soldiers stood around the kettle eating stew out of metal bowls.

"I've got to give these Gruns credit," said a soldier with long blond hair, "they knew how to cook."

Nemeris walked over to peer into his bowl. "Do you even know what kind of meat that is?"

"It's treg meat," the blond soldier said. "What did you think it was?"

Nemeris sniffed the aroma coming off the kettle. "With Gruns, you never know."

"How many did they have working in there?" The soldier dipped his spoon into the bowl, drawing out a chunk of stringy meat.

"Looked like there were nine," Nemeris said. "Four of them are joining us along with a kid."

The young, blond man gathered the contents of the spoon into his mouth. "As long as there's enough room on the shippies."

"There should be," said Nemeris. "The others can ride on the supply cart, and Ambrielle here can ride with us."

The blond soldier glanced at Ambrielle, then back to Nemeris. "I've never seen you so welcoming to newcomers."

"Shut up, Dex." Nemeris playfully punched him in the stomach.

"Dex?" Ambrielle interjected with surprise. "As in Dexius?"

The blond soldier glanced up from the bowl, his hair falling over his eyes. Throwing his head back, he let gravity brush the hair away from his face. "That's right. Dexius at your service," he replied with a playful salute. He glanced at Nemeris. "I guess the tales of my heroics are beginning to spread beyond our inner circles."

Nemeris let out a good-natured snort. "Don't let his modesty fool you."

Ambrielle smiled, amused by their banter. "Of course, but I was wondering, do you know anyone named Gavian?"

Dexius paused, as if searching his memory. "Gavian?" he said. "I can't say I've heard of anyone by that name."

Ambrielle looked away in disappointment as her hopes that she had found Gavian's friend faded away. "Tavarian!" She suddenly realized Dexius wouldn't know him as Gavian. "Do you know Tavarian?"

Dexius set the crude metal spoon into the bowl, looking toward some tiny birds splashing in a puddle of rainwater. "Haven't seen him in years. We looked for him everywhere we could think of, but there was no sign of him anywhere. I figure he must be dead." Dexius's eyes locked with hers. "How do you know him?"

"He's alive!" said Ambrielle with delight. "I came here with him to find you and Darby!"

Dexius's face went slack. "What? Where is he?"

"Well, I don't know exactly," said Ambrielle. "We got separated when the Grundians took us. But I saw him in the nyalith!"

"If he's alive, then why didn't he come back to Strakenbridge?" said Dexius. "We waited for him. We spent a lot of time looking for him. Why would he just leave us like that?"

"He's been in another world the whole time," said Ambrielle. "That's where I met him. He didn't remember where he came from or how to get back."

"So, he sent you here to tell me this?" said Dexius. "Did he think I would believe it if it came from someone else?"

"He came here to tell you himself," said Ambrielle, "but we were caught by Grundians. They took me here and him somewhere else. I need to find him. Will you help me?"

"I have duties here," Dexius said. "I'm not going to abandon my team just because he finally decided to come back. I've wasted enough of my life already, worrying about him."

"But the Grundians have him!" Ambrielle said. "You're hunting them anyway."

"If we run across him, fine." Dexius said.

Nemeris squinted, staring at the bowl Dexius was holding. "Why does your stew sparkle?"

Ambrielle cocked her head to get a glimpse of the tiny shimmers floating and covering the thick broth. "Probably bits of the metal we were digging in the mines."

"Why would they put metal in their stew?" Nemeris stepped out of the way of a group of soldiers as they passed by.

"It's part of their beliefs." Ambrielle shrugged. "They think it makes them stronger."

Dexius dipped the spoon in and took another bite.

"You're still eating it?" Ambrielle crinkled her nose.

"This is the best thing I've had in weeks," said Dexius. "If it happens to make me as strong as a Grundian, I won't complain."

"You're putting a lot of faith in Grundian beliefs." Nemeris gently slapped Dexius on the arm. "I hope you have a strong stomach."

Ambrielle moved in front of Dexius as he took another bite. "There's something else you need to know."

Dexius picked up his spoon, leaning his head toward the bowl.

She wasn't sure he was still listening, which agitated her a bit, but she continued. "I think the Grundians are going to invade Rethia."

Dexius glanced up from the bowl. "What makes you think that?"

"I heard them saying they were going to a mountain with no road," said Ambrielle.

Moving the bowl away from his mouth, Dexius wiped his chin. "Why would they care about Rethia?"

Nemeris's eyes darted between them. "Do you two know each other?"

"They said something about there being a city whose people had not fled like the others," said Ambrielle, "that they were defying them."

"Rethia isn't defying them." Dexius smirked. "They don't even know Grundians exist."

"Well, that's not the way the Grundians see it," said Ambrielle.

Nemeris crossed his arms. "What are you guys talking about?"

Dexius's eyes moved to Nemeris and then back to Ambrielle. "How do Grundians know about Rethia?"

"Some voice was talking to them in the stone," said Ambrielle. "I think it must be some kind of Nulvarian. It wants the Grundians to kill everyone."

Nemeris stepped in closer. "Does this have anything to do with that strange being from the chamber?"

"I wonder if the Grundians would be able to get up there." Dexius stared off, not focusing on either one of them. "How many were going?"

"I think it said three fists or hordes maybe," Ambrielle said.

"Every fist leads their own horde," said Dexius. "That's a lot of Grundians. I wonder which fists it was."

"Grunch, Rugrug, and I can't remember the other one," Ambrielle said.

"Puvan? Snorp?" Dexius guessed. "Twick?"

"Twick!" Ambrielle said. "That's it."

Dexius and Nemeris glanced at each other. "I would love to get another shot at Twick," said Dexius.

Nemeris turned to Ambrielle. "Twick's horde wiped out Avalanche Brigade," said Nemeris. "Some of our friends were in that group. Though he's been involved in many battles, no one has been able to bring him down yet."

A woman with a scar across her cheek strode through the crowd of soldiers. "We've all had enough time to rest!" she shouted, putting on a rather odd-shaped helmet. "We need to get moving!" A gust of wind swept her long, brown hair swept off her armored shoulders.

Nemeris draped his arm around Ambrielle, leading her toward a magnificent, enigmatic creature. Its body was adorned with burgundy-hued fur akin to the delicate down of fledglings. A sinuous neck, resembling that of a serpent, boasted scales as dark as night, extending gracefully toward a matching tail. The creature's form widened slightly along its back, accommodating a spacious saddle capable of holding up to six individuals. Crowned by two stubby horns, its countenance displayed large, round eyes that exuded a sense of wisdom. Its haunches, elongated yet bent at the hip and knees, spoke of both agility and strength.

"What kind of animal is this?" Ambrielle asked, when she took the rope ladder that lay over the side of the creature.

Nemeris kept his hand on her back to make sure she didn't fall as she climbed. "You've never seen a brontha?"

Ambrielle settled into one of the saddles, placing her satchel in front of her. "What about those other ones?" She pointed toward a long, slender creature with outstretched legs bent out wide.

"Those are jagstriders." Nemeris climbed onto the brontha. "They aren't good for carrying a lot of riders, but they are excellent over rough terrain like this."

"And what about those?" Ambrielle pointed behind them toward the animals hauling wooden carts. Thomin waved to her after he climbed onto one of the carts. She smiled and waved back.

"Those are docimares," said Nemeris. "We use them to carry supplies and people."

"Oh, I've heard of those!" exclaimed Ambrielle.

"They're pretty common around here," said Nemeris.

The column began to slowly move forward. Ambrielle held tight when the brontha lurched ahead. It seemed to pick up speed as it found its rhythm. It was surreal riding this strange creature across an alien world with the dangers of war around them. She'd never pictured actually doing anything like this. It was exhilarating and a bit nerve-wracking. Staring ahead at the animals and soldiers marching along with them, Ambrielle lost any concept of how long they rode.

After a while, they came to a halt, the oppressive heat of the afternoon sun casting a hazy glow over their surroundings. The constant cloud cover seemed to intensify the humidity, making the air thick and muggy. Ambrielle, feeling the stiffness in her limbs, eagerly climbed down from the brontha, her muscles yearning for some respite. As she stretched her arms and legs, her gaze drifted toward Thomin, who was diligently assisting the young men in carrying a heavy trough for the animals to drink from. After that, he carried an armful of wooden flasks, handing one to each group for them to share.

Something about Thomin's youthful determination and willingness to help tugged at Ambrielle's heartstrings. She sensed a kinship with him. He had lost his family and needed a sense of belonging somewhere. She felt for him with all the challenges he faced as a kid in this harsh world.

Leaving her tiredness behind, Ambrielle strode to him, a warm smile gracing her lips. When she approached, Thomin looked up, surprise mingling with curiosity in his eyes. Without hesitation, Ambrielle initiated the conversation, her voice gentle and reassuring.

"You're doing a great job helping out here," she said. "I've noticed how hard you work and how much you care for others."

Thomin's face lit up. He shifted nervously, as if not accustomed to receiving such positive attention. "I . . . I try my best," he stammered, a touch of uncertainty in his voice.

Ambrielle placed a reassuring hand on Thomin's shoulder, offering him a comforting presence. "You have a caring heart, and that is something you don't find often enough. It makes you special. As hard as this war may be, the kindness you show to others will protect us. It's just as important as fighting against the Grundians."

Smiling confidently, Thomin handed her a flask and hurried off to other thirsty soldiers. Ambrielle took a drink from the flask, noticing Dexius walking by with a determined look on his face.

"Where are you going?" Ambrielle asked, offering the flask to him.

He took a quick drink and handed the container back to her. "I'm going to talk to Captain Enira about what you heard." Dexius turned back slightly while he walked away. "Three Grundian hordes are more than we could usually handle, but I have an idea."

Ambrielle's heart fluttered with a glimmer of hope, the ember of possibility flickering within her. Dexius's confidence was infectious, kindling the flame of determination in her own spirit. Yet, even as hope blossomed, it was tempered by the thought of Gavian out there, separated from them in the vast unknown. The ache of his absence reverberated through her being and sparked a yearning to reunite and face these trials together.

THE VISION FROM the nyalith faded, slipping away from Gavian's grasp like mist dissolving under the sun's warm touch. He returned to the crystal stone again and again, desperately seeking a glimpse of Ambrielle, only to be met with an empty void.

The forest loomed around Gavian, its once-majestic trees now contorted and gnarled, like ancient sentinels twisted by malevolent forces. Branches stretched out like skeletal fingers, casting long shadows that danced with a sinister grace upon the forest floor.

Yet, even in the face of the forest's malevolence, Gavian pressed forward, refusing to succumb to the despair that threatened to engulf him. He now knew Ambrielle was out there, and he would not rest until he found her.

"They got the shippy fixed!" shouted Darby, shaking him out of his stupor. She ran beside him as he climbed to his feet. "Why didn't you answer me?"

"Sorry." Gavian rubbed his forehead, trying to get the numb feeling out of his head. "I saw her in the stone."

Darby wrapped an arm around his waist while he stared at the tall stone. "Ambrielle?"

Gavian nodded his head yes, and something caught his attention ahead. In the midst of the densest part of the corrupted forest stood a monument. It had some dark grime nestled into the square pockets of its textured surface but was otherwise white. Some of it had sunk into the muck, but Gavian recognized it as one of the smaller Cereveshian akreums.

"What is that?" Darby gazed at the object surrounded by oozing trees.

Gavian wasn't sure what to say. The answer would require a lengthy explanation that would lead to more questions. His mind burned with thoughts of Ambrielle. "It's sort of a resting place."

"Oh, you mean someone is buried there?" Darby said.

Lifting his boot from the rotting ooze, Gavian stepped toward a group of soldiers circled near where the shippy had been stuck. "Pretty much, yes."

As they neared the soldiers, he began to sense something wasn't right. The low growl of a cornered animal reverberated in their midst as Bradwyn, Vilura, and the others backed away from the source of the sound.

"Don't hurt her!" Bradwyn yelled. "She's just spooked, that's all!"

"She's rabid!" Hilvan drew his sword. "If we don't put her down, she'll kill someone!"

Flumpy stood in the middle of the group, baring her fangs with her fur standing rigid down her spine.

"No!" Darby ran toward them, shoving her way through the others toward the beast. Bradwyn managed to grab her arm, pulling Darby back when Flumpy clapped her jaws at her.

"She's not herself!" Bradwyn said, pushing Darby behind him.

As Gavian moved into the circle near Darby and Bradwyn, Flumpy lunged at him. Gavian fell backward, and Bradwyn tackled the beast, shoving her into the dirt. Flumpy bucked wildly, trying to shake Bradwyn loose. Bradwyn held on for a few moments, but soon the creature flung him off. The soldiers drew their weapons when Flumpy charged at Bradwyn. While the mad beast tried to attack him, a large rope net fell over her, pulling the animal off her feet.

Vilura tugged on the rope until Flumpy could no longer move inside the net. The beast writhed and thrashed in the netting, but Vilura kept hold. Bradwyn got up slowly, lumbering over to help Vilura control Flumpy.

"This solves nothing!" Hilvan said. "This ravenous monster must be killed!"

Gavian turned to Darby, expecting her to react. She stood frozen with her eyes bulging. A familiar buzzing sound rose slowly from the dense forest behind them. Before Gavian could speak, he was caught in the mind-gripping influence of the Shadows.

Slay this vile beast! it whispered into his mind. *Save your friends! Be the hero you always wanted to be! They lack the will to do it! Free them from their ambivalence!*

Gavian removed the sword from his back. There was logic to what the voice in his head was saying. But it was without wisdom. Trudging across the vile muck, he made his way past the stone and into the thick forest ahead, following the vibrating sound.

His mind was attacked again. *If you favor the animal over the others, then return and protect it! They gather now to kill it! Your indifference is worse than making the wrong choice!*

Ignoring the Shadow's temptations, Gavian quickened his pace, cutting through branches with the sword. With the buzzing reaching an irritating level, he brushed back the leaves to reveal his dread. Not all Nulthereals had been eliminated from Isodonia.

The warning boils within you even though you ignore it, the Shadow whispered. *Soon they will all be raving, mindless beasts. It is not too late to run.*

His pulse quickened as he furiously slashed through the heavy under-growth, closing in on the shadowy Nulthereal.

Each step you take only hastens the ruin of your world.

Gavian sliced through the last vine. Facing the Shadow, he brandished his blade. Before his strike could land, the Nulthereal ensnared him into its current. Lifting Gavian's feet from the ground, it swept him toward the Shadow.

If you are fortunate, you will become part of the mindstream.

He pressed the switch on his sword, allowing energy from the roken-stones to flow. The blade vibrated into a blur, weightless in his hand. Gavian brandished the sword, the black mekkadium on the end of the blade making contact with the Shadow and ripping a physical tear into the being. His immediate second blow struck the weakened area, deepening the cavity.

Gavian dropped to the ground, reaching his arms and feet under him to catch his fall. The Shadow's bright disk of energy faded into smoke when its form crumbled into a pile of rock and dust. The pulsing buzz had stopped.

Amidst the hushed silence, the crackling of brittle leaves crushed underfoot broke the tension. Gavian swiftly turned, his senses heightened, only to find Darby standing there, her bow drawn and ready for any threat that might emerge.

Darby's gaze fixed on Gavian, while curiosity and concern mingled in her voice as she spoke, "How did you manage to destroy it?" Her eyes darted between him and the remnants of the vanquished Shadow.

Gavian raised his sword, rotating it in his hand and staring at its tip. "I don't understand everything that happened," he said, "but when the Blight Whidge connected to Malidora and me, we were somehow able to open its energy field. Some of the Shadow spilled onto the sword, turning the end to mekkadium."

"What's mekkadium?" She moved to get a closer look at the blade.

"I think it's a physical form of the Shadows. Maybe something in-between," Gavian said. "Whatever it is, it can touch them."

Darby walked past Gavian to the pile of iridescent black rock that remained of the Nulthereal. "So, if I used these shards?"

"Yes, good idea, take some," Gavian said.

She scooped up two handfuls of stone pieces and placed them in her pouch. When they returned to the shippy, Flumpy was still in the rope net but had calmed down. The arguing seemed to have stopped since the soldiers were working together to get the shippy's shafts reattached to the docimare's harness. Once they got it connected, they began on their way out of the black forest.

Darby and Gavian followed as the column moved out of the rotting forest.

"Do you think this is really it?" Gavian said, raising his sword. "Stormwaker?"

Staring at the ground beneath her while she stepped through the thick sludge, Darby spoke, "Is it a legendary sword with its own name? Who knows."

Slowing his pace, Gavian watched ahead. The soldiers reached the living part of the woods. "What do you know about this sword then?"

"Like I told you," said Darby, "it's a rokensword. It has special parts that connect the energy of the rokenstone to the blade."

"So one of many?" Gavian asked.

"Not many, but possibly more," she said.

"Do you recognize this one?" Gavian said. "I found it in your house in Muloken."

Darby looked away before speaking. "The hilt was an heirloom of my mother's," said Darby, "passed down through the family. She didn't let us see it much and never talked about it."

"It should be yours then," said Gavian.

"Like I told you before, I want you to keep it," said Darby. "It was designed to help defend this land. You reforged it and used it for that purpose. I believe you were meant to find it."

Gavian looked at the sword, recalling the blacksmith Ibis helping him remake the blade by using the same metals. "Why did she allow it to remain broken?"

"We'd better catch up to the shippy before they leave us," Darby said as she sped up, running toward the back of the column.

The column moved out of the woods into orange grassy fields. Darby and Gavian climbed in with Bradwyn and Vilura. Flumpy had fallen asleep, still trapped in the netting.

"I don't know what got into her," Bradwyn said. "Captain Holkson might not let me hunt with her again."

"Something must have frightened her," said Vilura. "She may be tame, but she still has animal instincts. If they see her calm like this for long enough, they'll forget about it."

"I hope you're right," Bradwyn said, staring out into the uneven plains. The column moved between two big patches of water that had settled into small basins. White flowers danced in the soft breeze as they moved toward a row of three cliffs of stone.

"You know they used vorrens in the Battle of Strakenbridge," said Vilura.

Bradwyn rolled his eyes. "We can't talk about anything without it leading to some battle story."

"At least my stories are more interesting than listening to you snore for most of the ride," Vilura said.

Darby stood from her seat, pointing ahead. Something was running in front of the distant cliffs. The column came to a halt, everyone stopping to watch the Grundians.

"Looks like a horde of them," said Bradwyn. "You don't usually see them running like that."

"Where do you think they're heading?" Darby asked.

"They're going south," said Vilura, "but not far enough to attack the Gulflands."

"Are we going to fight them?" Gavian wondered.

"Too many for us," said Vilura. "We'd need another brigade to take them on."

"Even with that sword of yours, I'm afraid," Bradwyn added.

"Look!" Vilura said. "See that big one? That's Rugrug!"

"Who's Rugrug?" said Gavian.

"Each horde has a fist, which is somewhat of a leader," said Vilura. "We've encountered him before but have never been able to bring him down."

"You usually don't find an entire horde moving together like this," said Bradwyn. "They send out smaller groups to attack."

"They would have to leave their hideout mostly unguarded," said Vilura.

Darby's eyes lit up with a mischievous spark. "We need to find it," she declared. "We could set some booby traps in there for when they return."

"That would be quite satisfying," Bradwyn chimed in, a sly smile curling on his lips. "Maybe they'll let Flumpy track for us again."

Gavian, feeling the weight of his own urgency, couldn't contain his frustration any longer. "Are we still following the same trail?" he blurted out, his exasperation seeping into his words. "I didn't join you to fight in this war. I came to find Ambrielle."

"Navigating this war-torn land requires caution," said Bradwyn. "We'll find your Ambrielle. Just try to be patient."

Gavian took a deep breath, allowing Bradwyn's words to resonate within him. He closed his eyes for a moment, feeling the rhythmic beat of his heart gradually slowing. With each pulse, he reminded himself they shared a common goal. Though they might have different priorities, they were all looking for the Grundians who took Ambrielle.

Leaving a trail of dust behind them, the Grundian horde finally rumbled out of view. The halo of the obscured sun began to settle behind the trees, and a quiet serenity contrasted with the recent tension. The column started up again. Winding between the hills, they continued until they came to a small scattering of trees.

The sky had grown dark by the time they climbed off the shippy. The ghostly glow of the blue moon took the place of the sun. Darby pushed a stack of crates to the edge of the shippy. Gavian took one of them and followed the others into the thicket ahead. Everything seemed so different at night, closed off and mysterious. All was quiet, as if the world itself held its breath in anticipated dread, waiting for what the night might bring. The crate grew heavier in his hands as he made his way to the campsite. At last, he reached the location the others had been stacking the crates, breathing out his relief when he set the wooden box down.

A fire was started, and tents were erected. Wooden bowls were distributed, containing a warm concoction of a gray mash of beans and water. It tasted okay in the beginning, but after several bites, Gavian soon grew tired of it. Darby downed her bowl quickly, taking out a knife to shape the mekkadium pieces into arrowheads. Gavian bore through it and ate it all, not knowing when his next meal might come.

As he finished eating, someone strode toward him in the firelight, tossing a thick wooden stick at him. "You have potential for a filler. If you want to improve and use that sword of yours properly, show me what you've got."

Gavian caught the smooth wooden stick and followed Hilvan, who walked away from the camp. Hilvan raised his wooden sword. "See if you can hit me." He motioned for Gavian to attack.

Gavian rushed toward him, swinging at Hilvan's right side, then his left. Hilvan blocked both and poked his sword into Gavian's gut.

"Surely, you can do better than that," Hilvan said, as he waited for Gavian to recover since he was currently doubled over trying to regain his breath after the blow. "Attack again when you are ready."

When Gavian could stand again, he raised the wooden sword. This time he charged at Hilvan with a flurry of tight arcing strikes. Hilvan parried them all with relative ease. Gavian came at him again, even faster. Hilvan dodged, trying to gain an opening between Gavian's swift attacks. He blocked each of Gavian's blows until one got through, hitting him in the chest.

Gavian spotted Darby watching from the camp. He was glad someone had seen him beat Hilvan. Brushing off his tunic, Hilvan put his sword behind his back. "Good. I won't have to go easy on you. You have speed, which is nice, but your biggest weakness is your footwork."

"I thought my stance was fine." Gavian spun the wooden sword in his hand.

Hilvan stepped toward him. "Your initial stance is good, but you come out of it once the fight starts. Let's start there. Stand with your feet shoulder width apart and keep your weight centered between them."

Gavian nodded, gripping the sword tightly and shifting his weight back and forth, trying to find the right balance.

"Good," Hilvan said, nodding encouragingly. "Now take a step forward with your left foot. Keep your knees bent and your weight centered."

Gavian followed Hilvan's instructions, taking slow, deliberate steps. He stumbled a few times, but gradually began to find his rhythm.

Excellent," Hilvan said, a note of approval in his voice. "Now, let's work on your strikes." He took up a defensive stance and gestured for Gavian to attack.

Gavian lunged forward, swinging his wooden sword wildly. Hilvan deflected the blow easily, then countered with a fleeting strike of his own. Gavian stumbled back, but quickly regained his balance and raised his sword again.

They continued working at it until some of the others headed for the tents to get some rest. "We'll continue tomorrow," Hilvan said, as he made his way to one of the tents. The chill of the night air settled on them, and many soldiers huddled together for warmth around the fire. Bradwyn had tied Flumpy to a tree, feeding her through the netting. All Gavian could think about was seeing Ambrielle again. Pushing back negative thoughts that tried to creep into his mind, he played scenarios in his head. What would he say to her when they finally found each other again?

Even when they were recently together, he'd felt a gulf between them. Had her feelings changed while they'd been apart? She had been excited to see him, but something wasn't quite the same.

CHAPTER 15

FROM ATOP THE brontha, Ambrielle spotted Thomin carrying containers of water and passing them out to the soldiers again. It seemed like the boy had found his place within the group. They each took a drink and handed it to the next person. Now that he was out of the cave, he seemed fully alive, smiling and talking to the soldiers. It was easy for the thirsty to like someone handing out refreshments, a great way for Thomin to get to know everyone.

"You seem to be getting popular around here," Ambrielle said, as he handed her one of the containers.

Thomin smiled. "Captain said if I keep doing a good job, they'll teach me how to fight!"

"But then we'll lose our best assistant." Ambrielle took a drink, then fiddled with the cap of the container.

Thomin didn't stop moving the whole time he waited for them each to take a drink. "Don't worry, I'll still be an assistant when I become a lancer. I can do both."

"Both?" Ambrielle teased. "The captain better look out. You'll be taking her job before long."

Thomin shook his head. "I don't think so. Captain Enira is

the best." After Nemeris handed Thomin the container, the boy waved and quickly ran off to the next group.

Ambrielle held tight to the saddle when the brontha leaned into a depression on the rocky surface. The restless night had come and gone. Heavy clouds hung low, draped like a leaden shroud, suffusing the landscape with a somber ambience. The trees thinned out, their forms becoming fewer and farther between, allowing glimpses of the vastness beyond.

"What did you tell Enira?" Nemeris asked Dexius.

Rubbing his stomach, Dexius leaned back in the saddle. "I told her what Ambrielle heard."

Ambrielle inquired, "But what about the idea you mentioned?"

Dexius put his hand to his mouth for a moment before answering. "Even though there are three hordes of Gruns, if we can catch them while they are climbing the mountain, we would have a huge advantage."

Nemeris sat up straight in the saddle. "We could take out three hordes by ourselves!"

"That would make a big difference in this war," Dexius said.

"I want to find Gavian first," Ambrielle said. "Are we even looking for him?"

"We don't know where to look," said Dexius. "Even if we did, we have bigger problems right now."

The brontha passed a low-hanging branch, and Nemeris slid forward to duck under it. "So why aren't we heading south?"

"Because—" Dexius grunted, pressed his lips together tightly, and wrinkled up his brow as he shuffled on the saddle. His stomach loudly grumbled in protest. "Slow up," Dexius said to the driver. "I'll catch up in a bit."

"Because what?" said Ambrielle, while Dexius moved out of the saddle and descended the rope ladder. When his feet touched the ground, he ran into the trees, holding his stomach. Ambrielle and Nemeris glanced at each other, making Ambrielle begin to chuckle.

After a while, the convoy came into a green meadow, and Ambrielle spotted Dexius running full speed behind the brontha. When he caught up, Nemeris and Ambrielle helped pull him up.

"I take it your stomach rejected the Grundian belief system." Nemeris grinned.

Ambrielle giggled as Dexius closed his eyes, seemingly exhausted. The brontha picked up speed once Dexius was securely back in the saddle.

After catching up with the rest of the convoy, they rode on for a while, and the landscape changed to rough, reddened stone as far as Ambrielle could see. Towering columns of rock filled the area. Some were smooth and polished, shaped by the master crafting of wind and water.

In stark contrast, other columns appeared jagged and rugged, like they'd been violently torn from the earth by some unfathomable force. These towering monoliths bore the scars of a tumultuous past, their surfaces pitted and scarred as if bearing witness to a great cosmic battle.

Some of the formations bore the remnants of old sculptures of some unknown race. The land seemed to hold secrets of forgotten civilizations and untold tales from ages long past. "Who made these carvings in the stone?" Ambrielle asked, as they passed by.

Before Nemeris could answer, a clamor rose from the riders ahead. "Incoming! Brace yourselves! Defend the convoy!"

A large stone hit the ground nearby, dredging up dirt, bouncing and rolling toward the convoy. The line of soldiers and mounted creatures scattered apart, kicking up dust. The stone fortunately came to a stop without touching the convoy.

Dexius readied his bow while two Grundians charged toward their left flank. Firing an arrow through the haze, he hit his target, but his arrow missed any vital points. Volleys of arrows from other archers rained down on the two Grundians, but they were not deterred.

Another boulder was thrown toward the scattered brigade, directly hitting one of the shippies behind them. Ambrielle gasped after she saw the cart smashed to shreds. Dexius continued firing along with the other archers, until one of the Grundians was brought down. A group of lancers on jagstriders swiftly charged at the lone Grundian, who clutched another stone. Encircled by the lancers, the towering giant met his demise before he could hurl the next stone.

With the two Grundians dead, the brigade came together, halting while they regrouped. Ambrielle sat still and quiet in the saddle, hoping her heart would slow down. She felt cold perspiration on her neck as she looked at Dexius and Nemeris sitting calmly, like they were simply waiting to get moving again.

"How do you guys deal with this so well?" Ambrielle asked.

Dexius looked at her. "After you go through this long enough, you don't react to it as much."

"But it doesn't make it any easier," said Nemeris.

A somber procession of soldiers slowly passed by, bearing the weight of a fallen comrade from the shippy's wreckage. Ambrielle caught glimpses of two more bodies being carried, their forms crushed and mangled, a devastating sight that threatened to overwhelm her. She averted her gaze, unable to bear the magnitude of the devastation that unfolded before her eyes. Yet, a force beyond her control compelled her to look once more, and in that heart-wrenching moment, she recognized the lifeless figure being carried past.

A wave of dizziness washed over Ambrielle as the soldiers continued their solemn march. Ambrielle dismounted the brontha and raced after them, her heart pounding with desperation. "Can you help him?" she pleaded, her voice strained with anguish, directed toward the soldiers who bore the lifeless body. In her turmoil, memories of the healing beam within her silbrace surged to the forefront of her mind, a flicker of hope that could mend and regenerate cells with remarkable speed. "If not, I have something that will work! Please!"

One of the soldiers walking in step with the mournful procession turned around, his expression weighed down by sorrow. "I'm afraid it's too late for that," he uttered with a heavy sigh. "We must lay them to rest."

"But Thomin," Ambrielle's voice trembled, her eyes welling with tears. "He's just a boy. He can't be . . . He's too young to be . . ." Her words faltered, her heart breaking at the thought of such a vibrant soul snuffed out so prematurely.

In that moment, grief enveloped Ambrielle, casting a shadow over her world. The magnitude of the loss, the unfairness of it all, threatened to consume her. She stood there, stunned and devastated, her spirit crushed under the weight of unbearable sadness.

Ambrielle, filled with a mix of desperation and despair, continued to pursue the soldiers' grim procession. Dexius caught up to her and stood by her side, his touch a gentle anchor on her arm. His voice, a soft solace, reached her ears. "It's going to be okay," he whispered. "Life doesn't always make sense."

She turned to face him, her cheeks streaked with tears. Seeking comfort, she buried her face in Dexius's chest. Gasping breaths escaped her as she struggled to make sense of his words. However, her mind was consumed by darkness, unable to see beyond the weight of the thick, suffocating clouds that shrouded Isodonia. She feared the possibility of never reuniting with Gavian, their love lost amidst the chaos of war. The endless conflict threatened to devour all life on Isodonia, leaving nothing but desolation in its wake. The mere thought that the Shadows, the embodiment of malevolence, would persist to drain the life force from the universe intensified her despair.

Ambrielle wanted to go back home, to return to the safety of her room. She would crawl under the covers of her bed, never to return to the outside world again.

❦

Ambrielle watched the skies as the day wore on, hoping she would spot Wegin returning to her with good news. The column turned, and they approached a deep canyon stretching out ahead of them. The death of Thomin clouded everything in her mind. If he had a destiny, a purpose, why had he not been allowed to fulfill it? Did anything have a purpose? Was the Everance indifferent to it all, as Gavian said?

"Bloodstone Gorge." Nemeris nudged her as the rest of them gazed at the enormous red formations of rock.

The brontha strode along parallel to the ravine, following the rest of the cavalcade at a safe distance from the rim. "The home to many Grundian hordes," said Dexius.

"Do any of them still live here?" Ambrielle's golden hair blew across her face when she turned to him.

Dexius looked at her like she was joking. "Most of them stay here all the time. It's normally only Grunch's horde that lives in the vibrant lands."

"Shouldn't we be avoiding this place?" said Ambrielle, not wanting to see another Grundian ever again. She hated them.

"Captain Enira wants to have a look at Dimcut Pass," said Dexius. "If Rugrug's and Twick's hordes have truly gone to Rethia, it should be obvious. That will make her more likely to make the journey to Rethia. We'll take out as many Gruns as we safely can before heading to Strakenbridge."

Nemeris glanced up at a formation of large birds, nearly camouflaged against the stirring gray clouds as they glided on the wind. "We won't actually be going into the gorge."

"No one ever goes in," said Dexius.

After riding for a while, they came to a sloped divide along the edge. A rocky path covered in red dust coursed down along the canyon wall. When the company came to a stop, a few of the soldiers dismounted to examine the area. When the others started climbing off the brontha, Ambrielle followed their lead. She needed to stretch her legs if nothing else.

Ambrielle watched the captain and some others walk over to the road, kneeling to examine the clay. They were talking back and forth, but Ambrielle could not hear what was being said. Inching closer, she tried to get within earshot of them. Dexius moved in front of her, shaking his head as if warning her not to get in the captain's way.

"This is closer than anyone has been to Bloodstone in some time," Thakia said, reaching both hands toward the sky and arching her back as she stretched. "Other than the giants."

Ambrielle still didn't care much for Thakia, wondering why she couldn't have been like most of the others and fled to the Gulflands.

A howling call echoed through the canyon, attracting Dexius's attention momentarily. "Just another day for Storm Brigade."

"What do you think they are saying?" Ambrielle wondered, as Captain Enira stood, pointing down the path that led into the gorge.

Nemeris kicked at a rock embedded in the hard dirt. "Hopefully they didn't find anything."

"Why not?" Dexius asked.

"We just got done fighting in Grungal," said Nemeris. "I need more time between the stress of potentially dying a horrible death."

Dexius affectionately thumped him on the shoulder. "I hear you. I didn't expect this war would last two years. But the sooner we fight, the sooner we get this over with."

"You may have been fighting for two years," said Nemeris, "but I've seen this my whole life. I've only known a few years of what it was like to be normal before the fighting started again. That was my only respite."

"What other wars have you been in?" asked Ambrielle.

"Nemeris is from Varkandor, the land across the sea," said Dexius. "He came over here when it was destroyed."

"Like Malidora?" Ambrielle said.

"Tav told you about her?" Dexius said. "She was from Arkanthis; Nemeris came from—"

"Lethoria," said Nemeris. "It bordered Arkanthis. As much as Dexius talks about this Malidora, you'd think I would have heard about her before coming here."

"What? I don't talk about her," Dexius said.

Captain Enira began walking toward them. "We're taking a scout team into the gorge," she bellowed. "There's a Grundian cave not far in. We have concluded that it is abandoned, at least temporarily. We'll be setting big game traps inside for when they return. It should be quick, just in and out. Do we have any volunteers?"

With a lift of his brow, Dexius glanced back and forth between Ambrielle and Nemeris. A few of the soldiers stepped forward. "We can't let them be the first to set foot in Bloodstone." Dexius moved beside the other volunteers. Nemeris let out a weary breath and shuffled alongside him.

Perhaps out of ignorance of the depth of danger this incursion involved, Ambrielle felt compelled to go with them. After what the giants did to Thomin, she wanted a part in their demise. As she walked ahead into the group, Nemeris and Dexius glared at her. "You?" Dexius said, while a few other volunteers came forward.

"I don't see why not," Ambrielle remarked, testing her silbrace to make sure it still had power.

"You don't strike me as someone . . ." Dexius paused, "someone who's inclined to take risks."

Ambrielle tilted her head slightly, her gaze unwavering. "I faced The Hollow and survived, and I crossed through two worlds to get here just to help Gavian find you. I've been captured and forced to work for the Grundians, and before you try to claim credit for my rescue, you wouldn't have located Grungal if it weren't for Wegin. Does that strike you as someone afraid to take risks?"

"She did help fend off some of the Grundians in the cave," Nemeris interjected. "In case I hadn't mentioned it."

Dexius cocked his head back, conceding the point. "I stand corrected."

"You're going to let a filler on a mission like this?" one of the soldiers chimed in.

"I'm accepting any volunteers who are willing," Enira asserted confidently.

Captain Enira led them down the path, while the rest of the group watched over the animals and supplies. Ambrielle wished she had something to tie her hair back because it kept getting in her face.

Enveloped in the depths of her grief, Ambrielle embraced the darkness that consumed her. The allure of exploring uncharted realms, untouched by the presence of others, beckoned to her with a different purpose—one driven by vengeance. She now saw them as a battleground where she could help to exact retribution upon the dangerous giants that inhabited them.

Ambrielle disregarded the inherent risks that lay ahead, fueled by a singular desire to confront those who had caused her immense pain. The territory, teeming with perilous beings, held little sway over her decision. Blinded by her grief and a burning need for justice, she marched forward.

Several red lizards scattered along the vertical wall beside them, making Ambrielle jump from the sudden movement. The closer they moved to the canyon floor, the damper the air began to feel. The musty smell of dirt and minerals grew more intense. Vertical rock formations with red and purple layers stood out from the ground below them. A great waterfall spilled over the rim in the distance, falling into a basin at the bottom.

Reaching the canyon floor, they moved along a footpath that divided the dense foliage. Vines with large leaves, ferns, wide splaying bushes, and wispy trees made up the environment around them. Giant blue geodes lay partially exposed underneath layers of rock. Red crystal formations were abundant and much bigger than those she had seen in the other parts of Isodonia.

"This is like a whole world of its own," said Ambrielle, glancing at the stares of the others around her and forgetting they were trying to keep their presence unknown. Small birds called to them from the tops of trees. A group of small, fur-covered creatures scurried off the path into the thick vines as they walked by.

The ground became soft and mushy when they entered the basin. The waterfall above thundered into a plunge pool in the canyon bed, flowing into a river that carved through the middle of the gorge. Not far from the plunge basin was the mouth of a cave big enough for a giant.

Primitive carvings adorned the wall around the cave. Two stick figures with their hands raised above their heads, each holding an object in both hands. After they moved around one of the tall formations of stone, the flame of torches inside the cavern became visible.

Captain Enira signaled them toward the cave opening. As they reached the entrance, Dexius and Nemeris leaned in, listening for any sound, but the roar of the falls made it difficult. The carvings around the opening made more sense up close. They portrayed giants breaking an animal in half above their heads, perhaps serving as a warning to those who would be foolish enough to enter.

Enira nudged Dexius and Nemeris inside. Reaching back to tug on Ambrielle's sleeve, Dexius pulled her along with them as the rest of the soldiers entered on the other side of the captain.

"I need the last five of you to watch the entrance," Enira said. "Warn us if there is danger. If we run out, you'll need to cover our escape."

Shadows danced in the orange glows cast by the torches above, giving life to a two-dimensional world on the stone surface. Ambrielle watched the interplay of shadow and light imprinted by the three-dimensional reality beyond the walls of the cave. The Grundians had only a rudimentary perception of the environment they inhabited. Without their strength to bully other species, they were nothing. It made Ambrielle wonder what could lie beyond her own perception. Could her reality merely be the reflection of higher dimensions of space and time?

The scent of burning wood filled the cavern. She could feel her steps angling with the tunnel sloping downward, eventually flattening out when they entered a larger chamber. Huge, sloppily made wooden boxes lay along the sides of the hollow room. With the sound of the waterfall dampened, Captain Enira halted the group, listening for any sound in the tunnel ahead. Rhythmic droplets fell into shallow pools, like a heartbeat in the dark.

Leaving the room behind, they entered the tunnel before them. Though they moved as quietly as they could, the sound of their footsteps bounced around the cavern walls.

"You are bold to enter," rose a deep voice from somewhere in the cave.

The group hesitated, exchanging apprehensive glances in the ghostly flame, uncertain of how to proceed.

"Come closer," it said. "I know you are there."

Ambrielle and some of the others eased back. Captain Enira motioned for the others to back up. "What do you wish us to do?" she called out to the darkness ahead.

The low voice from within the depths of the cave responded with a hint of resignation, "If you have come to kill me, I welcome it."

"You wish to fight?" Captain Enira said.

The rustling sound of something stirred deeper in the tunnel. "There is no fight left. I wish to die like a Grundian. To swords and bolts of steel, not of weakness and suffering."

"Who are you?" said Enira, her voice firm but curious.

"I am Thud," he replied, his voice echoing through the chamber. "My horde left me here to die."

A wicked canopy loomed overhead, adorned with menacing stalactites that seemed to stretch downward, reaching toward them.

"My leg is broken." Thud's voice carried a tinge of bitterness. "I would have slowed them down."

"Where did they all go?" Enira probed.

"Come into my chamber," Thud beckoned, his voice carrying a sense of urgency. "Promise a swift end and I will tell you."

"Sounds like a trap to me." Enira's words bounced off the cavern walls. "How do I know you can't walk? For all I know you are waiting to strike as soon as I enter."

The giant's deep voice rumbled in response. "If I could walk, you'd already be dead."

"Fair point," Enira conceded, her tone still guarded. "But why would you help us find the rest of your horde?"

A heavy sigh escaped the giant's lips. "They are not themselves," said the giant. "The dark mind has taken them."

"What dark mind?" Enira's eyes narrowed. The cave seemed to grow darker, as if the shadows were rising up to consume the torches' light.

"It is called Ogolameth," said the giant. "It once controlled my thoughts. Now that I am useless, it has left me alone. As long as we keep winning its battles, the monster will control us. Maybe if you can stop them, Ogolameth will leave the others alone too."

Captain Enira crept further into the tunnel. Ambrielle and the others began to follow. Rounding a corner she stopped, staring at something out of view.

In the corner of the wide-open chamber sat a Grundian leaning against the wall. Surrounded by the bones of small animals, the Grundian who called himself Thud appeared sickly and frail. It seemed he had not been brought food or water in days.

As the swordmasters brandished their swords, Dexius took an arrow from his quiver, aiming his bow at the Grundian.

"Who is this Ogolameth that you spoke of?" Captain Enira inquired.

"I've told you, it is a darkness," Thud explained. "A dark mind giving commands."

"What does it tell you?" Enira pressed.

"Its words are lost to me now," Thud admitted. "Only images are left. It showed us all the Grundians in the world. Even the Gurrians in the icy north few of us had seen before. It made us forget our disagreements. We were called to unite and destroy the cities of kips. Take it all for the Grundians."

"Where did it tell the others to go?" Enira questioned further.

"To a mountain in the south," Thud revealed. "Ogolameth needs more essence. It wants to move toward Strakenbridge. The Gurrians will attack Tildenhal, while Grundians attack the mountain."

Ambrielle exchanged a knowing glance with Dexius.

"They're already moving toward Tildenhal?" Enira exclaimed. "Ekendale can launch a counteroffensive from their rear."

"We do not argue," Thud stated firmly. "We only do what Ogolameth asks."

"What sort of essence does this dark mind need?" Enira probed.

"It comes from living creatures," Thud explained, "or the recently dead. If it gets enough of it,

Ogolameth can bring its full form into the world."

"What happens then?" Enira wondered.

"It can move now, but only slowly. It must be cautious," said Thud. "If it gains its full power, it won't need us anymore, it will be able to get the essence for itself."

"So we need to attack it now, before it reaches full strength," said Enira.

"I would tell you if I knew where it is," said Thud. "All I know is that it has been moving a great distance, slowly toward Strakenbridge. Though it wants to stay hidden, it also wants to be close when the attack begins."

Ambrielle checked the contents of her bag. If only she knew how to use the rectangular metal block the Cereveshian had given her.

"What else can you tell us?" said Enira.

"That is all I know," said the Grundian. "Will you hold up your end of the bargain?"

Captain Enira stepped past the rest of the group. "Dexius . . ."

Dexius drew back the string. "Wait!" said Ambrielle, as she grabbed Dexius's shoulder. Taking a deep breath, Dexius lowered his bow, glaring at Ambrielle.

"The other Grundians, was there a young man with them?" Ambrielle lifted her hand into the air above her head. "About this tall. Dark brown hair, blue eyes." Her arms tightened while she waited for the answer.

"There were no kips," said Thud. Ambrielle dropped her shoulders in defeat. She didn't really expect the answer she wanted. This was becoming a cruel joke.

The others put away their weapons and started out of the cave. Ambrielle fell in line with them while Dexius's bow groaned from the tension. A muted thwack, a gentle whisper, and then a wet, hollow impact in rapid succession sounded behind her. The Grundian choked for breath for a moment before making a loud percussive sound against the floor. Ambrielle couldn't help but look back, wanting to watch the Grundian die. She saw Dexius retrieve his arrow from the stained throat of the Grundian. She quickly faced away. It brought her no solace for Thomin's death.

CHAPTER 16

GAVIAN WAS BARELY able to parry the attack as Hilvan lunged. With his weight shifted to his right foot, he was unable to quickly counter the strike. Taking advantage, Hilvan swung his wooden sword to Gavian's left, forcing him to overcompensate while stopping the blow. Gavian was unable to get back into position in time to stop the strike to his right arm. He grimaced, dropping the wooden sword and rubbing the ache.

"Let's work on your cutting technique a bit more," said Hilvan. He moved to one of the tree stumps at the edge of the forest.

Gavian grew frustrated. "I don't know why we spend so much time on cutting technique. My sword goes through anything when it's powered on."

"Don't be too reliant on your dangerous weapon. If you are going to wield a weapon with that kind of power, you need to have the hands of a master, not some novice like you are now. We'll use our real weapons for this. Pay attention to your grip on the sword," Hilvan instructed. "You want to have a firm grip, but not so tight that it tires your arm."

Gavian gritted his teeth. He might not be a master, but he was more than a novice. Taking a deep breath, he adjusted his grip. He held the hilt of the sword tightly, but not too tightly. Hilvan nodded in approval before turning to a nearby tree stump.

"Now, watch closely," Hilvan said, as he raised the sword

above his head. "To properly cut through an object, you need to use your whole body, not just your arms."

He brought the sword down, slicing through the stump with ease. Gavian had seen him do this many times but had not been able to replicate the result. Hilvan stepped back for him to take a turn.

"Remember, don't just use your arm," Hilvan reminded him, "use your whole body, from your feet up to your shoulders."

Gavian took a deep breath, steadying himself before raising the sword above his head. He brought the sword down, slicing through the stump with all his might. The sword cut through most of the wood with a loud thud, and Gavian felt a surge of satisfaction. It was better than he had done before.

"Good," Hilvan said. "Now try it again, but this time, try to be more fluid, like you're cutting through air. Practice the swing before you try it on the tree again.

Gavian nodded, taking a moment to focus before raising the sword again. He brought it down, slicing through the air in a fluid motion, imagining the stump in front of him. The sword cut through the air with a swishing sound, and Gavian felt a sense of accomplishment.

Hilvan turned when a man came running out of the woods. Soldiers readied their weapons as the man closed in. He finally came to a stop, his chest heaving as he tried to catch his breath. The man kept trying to speak, but nothing more than huffs and grunts came out. Pointing to the line of trees on the eastern horizon, he seemed to want to show them something.

More soldiers, including Darby, Bradwyn, and Vilura, came over to see what was going on. After resting for a moment, the man was able to stammer his way through a sentence. "Ekendale is destroyed!" he said frantically. "The Grundians! They'll be heading for Tildenhal next!"

"Are you sure?" said Bradwyn. "They couldn't have destroyed it that quickly."

"They broke through the gate!" said the man. "They slaughtered everyone in sight! Soldiers and civilians alike!"

"That's hard to believe," said Vilura. "Ekendale is known for their prowess in combat. How could they have been beaten by Grundians?"

"It's true," said a woman, as she came out of hiding from the underbrush. She came forward with several others coming behind her, all with tattered, dirty clothing.

"The Grundians appeared to be massing near the northeast gate," the man said. "So they moved most of their defenses there. But the main force attacked from the south."

"That seems too clever for Grundians," said Bradwyn.

The man brushed the wet hair from his eyes. "That's exactly what the soldiers said."

"Since when do Grundians use strategy?" Vilura said.

"If they take Tildenhal, they could open the dam," said Bradwyn. "Would they be able to flood Strakenbridge?"

"I don't think so," said Vilura. "Strakenbridge was built long before Tildenhal had their dams. It would flood some of the croplands though. If they are using strategy now, they could starve us out."

"Help yourself to the stew." Darby guided the man to the camp, pressing her hand gently against his back. "You must be hungry."

"You should join us," Gavian said. "All of you. We could use your help."

"We're not soldiers," said one of the women. "I'm afraid we wouldn't be much use to you."

"There's more to being a soldier than fighting," said Gavian. "I wasn't much of a fighter when I started, but sometimes skills are born out of necessity."

"If you can use a seamstress, I will join," said the woman. "I would be glad to contribute something to the war effort."

"Thank you," said Gavian. "Hopefully you all will stay with us."

The woman quickly bowed her head to Gavian and followed Darby to get food.

"That's all we need," said Hilvan. "More fillers."

"Why do you call them that?" said Gavian. "You deride people abandoning their towns instead of fighting for them, and then when people join, you treat them like second-rate citizens."

"What are you talking about?" said Hilvan. "I treat everyone here the same."

"Then stop dividing us," said Gavian. "Calling us fillers isn't exactly welcoming. It makes us stay together in our own little group. If you wonder why people aren't joining you, that might be one reason."

Hilvan stared at Gavian. "If you are done with your little speech, we can proceed with this training exercise, or we can go back to our 'little groups,' as you put it."

Gavian raised the wooden practice sword into a defensive posture. Hilvan charged Gavian. He went through a combination of attacks that he had taught Gavian, who parried them all but the last blow. Rubbing his shoulder, Gavian sat up in the grass as Hilvan walked over. "I thought you knew what was coming by now."

"I got ahead of myself," said Gavian.

Hilvan extended his hand and helped him to his feet. "You are thinking too much. After a few more days, you will start to react instead. That will be all for now. Let's use at least some of this time to unwind."

"Thanks for helping me." Gavian walked slowly back to the camp, finding a place to lie down. The soft grass cradled his weary body, surrounding him in its mossy scent. He watched the layers of clouds of the lower atmosphere pass by each other. White streaming clouds and light gray whisps passed by a field of dark gray. He heard someone shuffling through the grass, but he didn't bother to move and check to see who was there.

He recognized the red of her cloak when she lay beside him. "Do you think there are signs in the clouds?" Darby said, leaning on her side.

"What do you mean?" Gavian wondered.

She rolled onto her back, gazing up at the sky. "Sometimes the clouds form familiar shapes. I like to think they can show us the future."

"Oh," said Gavian, as he watched the clouds drift by. "Not unless you think a docimare jumping over a bird is significant."

Darby chuckled for a moment before going silent, as if lost in her thoughts while she observed the formations of clouds. The sounds of people at the camp faded into white noise, and his mind sailed across the sky.

"We'll find Ambrielle," Darby assured him.

Gavian shifted to his side. "Did you see that in the clouds?"

"Not exactly," she giggled. "I just know we will."

"Everything seems to be going wrong," he said. "I thought I was going to find you and Dex, and that we would all catch up on what we've been doing the last few years. Maybe I could even convince you both to come see some of the other worlds. There are problems out there too, beyond these skies. It seems like everywhere I go, there are problems. Makes me wonder if I should have come back. Maybe you and Dex would have been better off."

Darby slid closer to him, resting her elbow on the ground and propping her head on her hand. "Gav, things weren't exactly great while you were gone." Her auburn braids slid across her cheek. "This war has been going on well before you came back. It's been getting worse every day. Maybe you came back at the perfect time. When we need you the most."

"You're beginning to sound like Ambrielle," said Gavian. "She thinks there's a greater plan for the universe, and if we stay true to who we are and follow what we know is right, everything will fall into place when it is supposed to."

"I like that sentiment," said Darby. "I do believe in fate, but I can't reconcile the idea that everything that has happened in my life needed to happen."

"She would say the bad prepares us for the good," Gavian said.

"The bad prepares us for the good?" Darby repeated. "Do you mean we learn from bad experiences and grow from them and are better people because of it?"

"Something like that," said Gavian. "I think she means—"

"Like your sword practice," said Darby. "You keep getting beaten by Hilvan, but then you learn how to defend it. So, then he throws something new at you, and you lose again, and so on. If you lose enough and learn from it, one day you'll be ready for anything and become a master swordsman."

"Yeah, that's exactly it," said Gavian. "Though I'm not getting any better yet."

"You've gotten so much better since you first started!" Darby said. "I should have used the time I was learning how to use a bow as my example."

"No, it's fine," Gavian said. "I guess it's just a little frustrating thinking about how much losing is in front of me."

Returning his attention to the clouds, he watched two of them that seemed to collide and merge together. After a few moments of quiet, Darby spoke again, "Do you want to hear another story about Stormwaker?"

"You know some too?" Gavian said.

The light made a halo effect on the loose strands of her hair. "I know a few. They're not exactly the mythic ones that Vilura tells."

"I'm listening," he said, as he lay flat with his hands folded on his chest.

"Centuries ago, this part of Nalacea was known as Rokendor," said Darby.

"Rokendor?" Gavian inquired. "Is this about the Roken Order you mentioned years ago?"

"If you'll let me tell the story," she said.

"Right, okay go ahead."

"Rokendor was an empire, divided by six houses that divided the regions of the land," Darby said. As with any great empire, some houses were more well connected than others, some were well liked, and others were less so.

"There were arguments over property, money, and even the occasional woman. Threats were common outside the empire as well. Over time, land was conquered and taken back; Rokendor was reshaped several times. There was a blacksmith and craftsman named Grendon Thett, who dabbled with stones that attracted and absorbed lightning."

"Vilura mentioned him," said Gavian, "the one who was worthy of the sword."

"This story is a bit different," said Darby. "Grendon Thett forged the sword and, using rare metals and materials, designed it to use the stones' power. The sword was used in many battles and gained a reputation for making those who carried it invincible, and it was given the name Stormwaker.

"After Grendon passed away, the Thett family gave the sword to the aurent to defend the empire. It became tradition with each new aurent that they would present the sword to the aurent, and the aurent would, in turn, choose someone in their house worthy of carrying it.

"Time went on and peace continued until, after some marriages and a few untimely deaths, Talyrian Reth was in line to become the next aurent. Some of the other houses accused Talyrian of bribery, blackmail, and even murder to position himself as aurent. Some houses, especially Houses Larken and Nolgin, knew that, after their disagreements with House Reth, if Talyrian became aurent, they would suffer under his rule."

"Wait House Reth? As in Rethia?"

"I'm not an expert on this. I'm just telling the story," Darby said. "So, the houses became divided over this, and many called on Merek Thett to deny Aurent Talyrian the sword and keep it himself. Merek agreed to delay the presentation and called on the houses to come together around the new aurent as they had always done. But he told them that, eventually, he had to present Stormwaker to Aurent Talyrian because it was his duty.

"This enraged Talyrian since the presentation had never been delayed like this, and he threatened Merek Thett in his own house. Merek's son Dagion defended his father, wielding Stormwaker against Aurent Talyrian and slaying him. This started a war between the houses and led to House Reth having to flee Rokendor and hide where no one could find them.

"After the houses continued fighting and arguing over who should have the sword, they came after Merek Thett, who said it could only be given to a member of House Reth, as they still had the rightful claim to Stormwaker. Merek destroyed the sword and went into hiding, vowing that, like the empire of Rokendor, it could only be made whole again by the other houses reconciling with House Reth. He was right. Rokendor was forever divided; it crumbled and faded over the years. It is forgotten now in most parts of the world to all but the most studied scholars."

"Is this true or did you make this up?" Gavian asked.

"This was from chronicles I read in Muloken and Strakenbridge," Darby said.

"Where did House Reth hide?" Gavian asked.

"There is only speculation; they may have sailed over the sea to Varkandor or maybe they hid in one of the many caverns in Isodonia." Darby lifted her eyes to meet Gavian's. "It's even possible they found sanctuary on one of the mountains, destroying the path to ensure they couldn't be attacked."

"This is . . ." Gavian started, "this is a lot to take in. This sword, it really is Stormwaker?"

"I'm only telling the story as I read it. Beyond that I can't say with any certainty," said Darby.

"What about the Roken Order?"

"They are descendants of Dagion Thett," said Darby. "They were under strict vows never to reforge the sword, except in the unlikely event that a descendant of Reth returned and could satisfactorily prove they would only use it in the service of Rokendor and that they would bring the noble houses together."

A chill went down Gavian's spine. "That can't be real."

"It almost seems like fate, doesn't it?" quipped Darby, arching her left eyebrow.

Even as heroic fantasies flashed through his mind, he did not want to get carried away with illusions. "I'm still learning how to use the sword," he said. "Even if I were some descendant of this Reth person, I wouldn't be able to do all that."

"You technically can't because Rokendor no longer exists, and the noble houses have long since faded away. But part of them remain in the people of Nalacea. You can still bring them together to fight against the Grundians."

"Why did you never tell me this before?" said Gavian.

"I only knew some of this before. I started to tell you the day I put the rokenstone into the sword," said Darby. "It didn't seem like the right time with everything that was going on."

"Hilvan is still so much better than me," he said, as he touched the hilt of the sword beside him. "I wish I could be as good as him."

"You're closer than you think. Have faith in yourself," Darby said reassuringly. "There's often more happening than what your eyes tell you."

"In Rokendor, the noble houses carefully selected warriors who possessed not only exceptional combat prowess but also the capacity to mediate conflicts, resolve disputes, and foster harmony," Darby explained. "These individuals were intended to embody the very ideals and values cherished by Rokendor. In one of the ancient tomes, they were referred to as Stormwakers, entrusted with formidable blades of immense power. Their motto, 'Through Virtue, We Prevail,' guided their actions. And I believe that you, more than anyone else, embody those qualities."

"I appreciate you saying that. That is everything I would like to be," he replied, "but it sounds more like Ambrielle."

Darby's eyes met his for a moment and then looked away. "They are lofty ideals, ones we all should strive for, even though the best of us fall short at times. But I don't think you give yourself enough credit."

Gavian wasn't sure how to respond. As much as he liked the idea of receiving compliments, it made him flustered when he was given one. "Has Dexius heard about any of this?"

"I haven't brought up anything about the sword," Darby said. "The last thing I want is to give you two something else to argue about."

"Between the two possibilities, which do you think is more likely? That Stormwaker refers to a sword or to the warriors who wielded weapons like that?" he asked.

"I find myself wavering on that," Darby admitted. "Perhaps both hold some truth. It could have originated as a sword and later evolved into a title bestowed upon the warriors."

They settled in the grass, daydreaming as they watched the breeze carry the lower clouds along the covered sky. Darby was one of the few people he could spend time with silently and not feel awkward. She seemed to enjoy quiet moments as much as he did. Knowing she was there was enough.

"What is that up there?" Darby asked. A round object flew against the cloudy sky.

Gavian sat up, watching it as it came to a stop, floating in place. The object began moving again, heading straight toward him. He took Darby's hand and stood up. The white surface of the flying craft gleamed in the light while it descended, maintaining its direction.

"Gavian! I finally found you!" Wegin's metallic voice cut through the air, drawing Gavian's attention. "Ambrielle wanted you to know she is safe. She is with a group called Storm Brigade."

A surge of relief and excitement washed over Gavian's face. "Take me to her!" he exclaimed eagerly, his heart pounding with anticipation.

"Storm Brigade? That's Dex's unit," Darby said. "Where are they at?"

Wegin processed the information swiftly. "I'll access the tracking data to determine her current coordinates," the synthetic assistant replied. "She is currently located at X Position 361 units, Y Position 15835 units."

"What does that mean, Wegin?" Gavian furrowed his brow, trying to make sense of the unfamiliar terms. "Can you guide us to her?"

Wegin took charge of the moment with a confident declaration, "Follow me!" He beckoned, his metallic frame propelled forward, serving as a beacon of hope.

CHAPTER 17

THE STEEP CLIMB up the path had tired them all out. Ambrielle found a small rise in the rock formations creating a nook to sit in and lean her back on. Captain Enira and the other leaders stood away from the group, privately discussing their next moves. Soon they would be heading to Rethia to catch the Grundians off guard. For them it was solely about killing as many Grundians as possible before they could mount a counterattack. Though the Grundians deserved nothing more than to be slaughtered for their deeds, Ambrielle wanted to see Rethia saved. For Gavian's sake if nothing else.

She understood, for they knew nothing of an isolated town on top of the mountain. It seemed wrong to be heading to Rethia without Gavian. Dexius had been oddly quiet. He hadn't said anything to make his feelings known about this attack on his former home.

Even if they succeeded in saving Rethia, they were a long way from this being over. There were apparently still Gurrians from the northern regions heading to a place called Tildenhal at this very moment. Then there was the Nulvarian called Ogolameth, potentially one of the Primevus that Dracos'Arkon spoke of. With every living thing killed it was gaining even more power.

She debated within herself the validity of everything happening for a reason. It was a comforting notion that aided her in coping with the car accident that had claimed her mother's life. However, in the depths of her mind, there lingered a shadow of doubt, leaving her questioning whether it was her own guilt that propelled such beliefs.

The day her mother had passed away, if Ambrielle had returned home on time, she could have pedaled her bike through the woods to the store. It wasn't a long distance, but her mother had to briefly navigate the highway to reach it. Ambrielle believed she could have averted the entire incident, sparing them from the tragedy.

She couldn't bear the weight of a lifetime burdened with the belief that it was solely her fault. If everything unfolded according to a greater plan, then perhaps it was inevitable, beyond her comprehension. The notion of a purpose beyond her understanding offered absolution from the suffocating guilt.

Grappling with her conflicting thoughts, she needed a distraction. Opening her satchel, Ambrielle took out the square metal piece the Cereveshian geologist had given her in the akreum. It was supposed to open into a geowave the automatons used to dig out rock in the mines. The square piece was a dark copper material with a black binding around the edges. The surface was smooth except for a small patch of rough scale. Running her fingers over it, she could find no discernable buttons or latches that might open it. The rectangular piece of metal felt heavy for something of its size, leading her to believe that it was very dense. That being the case, it had to be nearly solid; how could there be much inside it?

After trying to pry it apart, twist it, and slide it open, she gave up and put it back in her bag. Maybe Gavian would be able to figure it out. If only he were here.

She stared at the swirling sky as her thoughts drifted into mindlessness. The sound of boots scraping on the crusty dirt nearby shook her back to her surroundings. Dexius sat beside her, leaning against another part of the same stone. "I hope you don't mind," he said.

"Me or the rock?" she smiled.

A faint grin appeared on his face but quickly vanished. "What do you plan to do now? Are you coming with us?"

"I'm not sure what to do," said Ambrielle. "I still need to find Gavian."

Dexius slid his boots toward him, bending his knees into his chest. "If you leave, where would you go? Would you be okay alone out here?"

"Well, I've survived being alone in a desert," said Ambrielle.

He turned to look at her. "Was it in the middle of a war with giants roaming about everywhere?"

"No, but there were Nulthereals," she said.

"Oh, you've seen those too," he said.

"This war goes far beyond your world, I'm afraid," Ambrielle said. "Gavian and I are trying to figure out a way to stop all of it. I'm beginning to think it's impossible."

Dexius removed the pouch from around his shoulder. "They can defend their own homes; we've got enough problems here."

"The Nulvarians want to destroy the whole universe," she said. "It doesn't matter where we fight them, we have to defeat them."

"I know Thud said there was no kip with them." Dexius reached into the pouch and took out a handful of puffy, white pieces, "but that was only one horde. You said there were three going to Rethia. Gavian could be with one of them."

"So, you want me to come with you?" Ambrielle said.

"I'd hate for you to be out here alone." He tossed one of the pieces in his mouth and started chewing. "It would be dangerous for me, and I've had experience living off the land. I know sometimes people do dangerous things because they feel, if they don't, they aren't doing enough. I don't think you would be doing yourself or Gavian any good."

Ambrielle watched as he ate. "What are those?"

Dexius paused chewing to speak. "Relda seeds, you want some?" He took a handful from his pouch to give to her.

"I'll try a few," she said, holding out her hand. She put one into her mouth, anticipating the taste.

"I roasted them over a fire," Dexius added.

Ambrielle finished one of the slightly crunchy seeds, focusing on the taste and texture. "Reminds me of popcorn."

Dexius cleared his throat. "Maybe Gavian told the Grundians about Rethia," he said. "How else would they know about it? That proves he's with them."

Ambrielle shook her head. "He wouldn't do that. I had the impression that Ogolameth has some kind of far-reaching vision."

"You mean it could see us now?" Dexius said. "Maybe it knows our plan already."

"There must be limits to its vision," said Ambrielle. "Otherwise, we probably wouldn't have been as successful in killing his Grundian minions."

"I hope you're right," he said. "There aren't many I care about on Rethia, but my sister is there. I may not have been the best brother she could have had, but I won't let anything happen her."

"Attention! I want everyone and everything packed up and ready to move in five minutes!" shouted Captain Enira.

Dexius turned to Ambrielle, raising his brow. "Better make a decision."

Ambrielle pushed herself up, brushing the red dust from her clothing. "I don't know what to do. I guess I'll stick with you."

❧

The convoy started up again, moving them from the dusty canyon vista to yellow plains. Two huge gray stones rose out of the tall grass ahead. They appeared to be almost two parts of the same stone. Maybe they once were and were split apart by the elements over time. A tree growing between the two stones could be seen after they moved closer, its branches wrapping around both as if trying to hold the boulders together.

"Have you ever been in love before?" Ambrielle realized she had caught him off guard by the look in his eyes.

After squirming in his seat for a moment, he began to answer, "There's people I care about, but I don't know if that's the same thing as love."

"I would call that love," Ambrielle said. "But what about a girlfriend, anything like that?"

"Girlfriend?" Dexius's bottom lip twitched.

"Like someone you are attracted to," Ambrielle clarified.

"Oh, you mean have I taken a lady?" asked Dexius.

"That works." Ambrielle nodded.

"Well I would have, but with the war going on there hasn't been much time for things like that," said Dexius. "Why do you ask?"

"Gavian never really tells how he feels about me," said Ambrielle.

Dexius looked at Nemeris, as if hoping he would do something to save him from her questions.

"I would want to spend as much time with her as possible," said Nemeris. "There's a garden on the west side of Strakenbridge, enclosed in cobblestone walls. There are flowers of every color and scent. It's like being in paradise. I would take her walking there. We would talk about the statues and read the plaques that told their stories. And in the middle of the garden is a pool filled with fish."

The description painted a lovely scene in Ambrielle's mind. "That would be so nice. I wish he would take me places like that."

"From what you've told me, it sounds like you've been too busy traveling to other worlds and fighting the Shadows," Dexius said.

"I suppose you're right, there hasn't been much time," said Ambrielle. "Still, it would be nice to have some indication that he likes me."

Something caught her eye to their left, flying against the wind. The white object barely contrasted with the clouds but for the lights around it.

"Wegin!" Ambrielle shouted, and she stood up in the shippy.

He floated down, matching the speed of the shippy to stay with her. "Ambrielle, I'm pleased I was able to find you so quickly."

"Did you find Gavian?" She nearly burst trying to get the words out.

"Look!" Wegin said, moving out of her view.

A dusty haze hung in the air over the hill from the direction Wegin had come. Ambrielle gazed in the distance while some creatures mounted by soldiers came into view. They were moving fast, kicking up dust underneath the yellow grass.

"Driver! Slow down!" yelled Ambrielle. As soon as the shippy slowed, Ambrielle climbed over the side and into the field. For a moment, she stood waiting for the column of soldiers, not wanting to get her hopes up too much. But soon that sentiment vanished, and she sprinted toward the other convoy.

She ran at an angle that took her far enough out of their way as they passed. The faster animals sped by, and there were two shippies taking up the rear. Ambrielle gazed at the soldiers on the first cart, but they barely seemed to notice her.

As the second one approached, she saw someone stand. He waved frantically as the cart went by. It was Gavian! Sprinting behind it while it sped behind the Storm Brigade convoy, she began to run out of breath.

Though winded, she didn't slow down. The cart came to a near stop, and he leapt out and started toward her. She finally slowed to catch her breath as he caught her in his arms.

"I didn't think I would ever see you again!" he said, holding her tight.

She slumped her head onto his shoulder. As much as she wanted him to hold her, she needed room to breathe. She pushed against him, and he seemed to realize she was gasping for air. He moved his hands to her side, rubbing her back gently while she took in deep breaths. She shouldn't have run so fast or at all. It made no sense in hindsight, but the impulse took over.

As Ambrielle's breathing slowed, Gavian tenderly brushed the strands of hair from her cheek. In response, she drew him closer, and their lips met in a passionate embrace. In that moment, it was as if they were both transported to another realm, their bodies and souls entwined in perfect harmony. Together, they sang a wordless song of enchantment.

The sound of clapping woke them out of the surreal daydream. Ambrielle's cheeks reddened as she noticed members from both convoys applauding. Gavian took her hand and started toward the shippy he had been riding on. Nearly too embarrassed to go near them, Ambrielle hesitantly walked with him.

He brought her over to one of the shippies in the other column. Gavian stretched out his hand, directing her attention to a lovely girl with shy eyes but a huge smile on her face. "Ambrielle, this is Darby," he said. "She helped save me from Grunch!"

"I knew you would find her!" said Darby, still smiling.

This young woman wearing a dark red cloak was nothing like Gavian had described. "The same Darby you were looking for?"

Darby seemed to notice the confusion on her face. "Gavian didn't recognize me at first. It's been a few years."

"Thank you for helping Gavian," Ambrielle said. "I'm happy to finally meet you."

"Gavian has been telling us all about you!" said Darby. "You're as pretty as he described."

The news filled her with a warm glowing energy, prompting her to give Gavian another hug. For the first time since Thomin's death, she felt a sense of hope, like a light at the end of a long, dark tunnel.

As Vilura and Bradwyn introduced themselves, a big, furry creature poked its head between them. Ambrielle stepped back. Her instinct was to run, but seeing everyone else so calm around the beast, she nervously paused. "And this is Flumpy," said Darby, wrapping her arms around the creature that had something of a dog's head with a bear's body. She glanced around as the soldiers from the two brigades moved about, greeting each other and beginning to share stories. Ambrielle was surprised Dexius had not yet come over.

She wrapped her hand into Gavian's, gently tugging him toward the shippy where Dexius sat next to Nemeris. "Look who I found!" she said, poking Dexius on the shoulder. He turned around slowly. Gavian's eyes lit up when he recognized his old friend.

Climbing into the cart, Gavian stepped toward Dexius, but he remained in the seat. He kneeled in front of him, affectionately slapping Dexius on the arm. "It feels like it's been a lifetime since I last saw you." The smile faded from Gavian's face as Dexius didn't react. "You look so different now, maybe it's the hair."

"I haven't cut it in a while," said Dexius.

Gavian stood, giving him some space. "I'm glad you and Darby are okay." He climbed down from the shippy while Darby came over. "Dex, I would have come back sooner, but something strange happened."

"You went into another world. Lost your memory," he said. "Ambrielle told me."

"I would have never left you and Darby if I had known," said Gavian. "Only recently did I finally remember it all."

"I guess you can go back now," Dexius said. "If that's what you came to tell me."

Gavian's eyes darted around while he searched for what to say. "I came back to see you, to finish what we started. If you and Darby are in danger in this war, I will help."

"Suit yourself," said Dexius. "But we've been fine so far without you, and we'll continue to be fine."

"What did Ambrielle tell you exactly?" Gavian said.

Ambrielle huffed at the implication that she had done something wrong. "I told him everything you told me."

"It's fine," said Dexius. "She explained what happened, I get it. But if you expected me to be the same person I was when you left, you might be disappointed. A lot has changed."

"I know things have changed, but we're still a family," Gavian said.

"We were never that much alike," said Dexius. "We were bound to grow apart eventually."

"What has gotten into you, Dexius?" said Darby. "You were beside yourself trying to find Gavian. I helped you look for him for months, and now we've found him again and you're going to act as though you don't care."

"What are you doing with Inferno Brigade?" said Dexius. "I told you to stay away from the fighting."

"Maybe I don't want to follow your orders anymore!" Darby said. "The scout team joined up with Inferno, and you know what? They actually believe in me! They know I can fight. I killed some Grundians! I even killed Grunch!" Darby stormed off toward the shippy they rode in. Ambrielle began to follow her, as Gavian took one last glance at Dexius before walking away.

CHAPTER 18

S THE TWO brigades thundered across the vast expanse of grassy plains, Ambrielle's heart was caught between conflicting emotions. Perched atop the sleek shippy of the formidable Inferno Brigade, she felt the rush of adrenaline coursing through her veins. The wind tousled her hair, carrying both the thrill of the moment and the weight of uncertainty.

Her gaze shifted to Gavian, riding steadfastly by her side. In that fleeting glance, a whirlwind of emotions swirled within her. Gratitude washed over her, making her feel thankful for their reunion amidst the chaos and devastation. The sheer fact that they were together again, fighting side by side, was a bittersweet reminder of the loss she had endured.

Having reunited, along with finding Darby and Dexius and meeting Vilura and Bradwyn, they traded stories of the past few days while Nemeris and Dexius remained on the brontha. Their new goal was to save Rethia, though Ambrielle was thinking further than that. They had to defeat Ogolameth. Hopefully defending Rethia would help them accomplish that.

"It's amazing how both brigades have come together like this," Gavian said. "It's like it was meant to be."

With a heavy sigh, Ambrielle's voice trembled. "Meant to be?" she repeated, her tone tinged with bitterness. "This hasn't turned out at all like it was supposed to." Her words hung in the air, carrying the weight of shattered expectations.

Her voice strained with disillusionment, she continued, "It took Wegin for us to find each other. There wasn't any kind of universal force guiding us." The words spilled out as if the very fabric of destiny had unraveled before her eyes.

Wegin's lights blinked on and off at the mention of his name. "Pleased to be of service."

"I'm sorry, Ambrielle, I didn't mean to downplay anything. It's just, through all the adversity, we are here together," said Gavian. "We found Darby and Dexius. It's definitely not perfect. Dexius hates me."

"He doesn't hate you," said Darby. "When you didn't come back to Strakenbridge, he left to go looking for you. He wanted me to stay with Wynnotha, but I wasn't about to risk him not returning too. We stayed in Grenova for a while, hoping to find some sign of you. When we returned, Wynnotha had passed away. It was a hard time for him. For both of us."

"If I could take it all back, I would," said Gavian. "Except meeting Ambrielle, of course," he corrected, quickly turning to her.

"I don't tell you this to make you feel bad," said Darby. "I just wanted you to know what Dexius has been through."

"You went through the same thing," Gavian said.

"Tragedies affect everyone differently," Darby said. "I haven't had the same experiences he has."

"Make sure you have your head right before we get to the mountain," said Bradwyn. "This is the best chance we will get to significantly reduce the Grundians' numbers."

"Do we still have that weapon?" Vilura wondered, as she leaned over to look behind the seats.

Gavian reached behind the seats on the other side and lifted a staff.

"My bladestaff!" Ambrielle reached for it excitedly. "How did you find it?"

"It was in the grass when we were following the Grundian tracks trying to find where they took you," said Gavian.

"This plan reminds me of the Ambush at Lekin's Hill," Vilura said.

Bradwyn mumbled something when she began to tell the story. As

Vilura spoke, Ambrielle's mind wandered to all the things that lay beyond their impending battle with the Grundians. There was so much more ahead of them. They had to find a way to seal the rift. They had to deal with Ogolameth, and all the Gaith who waited outside the universe sending the Shadows to end all worlds. Ambrielle reached into her bag and pulled out the metal square . "Gavian, see if you can open this."

"What is it?" he said, after she handed it to him.

"A Cereveshian geowave I got from the mine," Ambrielle said. "If it works, we may be able to use it against this mind that is controlling the Grundians. Especially if there are any more Nulthereals like you saw recently."

Vilura overheard Ambrielle and stopped in the middle of her story. "How is sound going to help us?"

"Well, it's a bit complicated," Ambrielle said, "but the Shadows have some kind of essence or energy surrounding them that allows them to exist in this realm and—"

"Maybe it plays some really annoying music, like the stuff they play at Misty Moon Inn," Bradwyn joked. "Could we use it on the Grundians?"

"I've got a feeling they aren't big fans of the lute," Darby added with a chuckle.

Gavian pretended to be offended. "Don't underestimate the power of a good lute solo." Noticing Ambrielle's glare, he cleared his throat and began working with the metal piece she had handed him.

⊰

As it began to grow dark, the convoy came to a halt in the middle of a forest glade. Ambrielle and Gavian helped Darby, Bradwyn, Vilura, and some of the other soldiers set up tents. Dexius, Nemeris, and several others took axes into the woods to gather wood for a fire. By the time the tents were finished, they had the fire blazing.

Ambrielle got in line with Gavian where they were serving bowls of something that looked like a cross between oatmeal and wet cement. Everyone gathered in groups around the fire to eat.

"This is the same gruel we had at breakfast," muttered Gavian, as he sat beside her.

Ambrielle took a tentative spoonful and chewed thoughtfully. "It's not that bad," she said, trying to sound optimistic. "It's softer than it looks. It's like . . . eating mud made out of bread."

Gavian laughed. "That's not exactly selling me on it."

"Well, at least we won't be hungry." Ambrielle shrugged. "Whatever your favorite food is, imagine you're eating that instead. I tried imagining it was margherita pizza, and it kinda worked."

"I don't think I have a favorite food," Gavian confessed, his tone tinged with disappointment. "The Darterrans practically lived on escradas, and Rethian cuisine didn't quite impress me either. Gavian prepared for the worst as he took a bite. "If we survive this war, I'm going to find some real food somewhere, a proper feast."

Ambrielle's eyes sparkled with amusement. "Are you going alone on this culinary quest?"

Gavian chuckled. "Only long enough to find the finest cuisine in the universe, then I am taking you there."

Wegin's artificial voice chimed in, "I have gathered data on countless gastronomic establishments across the cosmos. From gourmet restaurants on celestial cruisers, to exotic food stalls on distant planets, I can assist in planning our culinary quest."

"I don't remember inviting you Wegin,"—Gavian laughed—"but you are welcome to make suggestions."

Ambrielle's grin widened. "Be careful what you say, Gav. I'm going to hold you to this."

Vilura, seeming a bit confused by the conversation, added, "Oh, do you know what they had to eat during the Heldon Offensive?"

"She's got a story for everything," Bradwyn said.

Everyone grew silent when they heard boots crunching on dry grass coming close to them. "How are you all doing this evening?" Hilvan greeted them.

"Just fine, Hilvan, just fine," Vilura responded, her voice filled with casual assurance.

"You know you are all welcome to sit with us anytime," said Hilvan. "We're all soldiers. You don't have to separate yourselves."

"We'll keep that in mind," Bradwyn replied with a nod.

Gavian smiled. "Vilura was just telling us a story about the Heldon Offensive."

Hilvan's eyes lit up with interest, and he settled down on the grass next to Vilura. "You know about the Heldon Offensive? My grandfather fought in that war. I have a tale you probably haven't heard."

Bradwyn let out an exaggerated sigh as Hilvan launched into his story.

As everyone finished eating, they put the containers into stacks on the supply cart and filed into the tents. Ambrielle gave Gavian a quick kiss before the men separated from the women. Darby gave Flumpy a hug, and she, Ambrielle, and Vilura headed to one of the women's tents.

After setting her bladestaff on the ground beside her, Ambrielle wrapped the blanket tightly around her. The once-radiant blaze of the fire had been reduced to a mere flicker. It was at least some comfort that she had the light on her silbrace if she needed it.

Darby seemed to be already asleep next to her since her breathing had slowed. Seeing her resting peacefully put her mind at ease and soon Ambrielle joined her, slipping beyond the boundaries of the waking world.

⤎

Deep in the dark of night, Ambrielle awoke. Darby restlessly rolled over, back and forth. Thoughts raced through Ambrielle's mind as she closed her eyes to go back to sleep. The dangers they faced ahead and the losses they might endure weighed heavy on her heart.

Her mind raced with notions, tangled images of disturbing violence and death. Whispered voices planted seeds. Sprouting in her head, thoughts branched endlessly in her consciousness.

You don't belong here. One voice dominated the rest like an invasive weed. *You will die for nothing if you stay. He will abandon you. This may be your last chance to leave.*

She'd always had doubts, but they were minor. Insecurities tended to crop up when things were going well. These thoughts were strong. Why would Gavian put so much effort into finding her on Earth if he didn't truly care about her?

Ambrielle opened her eyes when the sounds of grunting and rustling came from outside the tent. Soldiers began to scramble in the dark as Ambrielle peeked through the flap.

"Let me go! Are you crazy!" screamed a soldier with long black hair, while another woman dragged her out of the tent.

Three soldiers ran over and grabbed the long-haired woman, pulling her off the other one. Once she was subdued, the other soldier got up and ran toward her attacker. One of the soldiers let go of her to prevent the other from getting to her.

"She was sneaking out to Robit's tent!" shouted the long-haired soldier.

The woman brushed the grit out of her short dark hair. "I told you I was getting a drink!"

"You're lying!" said the other.

"Both of you shut up so we can get some sleep!" said one of the men coming out of his tent.

"This doesn't concern you!" shouted the woman with long hair. "Get out of our business!"

"Who can sleep with all this screeching out here!" said another.

Another man came out of a tent. "Someone get Robit so he can shut them both up."

A faint vibration buzzed in Ambrielle's head, causing a dull ache. Her concentration went in and out as the chaos grew around her. The arguing was spreading. Others were close to coming to blows.

Erratic gasps of breath caught Ambrielle's attention, and she turned to see Darby standing there, a haunted look in her eyes. Her gaze seemed distant, lost in the void of her memories.

"Darby, what's happening?" Ambrielle's voice trembled with concern, the buzzing sound intensifying. But Darby remained unresponsive, trapped in the grip of her own thoughts. Her eyes darted from soldier to soldier, a mixture of fear and vulnerability etched across her face.

Ambrielle gently reached out, placing a hand on Darby's shoulder, hoping to ground her in the present moment. "Darby, it's me, Ambrielle. You're safe. I'm here with you."

She understood Darby's past experiences had left scars, ones that resurfaced in moments like these. She stood by her side, offering support and understanding, knowing that sometimes words were not enough. Ambrielle knew she had to stop this before the Shadows' influence on the soldiers got out of hand.

She ran into their tent, putting on her boots and grabbing the bladestaff. Wegin's lights turned on as he rose from the ground. "This might be dangerous Wegin, stay here," Ambrielle whispered.

The speed of the vibration outside slowed and sped up while it modulated. Her hands began to shake with the familiar sound buzzing through her bones. Turning on her silbrace light, Ambrielle dashed away from the camp and into the forest.

Yes, come find us. We will be your escape from this world.

As the trees covered the light of the campfire behind her, the sense of being alone crept in. Except for one time on Earth when she had gotten lost, Ambrielle avoided walking through the woods after dark, especially by herself. She told herself she wouldn't go much farther away from the camp, but as the volume of the buzzing increased, she kept going. The Nulthereal had to be close.

Just a little further, the Shadow hissed. *Don't you want to see what lies beyond this threshold? Energy is precious, don't make us waste it to reach you. Step forward and claim what should be yours.*

The haunting songs of night birds and the steady droning of insects did little to calm her nerves. Shadows turned and stretched in the light of her silbrace while she walked. Above the treetops, twinkling paths filled the skies. Brightflies moved in their own highways under the dark swirling clouds.

Straight ahead. Abandon the path others have laid before you. Cast away the burdens weighing on your shoulders. Take control and become a master of your own fate. We are your doorway into the mindstream. Your true potential lies within.

"Get out of my head!" said Ambrielle. She swung the bladestaff at the hovering Shadow. Its bristling white edges rippled, and it reshaped itself to dodge her attack. The energy pulsed around it, protecting the Nulthereal from the material universe. Swinging the other end of the staff around, Ambrielle struck the Shadow.

The white glow began to dissipate, clinging to the dark shape. Around the weakened area, the Shadow hardened into stone. With part of it now corporeal, Ambrielle ignited the laser on her silbrace as it charged toward her, burning a hole straight through it. Chunks of rock and dust burst, and the Nulthereal fell to the grass in several pieces.

Before Ambrielle could relax, more buzzing rose around her. A Nulthereal manifested directly behind her, close enough to use its invisible force to pull her further toward it. Caught in its grip, she was unable to move except further toward the Shadow. She tried to turn and face the Nulthereal but was only able to turn her shoulder to it.

At the last remaining moment, Ambrielle bent her body backward at the Shadow, swinging the end of the bladestaff into it. The mekkadium blade connected, turning the Nulthereal into a physical surface. The grip on her was released.

❧

Gavian woke to the sound of Flumpy growling. Bradwyn immediately grabbed the rope netting and tossed it over her, pulling the drawstring tight. Hearing the commotion outside, Gavian burst out of the tent, surveying the wild scene before him.

"Everyone back to your tents, now!" Captain Holkson shouted, but no one seemed to listen.

A distant buzzing droned beyond the edge of the campsite. Standing a few paces away, Dexius scowled. He turned to Gavian for a moment before walking toward the melee.

"Don't listen to them!" Gavian tried to yell over the noise. "Ignore the whispers in your mind!"

Dexius pulled one of the soldiers from the crowd, trying to calm him down. The buzzing continued and grew louder the closer Gavian moved to the arguing soldiers. *Behold these deluded imbeciles.* A whisper entwined with his thoughts. *You have no use for them. With your mighty weapon, you can take the giants alone. You can carve out your own name into history as a legend.*

Clutching his head, Gavian attempted to stop the rush of thoughts. He stumbled away from the group. Shoving one of the soldiers away from the fight, Dexius tried his best to break it up. He needed to help Dexius. They had to stop this, but Gavian had to right himself first.

Near one of the women's tents, he saw Darby head into the dark woods with her bow in hand.

"Darby!" Gavian called after her as she disappeared into the night.

Dashing back to his tent, Gavian grabbed his sword and ran into the woods toward the persistent buzzing.

The sound of his own breathing blocked out everything else while he ran between the tall trees. Gavian stopped and listened. The buzzing was less consistent than before. It slowed its speed erratically. Racing toward the sound, Gavian pushed through the branches with his body.

Why waste your time on the girl? She has already forsaken you. When you save this land, you will find a more deserving companion. One who will appreciate your power and cunning. One who will bow to your every whim.

Tightening his grip on the sword, Gavian continued toward the sound. He knew these were only fears, not thoughts of his own making. Crossing a thin trail through the forest, Gavian noticed several holes in the dirt. Trees had been completely uprooted, but the trees themselves were nowhere to be found.

Do not be afraid of the darkness. For it is only when you fully embrace the dark that you will truly see the light.

The buzzing suddenly grew loud, and something ahead disturbed the thicket. Bushes, vines, and trees snapped, flying toward the dark object behind them. The Nulthereal flew toward him as the nearby foliage was pulled in. Against every instinct, Gavian charged the Shadow, entering its invisible grip. He pulled in close and slashed at it with the darkened end of the blade.

With the momentum of his swing taking him away from the Shadow, Gavian swiveled on his toes, spinning the blade around to strike it again. The Nulthereal split in two vertical halves as it materialized, breaking into smaller bits when they hit the ground. He slowed his breath, a new buzzing emanating to his left.

Running into the dark, Gavian found Ambrielle swarmed by Shadows. She swung her staff at a Nulthereal, breaking off bits of stone before bringing the other end around to thrust it into the center of the Shadow. The Nulthereal imploded, crumbling into a pile of dust.

The blue glow of the moonlight reflected on the sweat of her forehead.

She tried to catch her breath while the other Shadows moved in. Gavian charged at them, flourishing his blade as arrow after arrow rained onto them. Ambrielle and Gavian made quick work of the weakened forms of the Nulthereals, splitting and shattering them with ease. When the last Shadow was sundered, they turned to find Darby ready, if necessary, for her next shot.

"If only I had these arrows a few years ago," Darby said, pulling her arrows from the piles of dust.

Gavian glanced at her with a grin. "Could you shoot like that back then?"

"Maybe not,"—Darby smirked—"but I'm a quick learner."

"Do you think that's all of them?" Ambrielle's eyes darted nervously between the surrounding trees.

Gavian held his breath to listen. "I don't hear them anymore."

When they returned to the camp, five soldiers sat on the ground near the embers of the fire while someone cleaned and bandaged their wounds. The arguing had subsided. Vilura was dressing a cut on someone's head when she turned around to see Ambrielle and Gavian walking up. She shot them a hasty grin before returning her attention to the wrapping.

"I thought you said he destroyed them all." Dexius glared at Ambrielle as he made his way toward them.

Gavian inhaled deeply, releasing the air slowly. "We destroyed the Blight Whidge and two Nulthereals, but they took Malidora before I could stop them. I was transported to another place. I forgot everything until recently. I don't know how many there are. That's part of the reason I came back, so we could make sure we finished what we started."

"The seal connecting The Hollow is broken," said Ambrielle. "We have to find a way to close it."

"How do we know the Blight Whidge is really dead," Dexius said. "Convenient that Malidora isn't here to corroborate your story."

"This time I'm not leaving until we get them all and close the rift," said Gavian.

"We should all get some rest," Darby said. "We have a long day ahead tomorrow."

Ambrielle and Darby moved back to their tent. So did many of the others. Gavian lay on the blanket with images of Rethia playing through his mind. Lirah flipping the curls of her long white hair as they stared out at the sea of clouds. His older sister, Valea, teasing him one minute and offering advice and encouragement the next. Gavian tightened the blanket around him, and before long, he drifted off to sleep.

CHAPTER 19

AMBRIELLE FOLLOWED GAVIAN'S lead after he climbed into the wooden shippy. She couldn't help but feel a tinge of self-consciousness as her fingers nervously weaved through her hair, attempting to tame the flat, frizzy mess it had become. The relentless humidity of their journey had taken its toll, leaving her locks in a disheveled state. Beside her, Wegin drifted in the air, floating near her shoulder.

Darby carried a pair of bows and quivers, and Dexius followed her toward the shippy but stopped when he noticed Ambrielle and Gavian. He turned and moved to the other shippy, but there was no room left.

"Too late, that one is full." Darby pulled him by the arm with him glaring at her.

Dexius reluctantly grabbed his bow and quiver from Darby and climbed in. Bradwyn and Vilura moved next to Ambrielle to make it easier for them to settle in. Refusing to look at Gavian across from him, Dexius turned his body toward Darby and stared toward the forest.

Long branches scraped by them while the shippy pressed between the trees. Ambrielle glanced between Gavian, Darby, and Dexius, but no one was talking. Since she was somewhat of a neutral party in this silent feud, Ambrielle felt as though it was on her to start a conversation.

"Gavian told me you are quite the hunter," Ambrielle said, as she shielded her face from the ends of some long thin tree limbs.

Dexius continued to watch the trees pass by. She began to wonder if he was going to ignore her too, until finally, he cleared his throat. "I haven't been hunting in months. I'm an archer now, a marksman."

"He's the best marksman in the alliance!" Darby said, her thick auburn hair bouncing along with the movements of the shippy.

Brushing away an insect that buzzed around his ear, Dexius sat up straight and stretched before slumping against the side rail. "Best in Storm Brigade maybe. Jamus has me beat."

"That's debatable." Darby rocked on the edge of the seat, holding on to prevent herself from falling forward. "Have you heard anything from him or Blizzard Brigade recently?"

"Not since our last rendezvous," said Dexius. "I would guess they are keeping a distant eye on Tildenhal."

"Dexius is right," said Bradwyn. "They could ambush the Grundians' position when they attack."

"Even if the giants razed Ekendale, they surely suffered heavy losses," said Vilura. "If they somehow defeat Tildenhal, there won't be enough of them left to be a serious threat to Strakenbridge. They'll be dependent on the Grundian hordes on this side of the river. If we can take them down here, we win, the war is over."

"You make it sound easy," said Gavian.

Ambrielle smoothed out the skirt over her gray leggings. "How far is Tildenhal from Strakenbridge?"

Wegin lit up. "Unfortunately, all the landmarks on the solisphere are akreums. I can see the shape of the terrain but there are no cities marked."

"I don't know the measurements." Dexius righted himself after his side of the shippy dipped into the uneven ground on the dirt path. "About a half-day's journey. With a fast mount, maybe less."

Pressing her lips together, Ambrielle hesitated but decided to ask anyway. "Do you think we'll be able to save Rethia?"

Darby breathed in, filling her cheeks with air as she leaned back in her seat. The shippy moved out of the forest into an open field. A small grassy hill stood ahead of the column. Dexius shielded his eyes from the sun. "Of all the cities we could save from the Grundians, it's truly a shame that it would be Rethia," he said, turning to Darby. "They are the least deserving."

"But what about your sister?" Gavian blurted out. "What about Lirah?"

Dexius crossed his arms, resting them on his chest. "Yes, yes, of course, there are a few among them I care about. But for the rest of them, I would watch while the Grundians tore that place to shreds. They tossed us off the mountain like garbage. Is there no justice in this world that we are now made to help them?"

"I thought this would be good for you," Darby said, glaring at him. "A way to reconcile with a past that haunts you. You've done that for me. More than showing me how to use a bow, you taught me to stand up for myself. You were there for me when no one else was left."

Dexius shuffled uncomfortably in his seat, but let her speak.

"You act as if you are better than them, yet when it comes time to show it, you prove yourself wrong," she continued. "As much as you've accomplished these last few years, there is always something holding you back. I know you said you had forgiven the Rethians. That you have moved past that. But you haven't. You're still holding those feelings in. The same emotions the Shadows drew out of you. No matter what you think, if anything happened to Rethia, it would hurt you."

"Darby," Dexius said, as the shippy tilted up the hill. "Do we really have to talk about this right now?" He glanced at Ambrielle, Bradwyn, and Vilura. "I appreciate you looking out for me, and you're right, I shouldn't have said that. But this is about the war, not Rethia. I don't wish anything bad to happen to them, but I'm not risking my life to save them either."

"Now that Muloken is gone. I feel there is a wound that will never heal. I wish I still had a chance to protect it," said Darby. "Even after everything that happened there."

The wheels of the shippy cart clunked onto a wooden bridge over a small winding stream at the bottom of the hill. Passing more abandoned towns on the road, they traveled from grassy plains to hard-crusted desolation pocketed with pools of the last rain. The mountain of Rethia loomed into view, and Ambrielle couldn't help but notice the tension etched on Gavian's face.

As they approached the base of the mountain, the haze of the sun settled behind the distant trees. The soldiers climbed off their mounts and filed out of the shippy as they came to a rest. Grabbing her bladestaff, Ambrielle leapt over the siderail onto the soft grass. Gavian strapped on his sheath, and Darby and Dexius put on their arrow-filled quivers.

A pathway wound around the outside of the mountain, coming to an abrupt stop. Massive logs of tall trees bridged the gap up into the clouds.

"We're too late," said Dexius. "They already found a way up the mountain."

The color left Gavian's face as he stared at the Grundian-made bridge. Ambrielle wrapped her arms around him, leaning her cheek against his shoulder.

"What now?" said Bradwyn, holding Flumpy's leash.

Captain Enira glared up at the clouds covering the top of the mountain. "I say we wait. The path down the mountain is a natural choke point. We can camp here tonight. Reinforce defensive positions, dig trenches. As they are coming down the mountain, we strike."

Gavian was about to speak up when Dexius stepped forward. "We're just going to wait until after they slaughter everyone on the mountain?" said Dexius.

"They had their chance to leave," said Enira. "I assume they are confident in their defenses. If all goes well, they will force the Grundians to retreat, and we will be here to ambush them when they do."

"I agree," said Holkson. "What are you all standing around for? You heard the captain, get to it!"

Dexius and Gavian looked at each other while everyone ran to start a chain, passing tools and supplies out of the shippies.

"I want two firing angles on that choke point! Give me trenches at the base of the path and one here!" Enira pointed.

Captain Holkson walked over as they started digging. "Slope the backside of those trenches. Make it easy to climb out if we need to retreat."

By the time the trenches were dug, the sun had vanished without a trace. They did not build a fire this time, to keep their presence unknown. Ambrielle worried Ogolameth knew they were here. She had little doubt that it had sent the Nulthereals to their camp last night, making them fight amongst themselves. The same thing could happen again here.

Bradwyn and some others were assigned to guard duty through the night. The rest were ordered into their tents, so Ambrielle had to separate from Gavian to go with the women.

"If only we had arrived sooner," Gavian said. "Or is this happening for a reason?"

She gave him a quick kiss. "I hope there *is* a reason for all this." It was the most positive message she could muster at this moment, considering they were in a war with people dying around them.

Ambrielle stepped into the tent, finding Darby already inside arranging a blanket for her. She settled down, her mind filled with thoughts of the impending danger and uncertainty. How could they possibly find rest in such troubled times? Shifting onto her other side, Ambrielle caught sight of Darby, who met her gaze.

❧

Gavian bided his time, patiently waiting for the others to fall asleep. Seizing the moment, he snatched his sheathed sword and skillfully slipped out of the tent, careful not to disturb the others. Navigating through the sleeping figures, he caught sight of a vigilant soldier on duty. With a cautious maneuver, he veered wide, skillfully evading the guard's line of sight and discreetly retracing his steps, making his way back to the path.

As he started up the mountain, the sound of moving gravel gave him pause. The noise had not come from his own feet, but somewhere behind him. Something rubbed against his leg. Gavian swatted at his trousers, finding a big soft clump of fur. He nearly jumped out of his skin as he drew back his hand. Then he realized it was only Flumpy. He had never been so relieved to see a huge fur-covered beast.

As he stroked her hair, Gavian noticed Bradwyn standing in the shadows nearby.

"Going up the mountain?" Bradwyn asked.

"Just getting some fresh air," said Gavian.

"The captain thought you might," Bradwyn said. "If you're going up there, at least come down with some information we can use. Let us know how many Gruns there are."

Gavian nodded and started up the path. In the hazy moonlight, he made his way around the mountain to where the path was broken. Stepping onto the huge logs lodged in the rock, he carefully climbed the makeshift bridge. It was made with two logs with a gap between them large enough for him to slip through. He had to take it slower than he wanted, having to balance on one log. It wasn't difficult but the height made it feel as though a current was flowing through his body.

He passed through the clouds into the dark star-filled sky. Once at the top, Gavian moved into the shadows cast by the moonlit trees. It was well after curfew. All but the peace control officers would be in their homes asleep.

As he passed the campus grounds, two Grundians were breaking through the wall of the schoolhouses with their hammers. While their backs were to him, Gavian crept across the road and back into the shadows on the other side.

Chaotic yells and screams sounded in the distance when he entered the Deralawn district. Periodic crashes and loud banging rang out in the night. His heart pounded in his chest as his breaths came quick and short. In the blue light of the moon, it became apparent that the Grundians had been down this road already. Houses had been torn apart; people lay in their yards, unmoving.

The scene was surreal, like something out of a nightmare. His breathing grew louder while he made his way to Lirah's house. Gavian stepped over the broken fence where the gate he had built once stood. Stepping into the ruins of the house through one of the holes in the wall, he turned on his silbrace light.

Shadows rose and fell when the light passed by the smashed table and other furniture. The floorboards creaked while he moved slowly from the kitchen to the hallway. He stopped at Lirah's bedroom. As he entered through the doorway, he almost turned around and ran. Images flickered in his mind, so many memories of being in this house as a kid. He had never expected things to turn out like this. It was like he was seeing the most insane of all possibilities play out.

The room was pitch black since his silbrace remained pointed at the floor. He wasn't sure he could bear to see what the light might reveal. Maybe he was better off never knowing what happened to her. But what if she was hurt and needed help? He had to face it, just in case.

Lifting the silbrace, he shined the light into the corner of the room, across the floor, and then to the bed. No one was there. The floor groaned again when he moved back into the hall. Walking past Lirah's room, he continued to check the others.

As he shined the light into another bedroom, Gavian found two people lying still. On the floor was a man and, on the bed, a woman. Both were bloodied, removing any doubt as to whether they were dead. Gavian's heart sank when he recognized the woman lying before him as Lirah's mother. Despite the blood that covered her face, he could see the kindness in her eyes that had always greeted him warmly. The surreal setting dulled the shock of discovering her in such a state, shielding him from the full horror of it all.

Leaving the house, Gavian returned to the shadows, hurriedly walking down the road toward his old home. As he came to the where the roads branched off, a group of Grundians bounded down the other path. Gavian crouched in the dark while they turned onto the other roadway.

As soon as they disappeared from view, he rushed down the road. Every house he passed was in ruins, with debris strewn everywhere. Countless Rethians lay still and lifeless on the sandy road, their blood mixing with the sand. The place he had known so well, which had been so familiar to him for most of his life, was now an unrecognizable and desolate wasteland.

Gavian stood frozen before the remnants of his once-beloved home. The roof lay in shambles, and the door was now a jagged opening in the wall. As he trembled, he stepped forward into the abyss, his light casting a dim glow over the familiar space. Debris from the ruined walls and collapsed ceiling littered the kitchen area, obscuring what was once the dining table. In the midst of the destruction, he spotted a broken support beam jutting out at an odd angle, further unsettling him.

He checked his old room. It wasn't that he expected to find anyone there, but more to see what might have been his fate if he had stayed in Rethia. The bed was overturned. His shelves that once held his collection of interesting rocks were crushed. It was no longer the same room he remembered.

Gavian checked Valea's room. No one in there. He moved to the end of the hall to his parents' room. His baby brother's crib was no longer there.

No sign of anyone. He leaned against the splintered wall, with the sounds of distant destruction tolling. It was almost comforting to hear it far away, but he knew it only meant others were suffering.

Stepping back into the moonlight, Gavian stood outside the house, uncertain what to do next. What had the Grundians done with Lirah? His family? Could they have managed to get away? If he had been here through this, what would he have done? Where might he have gone?

A spark flashed into his head, and Gavian raced down the road toward the Plentyfield farming region. The blue moon danced on the currents as he came to the river. Rushing through the trees, he ran toward the edge of the mountain. It was his and Lirah's secret spot where they would stand at the wooden fence near the waterfall and gaze at the clouds below.

He hoped to find Lirah hiding here, but instead there were others. Four of them, including a small child, huddled together. They seemed startled when Gavian came out of the woods. He started to leave, when one of them spoke. "It's okay, you can hide with us," a man's voice called out. Gavian's ears perked up, recognizing a hint of familiarity in the tone. His mind raced to piece together the puzzle, the voice triggering a distant memory that tugged at the corners of his consciousness.

Gavian crept toward the fence to sit near them. "Where did everyone else go?" he said. "I can't find my family."

"Hopefully they found a place to hide," said one of the women. "It's best to wait this out. Whatever those giants are looking for, they'll move on once they get it."

"They want to kill us all," said Gavian.

As the moonlight shone on her face, the shadows on her features parted, and one of the women turned to face Gavian. Her voice sounded familiar as she called out his name, "Tav?"

Gavian narrowed his eyes, trying to see her clearly. And then, recognition dawned on him when he gazed into her eyes. "Valea?" he said in disbelief.

They all moved toward him, coming out of the shadows into the dim light. "Tavarian!" his mother called out. That name had become unfamiliar to him. She grabbed hold of him, putting her arms around him as well as she could in the dark. "Why did you wait so long to come back?"

"Of all the times to come home, you pick now?" Valea said incredulously.

His father hugged him and then backed up to look at him again. "You shouldn't have come back at all."

Gavian leaned against the fence post. "I had hoped to get here before they did."

"How would that have been any better?" his mother asked.

He opened his mouth to speak. Though he hadn't even formed the response in his head yet, it likely would not have come out well. Instead, he gathered his thoughts first. "There's an army here, at the foot of the mountain. The plan was to kill the Grundians while they were climbing the mountain, but we were too late."

"You joined an army?" his mother nervously asked.

"The whole world below the mountain is at war. These giants are killing everyone in every town they come to."

"Why fight their wars?" his father said. "You could have just come back up here and told everyone what it is like down there. We could have prepared for this."

"The council would have killed me if I'd come back," Gavian said.

"What are you talking about?" said his mother. "The council has been hoping you and the other Descenders would have returned by now."

Gavian glanced at Valea. "You didn't tell them."

"You told me not to!" Valea said.

"I'm just surprised you did what I asked for once," said Gavian. "They tried to kill all of us Descenders. That's what the Descension is about. Their attempts to control the food supply leads to a shortage. It necessitates reducing the number of mouths that have to be fed."

"Where did you get an idea like that?" his father said.

"Because when I came back, they imprisoned me," said Gavian. "After I escaped, I had to leave Rethia again. They would have come after all of us."

"I find this a bit hard to believe," his father said.

A loud crash thundered nearby, and screams sounded on the other side of the woods.

"We can't stay here for long," Gavian said, as the Grundians grunted and cheered. "I can lead you to the camp."

"They won't find us here," said Valea. "No one knows about this place but you and I."

"And Lirah," Gavian said, heat rushing into his face. "I found her parents in her house. They were both dead."

Valea visibly swallowed hard. "I fear how many others suffered the same fate. You might be pleased to know that Lirah doesn't live there anymore."

"Why would—?" Gavian suddenly realized what might have changed. "Oh, Neylin?"

"Yes," Valea said. "They are married now."

"I need to find her," said Gavian. A chorus of Grundian howls rose.

"Tavarian, you need to let her go," his mother said. "Let her husband take care of her."

Thoughts swam through Gavian's mind. Should he depend on Neylin to keep her safe? If something happened to her, would he regret not doing something to help? "Neylin won't be able to fight Grundians."

"What makes you think you can?" said his father.

Gavian stood and unsheathed his sword. "Because I have this." He moved into the thicket. Neylin's parents lived in the Rivercut district. It was likely that he and Lirah lived in the same area.

"Tavarian!" his mother called out as he moved back into the woods.

"I'll be back soon."

CHAPTER 20

GAVIAN CAME OUT on the road that went by the Plentyfield district. The river twisted away from the road between two hills, leading to a few small plantations beyond. Leaving the road, Gavian stayed under the large sigamoss trees while he ran. As he moved past a group of Grundians relentlessly pounding buildings with their fists and clubs, he slowed his pace, trying to avoid drawing their attention. They seemed to be too focused on destruction to hear his steps in the thick blanket of leaves on the ground.

Gavian crossed the bridge where the river darted from the Plentyfield region to Rivercut. The houses here were still intact, giving him some hope that he might find them alive. Several Rethians stood outside their homes. They didn't seem to understand yet what was happening.

After passing a few houses, Gavian noticed a young woman with long curly white hair holding a blond-haired man. It was her. Sheathing his sword, he quietly strode toward them.

"Lirah?" he said, crossing the road.

"Who's out there?" Neylin said. "You shouldn't be on the roads after curfew."

"You need to leave," said Gavian. "They're going to kill everyone in Rethia."

"What?" Lirah said. "Who?"

"You hear that?" Gavian paused to allow them to focus on the sounds of crashing, banging, and cheering. "Grundians are attacking Rethia." He stepped into the moonlight a few feet away from them. Lirah's mouth fell open as she began to recognize his face.

"Tavarian!" she said. "What are you doing back? The peace control officers will throw you in the dungeon!"

"The peace officers are dead," said Gavian. "Rethia is under attack by giants. We have to get out of here."

"We can't leave Rethia," said Neylin. "You may be able to live on Root-core, but the toxic clouds would kill us."

"They're not toxic," Gavian said. "It was all a lie. Come with me. These giants are not going to stop until everything and everyone are destroyed."

"I can't take that chance," said Neylin.

Lirah held Neylin's hand. "I've known Tavarian all my life. He would never lead us astray."

Neylin grimaced and glanced at Gavian.

"If you won't trust *him*, place your faith in me," Lirah said.

The building across the road began to shake from the pummeling it was taking. The banging turned into crunches, and then two Grundians crashed through the back of the house and into the street. A group of Rethians began running, but one of the Grundians quickly caught up with its long strides. The giant swung his club at the fleeing Rethians, knocking two of them across the sandy road.

Lirah froze when the two Grundians turned their attention to them. Neylin grabbed her hand, tugging her as he ran toward the river. Gavian drew his weapon as the giants thundered after them. Igniting the roken-stone in the hilt, he charged the nearest giant. The vibrating blade slashed deep into the Grundian's side, sending chaining bolts of energy through its body. The street flashed with violet light while the blade bristled with power. As he turned to face the other giant, the power surrounding the sword discharged, branching through the air to his target. The other Grundian fell too, its body smoking after it hit the ground.

Gavian disengaged the rokenstone, and the blurred blade came into focus. Lirah and Neylin stared back in apparent disbelief as he put the sword back in its sheath.

"How did you do that?" Lirah's pale blue eyes opened wide.

Gavian pointed toward the bridge. "Hurry! We need to go."

They crossed the river, heading toward the farming district. Keeping to the shadows, they moved among the trees. They passed other streets, and Lirah and Neylin began to see the destruction the Grundians had wrought.

Lirah held her hand to her lips, tears beginning to bead on her eyelashes. "Why are they doing this?"

Dead Rethians lay in the road. Some houses were completely flattened.

"How did you use that light you used back there?" said Neylin. "What was that?"

"A rokenstone," said Gavian.

"You found them?" Neylin wondered. "It's a shame you didn't find them sooner. Maybe you could have stopped this from happening."

"Yeah," Gavian said, as the images came back of the control officers throwing him in a cell, the rokenstones spilling out onto the floor. "I did try."

"Of course," Neylin said. "I don't mean to disparage you. You are the first that has ever returned!"

"Is it all destroyed?" Lirah wiped her eyes.

"I'm not sure if they've reached everywhere," Gavian said. "But Deralawn is—"

"Deralawn is destroyed?" Lirah's eyes narrowed. "My parent's house too?"

Gavian tucked his lower lip under his upper one, unsure what to say.

"We have to go there now!" Lirah started to run down the road, carelessly stepping out of the shadows.

Gavian caught her by the arm. "I've been there already. The house is demolished."

"They must have left," Lirah said. "We have to find them!" She tried to jerk away from his grip.

"It's too dangerous." Gavian looked at Neylin, who tried to calm her down by stroking her hair.

"I don't care!" Lirah said. "We have to help them! You can kill these giants with your sword!"

Gavian turned away, he could avoid it no longer, but he couldn't bear to see her face when he told her. "They were in the house. They're gone."

Lirah froze. All expression left her face, as though her spirit was no longer inside. "No. Did you try to wake them up? They're hard to wake sometimes."

"Lirah," Gavian said. "I'm certain."

Neylin wrapped his arms around her. She tried to push him away, as though accepting his embrace was accepting the reality of their fate. He held her tight until she stopped fighting him, burying her face into his shoulder.

It pained Gavian to hear her like this. As he began to draw his focus away, the banging and crashing sounds returned. "I'm sorry Lirah, but we need to go. There's an army here at the base of the mountain. We need to get you there, where it's safe."

Neylin urged Lirah on while they walked toward the forest by the river. The chaotic sounds of the Grundians grew more and more distant after they reached the scattered moonlight at the edge of the woods.

"Stay here in the dark, I'll be right back," said Gavian, weaving between the thin trunks of the trees.

He came out onto the open cliff where his family huddled together by the fence.

"I found Lirah," Gavian said. "But the giants are spreading through all the districts. We have to get off the mountain before they search the forests."

His mother glanced at his father, who seemed to be mulling it over in his head. "All right," he said. "Lead the way."

Gavian walked back through the woods, directing them to the spot where Lirah and Neylin waited in the shadows. Valea held their little brother's hand as they stepped out of the forest to the tall grass near the road.

"Is she okay?" said his mother, while Neylin consoled Lirah. Gavian took his mother far enough away from Lirah that she wouldn't hear. "She lost her parents," he whispered.

"Poor dear," she said, with everyone gathering near each other. Keeping out of the moonlight, Gavian led them through the bushes off the road toward the main town square where the path down the mountain started. As they passed what was left of Gavian's old home, two Grundians came onto the road behind them.

"Nothing left here to break," said one of the giants.

"Then break the trees down," said the other. "Make sure there's no place left to hide."

They spread out. One of the giants left the road, stomping into the thicket nearby. He snorted and then stopped, beginning to sniff the air. "I smell kips."

"Where?" said the other. "Show me."

Gavian watched them through the grass, afraid to move and risk making a sound. The Grundian continued sniffing as he stepped into the tall grass, heading straight for them. Slowly sliding the sword from its sheath, Gavian kept his eyes on the giant. The rokenstone was solid black now, as if all the energy had dissipated. He moved the rokenstone into position on the hilt. The blade vibrated for a moment and stopped.

Perhaps they could run for it and lose the giants in the forest. But it was only two of them. He didn't need rokenstones to give him the strength to fight the giants.

Gavian stood, assuming a defensive stance and leading the giants' attention away from the others. The first Grundian swung his massive fist. Gavian dodged the attack and brought the sword deep into the side of the giant. The other Grundian approached from the side, raising his club at Gavian. As he attempted to use the sword, it didn't budge. It was stuck deep in the Grundian's thick hide, taking Gavian with him when he fell to the ground.

"Tav!" his father called out while the giant swung the wooden club. Gavian released his grip on the sword, and his father shoved him hard into the sand. A blunt smack sounded as his father tumbled across the road. Voices crying out, Gavian ignited the short laser blade in his silbrace, stabbing into the Grundian before he could rebound. The giant's body collapsed into the street. His father lay near one of the broken houses . . . motionless . . . dead.

Before Gavian could absorb the shock of what had just happened, a familiar sound went through the air, impaling him with fear. A whooshing hiss came from shadows ahead, followed by a screech. Gavian dashed into the foliage. The others remained out of sight as he motioned for everyone to hide in the grass. He tried to quiet his breathing, taking short breaths but not getting enough air. Footsteps came closer. His breathing grew uncomfortable. Risking a deep breath, he inhaled slowly, as quietly as possible.

The whooshing screech sound rose again, this time much closer. The robed figure, wearing a silver mask underneath its hood, stepped into the blue moonlight, the being Ogolameth referred to as Pythus. Gavian shivered when he drew another breath. Pythus drew a silver sword from his robe and kneeled to one of the dead Grundians. He held the sword over the body and a glowing white energy began to emerge. Like smoke, it wafted from the corpse to the blade. While the energy poured from the dead Grundian, its face began to shrivel. The body's skin withered and turned hard like stone.

Gavian stared in horror while the dark figure made his way to the other Grundian, draining the essence from him into the blade. Their hardened faces became hollow. Gavian's hands began to shake as the cloaked man stepped closer.

Pythus stood, moving across the street toward the body of Gavian's father. A trembling feeling rose in Gavian's chest, moving toward his throat. He watched the dark figure kneel to one knee. Gavian rose from his hiding place in the tall weeds. "No!"

He heard nothing other than the beating of his own heart as he ripped the sword from the Grundian's side and lunged toward the cloaked man with the silver mask. The dark figure stood, deftly parrying Gavian's furious strikes with the silver sword. Hacking at the robed man, Gavian left himself open to counterattack, but Pythus blocked the strike. The masked man stabbed at his side, forcing Gavian to tumble awkwardly out of the way.

"You come to me like a moth to a flame," hissed Pythus.

Gavian regained his footing, circling the masked man, who stood quietly staring back at him. The dark being inhaled with a whooshing breath, exhaling a crying shriek as he lowered his stance. "There is work to be done," the being said in a raspy voice. "Either run or surrender your life blood to me."

Easing toward the robed man, Gavian tried to calm himself. Too much aggression would lead to mistakes. Swinging at the silver mask, Gavian tested the man's defenses. The cloaked being parried easily, barely moving his blade. Backing out of the man's reach, Gavian tightened the grip on his sword. The hooded man was patient, seemingly waiting for Gavian to make a mistake.

Gavian launched another series of quick, short blows, intent on observing how the man defended blows of different levels and angle. They were all effortlessly deflected, with no apparent weaknesses in his form.

The cloaked man swung at Gavian's feet, and he leapt back. Gavian moved in, but the masked being thrust his weapon. Batting the blade away with his heavy sword, Gavian quickly took advantage of the opening. Slashing at the hooded man, his sword found nothing but air as Pythus dodged the attack.

Pythus moved toward him, spinning the sword in his hand, launching lightning-fast swing combinations. Gavian's reflexes took over, and he tried to match the speed.

Gavian was caught out of his stance, but he deflected the last blow. As their blades locked, Pythus pressed his strength onto the rokensword, forcing Gavian's own double-edged sword toward him. As much as he tried to force the swords back, the dark being's strength was too great.

Igniting his lightblade, Gavian attempted to cut through the silver sword of Pythus. To his surprise, Pythus's silver sword reflected the light, bending the laser blade back onto itself and destroying the housing in the silbrace.

Pythus continued to press Gavian's sword into his skin, drawing the first trickle of blood. Gavian watched the wraith's finger reach for the ring under his sword's cross guard. Was this small cut all the sword needed to siphon his life essence? A crackle of leaves turned the dark figure's attention behind him. His gloved hand reached to catch a sharp splintered board as it swung toward his head. Yanking the board, the cloaked man pulled the attacker toward him before backhanding her. Valea stumbled backward from the blow, falling onto the road.

As the dark being brought his attention back to Gavian, something whistled through the night air, ending quickly with a wet thud. Violet power bristled over the hooded man's body while he tried to pull out the rokenstone arrow. Gavian distanced himself from the lightning that was engulfing the masked figure. The black-robed man howled, breathing another whooshing breath before rushing off into the darkness.

Gavian slowly made it to his feet as Darby, Ambrielle, and Wegin came into the moonlight. He offered his hand to Valea, helping her up while she rubbed her reddened cheek. "You shouldn't have risked yourself like that."

Dusting off her dress, Valea looked at the cut on his chest. "I wasn't going to let that thing kill you too."

"I don't want anyone else dying because of me," Gavian said.

"What were you doing trying to fight that wraith alone?" said Darby.

"My rokenstone is dead." Gavian put his sword back into the sheath. "If it was energized, I would have killed him easily."

"Don't be so sure," said Darby. "Until now, I've never seen anything survive my rokenhead arrows."

"How many of those do you have left?" Gavian said. "Do you think one will fit in my sword?"

"That was my last one," said Darby. "You'll have to hope it storms soon or you find more rokenstones."

Gavian turned to Valea kneeling beside their father, who was lying near the road.

"What should we do?" Valea said. "We can't let that monster come back for him."

The sword had betrayed him, allowing him great power until it came time to save his family. Now his father was gone because of it. Gavian's chest tightened as he shifted the blame on himself. It was his fault that his father was dead. If he had been smarter, he could have defeated those two Grundians with ease. He wasn't as skilled as he thought he was. Now he would have to be reminded of that mistake for the rest of his life. Maybe he deserved it. It should have been him lying in the road. "Darby, do you have that shovel with you?"

"Yes, it's in my pack," she said, as she took off the backpack and set it on the ground.

Ambrielle rubbed the back of his shoulder while he waited. "Gavian, why did you leave the camp without telling us?"

"Not right now, please," he said, taking the hand shovel from Darby and moving beside his father.

Ambrielle followed him, and he began digging with the shovel. "I'm not scolding you, Gavian. I just . . . I want us to be a team."

"Could you and Darby please help my mother and Lirah get to the mountain path?" Gavian asked. "We will meet you there."

Ambrielle nodded. "Of course."

"Keep them safe, Wegin," said Gavian.

Wegin responded in his metallic voice. "Certainly."

As they moved out of sight, Valea looked at Gavian. "Shouldn't we move him to our yard?"

Gavian continued digging as the noise from the Grundians rang out all over Rethia. "We don't have time and it doesn't really matter." Valea looked away from him, standing up with her arms folded. "I think he helped build this house." Gavian nodded toward the broken house nearby. "So, in a way, it's fitting."

Picking up the sharp board she'd tried to hit the cloaked man with, Valea used it to help dig the hole. Once they had a large enough space, they placed him into the hole and covered him. Gavian scattered some sand from the road over the area to try and hide the spot.

Nothing ever turned out the way he planned. The more he tried to be a hero, the more he failed. Maybe this was another hard lesson he needed to learn. He was still trying to prove his worth to others and to himself. When it seemed as though there was a path before him, he often used it as an opportunity to gain approval. He would do that no more. From now on, he would do what needed to be done to help when others needed him. If he planned to build a relationship with Ambrielle, he had to learn this. They had to complement each other.

CHAPTER 21

Gavian and Valea sought refuge behind a dense cluster of trees, concealing themselves from view in the outskirts of the town square. His eyes were fixed on the horizon, watching for any sign of approaching Grundians. Several lifeless giants littered the area, clear signs of a recent skirmish near the dilapidated mill. Gavian's gaze shifted, locking onto the familiar figures of Ambrielle, Darby, and Wegin gathered alongside his mother, little brother, and Lirah and Neylin. Valea exchanged a nod with Gavian, signaling it was time to make their move. With silent determination, they emerged from their arboreal sanctuary, cautiously venturing forth into the heart of the town.

His mother ran up and hugged them both with one hand while she held onto their brother with the other. Neylin continued to console Lirah, glancing at Gavian as they both sat on the dirt. He counted five dead Grundians, each with arrows in their necks.

"Where is Dexius?" Darby muttered, searching the area. "He said he'd be here by the time we got back."

Lirah raised her head from Neylin's shoulder. "Dex said he was going to find his sister. I saw him go into the Chamber of Elders."

"Dexius came up here too?" Gavian stood, dusting his trousers. "Why would his sister be in the council building?"

"I didn't ask," Lirah replied.

Gavian headed toward the building. "I'll be right back. You guys keep an eye out for Grundians." He tested the lightblade on his silbrace while he walked toward the Chamber of Elders. Darby did not acknowledge his request, instead following after him.

A puff of smoke appeared from the stem where his blade should be. It appeared to be done for. Gavian tried the lylace function, and the silbrace fired a long rope of light ahead of him. At least that still worked. The building lay in ruins as Gavian stepped through what used to be a doorway. If nothing else, this day had been the reckoning the council had long deserved. The first chamber they came to was where citizens were allowed to enter and bring their grievances before the council. They pretended to listen and made decisions accordingly.

Gavian stepped over the debris through the main chamber toward the back. What used to be bright red carpet was now covered in dust and flecks of wood. No sign of Dexius anywhere. Gavian entered the room where he had fought a peace officer to escape. The door ahead, leading to the dungeon, was standing open. There were shouts coming from inside. He moved onto the first step that led down into the dark.

"You may want to stay up here," Gavian said to Darby. "Last time I was here, there were prisoners. Crazy ones."

"Worse than Grundians?" Darby said.

"Good point," he said. "But you know, It's dirty down there. I just don't know if this is the place for—"

She let out a sigh. "Just go find Dex. If you're not back soon, I'm coming down there."

Before he made his way down, the sound of footsteps gave him pause. Startled, Gavian backed away as someone emerged from the dark interior and ran past him. An orange-haired woman holding the hand of a young girl ran across the red cloth covering the wooden floor. They moved past Gavian and Darby out into the open street.

Collecting himself after the scare, Gavian descended the stairs until he reached the uneven stone floor. Voices continued to echo down the dark hall.

"We gave you an honor," said a voice at the end of the hall. "The honor of helping your community."

"Stop lying!" said a voice that he recognized as Dexius's. "You sent us to die!"

Gavian paused, listening intently to the conversation.

"If we sent you to die, you would not be standing here right now," said another voice.

Dexius spoke again. "You knew the road was out. I only survived by pure luck. I just want to hear it from your mouth. Speak the truth, just for once."

"All we are guilty of is maintaining a community that was fair to everyone," said the voice of Councilor Ravaris, "one that was safe from the greed and selfishness of Rootcore. We have only ever done what was necessary to continue what our forebears started."

"You mean descendants of Talyrian Reth?" Gavian stepped lightly around the pools of water collected in the pockets of stone. A few of the prisoners on either side of the hall stretched their hands toward him through the bars of their cells.

"Where did you hear that name?" said one of the three robed councilors. Ravaris, Tanius, and Hiramian huddled against the wall. Dexius had his bow pointed at them through the bars of the cell. The air of intimidation they'd once possessed had now vanished. They seemed concerned, worried, afraid, having closed themselves in the dungeon for protection from the Grundian invasion.

"I heard he was a liar, a cheater, and a murderer. Just like all of you." Gavian stepped closer to the cell.

Ravaris moved toward the cell bars. "You've been told the lies of those who betrayed us. The title of aurent was never meant to stay in the hands of houses like Nolgin. It was intended to be passed to each house over time as they united in marriage. They let their personal hate for House Reth divide Rokendor."

"Regardless of what is true or not," Gavian said, "what you called unity in Rethia was tyranny and deceit. I intend to help unite whatever remains of the land below Rethia and defend it from this new threat."

Dexius looked at Gavian with confusion before turning back to the councilors. "If you wanted to rejoin the world, you should have done so long ago," said Dexius. "We could have traded with other cities for any supplies we lacked. Anything would have been better than sending kids to die every year because you couldn't manage resources."

"Son, you don't understand our burden, what our kin had to deal with just to survive," said Tanius. "Look outside. The House of Nolgin has sent these giants to finish us off. Even after all this time, they have not forgotten."

"Oh, *now* I'm your son?" Dexius stretched his arms out to the side. "It took all this for you to finally say it."

"Dexius, you have a lot of growing up to do still," Tanius said. "If anyone in Rethia had known about your mother and I, it would have caused mistrust in the council. I was as much of a father to you as I could be."

"A father? You were never there!" Dexius said. "You only ever scolded me, punished me. Shall I show you the scars?"

Dexius's words pierced through Gavian like a blade, and he felt the confusion etching across his face as he struggled to process the revelation unfolding before him.

"It was your mother, son. She didn't have the stomach for discipline. That was all left to me because of her absentminded laziness," said Tanius. "If she had done what she was supposed to, I could have been easier on you."

Dexius reached for his quiver, firing an arrow into Tanius's arm. "Don't put the blame on her!" The councilor shrieked while the gray robe began to turn dark where the arrow protruded.

"Dex!" Gavian called out. "Let's go. Find your sister and let's get out of here!"

Dexius turned to Gavian. "What do you think we should do with them?"

"Maybe we should leave them in the dungeon," said Gavian, timidly moving closer.

"They have the keys, they can get out whenever they want," said Dexius. "I thought you would be more creative."

Gavian took another few steps toward them. "Creative?"

"Don't forget what they did, what they've been doing for years," said Dexius. "Remember what the broken bodies looked like at the bottom of the mountain? Tiagra, Veras, Pilo, I never even found the others. We should do the same to them. Shove them over the side of the mountain."

The images blinked through Gavian's mind. "If we kill them like this, we'll be no better than them," Gavian said. "We'll become what the Shadows want us to be."

"This has nothing to do with the Shadows!" Dexius shouted, as he turned to Tanius. "Think of all the deaths they are responsible for."

"You told me you forgave him." Darby stepped into the torchlit hall. "You said you had moved past what he did to you. That you wanted to start a new life. Was that all a lie?"

Dexius lowered his bow. "Darby, you shouldn't be down here."

"Was it a lie?" she repeated.

Walking away from the cell, Dexius moved toward Darby. "It wasn't a lie, not at the time anyway. I thought I could forget until I saw him. They were all down here cowering in the dark. They did nothing to help save the community. They could have given some kind of warning to the rest of the city when the attack started here. But they only care about themselves."

"What they have done is monstrous. We all know that. I told you it wouldn't be easy," said Darby. "It may be one of the hardest things you ever have to do. If you walk away now, you still have the opportunity to forgive them, and you leave them the chance to one day realize what they have done." She rested her hand on his back. "I know you have the strength for this. You're one of the strongest people I know."

Dexius faced the councilors in the cell and then turned, walking past Gavian and Darby down the hall. Gavian glanced at the councilors once more before he left.

The distant roars and bellows of the Grundians returned as they came out of the chamber building. Gavian glanced at Dexius, who immediately turned away, making him wonder if Dexius was about to say something. Keeping his eyes toward the edge of the darkness where the torch's light dissipated, Gavian waited for him to speak. They stood in silence for a moment until Gavian faced him. "I had no idea Councilor Tanius was your father."

Dexius sucked air through his nose and rubbed a scratch on the side of his face. "I never told anyone the whole time I lived here. He threatened me and my mother." Looking off toward the distant trees, Dexius started again. "No one would have believed me anyway."

"The night before I left, when you mentioned what your father did to you," Gavian said. "Why didn't you say anything then?"

"I didn't want anyone to know my father was one of the councilors who sent us off to die," Dexius said. "Maybe I would have told you if you didn't run away."

"Dex, I didn't run away," Gavian said. "I didn't intend for any of this to happen. He scanned the ravaged town area while they stood in silence. Ambrielle was standing by his mother, Lirah, and Neylin. Gavian's eyes met hers, and she came walking over.

"We need to get back to camp," Dexius said, walking across the road toward the orange-haired woman and the young blonde girl. He gave the young girl a hug, talking to her as if he knew her well. Having never seen Dexius's mother or sister, Gavian could only assume it was them.

Wegin's lights blinked as Ambrielle put her arms around Gavian, leaning her head on his chest. He propped his head on her shoulder, playing the images of the last several minutes over and over in his head. Darby made her way toward Dexius, seeming to let Ambrielle and Gavian have a moment of privacy. Something Wegin apparently had not learned yet.

The thunderous sounds of the Grundians grew louder. Beneath their feet, the ground shook. He heard a gasp of breath come from Ambrielle. When Gavian turned, he saw something above the dark canopy of trees. An enormous Grundian, as big as Grunch, peered down at them.

"Twick!" Dexius shouted, reaching for his bow. Twick, the leader of one of the hordes Ogolameth called to destroy Rethia, charged through the trees straight at Gavian and Ambrielle.

Drawing his sword, Gavian shoved Ambrielle behind him as he backed up. Wegin soared into the starry sky, high above the danger. The ground beneath them shook with every step of the giant. Twick's shadow enveloped them when he closed in. There was no place left to run.

Gavian readied his sword, but the giant was too tall to strike anything but his legs. Twick leaned down, reaching for Gavian with his huge hand. Gavian slashed red lines into Twick's hand, but nothing seemed to deter him. Gavian and Ambrielle turned and ran. With them both out of Twick's reach, he pounded his fist into the ground, knocking them off their feet.

Leaping up, Gavian tried to evade Twick's hand as a high-pitched whistle screamed above him. Dexius's arrow plunged into Twick's neck. The giant toppled over with Gavian and Ambrielle scrambling between his feet to avoid his massive body crashing into the dirt. The impact was like an earthquake, vibrating everything in the area.

"One shot, one kill!" Dexius grinned while Gavian stumbled around the massive form of the Grundian.

Ambrielle dashed toward Gavian. "Are you okay?"

"I think so," he replied. "Are you?"

"Large creatures approaching quickly!" Wegin warned. A loud rustling sounded behind the Chamber of Elders. Dexius wheeled around, hurrying toward his mother and sister. Behind Gavian, a group of Grundians stormed into the town square, gathering around Twick. Gavian and Ambrielle glanced at each other before sprinting toward the path.

The area around them descended into chaos with more Grundians pouring in from the road ahead and blocking their way. "Gavian!" Dexius called out over the din. Ambrielle and Gavian swiftly weaved through the crowd of giants, fists whipping by them. Through the massive bodies of Grundians, Gavian could see Dexius urging everyone around him toward the path that led down the side of the mountain. Gavian and Ambrielle darted between the Grundians' feet, taking refuge in their shadows as they dashed from one giant to the next. Gavian shielded his eyes against the flying dirt, grasping Ambrielle's belt to ensure they stayed together.

"Go Dex!" Gavian yelled back. "Get everyone out of here! We'll catch up!" Suddenly, a Grundian swung its club at them, knocking down another giant in the process. Gavian raised his sword as another club came hurtling toward him. He braced for impact, realizing he didn't have the strength to soften that kind of force. Before it could land, Ambrielle drove her blad-estaff into the giant's side. Gavian followed with an arcing slash under the giant's ribs.

With a brief opening, they bolted for the mountain path. The stomping Grundians continued their chase as they moved onto the road. One of the giants roared after it fell over the mountain's edge, pushed off by the clumsy pursuit of the others.

After passing through the dense clouds of the lower atmosphere, Ambrielle and Gavian slowed. They had reached the first section of the makeshift bridge. Gavian reached for Ambrielle's hand. "Still trust me?"

"Trust is a process, Gavian," Ambrielle said, teasing his words back to him. "It takes time."

Her response caught him off guard. Though he couldn't see it through the vaporous clouds, he imagined her mischievous grin. It was enough to make him laugh to himself. "We don't seem to have the time for that right now," he said.

Ambrielle's hand slipped into his, their fingers intertwining with a reassuring grip. They stepped onto separate logs and ran, using each other's weight as a counterbalance. After winding around the mountain, the logs finally ended, taking them back onto the stone pathway.

The mountain path twisted behind the waterfall with the Grundians hot on their heels. Gavian and Ambrielle sprinted toward the bottom of the trail, trying as best they could to avoid stumbling over loose rocks. Ambrielle dropped the satchel she was carrying, some of its contents spilling out onto the road, but she briskly picked it up while continuing to run.

Spinning down the slope, the metal square bounced, somehow growing larger with each impact. After snaring one of the extra cells for her silbrace, she reached for the metal piece as it slid to a stop ahead of them. She picked it up, but the square metal object had transformed into something resembling a gun. Ambrielle strapped the bladestaff over her shoulder so she could carry it.

The trees on the mountainside below began to shake violently. Gavian recognized the huge, shelled creature he had encountered the first time he ever left the mountain. Arrows flew above their heads, hitting some of the Grundians behind them. Storm and Inferno archers were alert and firing, taking out some of the giants and causing them to tumble down the path. They bowled some of the Grundians over, while others were able to avoid them. The avalanche of Grundians was gaining speed, and Gavian knew they couldn't outrun it.

Grabbing Ambrielle's hand, he leapt off the side of the road, landing on the creature's shell while it chewed on the trees. They held on tight with the creature swaying back and forth and trying to shake them off. Finally, they went flying off the shell, hurtling toward the surface below.

They landed with a painful smack in the pool at the bottom of the waterfall. Gasping for air, they climbed out of the icy water and looked up to see the Grundians charging toward the camp. The archers in the trenches fled as several giants barreled through, smashing everything in their path.

It was difficult to see what was happening, even in the ghostly moonlight. Captain Enira called out in the distance, shouting over the sounds of chaos. "Retreat!" she screamed. "There's too many of them!" The rumbling of bronthas, docimares, and shippy carts was soon drowned out by the thunder of Grundians.

The lights carried by Inferno and Storm soldiers trailed away in the distance. Ambrielle and Gavian walked through the darkness, stepping over the bodies of dead humans and giants. With all the riding creatures taken, it would be a long walk to Strakenbridge.

The sounds of the battle faded into the distance as Gavian collapsed to his knees. Finally, their heartbeats began to slow as they relaxed, leaning against each other. Sitting in silence, Gavian listened to the pattern of Ambrielle's breaths. He closed his eyes, starting to fall asleep.

⌘

Ambrielle jolted awake after having drifted off to sleep for a minute or two.

"Everything I try to do ends up failing," Gavian said.

"That's not true." Ambrielle sat beside him. "If it weren't for you, all of your family would be gone. You saved as many as you could."

"But not my father," Gavian said, pressing his hands hard against his face. "I don't even know if Darby and Dexius made it out."

"They were ahead of us. I'm sure they did," Ambrielle said, placing her hands on his shoulders.

"I never should have left the camp," Gavian said. "You were right. I don't know why I ever said that I didn't trust you. I always have. That's not why I didn't tell you."

"You can't expect to do it all by yourself, Gav," Ambrielle said. "If you planned to try to rescue anyone up there, you should have told me. Darby and Dexius too. We all would have helped from the start."

Gavian shook his head and looked away. "I thought I was doing the right thing. I didn't want you to get hurt."

"Nothing would hurt me more than if something happened to you," Ambrielle said.

He hung his head. "If there is a path I'm supposed to be on, I feel like I am so far away from it that I'll never find it again. I don't know what I should do anymore."

"Doing what you know is right," said Ambrielle, "that is the path."

"I don't know what is right anymore," he said. "If everything happens for a reason, what purpose does all this serve?"

"To weather the storm," said Ambrielle. She felt like she was consoling herself as much as she was trying to console Gavian. "To be better tomorrow than you were yesterday. To take what you're given and turn it into the best you can possibly be. Without resistance, you can't grow stronger. Just because things don't work out at first doesn't mean it was the wrong choice. When I was living on Mekkinspire with the Kavekkians, I had no idea where to look for a way back to Earth. If I had never found a way to go back, I at least felt useful and wanted, at least for the most part. But when I chose to see you against their wishes, I was banished."

"I guess I'm always getting you in trouble," said Gavian.

Ambrielle rolled her eyes. "What I'm trying to say is that my decision didn't go so well at first, but it turned out great in the end. You have to look beyond what is happening now and see what could happen in the future. Think about when you were captured by the Grundians. As bad as that situation was, you might never have met Darby otherwise."

"Sometimes the wrong choice is the right one?" Gavian gazed back at the mountain.

Ambrielle rubbed her soft hands over his shoulders. "Something like that."

Suddenly, she felt a rumble beneath her. There was a low crashing sound coming from the shadows ahead. The sound grew louder, joined by a chorus of rustling grass and leaves.

Ambrielle turned on her silbrace light and pointed it toward the dark. Several Grundians lumbered toward them. Some of them had apparently broken off from the chase of the soldiers to return to Rethia, far too many to fight. Gavian leapt to his feet, and they both dashed through the weeds away from the mountain.

Behind them, the Grundians roared ferociously, their pursuit relentless. Their massive forms loomed ominously, their thunderous footsteps drawing closer with every passing second. Ambrielle's feet pounded against the earth while they swiftly weaved through the tangled weeds that obscured their path.

Ambrielle and Gavian pushed themselves to the limits of their endurance, their breaths coming in gasps as they strained every muscle to outpace their ruthless pursuers. The adrenaline-fueled rush propelled Ambrielle forward, her determination and survival instincts overriding any fatigue or fear that threatened to consume her.

The ethereal glow of the moon attempted to penetrate the thick layer of clouds, casting a mesmerizing blue aura upon the surrounding sky. In the distance, the imposing silhouette of the other mountain loomed ahead, serving as a beacon in their desperate flight. As Ambrielle and Gavian pressed on, their frantic pace began to pay off, slowly increasing the distance between them and the weary Grundians, who seemed to tire with each passing moment.

Gradually slowing their pace, Ambrielle and Gavian sought to catch their breath, their bodies yearning for a momentary respite from the persistent pursuit. Amidst their panting, a familiar voice called out, "Ambrielle!" It was Wegin, the synthetic drone, flying down to their eye level. Relief washed over Ambrielle, and she waved in acknowledgment. "Where have you been, Wegin?" she asked.

Wegin hovered beside them. "I lost sight of you amidst those giants," he admitted. "I'm not programmed to handle dangerous situations like that."

Gavian eased his pace, chuckling lightly. "So, you were scared? I didn't think synthetics felt fear."

"I don't experience fear in the same way organic life forms do," Wegin explained matter-of-factly. "I am programmed to avoid damage."

Ambrielle grinned, finding amusement in the drone's response. "Ah, it must be nice being artificial. You can always blame everything on the programmer."

"I'm not quite sure what you're implying," Wegin replied, his tone slightly perplexed. "I wasn't blaming anyone. I was merely providing answers to your inquiries."

Ambrielle chuckled. "Of course, Wegin. I was just teasing."

Gavian, still catching his breath, interjected, "Did you see where the giants are?" There was a touch of trepidation in his voice.

"They are not far behind you," Wegin informed them with urgency. "You'll need to increase your speed to prevent them from catching up."

Ambrielle's weariness was palpable. "I don't know how much longer I can keep this up," she admitted.

As they ventured into a rocky basin flanked by dirt hills, their footsteps splashed through shallow water, each stride propelling them forward in a desperate bid to outpace the pursuing giants. After running for a stretch, Ambrielle's strength waned, and she leaned against a sturdy stone pillar, knowing they had only a few precious minutes to rest before Wegin alerted them once again. Gavian joined her, attempting to collect himself. "They're closing in. We must continue," said Wegin.

Ambrielle leaned heavily on the bladestaff, using it as a makeshift walking stick, as they hurried toward the towering mountain. Their pace oscillated between a brisk walk and a desperate sprint, the strain of their journey wearing on them throughout the seemingly endless night.

The distant roar of a waterfall filled the air, its sound guiding them through the dim light. Reaching the edge of a tranquil lake, Gavian abruptly halted and turned around, his expression tense. The pursuing Grundians were closing in faster than anticipated. Without hesitation, Gavian waded into the water, sloshing toward the mountain before pausing to assess their next move.

Ambrielle followed suit, her feet splashing through the cool embrace of the lake. Puzzled, she asked, "Are we going into the waterfall?"

Gavian hurriedly retreated to the sandy shore, his breaths ragged. "The water would slow us down too much. It won't slow down the Grundians, though." The thunderous footsteps of the giants echoed in the distance while Gavian swiftly circumnavigated the lake.

Ambrielle's eyes darted around, seeking guidance. "So, what's the plan now?" she inquired, her voice urgent.

"There's a cave somewhere along the mountainside, around here." He sprinted toward a patch of steam rising from the ground, its density increasing like billowing clouds of smoke.

Suddenly, with a resounding roar, a mighty plume of water surged from the rocks, soaring high into the sky before gracefully cascading into the waiting pool below. Ambrielle watched in awe as they veered around the spectacle, navigating through the hot vapors billowing from the rocky crevices.

Their path led them toward a narrow opening in the rugged stone wall, a gateway that seemed to beckon them forward with an irresistible allure of mystery and possibility. Ambrielle approached, a surge of electric energy coursing through her veins and infusing her with a familiar yet elusive sensation.

CHAPTER 22

IGNITING HER LIGHT, Ambrielle entered the mouth of the cave with Gavian. Gavian had to hunch over, carefully navigating the rocky ceiling, while Ambrielle found more ease in her movements since she was able to stand upright. The tunnel curved to the left, gradually obscuring the external light until they were enveloped in the cave's darkness. It was evident that the tunnel was too narrow for a massive Grundian to pass through.

Wegin's voice broke the silence, relaying information from the solisphere. "There is an akreum nearby," he stated. "Additionally, I am detecting an unusual concentration of energy in this vicinity."

Ambrielle's eyes lit up with anticipation. "Inside the cave?" she asked eagerly.

Wegin responded with a hint of uncertainty. "It is a possibility," he said. Ambrielle surged forward, her footsteps echoing through the winding path that snaked its way through the heart of the mountain. Gavian's voice called out to her, urging her to wait, and he quickly caught up when they entered a vast open chamber. Finally, the ceiling soared above them, granting Gavian the relief of standing tall. As they advanced, a rush of fresh, damp air enveloped them, replacing the staleness of the tunnel. The chamber they entered was saturated with a crisp earthy scent peculiar to the heart of the mountain.

Guided by the resounding rumble echoing in the distance, they ventured forth and arrived at a sprawling pool. Cascading from a cleft in the rugged ceiling, a torrent of water plummeted into the depths below. Ambrielle directed her light toward the glistening metallic formations nestled on the pool's bed. Meanwhile, Gavian circled the perimeter of the water, prompting Ambrielle to hasten her steps, not wanting him to make any discoveries before she did, driven by an odd sense of competition.

The section of the chamber came to an abrupt end, with Gavian's light reflecting off the rock ahead. As Ambrielle approached, she found a wall that was not naturally formed. It was the same white material the Cereveshians used to construct the akreums. While she and Gavian traced their light beams along the surface, they found an opening in the material.

The akreum, nestled within the cave's formations, lay exposed, but in a different manner from the akreums they had previously encountered. Where the others changed shape to form the doorway, this one was cut open with precision. Something had cleaved through the impenetrable Cereveshian material, leaving a jagged opening with black edges. Gavian directed his beam of light into the hollow center, while Ambrielle cautiously approached. The light from her silbrace would not reflect on the dark edges. At the periphery of the aperture, the air appeared to distort and ripple, accompanied by fleeting glimmers of tiny particles.

"Do not make contact with the edges," Wegin cautioned. "There is a peculiar phenomenon at play here, where matter seems to cease to exist."

Ambrielle stepped back. "Is it safe to go inside?"

"As long as you do not touch the edges," said Wegin.

As Ambrielle moved closer, she stumped the toe of her boot on a strange rectangular stone in the cavern floor. Kneeling to get a closer look, she found a stone with carvings. Gavian aimed his silbrace at the object, giving her an extra light to see. "What is it?"

"I don't know yet." She broke away the dirt caked over it. Gavian crouched beside her, helping to brush away the remaining dust. The object underneath was white stone but more organic than the Cereveshian metal. Several words were carved into its flat surface. They continued wiping away the dirt, revealing an inscription at the top.

"Can you tell what that says?" Ambrielle looked back at him.

Gavian leaned toward the stone for a closer look. "No, I've never seen writing like that."

"It is Ichtek writing," said Wegin, "but I have not been programmed to decipher it."

Gavian helped pry more of the hard chunks of dirt from the flat, white stone with his knife, until they revealed a carving of a circle with lines drawn out from it, resembling the sun. Beside the sun was a humanoid figure with a strange head shape and oddly bent legs.

"Is that supposed to be a Kavekkian?" Ambrielle wondered.

Gavian studied the drawing. "It's hard to say. It doesn't look quite right, but maybe it isn't a good depiction."

"Do you think Kavekkians ever came through that waterfall?" Ambrielle said.

Gavian peeled away more of the clay. "I guess it's possible. This stone looks really old."

"It appears to be a few million years old," said Wegin. "However, beyond a certain age, the accuracy of my scans become less certain."

As they continued to work on the stone, the breaks in the dirt revealed small letters Ambrielle could understand. They picked and brushed until they revealed a full word: *ADARA*. Below that was the word *AERON*.

"Names," Ambrielle said, as she continued to pick at the dirt stuck inside the carved letters. "They're all names."

Gavian leaned back to rest for a moment. "Names for what?"

"How should I know?" said Ambrielle.

Gavian started again, and they brushed over the column of names, revealing *AISLEN*, then *ALISTAIR*. Gavian pried into the clay over the next name, causing Ambrielle to gasp, rolling back off her knees to sit on the ground. *AMBRIELLE* was the next name on the white stone.

"Weird, someone else here had the same name," Gavian said.

"I think . . ." Ambrielle began, "I think this is one of the tablets of the ancients the Kavekkians found."

"What makes you think that?" said Gavian.

"That's where Maetha got the name Ambrielle," she said. "They normally used those names for the lightborn, the firstborn Kavekkian of the new year."

"Why did Maetha use one for you then?" Gavian said.

Ambrielle squinched her mouth side to side. "I guess because it was one of the only non-Kavekkian names she knew of. Or maybe she thought it would help make the vaesari council trust me more."

"I don't think it worked." Gavian smirked.

"Apparently not," she replied.

They went back to wiping the stone tablet, revealing the name *ARADEL*. Though it surprised Ambrielle at first, she quickly realized it made sense because Aradel was lightborn. They cleared more grime, and another surprising name was revealed: *GAVIAN*.

"What is this?" Gavian's breathing began to get louder. "Why is my name on here?"

Ambrielle leaned closer, making certain she was reading this correctly. "I don't know, but this is getting weird. It's like someone expected us to come here." A chill breathed down her back as she said it. Maybe there really was a plan for them. Despite the darkness and pain, maybe there was purpose. She had been wondering how destiny could exist if Thomin never got a chance to realize his. Surely, his path was not to die so young. Perhaps it was more complicated than that. Not only was there destiny, but there was also free will. If we truly have a choice, there is a chance we may never fulfill our purpose. The choices of others could even destroy the chance we have, and we could destroy theirs. Could it be that the path never went away, that even if something took you astray, you could still complete it?

"Expected us?" Gavian said. "Wegin just said it was millions of years old."

"We need to find out." She continued brushing the dust from the surface of the tablet. "I want to see what all the names are."

Gavian started at the bottom. They worked their way toward each other until they met. Once they had finished, two more names stood out among the rest: *KIDIRU* and *MALIDORA*. Kidiru was also lightborn, so he was named after this tablet, but the inclusion of Malidora's name was surprising.

"I'm not sure we should be here." Gavian began breathing rapidly. "I don't think we should be messing with this."

"I'm not so sure either," said Ambrielle as she stood. "But it must be important. If someone was expecting us to come here, they probably expected we would want to know what is inside."

"This is a whole new level of your things happening for a reason." Gavian stepped behind her while she stood inside the opening. "But what if it is a warning."

"Fear not the unknown, for therein lies the greatest data," Wegin recited. "It's an old Cereveshian proverb."

She entered the dark opening, her thoughts conflicted. An egg-shaped container stood ahead at the edge of a stairway, the same configuration as the vault interior in the Darterran caves. Something about this akreum was far more frightening than the others. With Gavian's footsteps behind her, she felt comfortable enough to go to the container. She froze when she realized the transparent seal of the container was broken.

Inside stood a Cereveshian, but its body was shriveled and hardened like petrified wood. Its eye sockets were dark and hollow, its mouth twisted open unnaturally, like the victims of Pythus. Dried orange liquid pooled underneath the being's solex. Ambrielle's first instinct was to run, but she noticed something that interested her, something else that differed from the other vault she'd encountered. In the akreum on Anatharia, the path down the steps ended, covered in the unbreakable material. But here, the material was cut open like the outside. A faint blue light reflected on the floor from the inside.

She would only go far enough to see what was inside, Ambrielle told herself as she took the first step down the stairs.

"I'm really starting to think we shouldn't be here," Gavian said when she neared the bottom of the stairs.

Blue light flooded into the chamber from somewhere within. With her courage beginning to wane, Ambrielle cautiously crept inside as Gavian hurried up behind her. A large stone column stood at the end of the tunnel ahead of them, the source of the blue light that bled through openings inside. The interior of the cave was naturally formed, except for one circular area that surrounded the blue light.

Marked with strange symbols, the rock surrounding the blue light was smooth and symmetrically shaped into a circle. They stepped down the tunnel leading toward the light, and unusual sounds began to rise into the chamber. Distant voices layered one over another. Murmurings and whispers, their words indecipherable. Among the cacophony, one voice was distinct among the rest.

"What happened? Was it destroyed?" Ambrielle and Gavian both jumped when the voice echoed from behind them. They whirled around but found no one. The voice sounded masculine with a strange inflection or accent.

"Who's there?" said Gavian, while they aimed their lights around the shaft heading back toward the doors. Indecipherable murmurs sounded as they crept toward the voices.

"Someone's talking," said the voice, much closer this time. "Whispering."

Gavian glanced at Ambrielle with her eyes growing wide. Raising his sword, he moved closer to the entrance. "Can you hear us?"

"It's communicating," said the voice. "I can almost make out the words."

"Yes, can you understand us?" Ambrielle's eyes scanned the tunnel around them.

"They want me to know what they are saying," the man said.

"Where are you?" said Gavian. "Can you come into the light?"

"It wants us . . . to come toward it," the man said.

They heard footsteps on the rocky floor of the shaft, sounding as if they were coming closer, but they still saw nothing. Gavian and Ambrielle turned as the sound moved past them.

"There are carvings in here," said the voice. "Old symbols of the Ichtek. We need to translate these."

Even though her heart warned against it, Ambrielle walked toward the sounds.

"There were voices . . . voices in my head." This time it was the voice of an anguished girl. "I must know. I must know what happened."

Ambrielle paused when the voices became faster, talking over each other.

"It . . . It looks like . . . forever . . ." the girl whispered from the circular chamber ahead. They should've been able to see anyone with all the blue light, but there was no one.

Ambrielle started toward the rotunda surrounding the bright but unstable light. "Do not get close to the light!" said a voice beside her, making Ambrielle stop again.

"Wegin, where are these voices coming from?" Ambrielle asked, as she was filled with unease.

"I only detect one other life form, but it appears to be in a state of stasis," Wegin replied, his top half rotating in contemplation. "Furthermore, I am unable to detect any electronic sources that could explain the origin of these voices. The exact source remains unknown and perplexing."

"It feels like I've been here before," a boy's voice remarked.

"Why do they all come?" the girl questioned.

"Lyleth, you keep repeating yourself," the boy pointed out.

"Why are there so many variables, Hegane?" Lyleth inquired.

"We need to break the loop," Hegane declared.

"How can we find the outcome if there are so many possibilities?" Lyleth pondered.

"But it still occupies different space."

"Maybe we should write them down."

"The universe is not a sphere, it's more like a crystal."

"Do you think there is an outcome that can free us?"

"With many facets reflecting the same light."

"We can leave this place, if we don't enter the rift again."

"Someone came near the cave today, in the universe's present time."

"What were their names?"

"When you looked into the light, what did you see?"

Ambrielle stepped back as the voices began overlapping each other, their words coming faster and overwhelming her. Gavian placed his hand on her shoulder, drawing her closer to him. "Maybe there was a wall there for a reason."

"We probably shouldn't be here," Ambrielle said, "but I want to understand."

"We have to, Hegane," Lyleth insisted. "If we don't go back, the energy will destroy everything."

"The rifts are all connected," Hegane explained. "There must be some kind of dimensional anomaly that mirrors this place across the universe."

"You know what you said about following your instincts?" Gavian said. "Right now, mine are telling me to get out of here."

Ambrielle turned to him. "But why was I drawn to this place if not to understand. Why are our names on the tablet?"

The voices continued multiplying until they were undecipherable. Ambrielle focused on the ethereal blue glow emanating from the central pillar. The light appeared to dance and flicker, like it had a life of its own. Ambrielle could almost feel it, as if it was aware of her presence, warning her not to come closer. "The rift," said Ambrielle, as she stared into its bright center. "That must be the rift Tetra'Novis and Dracos'Arkon told us about. The one in Anatharia was sealed, but this one has been opened."

"You mean that's how the Blight Whidge entered Isodonia?" Gavian asked.

"And Ogolameth," she said.

Gavian rubbed his chin. "I wonder why it would have destroyed Varkandor first."

"I don't know, but we need to find a way to seal it again." Ambrielle said.

"Why seal it if they can open it anyway?" said Gavian.

"Well, if the other one lasted four million years," said Ambrielle. "I think it's worth it."

As the weight of danger pressed on Ambrielle, they hastily departed the akreum, their footsteps echoing through the cavern. She felt a sense of unease when they passed by the weathered tablet inscribed with a haunting list of names. Ambrielle's light flickered, casting glimpses of its gentle glow upon the white metal surfaces strewn throughout the cave. Her eyes widened as she noticed a smaller akreum, untouched and nestled within the rugged slope of the rock.

Reaching out to touch it, she played the melody in her head. Her silbrace mimicked the tones, and the akreum transformed into a larger open vault. Stepping inside, Ambrielle found one of the glass eggs filled with pink smoke. This one was still intact.

The Cereveshian inside began to stir with the gas dissipating. It bolted upright, gasping for air before it started gagging and coughing. As the episode abated, the being climbed out of the bubble, trying to stand on its own while it leaned against the incubator.

"What is happening?" said the Cereveshian. "What has awakened me?"

"The voices near the rift," said Ambrielle, "do you know what they are?"

"You heard them?" the Cereveshian inquired. "We do not know what they are. Residual energy, dimensional interference, collective consciousness, there are several theories but no real data. How did you access the rift?"

"The seal around the rift is broken," said Ambrielle. "Can you help us close it?"

"You must be the awakener," he said. "I'm surprised you would choose me."

"I am Ambrielle," she told him. "Are you able to help?"

"Ambrielle the Awakener, it is my honor. I am Kyron." He coughed again briefly before stepping away from the stasis chamber.

"That doesn't sound like a Cereveshian name," Ambrielle said, as she watched him remove three small white spheres from one of the compartments.

Kyron handed the three objects to her. "It doesn't?" He twitched his small mouth back and forth before seemingly understanding what she meant. "Ah, yes, that is because I don't have an annex."

"An annex?" Ambrielle glanced from the objects in her hand back to the Cereveshian.

He leaned on the oblong extension from the floor, clearly tired. "Most Cereveshians fuse their minds with a duplicate of a great Cereveshian in their field. It greatly boosts their intelligence, essentially giving them two brains in one. If I were to merge with the mind of Thonaris, one of the great philosophers of old, my name would become something like Kyro'Thonar."

"That's crazy." Ambrielle had so many questions, but not nearly enough time to ask them. "So, you didn't want to?"

"I came to believe in the natural order of the Everance," said Kyron. "I would never be considered great among my kind or any others, but we all have a purpose in it, and they are all equally important no matter how great or small. Merging your mind with another erases who you were born to be."

Gavian turned off the light of his silbrace. "What do you consider your purpose to be?"

"Before I transcended this universe, I was a parametric," said Kyron, "one who designs and programs shapes into plastra material. It allowed me to use my creativity to create structures that I consider works of art. After trying and failing at so many things, I found that as a way to put my gifts to good use. Besides that, I also had the honor of being the one to create the seal around the rift and the akreum vault around that. Nothing can exist without a purpose."

"Do you feel like your purpose is invalid now that the seal has been broken?" Gavian asked.

"Not at all," Kyron said. "Nothing is forever in this finite universe. Generations fade to make room for others. But nothing can exist without purpose. The honor of sealing the rift is now yours." Kyron stepped over to a circular cut out in the floor. The circle rose from the floor as soon as he stood near, revealing an oblong device with many compartments. Setting each orb onto the top of the circular compartment, Kyron touched a blue glowing light in the lip of the compartment. The glowing light remained on his finger as he touched different points of the three orbs. He then handed them to Ambrielle. "This is plastra. I programmed each one to take a shape that will contain the breached area and merge with the rest of the akreum."

Ambrielle took them, examining one of them in her hand before carefully placing them in her bag. "How do you use them?"

"Hold one of the plastra orbs in your hand until it lights up," said Kyron. "Then place it near the akreum and move out of the way."

"Thank you, Kyron," Ambrielle said. "This will help a lot."

"As I said, it is the natural order," said Kyron. "What was once ours is now passed on to you."

"If you believe in the natural order," Ambrielle began, "is it natural to go to such lengths to leave this universe, putting your body in stasis so that your mind can move to another realm?"

"It does seem hypocritical, I suppose," said Kyron. "But when I heard about the Ureons' beliefs about the Everance, I had to go and meet them myself and learn more about their ways.

"What do you mean?" said Ambrielle.

"Unlike us Cereveshians, the Ureons in the realm of Averess are beings of strong emotion," said Kyron. "They are uniquely able to sense many other realms and the beings that live within them. They say that all the realms of the Everance interact and are dependent on each other in a great cosmic ecology. Radiance, essence, and energy can pass between realms, giving each other things they need. They also believe when you fade out of this existence you slip away from the constraints of being, into the eternal hyperdimensional omnisphere called the Afterglow."

"One of the others spoke of the Afterglow," said Ambrielle. "You go there when you die?"

"That is what the Ureons believe, and I will soon find out," said Kyron, stifling a cough.

"You can go back into the stasis chamber and live," said Ambrielle.

"You have given me an opportunity," said Kyron. "I have long outlived my time. This may be my only chance to discover the mysteries of the Afterglow."

"I don't want anyone else to die because I woke them," said Ambrielle. "Please don't make me the reason."

"It was only a thought. In truth, I am not ready. You would think after all this time I would be. But I am in the middle of important work in Averess. There is so much data to gather. So many new experiments to conduct. I suppose I may never feel ready, but as long as life is in my hands, I don't know if I will choose to leave it."

"Before we do anything, I have one more question," Gavian said. "If we close the rift, will we still be able to pass through the waterfall between here and Anatharia?"

"I was not aware the rift created a wormhole between two worlds," said Kyron. "Fascinating. I'm afraid I do not know the answer. It may or it may not close the connection."

"We had better not close it yet then," said Ambrielle. "We have to defeat Ogolameth first. We think he is the Primevus."

"Correct. If you close it now, you would prevent the Nulvarians' ability to transfer the energy of this world to their collection." said Kyron. "But it would not prevent Isodonia's destruction. If the Primevus is allowed to fester, it will grow enough to devour this world as they have done to others. As they nearly did to Anatharia."

"I need some way to get back home," Ambrielle said. "It can't be closed while we are here."

"Then you must find another to close it after you leave," said Kyron. "I would be the one to do it for you, but I do not think I will endure for much longer."

"To face Ogolameth, I have a geowave, but I don't know how to use it," said Ambrielle, taking the square metal piece and throwing it into the cavern floor, causing it to expand into the gun-shaped device the automatons used to dig.

"Ah yes," said Kyron. "It is old technology, but it should work. Aim it at the rock wall and fire. The rings at the top, one adjusts the frequency, one is amplitude, and the third is focus. Turn the rings until you get the right settings to break through the rock."

Ambrielle moved outside the akreum, firing a beam at the side of the cavern. It barely made a crack in the stone. Adjusting the rings, she continued firing, and the rock began to crumble. She turned them more and a hole opened, burrowing through the side of the cave.

"It works!" she said excitedly. Gavian peered out of the akreum to see. Ambrielle let go of the trigger and slammed the geowave into the ground, compressing it back into its compact form.

"Good," said Kyron. "Just make sure you do not put all the rings to their max settings. It could cause great damage to the area around you or even injury to yourself."

"Thank you, Kyron," Ambrielle said. "I hope you do reach the Afterglow one day."

"I hope so too," he said. "Keep to your purpose in the Everance and perhaps we will all see each other there one day."

"That would be nice," said Ambrielle.

Gavian and Ambrielle helped Kyron back into the glass chamber, waving goodbye while it sealed and filled with pink gas. They soon left the akreum and made their way back into the blinding light outside the cave. Even the covered sun of Isodonia was bright after being in the dark for a while. Ambrielle often wondered if her mother was still living in an afterlife. Kyron's words had given her hope. She couldn't get the image of the names on the stone out of her head. How was Gavian's name there? Even though her name was there because Maetha named her after it being on the tablet, the presence of Gavian and Malidora's names had to mean something.

"It's a long walk, but we should head for Strakenbridge," Gavian said, as they moved across the grassy steppes.

Ambrielle took another look back at the mountain, the waterfall not visible from this side. Her mind was a whirlwind. With everything Kyron had told them, she wished she had something to write it all down. Though much of it wasn't important for the mission, it resonated with Ambrielle. Still, she had to focus on what lay ahead. "Wegin, what's the best direction to go?"

"I am not familiar with the location of Strakenbridge," Wegin informed her. "But if it is the same way the brigades were heading, it would be this way." Wegin zoomed ahead then stopped, hovering in the air. Ambrielle and Gavian changed course, following after Wegin, who flew above them.

"Be on the lookout for Grundians," Gavian said. "We don't want to run into any more of them right now."

As they walked through the field, a group of flitterlyns danced in the air, gathering around one of the red crystals poking out of the ground. Ambrielle walked to them, leaning down to better see the small crystal. It was the same one that she had come across before, with beautifully formed facets that made it sparkle in the light.

Though she left it before to continue to be formed and perfected, coming across it again made Ambrielle begin to wonder if she was meant to have it. After all, nothing was certain. Letting it remain did not mean it would be perfected sometime in the future. It could just as easily be shattered or lost deep in the earth, never to be seen again. Ambrielle broke the shiny piece from the stem, holding it in the sunlight once more before placing it in her pouch.

After climbing the slopes of one of the hills, they passed into a small basin with a lake and several houses. Wandering between the houses, they made their way to a row of shops in the middle of town. A clapping sound intermittently played nearby. They approached the source of the sound at a blacksmith shop, its door hanging off the hinges, creaking back and forth in the gentle breeze.

Ambrielle followed Gavian as he peeked inside, greeted by the scent of metal and coal. At the center of the shop was the forge, now cold and empty. The bellows and tools were scattered haphazardly around it. This place, like many others in Isodonia, had been abandoned for weeks.

Leaving the deserted town behind, they came to an open forest. Hazy sunlight filtered through the trees while Wegin led them on. When they were drawn in further, a sudden noise caught their attention. It was a rustling sound, like something moving through the underbrush. Wegin stopped for a moment and then darted toward their right.

They followed him until they came upon movement ahead. A large, furry jagstrider grazed on fruit from the nearby trees. Its long tail curved upward as it continued to chew on the fruit.

"It has a saddle." Ambrielle scanned the trees around them. "Its rider must be nearby."

Wegin climbed higher into the air. He hovered for a moment before descending. "There is no one else nearby."

Gavian stepped closer, making the animal cautiously stop eating to watch him. "I think it was part of the convoy."

"How do you know that?" Ambrielle moved over next to him, studying the creature.

He slowly reached for the jagstrider's saddle bag. "I remember this symbol." He pointed to a mark that appeared to be burned into the leather saddle bag with a branding iron. It looked like a fire with curling flames. "I think it means Inferno Brigade."

The animal began turning itself toward Gavian. Uncertain what it planned to do, he stepped back a few feet to give it more space.

"He looks friendly." Ambrielle crept toward it, and the animal again stopped chewing on the fruit. After a moment, it lost interest in her and picked another piece of fruit from the tree. Ambrielle took a wide path around the creature, searching the branches of the trees for more fruit. She found one piece hanging low enough to reach and picked it. Examining it, she saw that the fruit was mostly red with a green netlike peel covering it.

As hungry as she was, she couldn't resist taking a bite. It had a lightly sweet taste and a soft pulpy texture. One of its tiny seeds got stuck in her teeth as she chewed. The net wrapping was a bit too firm, causing her to remove it from her mouth before finishing the bite.

With the rest of the fruit in hand, she slowly stepped toward the strange animal. She held the fruit toward the creature, and it took a few steps forward. It sniffed the fruit in her hand and took it in its mouth, getting Ambrielle's hand wet with thick saliva.

As the animal ate, Ambrielle moved around toward its side, stroking its thick hair. She once had a friend whose mother had horses. What little she had picked up from that experience she wasn't sure would apply here at all. Grabbing the saddle, Ambrielle hoisted herself onto the animal.

The creature leaned to its left side, turning around in a circle. Ambrielle held on tight, continuing to pet the furry creature. It straightened up and walked back over to the tree with her on its back to get more fruit.

"So, you're a rider now?" Gavian said, watching her from nearby.

"Yes." Ambrielle sat proudly on the animal. "Why not?" The jagstrider turned back and forth, as if unsure about a stranger being on its back. Ambrielle held on tight to avoid sliding off.

"Are you going to be able to stay on that thing?" Gavian said.

"Of course," she replied, trying to maintain her balance on the wobbling jagstrider.

Gavian cautiously moved toward the creature while it swayed back and forth. As he grabbed the saddle to climb up, the animal bellowed and turned away.

"You have to pet him first," Ambrielle said. "Let him know you are there."

"How do you know?" said Gavian, reaching for the saddle again.

"My best friend when I was a kid had horses," she said.

"Is this a horse?" Gavian began to stroke the creature's fur, and it stopped moving.

"No, but I guess some animals are the same no matter what planet it is." Ambrielle took hold of the reins.

He tried again, pulling himself up onto the saddle behind Ambrielle. She swung the reins, trying to make the animal move. "Go!" she said, and the creature moved, but not in the direction she'd wanted. It instead went over to the fruit trees to find more to eat.

"Yarvik always patted his docimare's side to get it started."

She supposed it was worth a try, and she gave the creature a pat, but nothing happened.

"He did it a lot harder than that," said Gavian.

Ambrielle hit the animal slightly harder, but it did nothing but snort.

"Do you want me to do it?" said Gavian.

"No," Ambrielle said. "Just give me a minute."

She slapped the side of the animal, and it raised its head. Ambrielle swatted it again, and it started trotting forward, but it was heading toward the trees again. Pulling the reins, she got it to turn around. After riding around the brush, she guided the creature onto a path between the trees. The animal wasn't extremely fast, but its trot was faster than they could comfortably run over a long period.

Wegin flew above them, able to keep up as the creature carried them past the wooded areas into the hilly plains. Ambrielle adjusted herself in the saddle after they had traveled for a while. She noticed something ahead of them. When they got closer, it became apparent that it was a man, two women, and two children.

Ambrielle pulled back on the reins, slowing the creature to a stop. The group continued walking hurriedly toward them.

"You're going the wrong way!" one of the women said.

Before Ambrielle could respond, the man rode up alongside them on his own animal. "Where did you acquire this jagstrider?"

Ambrielle hesitated, then began, "We—"

"It has been in the family for generations," Gavian interjected.

"We could really use one," the other woman chimed in. "Transporting children to the Gulflands is quite challenging."

Gavian replied, "You would need a larger animal for that. I'm not sure it would be comfortable with more than two of us."

The man suggested, "Why don't you come with us? There's nothing left in that direction."

"Tildenhal has fallen," one of the women added. "The remnants of the alliance have retreated to Strakenbridge."

"We have friends there," Ambrielle explained. "We can't abandon them."

"Surely they left with everyone else," one of the women insisted.

The man confidently stated, "I know how to care for these animals. Why don't you join us? We can take turns riding it."

"Sorry, but we have a mission," Gavian firmly replied. "If you're unwilling to stay and fight for this land, someone must."

"We have our children to consider," one of the women said.

"Then let us be on our way," Gavian declared. "If you truly care about this land, pray that we reach our destination in time."

He slapped the side of the jagstrider, and it began trotting again. Ambrielle looked back at the people as they drew away from them. "I feel bad not helping them."

"They're fortunate," said Gavian. "The people of Rethia were trapped; they were not able to flee. If no one stands up and fights for anything . . . there will be nowhere left to run."

"You're right," said Ambrielle, "but they did have children."

"Even more reason to fight," Gavian said. "I'm not talking about them, so much as everyone that abandoned this region. They think they can run while someone else does the fighting for them."

"They don't know what's coming," said Ambrielle. "The Shadows grow stronger with each city they raze."

"We have to save Strakenbridge," Gavian said. "If it falls, Isodonia falls with it."

They rode on for a while, until dark. Ambrielle gave the jagstrider a few gentle pats, and then she tied its leash to a tree. They made shelter nearby and settled in for the night. When dawn came, they awoke and resumed the journey.

"My brother, Ryan, would go crazy if he could see this." Ambrielle laughed as she glanced back at Gavian. "When he's not playing video games, he's in the woods playing with toy swords like he is on some great quest. He would absolutely idolize you."

He leaned closer over her shoulder. "Why me? I would think he would look up to you more than anyone."

"You're everything he wants to be," she said, pulling on the reins and guiding the jagstrider back on course. "I don't think he aspires to be a girl who has no idea what she wants to do when she's done with school."

Gavian gently brushed her hair to the side when it blew into his face. "But he surely wants to be a leader. One who is brave enough to face any challenge. Someone who puts others before herself. And perhaps even someone that can take on giants with a bladestaff."

She chuckled at the thought. "I haven't told him about any of this yet. Maybe one day I will."

Dreading to think how many days had gone by since she'd left home, Ambrielle wondered how she was going to explain this to her dad.

As twilight fell on them again, they came across a road leading in two directions as far as could be seen. Ambrielle looked up, smiling when she confirmed that Wegin was still with them. They turned onto the path and continued until they reached the bridge across the Vallohal River. Two guards lit the torches outside the gate while they approached. They began pulling both halves of the huge doors together as they reached the main entrance.

"Wait!" Gavian shouted. "You have to let us in!"

"The gate will open again tomorrow morning," said the guard.

Ambrielle eased the jagstrider up to one of the soldiers. "Our friends may be in there," she said. "Please. We've come all this way."

The other guard lifted one of the saddle bags. "You have weapons with you. We don't have time to check these in."

"What's that branded on the side?" the other soldier asked.

The guard leaned closer. "Inferno Brigade. Why didn't you say so?"

"Squeeze on through," said the soldier, as he pushed the door open a bit.

After they passed through the gate, Ambrielle slowed the animal. "Where might we find the others?"

"They should be in the barracks," said the soldier, while the two pushed the doors shut.

Ambrielle leaned back, whispering to Gavian. "Do you know where that is?"

He shook his head no.

"We're new to the unit," Ambrielle said. "Could you tell us how to get there?"

"I'm surprised they found anyone new to join," one of the soldiers said. They brought down the latch to lock the gate. "The center of town, between the four towers."

"Thank you." Ambrielle prodded the animal to move forward again.

One of the guards called out behind them, "You realize you have a very large insect following you?"

Ambrielle stiffened, searching the area around her. Wegin hovered by her shoulder. Breathing a sigh of relief, she said, "Oh, that's just Wegin. He's not an insect."

She guided the jagstrider down the cobblestone street. Stone structures of various sizes stood on each side of the street. They passed a crossroad with rows of smaller shops. Ambrielle guided the animal as Wegin floated above them. They turned onto another street toward four tall towers ahead.

As they reached the towers, Ambrielle pulled back on the reins to stop the jagstrider. Gavian jumped off and tied the rope to a railing by the steps of one of the barracks. They stepped through the doorway into a long corridor with closed doors on each side. The hall led to an open room. One of the soldiers ran the fletching of her arrows over the flame of a candle, while another sharpened his sword with a rough stone. Flumpy lay on the floor in front of one of the seats. Vilura and Bradwyn sat next to the vorren, stroking her hair.

Gavian rushed over and gave Flumpy a hug. "Have you seen Dexius or Darby?" he said, looking up at Vilura and Bradwyn.

"Not yet," said Vilura. "We got assigned to help with harvest evacuation duty as soon as we got back. Tildenhal has fallen, so they want to try to move some of the crops to higher ground in case the Gruns open the dam."

Ambrielle saw the concern on Gavian's face. She tried to be positive about Darby and Dexius. "Something must have slowed them down."

"Not everyone from Inferno and Storm has reported in yet," said Bradwyn, as he stroked Flumpy's hair.

Ambrielle felt a lump in her throat. She tried to quell her thoughts from seeking dark places while she sat next to Flumpy, sliding her hand through Flumpy's thick coat. As much as she hated to think about something bad happening to Darby or Dexius, her thoughts were on Gavian. With what already happened to his father, how would he deal with this?

"We were about to check the infirmary," said Vilura. "Darby and Dexius could be there."

Gavian paused before walking out the door. "I hope that's not where they are."

"If they are hurt, we could help them," said Ambrielle. "As you know, my silbrace can regenerate cells. It can't completely heal wounds, but it can do enough to make the healing process much faster."

"Let's go!" Gavian said. "Where is the infirmary?"

Ambrielle and Gavian followed the soldier's directions, crossing the courtyard to the stone building containing the infirmary. Spotting a nurse in the hallway, Ambrielle tried to flag her down. The nurse made a face, likely stressed and frustrated, having something important to get to.

"Can you tell us if anyone named Darby or Dexius is here?" Ambrielle asked, as Wegin hovered closely.

The nurse took a deep breath before she spoke. "I don't know everyone's name. We just got a lot of wounded from Tildenhal. Our infirmary has spilled over into the rest of the building. If you know how bad their injuries are, maybe you can find them easier. We've divided it up into three sections depending on the severity of the injuries. The north side are the most severe, and the south side are the least, with the middle being moderate."

"What side are we on now?" Ambrielle said.

"The north side," said the nurse.

They cautiously stepped into one of the larger rooms branching off the hallway. The air carried the metallic tang of blood and the pungent scent of antiseptic herbs. The room was filled with rows of makeshift mats, upon which most of the patients lay, their faces etched with exhaustion and pain. In the corner, bodies shrouded in cloth from head to toe lay still, a somber reminder of those who had succumbed to their injuries.

Ambrielle's stomach churned, a wave of nausea washing over her. Medics bustled around a row of wounded soldiers, their blood staining the floor beneath them, forming a gruesome mosaic of crimson. The groans and moans of the injured soldiers filled the room, mingling with the occasional whimper and cry of anguish. Ambrielle couldn't help but feel her shoulders tense up, the weight of the suffering around her bearing down on her empathetic spirit.

As they navigated through the harrowing scene, a pile of discarded, blood-soaked shirts crumpled on the floor caught Ambrielle's eye. Wegin moved around the room, scanning for Darby and Dexius.

"I could not locate either of them," Wegin said.

Gavian breathed a sigh of relief. They had not checked the other rooms in this part of the building, but she imagined that Gavian preferred to leave this area as much as she did. She was glad there were those who were strong enough to help people in brutal conditions such as this.

"Wait, I just thought of something," Ambrielle gasped. "My silbrace has a beam that can heal and regenerate cells."

Although she hated to see the horrible wounds of those around them, she had to help. She strode toward the first soldier covered in bloody bandages and rags. "I have something that may help," she told him. "Do you mind if I try?"

He nodded at Ambrielle, and she extended her arm to him, initiating the beam from her silbrace. She had used the regeneration beam on Gavian's wounds, and it might have been what saved his life. The soldier closed his eyes, and Ambrielle sustained the beam on his wounds. Gavian stood and watched as Ambrielle moved from soldier to soldier, healing those that could be healed. The silbrace ran out of power in the process, making her use the spare energy cell to continue. It couldn't help everyone, but she had to try.

They moved on to the middle part of the building that was more of an open lobby, letting them move by the chairs and bedding to check each person. These soldiers had cuts and broken bones, wounds that would heal. Ambrielle used the beam on them and was able to completely heal many of their wounds. The soldiers and nurses were astounded. People crowded around her while she moved between the wounded. After causing a stir, Ambrielle showed them that it was the silbrace doing it and not her. After helping everyone in the section, they still saw no sign of Darby or Dexius.

As they moved toward the south end of the building, a voice rose above the commotion behind them. "I shot him right in the neck and he fell. I kept grabbing arrows, firing one after the other, hitting them all. One shot, one kill."

Gavian's and Ambrielle's eyes met when they recognized the voice that continued talking from the end of the hall. "It was enough to hold them off for our group to retreat. That's when I saw you guys."

They stepped toward the room to the far right, where several soldiers and some plainly dressed commoners were sitting around the sides of the room. "That's when the big giant, Twick, came at me. He tried to crush me with his fists. I fired my arrow under his chin as he stood over me and brought him down with one shot."

Gavian followed the voice until he came to a stop near the corner of the room. Darby was wrapping bandages around Dexius's side and right arm. Lirah and Neylin were sitting next to him on his right, while Valea, Gavian's mother, and his little brother were on his left.

"Hey! You're all okay!" Gavian's voice quivered with a mixture of disbelief and overwhelming relief.

"I wouldn't exactly call this okay," Dexius said, lifting his wounded arm.

Darby, bounding forward, embraced Gavian tightly. "Gav!" she exclaimed, "Ambrielle!" Her voice filled with a blend of elation and lingering worry. "We were so afraid you didn't make it out of there!"

Gavian's mother, rising from her seat, approached him with open arms, enveloping him in a warm, motherly embrace. The weight of their separation melted away in that heartfelt moment. Darby and Valea joined in, their arms encircling Gavian.

"When we couldn't find any of you, I feared the worst." Gavian's voice trembled slightly as he spoke, the lingering fear still present in his words.

"We owe everything to Dexius!" Gavian's mother's voice brimmed with gratitude while she affectionately rubbed Dexius's shoulder. "If it weren't for his heroics, we would not be standing here right now."

Gavian smiled, turning his gaze toward Dexius. "Thank you, Dex."

In response, Dexius nodded to him.

"Dexius, I have something that may help with those cuts." Ambrielle displayed the silbrace. "If I may?"

"Go ahead." He turned his arm toward her.

She moved the beam around to each cut, until it couldn't help any further.

Dexius flexed his right arm. "Whatever you did, thanks, I think that does feel a bit better."

"You should have stayed close to Dexius," Gavian's mother said. "He would have gotten you out of there too!"

Gavian's smile began to vanish. "I got out on my own."

"It took you long enough to get here," she said.

"She's right, Dex," said Lirah. "We can't thank you enough. You are definitely our hero."

"I would never let anything happen to you," said Dexius. "Any of you."

"I'm glad I was able to help get you all to the camp," Gavian said.

"Yes, good thing you had that sword, Tav!" said Lirah.

Ambrielle noticed Gavian gritting his teeth. "Gavian is definitely my hero," she announced. "I would never have gotten off that mountain alive without him."

"Gavian?" his mother said.

"I go by Gavian now," said Gavian. "Long story."

"Oh. Yes, that's great that you two were able to make it here," said his mother. "Where did that nurse go? She was bringing hot tea, but Dexius needs a refill! I'll be right back!" She got out of the chair and walked out of the room.

"Well, I think I'm going to get some rest," Gavian said. "I'll let you carry on with the story."

"Well with, Tav," said Valea.

"Well with, everyone," he said and stepped out of the room. Ambrielle waved while she followed Gavian out of the building toward the barracks. He turned around outside the men's area, and Ambrielle wrapped her arms around him.

"That's what I love about you Gav," she said, as he puckered his face. "Even with all you've done, you aren't boastful. You don't help others for the glory."

"I wish I could say that was true, but—" Gavian stared back at her, his eyes wide open. "Love?"

"What?" Ambrielle was confused by his question.

He turned his full body to her. "This time you said 'love.'"

Ambrielle's focus moved around the room, and she avoided eye contact. "I guess I did."

"I love you, too." Gavian slid his arms around her waist, drawing her to him. He kissed her as she rested her hand on his chest. His arms felt tense at first, but the tension began to melt away. They drifted into a blissful dream, the kind she never wanted to wake up from. Ambrielle looked into his dark blue eyes when they separated. She turned to head toward the women's barracks, and he held onto her hand for a moment longer.

CHAPTER 24

"T**O YOUR STATIONS!**" The voice echoed down the hallway as Ambrielle rolled over in the bed. "Report to your stations immediately!" The women around her scrambled out of bed and began changing into their battle armor. The reality of the situation finally hit Ambrielle, and she popped up. She removed her robe and started putting on the blue outfit she had acquired in Elyravess. Grabbing her satchel, she moved into the line while everyone filed into the hall.

As the line moved outside, Wegin alerted her to Gavian's location among the men. Thunder rumbled in the distance, but the sky was no darker than usual. They marched away from the towers down the cobblestone street. Past the abandoned shops, they headed toward the eastern wall. Archers climbed the stone stairs leading to the alure, taking position behind the battlements. The swordsmen and lancers filled the area on the ground below.

The rumbling grew louder. Gavian moved out of formation and headed to her. "We don't have to do this," he said. "We can leave now and enter the waterfall. All you have to do is say so."

"Nearly every part of me is saying run,"—Ambrielle held her hands together to keep them from trembling—"and yet I feel compelled to stay."

"I think I know that feeling." Gavian turned, and a buzzing

rose up among the thunder. It was faint, but definitely there. Ambrielle froze. She could feel it vibrating through her body.

"I want to see what's out there," she said, as she ran toward the stairs that went up to the top of the wall, hearing Gavian's footsteps following after her. Once there, she hurried past the archers lined up between the parapets. At last, she saw Darby, sitting with her back against the stone bricks with Dexius beside her.

"See anything?" she asked.

"Not yet," Dexius said, "but the watchers in the tower spotted Grundians. They're coming from Tildenhal."

"What about you Wegin?" Ambrielle inquired. "Can you detect anything from here?"

"There are things here aside from the people, but you told me not to give you that information," said Wegin.

"What?" said Ambrielle. "What else is here?"

"Insects and rodents," Wegin replied. "If you wish, I can give more detailed information."

"No thank you," Ambrielle said. "That's not what I meant. There's something out there." Ambrielle leaned against the battlements, scanning the fields that led to the forests around them. "Do you guys feel it?"

Darby loaded arrows into her quiver, separating the mekkadium tips from the metal ones. "The Shadows."

"I don't see anything in all that open field." Dexius stood, staring out over the wall.

Something dark moved in the distance among the clouds, barely over the trees. "There's something out there"—Ambrielle pointed—"In the forest."

"Where?" Dexius put his hands on his hips. "Those dark clouds?"

"I don't think those are clouds." Ambrielle could almost hear its voice echoing through the ether. "It's Ogolameth."

Dexius glanced at her before returning his focus to the woods. "It's too big to be one of the Shadows."

Darby's eyes grew large while she watched. "I think she may be right."

Gavian squinted, looking into the distance. He grimaced and began to turn a bit pale. "If there's a Shadow that size, it could pull everything into it. Why would it even need the Grundians?"

"It needs more energy," Ambrielle remarked. "But once it gets it, no one will be able to stop it."

Darby turned to Ambrielle, her eyes full of determination. "What do we need to do?"

Ambrielle reached into her satchel, making sure the geowave was still there. "I have something that might stop it, but we can only use it once the creature moves over water."

Dexius crossed his arms, skepticism etched on his face. "If water is some kind of weakness, why wouldn't it just avoid it altogether?"

Ambrielle looked at Dexius, her gaze unwavering. "It will have no choice but to cross the river eventually, won't it? It will need to reach the Gulflands."

Dexius leaned against one of the merlons, his tone tinged with resignation. "You mean after Strakenbridge is destroyed?"

Ambrielle let out a frustrated breath. "We'll find a solution. We have to."

Dexius reached into his bag, taking out something and casually popping it into his mouth. "I have to say, this plan doesn't sound very promising."

Darby chimed in, "Well, it's close to the river. Maybe we can lure it closer somehow?"

Ambrielle considered Darby's suggestion. "Perhaps if one of us gets close enough, it might chase us."

Darby tilted her head, contemplating the idea. "On second thought, I don't think it would be that foolish."

Dexius wiped his hands on his shirt, dismissing the idea. "Yeah, that's not going to work."

Ambrielle's frustration grew. "Well, I'm open to other suggestions. I haven't heard any brilliant ideas from you guys yet."

Dexius placed another piece of food in his mouth, chewing thoughtfully. "Give me a minute. I'll think of something."

They all stared at Dexius, anticipation building while they awaited his next words.

Gavian rolled his eyes and began tapping his forehead with his finger. "Isn't there supposed to be a dam at Tildenhal?"

"Yes, there is," Darby said, as she watched the black smokey object in the distance. The trees around it swayed unnaturally.

"How wide would the river flow if the dam was opened up?" Gavian asked.

"I've never seen it open all the way," Dexius said. "They open it a little sometimes if there is too much flooding on the other side."

"The dam at Tildenhal creates a big lake around the castle." Darby moved back when a group of archers moved past them. "They use it to irrigate their crops."

Dexius clapped the residue from his hands. "And for defense."

"It's worth a try." Gavian shifted his weight from one foot to the other, like he was growing antsy.

"There's no one left in Tildenhal though," said Dexius. "How are we going to get them to open the dam?"

"We'll have to open it ourselves," Gavian declared.

Darby's brows furrowed as she processed the plan. "So, we head to the dam, open it, and then make it back in time to confront Ogolameth?"

Ambrielle nodded, her voice firm. "That's right. But we need to make sure we stay clear of the river ourselves in case things get out of control."

"Ogolameth will move away from the water by the time we get to it," Dexius said.

Ambrielle added, "One of us will need to stay close to Ogolameth. They can use the weapon as soon as the river floods."

Darby voiced her concern, "But how are we going to open the dam?"

"If it's mechanical, I should be able to figure it out," said Gavian. "I'll go to Tildenhal, and you all can prepare for that monster."

"Why is it always you who wants to go off on your own?" Dexius said. "Will you actually come back this time?"

"You go if you think you can figure out how to open the dam," Gavian said. "But if you can't do it, if this is your arrogance talking, then we're all doomed."

"Go ahead," Dexius muttered. "If you think you're so smart."

"Do I have a role to play in this plan?" Wegin asked, his lights blinking with curiosity.

"Just give us a heads-up about our surroundings, excluding the insects and rodents," Ambrielle said, turning to Dexius. "How long do you think it will take us to get out there?"

Dexius responded, "A while if we're walking."

Gavian interjected, "We found a jagstrider, but it's pretty slow."

"Slow?" Dexius exclaimed. "Those things are lightning fast."

Ambrielle expressed her surprise, "Really? Ours wasn't."

Darby chimed in with an explanation, "You have to know how to ride it. They use their speed mostly when they go after prey or when they get frightened."

"Well, what are we waiting for?" Ambrielle exclaimed eagerly.

Ambrielle, Gavian, Dexius, Darby, and Wegin rushed back toward the barracks where they had left the jagstrider.

"Gavian should take the strider," said Darby. "I'm not sure it can carry us all on its back. We'll borrow one of the big bronthas."

"Borrow?" Gavian said. "I hope you didn't pick up any bad habits from Malidora."

"Do you have a better idea?" she replied.

"Make sure you bring it back," said Gavian.

"We will," Darby said, rolling her eyes.

Gavian stroked the jagstrider's fur and climbed onto the saddle. Ambrielle fed it some of the fruit from her satchel while Darby untied the leash.

"As soon as you open the dam, come and find us," said Ambrielle.

Gavian leaned down to give her a kiss. "Stay hidden as long as you can."

"Well with you all," Gavian said, as he prodded the jagstrider into moving.

"For Rokendor." Darby winked at him, adjusting the strap on her quiver. "Take the road along the river and you'll find Tildenhal."

Gavian slapped the side of the jagstrider, and it began trotting forward. Pulling awkwardly on the reins, he guided the creature around the other direction. He gave the animal another hard pat and rode off onto another street.

Darby and Dexius led Ambrielle while they dashed toward the brontha stables with Wegin zooming along with them. They burst through the doorway, nearly running into a woman on a ladder, who was pouring feed into high troughs.

"Hey Darby, what's the rush?" the woman said.

"Oh, Ms. Mionie," said Darby. "I . . . uh . . . I wanted to show Ambrielle and Dexius the bronthas."

"Don't you know the city is under alert?" said Mionie. "Bronthas can sense fear, it's got them on edge."

"We're on a really important mission," Darby said. "One that could save Strakenbridge."

"I heard you took down Grunch," Mionie said. "I suppose if there's anyone that can save this city, it may as well be you." Mionie sighed. "Take Sorio, I've already fed him."

"Thank you Mionie!" said Darby, as she pulled on the stable gate. Ambrielle went over to help slide the gate open.

"I'll steer." Dexius climbed onto the saddle.

"Fine," Darby grumbled, climbing on behind him next, and then Ambrielle after her.

Dexius took the reins, and they rode on, the brontha's claws clicking on the street. Wegin trailed behind them when they approached the eastern gate. Before they passed through, one of the two guards outside held up a hand for them to stop. "Darby, this isn't the best time to be going for a ride."

"We're going on a scouting mission," said Darby. "If the Grundians are coming, we need to know where they are."

"They are coming," said the guard. "Maybe not today, but they are coming."

"I won't be long," said Darby.

"Don't go too far," said the guard. "If something is spotted, we will have to close the gates."

The guard stood aside, and Dexius snapped the reins, making the brontha start moving again. After passing through the gate, he steered the brontha around the base of the outer wall. Someone whistled above them as they passed the archers lined up around the battlements. Darby waved and Dexius pulled the brontha to a stop.

Dexius turned back to Ambrielle. "They'd let her get away with anything."

"We should all have their trust by now." Ambrielle held on to Darby as the brontha darted down the hill into the open field.

CHAPTER 25

AVIAN CROSSED THE bridge over the Vallohal as the jagstrider continued its slow trot. Guiding the creature onto the road to the east, he
heard loud stomping behind him. A large stone crashed into the dirt
not far from him. Gavian looked back to see several Grundians guarding
the road heading south.

More stones tumbled by, sending grass and dirt flying. Gavian smacked
the jagstrider's side, causing it to gallop for a moment before settling back
into its trot. Stones rained around them, so Gavian slapped the creature
again. This time, Gavian rapidly hit the saddle since splashes of soil began
to hit him. The jagstrider went from a gallop to a sprint.

He began to pull away from the Grundians, now outside of their throwing range. They must be the same Grundians that invaded Rethia. They
were likely positioned to ambush anyone going on the road south, once the
Gurrians on the other side of the river started their attack on Strakenbridge.
Fortunately for Gavian, they had not anticipated anyone going east.

After riding a while, the terrain became rocky, with the road sloping
upward. Crashing over rocks and small cliffs, the river was much wilder
in this region. As the road continued to rise, the river was now well
below him where it had carved out a valley through the rocky hills.

As he traveled down the road, a towering stone wall emerged

in the distance, spanning the width of the river from a nearby ridge. The wall boasted several massive doors, sealed with worn iron bars. Thick chains hung from slots in the wall, keeping a few of the doors open and allowing water to seep through. Overall, the dam mitigated enough water to stem the river's flow and create a sprawling lake on the other side.

The crest of the dam wall could be used as a bridge, though he didn't want to risk riding the jagstrider over such a precarious road. The side toward Strakenbridge was a steep drop into powerful rapids. On the other side, the water was much higher and appeared more calm but could be churning underneath the surface. The bridge itself led to a castle on the cliffside. After tying the jagstrider to the branches of a nearby tree, Gavian headed toward the dam.

He began to realize how high it was on the west side of the bridge when he started to walk across. Bricks on either side of the crest formed parapets, making him feel more secure as he walked across. In some areas, the parapets had worn down to nothing.

As he neared a large wooden door at the end of the crest, Gavian stepped onto a loose stone and lost his balance, nearly falling over the parapets into the river. After composing himself, he opened the door, venturing into the interior of the castle.

Gavian's breath caught in his throat after he stepped into the foreboding hallway, its massive stone walls casting long shadows that seemed to reach out for him. The air hung heavy with an eerie stillness, suffocating the usual sounds of life. Two diverging paths lay before him, disappearing into the darkness of the interior.

As he cautiously moved forward, the tapestries adorning the walls caught his eye. Once magnificent works of art, they now hung in tattered shreds. The floor beneath Gavian's feet betrayed the gruesome scenes that had unfolded within these walls. Slick with blood, it served as a macabre reminder of the recent battle. The fallen bodies of soldiers, both giant and human, bore the grim reality of the conflict that had ravaged this place.

As he emerged from the dark hallway, Gavian found himself standing at the edge of a flight of steps leading to a vast courtyard. Strewn across the ground were the remnants of shattered weapons and shields, lying scattered like discarded relics.

A beautiful garden, filled with vibrant flowers and lush ferns, stood against the face of darkness. Yet even this small oasis of beauty did not escape the grasp of death's relentless presence. A scavenger bird, its dark plumage mirroring the somber scene, pecked at the remains of a fallen warrior.

The mechanism for opening the doors had to be attached to the chains that were coming out of the dam wall. If that was the case, there had to be a way to access them. It had to be somewhere beneath him. Gavian started down the steps, hoping to find the answer.

As he neared the cobblestone streets below, an ominous whoosh pierced the air. Gavian froze. A shivering shriek soon followed, reverberating across the desolate courtyard. A dark figure emerged from the other end of the street. Gavian tried to quiet his breathing, but his heart raced. The black-robed figure had his back to him, pointing his silver blade to a group of corpses and collecting their smoky essence.

Gavian instinctively walked backward up the steps, keeping his gaze on Pythus. The masked ghoul turned around. Gavian started to run, but the being did not seem to notice him. Instead, he moved toward another group to gather their energy.

Gavian could hear the pulse inside his head while he watched the dark figure move to the bodies of humans and giants. If he hid long enough, perhaps the fiend would move on. But how much time did he have to wait? The Gurrians might already be at Strakenbridge by now. If this was even going to work, it would take time for the waters to reach Ogolameth.

There was no time to wait. He had taken it upon himself to accomplish this task. Whatever the cost, he had to get it done. For Ambrielle, for Darby, and even for Dexius. They were a team, a family, and they were counting on him. He felt he had already let them down once, and he could not do it again.

Sneaking quietly, Gavian made his way down the steps. The ghoulish creature moved toward another tangle of bodies. Gavian waited until Pythus began draining the corpses and dashed toward the bottom of the steps, hoping to find a way inside the wall of the dam.

As he neared the bottom, the masked being immediately turned, staring straight at him. Gavian was paralyzed, afraid to move.

"Like a moth to the flame," said Pythus, as he walked slowly toward Gavian, dragging the point of his sword along the cobblestones. "Are there more of you here? Or were you foolish enough to come alone?"

Gavian remained silent and still on the steps above the courtyard while the dark fiend continued to advance, speaking with a hissing voice. "Soon enough, all living energy on this world will be consumed by my blade."

Taking a few steps back, Gavian drew his sword.

Pythus halted, fixing his gaze on him. "It is a rare gift to encounter someone brave enough to face me." The masked being spun his sword into an upright position. "For that, I shall grant you a swift death."

Gavian assumed a defensive posture, taking advantage of the higher ground provided by the stairs. The ghoulish creature leapt into the air, sword poised to strike. Gavian deftly parried the attack, but the force of the blow sent him stumbling backward, walking up the steps. With lightning-fast reflexes, Gavian swung his blade, causing the creature to dodge nimbly out of the way, giving himself time to regain a solid footing.

With the higher ground advantage, Gavian had less to worry about in terms of the creature's sword reach, but the dark entity's relentless strikes at his legs caused him to move further up the stairs. Gavian's retreat came to an end when he reached the flat surface of the short hallway.

The dark being relentlessly delivered powerful blows, each clang of his sword reverberating through Gavian's arms as he struggled to defend himself. Pythus seemed determined to knock him out of his defensive stance, but Gavian knew he couldn't afford to keep retreating. Pythus pressed his attack unceasingly, keeping Gavian pinned on the defensive.

As Gavian deftly dodged one of his thrusts, Pythus followed up with a crushing blow that Gavian could barely withstand. Backing through the wooden door, Gavian stepped onto the crest of the dam, and the silence gave way to the roar of rushing water below. After blocking another high swing, Gavian took the initiative and lunged toward Pythus. The dark fiend parried the strike, but Gavian didn't give up. With a quick feint, he side-stepped Pythus's attack and delivered a brisk kick to his midsection. The blow caught Pythus off guard and sent him stumbling backward, giving Gavian a moment to catch his breath and prepare for the next assault.

"Impressive," Pythus remarked, as he took in a deep whooshing breath, letting it out with a shivering shriek. "But futile, nonetheless. Even if you could draw blood, I am immortal. There's enough essence in this blade to save me from a thousand deaths."

"At least you couldn't feed it to your master." Gavian lunged at Pythus, unleashing a rapid series of attacks aimed at his left side. However, Pythus parried each strike with ease, expending little energy in the process.

Pythus slashed hard at Gavian's head, forcing him to deflect it and leap back to avoid his next attack. "You are shortsighted. Once this universe is torn asunder, I will be a master of the Everance." The masked fiend stepped toward him, dodging Gavian's swing and thrusting his blade into Gavian's side.

Gavian fell forward, gasping for breath. Blood poured over his left hand as he clutched the wound. Pythus drew the silver sword to his masked face, staring at the blood dripping from the blade. He made the familiar whooshing shriek as his shoulders rose and fell with a deep breath. "There's nothing like the rush of victory. The feeling of your enemy's flesh giving way to your blade . . . such sweet satisfaction."

Gavian tried to push himself up, but his body wouldn't respond. He clutched at the wound, desperately trying to stem the flow of blood. How had it come to this? After all he had been through. All the challenges, the victories, and the failures. Losing love and finding it anew. Ambrielle and the others might never know what happened to him here. They might always believe he abandoned them when they needed him most.

"I haven't felt this in so long," Pythus said with a shivering hiss. "If only there were more like you. Fearless or stupid enough to stand instead of running from my presence."

A light rain began to fall. Gavian raised his eyes to the dark clouds moving above them. This would be the perfect time for a storm, for lightning to strike his sword and charge the rokenstone again. If Ambrielle had been right, that there was indeed a plan. If the Everance was more than chaos, this was the moment it would have to be revealed to him.

Pythus stood over him, lowering his sword. "I suppose I failed to give you the swift death I promised."

Bright energy poured from the hilt of the sword, wafting its way toward Gavian's wound. The puncture in his side turned bright white, and then the skin seemed to stitch back together and heal before his eyes.

"Consider it a gift," said Pythus. "A taste of immortality."

Gavian looked at his side. The wound was gone. He breathed a long deep breath in the moist air. Leaping to his feet, Gavian quickly resumed his defensive stance.

"I crave one more chance to feel the rush of battle and the satisfaction of victory." Pythus spun his blade upright.

Gavian seized the opportunity and lunged forward, striking at Pythus's chest. The blow was deftly parried, and Pythus countered with a quick jab at Gavian's midsection. Gavian barely managed to dodge the blow and swung his sword in a wide arc, aiming for Pythus's head. The fiend expertly blocked the attack and countered with a flurry of strikes, forcing Gavian to defend himself with all his might.

Refusing to disengage and catch his breath, Gavian pushed himself to the limits with renewed vigor from the blade's essence.

Pythus taunted Gavian as he effortlessly parried his attacks. "Your aggression will tire you out long before me," he said, "but it does allow me to ponder the type of killing stroke that would satisfy me the most."

Pythus effortlessly deflected Gavian's attacks and continued to provoke him. "I must say, I find decapitation to be the most gratifying of all. It's a shame you won't get to see it."

As Gavian circled around Pythus, his eyes caught sight of the loose stone on the bridge. He couldn't afford to step on it again and lose his footing. With potent agility, he ducked under Pythus's incoming blade, seizing the opportunity to retaliate with a powerful swing aimed at Pythus's shoulder. Anticipating the attack, Pythus rapidly twisted his upper body to block the strike, quickly regaining his stance. "Keep wearing yourself down, boy. I will soon have the opening I need."

Swiftly changing direction, Gavian slashed toward Pythus's right side. Gavian maintained his circling motion, attempting to find an opening that would catch Pythus off guard. However, Pythus proved to be equally agile, if not more so, countering Gavian's movements by circling in the same direction. Undeterred, Gavian kept an eye on Pythus's feet, trying to anticipate his moves. With a rapid succession of quick, albeit weaker, strikes, Gavian forced Pythus to defend and move toward the left, inching him closer to the treacherous loose stone on the bridge.

As soon as Pythus stepped onto the cracked stone, Gavian seized the opportunity. With a deft and decisive move, he leapt forward, capitalizing on Pythus's momentary loss of balance. While Pythus focused on regaining his stability, Gavian brought his sword down with force, slicing through Pythus's hand. A metallic clang echoed, the silver sword clashing against the ground while Pythus staggered back, writhing in pain. "You will pay for that, boy!"

Gavian swiftly retrieved the fallen sword and pointed it at Pythus. He pulled the ring located under the cross guard. A brilliant surge of energy was pulled from the fiend's wounded arm, coursing into the blade.

"Wait!" shouted Pythus. "The lives of thousands will be wasted!"

"No," said Gavian. The silver sword was soaked with the essence of Pythus. "They will be avenged."

Pythus collapsed to his knees. The black robes fell loose as his body began to shrivel. He tried reaching toward Gavian with his remaining hand, but he pitched backward, folding into an unnatural position on the stone. As Gavian siphoned the essence into the sword, the silver mask slipped off Pythus's face revealing wrinkled dark reptilian skin and large round black eyes now devoid of life. His alien face came to an elongated point where a snout met his chin, separated only by the crease of his small mouth. His body withered while the last bit of essence was drained.

The sword quivered in Gavian's grip, emanating a low, resonant hum that reverberated through his bones. The intensity of its power unsettled him, sending a shiver down his spine. Tentatively, he trailed his finger along the pulsating green crystal nestled within the black hilt, only to sense a profound presence lurking within. It was more than a mere sensation; it possessed an essence, a consciousness that seemed to gaze back at him, stirring a mix of curiosity and trepidation within his heart.

Gavian's breath came in rapid gasps as he removed the sheath from Pythus's lifeless form. After wiping the dark blood from the silver blade, he slid it into the sheath. Among the fiend's loose robes, something shiny caught his eye. There was an amulet around his neck. Gavian removed the black chain from the corpse, bringing it close for a better look at the green stone encased within. The stone was cut and polished with many facets.

Sensing its significance, Gavian placed the object in his pouch to examine later.

He strapped both the silver sword and his own sword onto his back, making his way to the steps. As he reached the cobblestone path through the courtyard, he turned back toward the steps and noticed an alcove in the base of the stairs. Inside was a door that surely led into the dam wall. Gavian turned the handle, expecting it to be locked. To his surprise, the door opened, leading to a long, dark hall. Switching on the silbrace light, Gavian crept through the darkness. The hall was filled with thick dust, dark mold, and cobwebs, and it stretched on as far as he could see. Water dribbled from the ceiling, collecting into puddles in the pockets of the coarse stone floor.

Large wheels were mounted in the walls and attached to chains. A circular rim stuck out from the wall below the wheels. Studying the machinery, Gavian grabbed one of the round metal rims and tried to turn it. It didn't budge. Unsure of which direction to turn the wheel, he tried the other way, but again, nothing moved. Gavian yanked on the ring wheel, putting his weight into it, but it didn't move at all. Slumping against the wall, he wrung his hands. Was everything working against him? He had come this far only to fail at opening the dam. He imagined Ambrielle hiding among the trees, waiting for the waters of the Vallohal River to sweep through the plains. Even if it was futile, he had to try. While he stood, Gavian contemplated his good fortune in not only surviving the fight with Pythus but defeating him. Perhaps there was a bit of destiny at play here. Gripping the wheel firmly, a surge of confidence welled up inside him. This time he knew, deep in his core, that he would succeed. There was no way he could let Ambrielle down.

CHAPTER 26

A MBRIELLE HELD TIGHT to Darby while Dexius guided the brontha
out of the long field on the eastern side of Strakenbridge and toward
the forest. Wegin flew above them, scanning the surrounding area.
The trees ahead swayed oddly, and one of them crashed to the ground at
the edge of the woods. Giants began pouring out of the forest, perhaps a
hundred of them. These giants were taller and lankier than the ones they
were familiar with. Covered in white fur, the Gurrians were every bit as
fearsome as the Grundians. Some carried clubs and crude hammers, while
others pulled carts filled with stones and spears.

Dexius pulled the brontha hard to the left, taking them away from
the rows of giants, hopefully out of range of any stones they could throw.
They headed toward a tall embankment. It was too high for the brontha to
climb. Dexius instead turned them to ride alongside the base of the ridge.

The Gurrians noticed they were there but ignored them, seemingly too
focused on Strakenbridge. While the last Gurrian passed by, Dexius continued to drive them between the forest and the embankment. Ambrielle
looked back as the Gurrians hurled stones at the walls of Strakenbridge.

Through volleys of arrows, the giants charged the outer wall, launching stones and spears. One giant fell from the barrage, but what
might have been a hundred more continued to close in.

The forest closed around her, blocking the view of the battle as Dexius guided the brontha into the trees. She drew her focus back to the mission at hand. If they failed, Strakenbridge would fall, the same way every other city before it had. The forest became denser, and Dexius turned onto a path the Gurrians had made through the thicket.

"Maybe I should have gone with Gavian," said Darby, as the brontha slowed to step across a thick log.

"What makes you say that?" Ambrielle asked.

"I was just thinking," said Darby, "there are three of us together, but he's all alone."

"Yes, but he shouldn't be in any danger, and hopefully it won't take long," said Ambrielle.

"I know," said Darby. "It's just . . . you ever get that feeling of dread for no reason?"

"You're scaring me," said Ambrielle, pulling the blue jewel on her necklace until the chain was properly positioned. "What do you think is going to happen to Gavian?"

"Nothing, I hope," said Darby. "Maybe I'm just afraid for all of us."

"That's what I was saying before, but no one would listen," Dexius said. "I don't know why we left this all up to him."

"Why do you always have such low expectations of Gavian?" said Ambrielle. "He has accomplished quite a lot."

"What has he accomplished on his own?" Dexius said. "The last time we depended on him, he left us stranded."

"If it weren't for him, you would still be carrying buckets of water for the Grundians," said Ambrielle.

Dexius tapped the sides of the brontha with his boots. "I'm sure whatever he told you was exaggerated."

"I think you're getting him confused with yourself, Dex. I've never heard Gav exaggerate." Darby turned around to Ambrielle, smiling.

"If you're both going to gang up on me, let's just focus on the mission," said Dexius, as the brontha climbed over the stone-covered terrain.

"There are large life forms in the vicinity!" Wegin alerted them from above.

The forest ahead began to darken with the clouds swirling overhead.

They pressed on until a crashing sounded through the thicket. Dexius halted the brontha. Tearing their way through the trees, a group of six woolly Gurrians moved into a small clearing nearby.

Two of the giants sat down to rest on a thick log, while the others lay among the ferns. Dexius grimaced because it didn't appear they were going to leave soon. The wall of rock on the other side was too steep to climb. Dexius turned the brontha around and guided it back the way they'd come. Darby drew the bow from the sling on her back.

"What are you doing?" Ambrielle whispered.

"We don't have time to wait," said Dexius quietly. "I'm going to try and go around."

As the brontha trotted away from the giants, one of them stood and pointed. Soon, they were all standing. Breaking off limbs from nearby trees, the Gurrians tossed anything they could find while they charged at them. Dexius clapped the brontha with his boots and drove them across the path of the incoming Gurrians.

"Someone hand me my bow!" Dexius said, as he seemed to be trying to outflank the Gurrians.

Darby pulled an arrow from her quiver and drew back the string. "I'm holding mine right now!"

Ambrielle reached behind Darby, trying to get Dexius's bow from his sling. Darby fired, hitting one of the giants in the forehead. He grunted in pain, pulling out the arrow and tossing it aside. The Gurrians chased, and Dexius prodded the brontha to speed up. Ambrielle got Dexius's bow loose and eased it into his hand.

Bending her leg, Darby got her boot on top of the saddle and swung her other leg to the other side of the brontha, hitting Dexius in the back of the head in the process.

"Watch what you're doing!" said Dexius.

"Sorry," said Darby, returning to the saddle and facing toward the back end of the brontha. "Now keep it steady."

"I need to turn, so I can take a shot," said Dexius.

"Just keep us steady," Darby said, as she loaded another arrow and drew back the string. Ambrielle ducked out of the way when Darby aimed and released her next arrow, striking the chasing Gurrian in the soft part of its neck. The giant tumbled, causing the one behind him to trip over its body.

The other four began to gain on them as Darby loaded the next arrow. The giants' long strides gave them an advantage over the slower brontha. They headed toward one of the strange rock pillars, causing the animal to veer around it.

Darby fired and missed the giant. "Keep straight and steady!"

"If you haven't noticed, there are trees and rocks in the way!" Dexius shouted back. One of the Gurrians was getting close.

"Keep us as steady as you can." Darby took another arrow and readied her bow. "I'm going to run out of arrows."

"Watch yourself!" Wegin shouted, whizzing by.

Ambrielle turned, feeling a gust of wind as the nearest Gurrian swiped at her, missing by only a few feet. The brontha began to climb uphill, jostling Darby, who was trying to aim. When the giant swung his fist at Ambrielle again, she took her bladestaff and thrust it into his head. She blinked before the impact, unsure where exactly it hit him. She looked back in time to see the giant face down in the grass.

"Now *that* was vicious!" said Dexius as he turned around.

Darby aimed and fired into the line of Gurrians behind them. The arrow stuck in one's chest but didn't stop him.

"I should be the one shooting," Dexius said.

"Maybe if someone didn't insist on driving!" replied Darby, reaching for another arrow. "*I* would actually be able to keep us steady!" The three remaining Gurrians continued to race after them as they came to an open part of the forest. Taking one foot out of the stirrups, Dexius leaned out away from the brontha. With his body turned toward the rear, he fired an arrow toward one of the Gurrians.

"One shot, one"—Dexius watched while the Gurrian he fired at kept running after them.

"You missed!" Darby said excitedly.

"I never miss," Dexius said, continuing to lean around them. "Something must have gotten in the way."

"Yeah, that's called missing," said Darby.

"Dexius! Look out!" Ambrielle said, as a thick tree limb was rapidly coming toward him.

Dexius grabbed the brontha's harness, pulling himself upright in the saddle before the tree hit him on the way by.

"Stay on the saddle Dex," said Darby as she fired, hitting the giant that Dexius had missed. "I've got this."

The river bent further into the forest, giving them less room to maneuver. With the last two Gurrians drawing closer, Darby aimed and fired, nailing her arrow into the neck of one of the giants. She reached for another arrow as the last one caught up to them. Ambrielle swung her bladestaff around to get in position to stab at the incoming giant. The end of the staff hit a tangle of vines in the trees above, nearly knocking it out of her grip. The blade on the end sliced through them, freeing the splintered half of a tree suspended in the mass. The Gurrian reached to grab her, but the broken tree fell onto his head, crushing him into the ground.

"Pure brilliance!" cheered Dexius.

Ambrielle lowered her staff with a sheepish grin. "I wish I could say that was on purpose."

"Who's to say it wasn't?" Dexius grinned as he urged the brontha on between the rocky pillars and trees.

"I'm getting some unusual data from the regions ahead," said Wegin. "Numerous life sources, all centered around one mass."

As they rode further, the forest transformed, the vegetation around them dying off. Some unnatural darkness was rapidly spreading through the forest. The trees were coated in a thick black syrup that oozed down their trunks and dripped from their branches. The bark was moist and fleshy, and the leaves, stringy and withered, hung limply from the boughs. Some trees had bent under the weight of the decay and could no longer support themselves. The ground was littered with dry, ashy remnants mixed with piles of sludge.

Dexius reined in the brontha, bringing them to a sudden halt. It wasn't until then that they all noticed it: an immense shadow looming over the forest. It was a palpable darkness, enveloped by flickering, intense energy. Six elongated limbs extended from its monstrous shape, plunging into the ground before them. Rows of red eyes, each of varying sizes, swiveled independently, trained on Strakenbridge.

"Hide," whispered Ambrielle.

Dexius turned the brontha around, moving out of the blackened forest and underneath the broader cover of the living trees.

What have you come to offer us? Ogolameth spoke the words into Ambrielle's mind. *Your essence or your mind?*

"Did you hear that?" Dexius whispered.

"Yes," said Ambrielle. Darby nodded her head. "It knows we are here."

To complete the sublimation of this world, I prefer your essence, said Ogolameth. *Give your tedious lives purpose, be part of the assimilation of the Everance.*

"The Everance?" said Darby. "What is that?"

Ambrielle stared at Ogolameth's moving eyes. "It is everything in existence. There are places beyond this universe."

"What's a universe?" Darby asked, making Ambrielle realize that, other than on Rethia, Darby had never even seen the sky above the thick clouds of the lower atmosphere.

Come closer, said Ogolameth. *This physical medium constrains my true form. With more essence, I could surge through this world with boundless power. I would no longer need these giants to level your cities. Lead merely a hundred of your kin to me, and I will drain the giants instead.*

"Don't listen to him," Ambrielle said. "He plans to drain us all."

You cannot resist for long, said Ogolameth. *I am a direct emanation of Vazerinaz the Unyielding. Your will belongs to him.*

"What?" said Dexius.

"I don't know," said Ambrielle. "Let's get out of here!"

Ogolameth's thunderous roar ripped through the air. "Come closer!" His voice echoed, tinged with an otherworldly malevolence. The brontha, driven by some unseen force, reared on its hind legs and surged forward, galloping heedlessly into the decaying depths of the forest. Despite Dexius's desperate attempts to rein it in, the animal disregarded his efforts, carrying them relentlessly closer to the looming presence of Ogolameth.

Sensing the impending danger, Ambrielle's instincts kicked in. "Jump!"

she cried out, launching herself off the back of the brontha and tumbling into the murky abyss of the rotting muck below.

Dexius wrapped his body around Darby, protecting her as he leapt from the brontha. Once they gathered themselves from the fall, they sprinted toward Ambrielle, looking back on the grim spectacle unfolding before their eyes. They could only watch in helpless horror while the brontha charged forward, succumbing to the sinister grip of one of Ogolameth's colossal tendrils. The once-majestic creature withered away before their very eyes, reduced to a mere skeletal frame ensnared in the clutches of the eldritch appendage, while its ethereal essence was mercilessly drained into the voracious entity that was Ogolameth.

Ambrielle tried to wipe the stains of dark ooze onto the ground while she walked toward the living forest. She turned around as a boiling, bubbling sound rose behind them. Erupting from the underside of Ogolameth, three drops of darkness fell to the ground. Each surrounded by their own protective discs of energy, they hovered over the ground.

If you come and give your essence, I will spare everyone else! Ogolameth's voice hissed into her head.

The three Nulthereals charged toward them. Ambrielle readied her bladestaff as they split in different directions to come at them from all sides. Wegin zoomed to her side.

"Don't listen to the voices Wegin!" Ambrielle advised.

Wegin orbited slowly around her. "I'm not picking up any voices, other than the three of yours."

"Okay, good," Ambrielle said, relieved that Ogolameth's influence did not seem to work on electronic brains like Wegin's.

"Dex, take some of these arrows!" Darby gave him a handful of arrows tipped with mekkadium.

Dexius swiftly placed all but one of the mekkadium arrows into his quiver, taking aim at the nearest Shadow barreling toward them. With a powerful shot, the arrow lodged itself into the amorphous surface, causing the Shadow to crack and weaken. "Darby, take out the ones on the right and left with one arrow each. Then, fire at will," he commanded.

Darby prepared her bow to take aim. With a focused shot, she hit the Shadow on the right with pinpoint accuracy.

Meanwhile, Dexius launched another arrow toward the weakened center of the Nulthereal, shattering it into pieces. Its disk of energy hurtled toward Ogolameth, merging with the essence surrounding him. Not missing a beat, Darby turned and let loose her next shot, aiming for the Shadow rapidly approaching Ambrielle. Wegin sped upward, moving out of the line of fire.

Projecting his light scanners toward the Shadows, Wegin pointed them out. "I will target the nearest enemy for you."

Dexius aimed his next shot at Wegin's target, a Nulthereal on Darby's side, firing two quick shots, the first impact weakening it. The second arrow disintegrated the Nulthereal, its energy returning to Ogolameth. Ambrielle charged forward, her bladestaff at the ready, and sliced through the remaining Nulthereal with ease, tearing it apart into chunks of rock, pebbles, and dust. Its ring of energy hung in the air for a moment before flying past them in the other direction. As they turned around, the energy flowed toward an approaching rider, absorbed into a silver sword raised in his hand.

CHAPTER 27

T HE TWISTED BRANCHES of the trees reached out like contorted limbs, their gnarled forms seeming to writhe with malevolence. The air grew heavy with a suffocating darkness, suffusing Ambrielle's senses with an unshakable feeling of foreboding. Sinister tendrils of blackness snaked through the undergrowth, curling and twisting with a life of their own. They seemed to grasp at her, their touch igniting a primal unease within her. Ogolameth loomed over the forest. His red eyes cast a haunting glow that pierced through the gloom of the forest. Each crimson gaze seemed to peer into the depths of their very souls.

Thunderous sounds reverberated through the air while Gavian approached, wielding a new blade.

"The essence contained in that sword belongs to me!" Ogolameth's voice echoed through the forest. "Bring it forth!"

Gavian quickly sheathed the sword. "Run! We need to find higher ground!" he shouted, stopping the agile jagstrider.

"We lost the brontha," Darby lamented, lowering her bow.

"Get on!" Gavian shouted, as the ground shook beneath them.

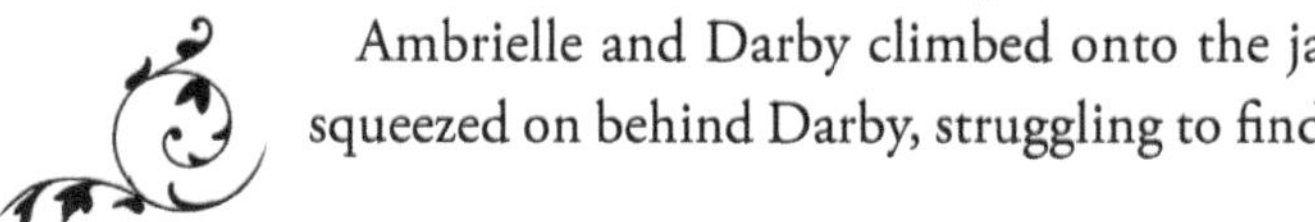

Ambrielle and Darby climbed onto the jagstrider, and Dexius squeezed on behind Darby, struggling to find enough room, while the ground continued to quake. Gavian spurred the animal into motion. "Where should we go?"

Wegin flew toward a nearby ridge. "You should be able to climb here!"

The jagstrider weaved through the trees, avoiding obstacles as they raced toward the ridge. They passed two Gurrians, one of whom had been felled by Darby's arrow, while the other gave chase.

As they reached the base of the cliff, water began to flood through the forest, rising quickly. Gavian urged the jagstrider on toward Wegin's position where there was a more gradual slope in the cliff wall. The water continued to rise, soon reaching Dexius's feet.

Meanwhile, the pursuing Gurrian was undeterred by the rushing waters and continued to waddle toward them. Suddenly, a massive wave surged toward them, sending water cascading over the saddle. The group struggled to maintain their balance with the current growing stronger, and the Gurrian drew ever closer.

Darby twisted her body on the strider, struggling to aim her bow at the approaching Gurrian. Dexius, behind her, shouted in protest. "You're about to push me off!"

As logs and debris floated by, she finally managed to fire, hitting the giant in the hand. Enraged, the giant yanked out the arrow and charged toward them. As the giant lunged at them again, he slipped and was swept away by the current.

The jagstrider, however, also lost its footing, and the river carried them all downstream. The strider kicked its hind legs and swam hard against the current, maneuvering along the ridge's edge. The water surged over the lower cliff, but the jagstrider used the slope of the ridge to ascend the mound. Finally, they reached the top, and the exhausted animal came to a halt. Ambrielle climbed off the creature and opened her satchel. Taking out the compacted geowave, she started to throw it on the ground, but was afraid it would fall into the water. Instead, she held the metal square while beating it hard against the rocks until it opened into the geowave.

Gavian, Darby, and Dexius followed after her as she ran across the ridge to get closer to Ogolameth. When they approached, more Shadows bubbled from Ogolameth and flew toward them. Ambrielle fired the geowave at the monster, its high-pitched waves barely audible. Nothing happened.

"Unknown objects coming in fast," Wegin reported, joining them on the ridge and using his scanner beam again to show the nearest target. He could calculate distance faster than any of them, and Ambrielle hoped that Dexius would use the advantage.

Dexius and Darby raised their bows to the incoming Nulthereals. "Like we did before," said Dexius. "Use your speed to weaken as many as you can. I'll use my precision to finish them off."

Rapidly drawing arrow after arrow from her quiver, Darby fired on the Nulthereals that Wegin pointed out. "You just want to still be able to say, 'one shot one kill,'" she joked.

"Maybe," replied Dexius, as he followed up her hits with precise shots that shattered the weakened Nulthereals.

"More giants approaching from the west and northwest," Wegin stated.

Gurrians emerged from around the flowing waters, scaling up the cliffside. While Dexius and Darby maintained their fire against the Nulthereals, one of the towering giants seized Dexius by the leg. Gavian rapidly made his way to the cliff's edge, witnessing Darby's arrow pierce the Gurrian's left eye. The giant relinquished its grip on Dexius, and both of them plummeted toward the unforgiving rocks below. Acting quickly, Gavian activated the lylace in his silbrace, catching Dexius.

As Gavian strained against the weight of Dexius, he braced his boots against the rocks near the edge to keep from being pulled over. Darby unleashed a flurry of arrows, fending off more Gurrians that climbed up after them. The projectiles found their marks, creating a brief respite in their assault. Amidst the chaos, Darby quickly moved to Gavian's side, her strong grip on his arm providing an anchor of support. Once Dexius's hands reached the edge of the cliff, Darby swiftly shifted her attention, rushing to his aid. Dexius found his footing and crawled back to solid ground. They all breathed a sigh of relief as they moved away from the precipice.

"Your feeble attempts at resistance amuse me. Can you not feel the weight of your insignificance against the might of my eternal power?" Ogolameth's voice resonated. He seemed to have abandoned the seductive whispers in their mind, now seeking to break their resolve. Moving slowly, he inched toward the cliff wall, continuing to boil Shadows from his body to attack them.

"Your futile defiance only serves to deepen the darkness that will envelop your souls," Ogolameth murmured ominously.

Dexius grabbed his bow, and he and Darby went back to work defending the cliff. Against Kyron's advice, Ambrielle turned all three dials to the max. She raised the geowave, her arms tingling. She began to feel weak. Gavian ran to her screaming, but she couldn't hear his shouts. Ogolameth was draining the life essence from her. Her conscious thoughts faded into nothingness.

Lightning shot into her veins as the feeling of life burst into her. Gavian held her against his body while he poured the essence from Pythus's sword into her. With renewed strength, Ambrielle grabbed the geowave from the ground.

With venomous malice, Ogolameth spoke again, "Embrace the despair, for in the end, all will be swallowed by the eternal night."

As Dexius continued firing, he bumped into Gavian, forcefully nudging him toward Ambrielle, as he positioned himself to shield Gavian from a group of approaching Nulthereals. He joined Darby in a seamless rhythm, firing mekkadium arrows that picked off the encroaching Shadows with precision. Gavian held onto Ambrielle, preventing Ogolameth from siphoning the life from her by filling her with the energy in the sword. Ambrielle pressed the trigger, dividing the air with the geowave's rippling beam.

Everything around them was silenced with the pulse beam rippling into the energy shield of Ogolameth. With gritted teeth, Ambrielle held tight as every ounce of the geowave's energy erupted. She refused to relent, and the life essence surrounding Ogolameth began to fracture and crumble.

"Nothing will stop the Gaith from destroying your universe!" growled Ogolameth. "Nothing!"

The organic energy that separated Ogolameth from the matter of the universe dissipated, leaving only a pattern of small particles in the air. Ogolameth's dark aethrum form spilled into the waters. As it solidified, the aethrum piled high above the river until it formed a massive black stone pillar, a smaller version of Mekkinspire.

Ambrielle released the trigger of the geowave and lowered it to the ground. The essence energy that had sustained Ogolameth's form in the physical universe surged into the silver sword, knocking Gavian off his feet. He blinked rapidly, dazed, as the sword glowed with intense green light. Ambrielle offered her hand, helping him to his feet.

"How did you manage to steal that sword from Pythus?" Ambrielle inquired, her gaze transfixed on the gleaming blade resting on Gavian's back.

Gavian grasped the hilt, his fingers tracing the intricate engravings. "His essence now resides within the blade," he revealed, a bit of solemn pride in his voice.

Ambrielle's eyebrows shot up in astonishment. "So, you defeated him? How?"

Gavian nodded. "If you grind a blade down enough, eventually it becomes sharp," he added with a smirk.

Ambrielle shook her head, trying to hide her smile. She wasn't sure if he was making fun of her or not but felt good knowing he had been listening to her words all this time. She had never seen this level of confidence in his eyes. "I wonder if you should keep that sword with you. With all the evil things it has done."

"Why wouldn't I?" Gavian said. "The evil was Pythus, not the sword. We can use it for good."

Their attention was soon drawn back to Strakenbridge. The Gurrians were retreating toward the north, heading away from the rising currents of the river. They climbed back onto the jagstrider and rode across the ridge to the western gate.

They navigated through the streets, the soldiers cheering with confused joy. Some attended to the wounded, while others jumped up and down, holding their hands high. Wegin's upper half spun back and forth while he took in all the various types of data. Dexius nearly fell off the jagstrider as he pumped his fist and shouted along with them. Darby's face broke into a huge smile, and she waved to everyone they passed. Ambrielle sat as tall as she could on the back of the animal, needing to express her elation. Meanwhile, Gavian remained solemn, as if savoring the moment.

However, when they approached the eastern wall, the sight of dead

Gurrians, Grundians, and soldiers littering the street filled them with dread. The once-lively street now felt like a battlefield. The destruction of the wall had allowed the giants to enter the city, and the wounded were being loaded onto carts pulled by docimares. Some soldiers were celebrating the victory, but others looked distraught at the loss of their comrades. A mix of sadness and anger stirred within Ambrielle as she surveyed the destruction and the loss of life. They had won, but at what cost?

She realized that destiny or fate wasn't always pretty. Many times, the storm was too great. There's no guarantee you will survive to learn from your mistakes. Sometimes life ends before it is given the chance to grow stronger.

"I wish I had more energy left in my silbrace," said Ambrielle, watching bloodied and bruised young men and women being lifted into the carts.

Gavian turned to her. "Do you think there is time to get back to Solsellion for more energy cells?"

"It's two days to get back to the waterfall"—Ambrielle's heart sank at the thought—"then back. Anyone critical would be dead, especially without modern medicine even by Earth standards."

"Maybe there is something we can do." Gavian's eyes were fixed on the stained cobblestone street. "I just feel a little weird about doing it."

"What do you mean?" Ambrielle titled her head, waiting for his response.

Gavian stopped the strider and dismounted. His eyes reflected a storm of conflict, determined but hesitant. Heading toward the carts of wounded soldiers, he removed the sheath with the silver sword. Keeping the blade covered, Gavian raised the pulsing crystal in the pommel toward them. "May I see your wounds?" he asked one of the soldiers being tended to. The soldier nodded yes, and the nurse moved aside revealing many cuts and puncture wounds in the man's side. The life energy of the blade flowed into his wounds, healing some completely while improving others. Ambrielle rushed over, with several of the soldiers waving their hands, hoping their wounds could be healed as well.

Ambrielle's mouth dropped open as she recognized the sword's power. It healed better than even the beam of her silbrace. She hurried toward the broken wall with Wegin, searching for more injured. Darby and Dexius joined her and signaled Gavian to bring the sword to them. By the time the sun began to edge behind the walls, all but the most severe wounds had been healed or improved. They unfortunately still lost a few who were beyond the healing of the essence energy to save.

The Everance might not be completely fair and just, but it was not without hope. It was a constant battle of righting what was wrong, an unyielding pursuit of balance and righteousness. It required the courage to confront the shadows lurking within oneself, those hidden depths that threatened to consume and corrupt. It demanded the unwavering resolve to illuminate those shadows, to shed light upon the darkness and disperse it with the radiance of truth and goodness. It was through this transformative journey, both within and without, that the flickering flames of hope grew brighter, dispelling the shadows that sought to engulf the world.

The silver blade of Pythus had accomplished great things, but Gavian was nonetheless troubled by it. A feeling rose in the pit of his stomach, the nauseating pang of guilt for using this kind of power. Something lurked deep within the blade that he did not understand or want to. A sword with the power to take life and give it to others was not something created of a virtuous mind. Gavian's true blade remained the rokensword—Storm-waker, if it truly was the legendary blade. Even if it wasn't, he would do his best to make it legendary, to use it honorably to defend and protect others. He would only use the silver blade of Pythus as a last resort, until the last bit of essence was gone from it.

As night approached, many of the soldiers sat around a bonfire. The air was filled with chatter of stories being told, from tragic to heroic. "I don't know." One of the archers shook his head in disbelief as he spoke to Dexius. "They were systematically destroying our defenses. They broke through the walls, and the archers had to fall back, while the lancers and swordsmen tried to stop them from advancing into the city. Several giants breached the wall, we would have been done for, but they got sloppy. I don't know what hap-pened, but it was like they suddenly didn't know what to do. They seemed confused and clustered together. We surrounded them and started picking them off one by one while the lancers kept them from getting to us."

Ambrielle put her hands gently on Gavian's shoulders. "I've never felt more certain that I am exactly where I was meant to be."

"Neither have I." Gavian leaned forward. "Even though so much went wrong. I failed as much as I succeeded. I don't know if there is an actual plan, but there does seem to be an order beyond us that exists to tame the chaos."

Resting her head on his shoulder, she brushed lightly over the scrapes and scratches on his arm. "Weathering the storm. If it were easy, we would never grow. That's the point. It's not how you face the good times, it's how we deal with the bad. I've always said just because there's a reason doesn't mean we will enjoy all of it."

"I wish my father were here so he could see that I did something right," said Gavian.

"I'm sure he knows. That's why he protected you from the giants," Ambrielle said. "I wish I could tell my mother about all this when I get home. Even though she would never believe me,"—her fingers searched for the blue jewel on her necklace, making sure it was still there—"but I feel like she's somehow been with me this whole time. Maybe there really is an Afterglow or some kind of afterlife." As if reading her thoughts, Gavian drew her to him, wrapping his arms around her.

After night fell over the city, everyone moved to another area, untouched by the stains of battle. The soldiers and citizens continued their celebration, lighting torches in the center of town near the fountain. Perhaps caught up in the exhilaration of the moment, their victory against all odds, most everyone put aside the grief of loss and came together for what they had left. The pleasing smells of smoked meats filled the area as musicians brought out horns and stringed instruments to entertain. Though different from the instruments Ambrielle knew on Earth, they served the same purpose.

Many of the women had changed into brightly colored dresses. Some of the citizens began to dance to the lively music. Their dance was unfamiliar with lots of stepping and swaying. A soldier stepped out of the crowd toward Darby and Dexius next to them.

"Nemeris!" Ambrielle shouted in surprise. It was the first time she had seen him since Rethia. Until now she'd had no idea if he'd survived. He flashed a smile at Ambrielle and turned to Darby, who peered up at him shyly.

"Ah, I see it in your eyes. Life without dancing is like a day without laughter: dull and utterly wasted." Nemeris held out his hand to Darby.

Darby chuckled and gave him her hand. "The very words I live by."

"What are you doing, Nem?" Dexius said. "Darby has had a rough week. There are plenty of other girls around here."

"It's only a dance," Ambrielle told him. "Let her have some fun."

Dexius shrugged while Darby walked with Nemeris into the group, dancing around the fountain. Ambrielle couldn't help but laugh as they moved together in uncoordinated motions. Gavian leaned to Ambrielle, kissing her on the cheek near her nose. She glanced up at him, wrapping her hands on the back of his neck when he kissed her cheek. Before he drew away, she pulled his face to hers, kissing him on the lips. With a smile, she grabbed his hand and pulled him toward the group of people dancing. He shook his head, standing firm on the cobblestones. "My motto is don't make a fool of yourself."

Ambrielle tugged on his arm. "But where's the fun in that?" She pulled until he finally gave in and let her guide him to the group.

"We never danced in Rethia," Gavian said, putting his hands on her waist. "I have no idea what to do."

She had never been fond of dancing, at least not in front of people, but something about the moment, or maybe it was everything that had led to this moment, made her cast aside her usual inhibitions and try something new. The music and atmosphere were infectious. "Don't worry, neither do I."

As ridiculous as she felt, she couldn't help but laugh at herself and at Gavian since they couldn't accomplish anything resembling synchronization. Before long, she stopped thinking about how she appeared and relaxed. She let the music guide them as they moved in unison with the other dancers.

"Who is that dancing with Vilura?" Ambrielle asked, while they followed the others.

Gavian slowed his movements, searching the crowd. He seemed to have a pleased look on his face when he spotted her. "Oh, that's Hilvan, the swordmaster."

Wegin seemed as though he was beginning to understand the celebration. He soared over to Ambrielle and Gavian, flashing his lights in changing colors while orbiting around them as they circled the fountain with the group. They spotted Lirah and Neylin joining in the dance too. Ambrielle felt like the pieces that remained of this world were falling into place. Lirah waved to them when they passed by.

Even though many of the others exchanged dancing partners, Ambrielle wasn't about to let go of Gavian. He turned her as they danced, drawing her attention to two people heading into the group. Vilura was now dancing with Dexius, and Ambrielle couldn't help but notice that the two of them moved surprisingly well together.

As it grew late, the celebration outside began to subside. Ambrielle, Darby, Gavian, and Dexius returned to the barracks for the night. Laying in the small bed, it was the first time Ambrielle could relax and process everything that had happened recently. She wanted to recount it all, every detail. While she debated where to begin, Ambrielle's consciousness slipped out of the waking world as she fell asleep.

CHAPTER 28

Gavian stood outside the entrance of the women's barracks, scanning the area for any sign of Ambrielle or Darby. Could they have left before he woke up? After waiting a little longer, he decided to venture away from the building and search for them. Making his way down a short street toward one of the towering structures in the city center, he witnessed a bustling scene of soldiers and workers engaged in the rebuilding efforts. Carrying stones, hammering, and sawing wood, the city was alive with activity.

Away from the bustling activity, a woman sat against one of the buildings, her quiet sobs resonating against the sounds of construction. Others gathered around her, offering consolation in their own empathetic silence. She was just one of many, others likely confined within the walls of their homes, mourning the irreplaceable losses. In that moment, his thoughts gravitated toward his own father, recognizing that every future occurrence would be accompanied by an unrelenting yearning—an ache to share these significant moments, to bask in the presence of his father's guidance and wisdom once more.

 Though stone walls and buildings could be rebuilt, the lives of the residents would forever bear the scars of this battle. Even though the city strove to regain its former glory, the journey

toward a semblance of normalcy seemed insurmountable for these afflicted souls. Yet, amidst the despair, he felt a glimmer of hope—their victory at least afforded an opportunity to begin anew, to reclaim what was lost, and to heal.

Suddenly, someone cleared their throat behind Gavian, prompting him to turn around. It was Dexius, his usually confident face now adorned with a rare look of uncertainty.

"Hey Gavian," Dexius began, clearing his throat once more. "I just wanted to say thank you."

Gavian raised an eyebrow, his jaw relaxing. "Thank me? For what?"

Dexius shifted his weight uncomfortably. "For saving my life back there. I don't know how you managed to pull me up that cliff, but I owe you one. If it weren't for you, I would be a goner."

A sheepish smile formed on Gavian's face as he scratched the back of his head. "I suppose we're even then. You've saved my life too, more times than I probably realize."

Dexius nodded, a hint of pride in his expression. "We made a pretty good team."

"We always have," Gavian agreed, his gaze fixed on the stone street. He felt a nagging urge to say something more. "How is your family doing now? Your mother and your sister?"

"They're fine," said Dexius. "Although, apart from my sister, I don't truly consider them family. Not my true family, at least."

Gavian's heart sank while he wondered if Dexius included him in that genuine family he spoke of. "I know I've said it before, but I am sorry I left Isodonia," said Gavian. "It was never my intention to abandon you and Darby like that."

"Well, you did come back," Dexius acknowledged. "And we never would have accomplished all this without you."

Gavian rubbed his face, ensuring no tears escaped his eyes. "As you said, we made a pretty good team."

⚘

Ambrielle meandered through the solemn corridors formed by columns of exquisitely carved stone. Her gaze fixated on the intricate patterns adorning the massive blocks that composed the street's corner. The euphoria of triumph and the jubilation of the previous night's revelries had dissipated, replaced by the weighty burden of war that consumed her every thought. The haunting image of Thomin's lifeless form lingered relentlessly in her mind.

In the larger picture he may have been just one boy, but to her he represented all of the lives lost in this war. Even though victory had been achieved, the cost weighed heavily upon her heart. This world had been irreparably stripped of so much, a relentless tide of irreplaceable souls forever lost. It felt as though the very fabric of the universe had been tainted and could never be fully restored to its former essence.

The deep-seated wound of grief she had carried since her mother's passing had been reopened, its pain mingling with the fresh sorrow of this war. Ambrielle wasn't sure if it would ever heal. In her moments of despair, she clung to a fragile strand of hope—time. Perhaps with its passage, her memories would gradually relinquish their grip on these tormenting thoughts, allowing her to move forward and find solace in the ever-changing currents of life.

Amidst the overwhelming weight of sorrow, she directed her thoughts to all she had to be thankful for. Ambrielle still had her father and her little brother. Her relationship with Gavian was growing stronger by the day. New friendships had been formed, and she had accomplished more than she ever thought she was capable of. She reflected on the remarkable journey she had embarked upon, surpassing her own expectations and embracing her untapped potential. The universe, vast and mysterious, unfurled before her with countless reasons to persist. There was enough beauty, love, and possibility to fuel her unyielding determination. For the sake of her loved ones, for the future she dared to envision, she would strive to bring an end to the Shadows forever.

Ambrielle's steps slowed as she approached a brick ledge where Darby sat quietly. The air around them seemed hushed, as if nature itself held its breath in reverence. Wegin, ever watchful, hovered by Ambrielle's left shoulder, casting a gentle glow.

Darby's gaze was fixed upon the vibrant flowers that adorned the small garden, their petals kissed by the soft rays of the covered sun. In her hands, she held a worn book, its pages filled with her musings and discoveries. With deliberate care, she selected different colored stones, rubbing their dust onto the pages.

When she noticed Ambrielle, Darby closed the book and set it in her lap.

"Were you drawing?" Ambrielle asked.

Darby held the book tightly. "Just trying to find something to do."

"May I see it?" Ambrielle said.

Hesitating for a moment, Darby reluctantly handed the book to her. "It's not very good."

Ambrielle looked at the sketch of a white flower with pink speckles. The drawing was quite detailed, especially considering the chalky stones she had to work with. "It's beautiful, why would you think it's not good?"

Darby glanced at the flower. "It doesn't look exactly right."

"It doesn't have to look exactly like it," said Ambrielle. "It's your interpretation, an expression of your feelings and how you see the world."

"It's a lidradary," said Darby with a hint of sadness in her voice. "My mother's favorite flower."

Ambrielle smiled. "I'm sure she would love it."

Darby's face lit up as she glanced at Ambrielle. "What are you going to do now? Are you going to stay in Strakenbridge?"

"I'm afraid I can't." Ambrielle adjusted her necklace, making sure the blue jewel was centered. "I have to check on things at home. Aside from that, we have to try and stop the Nulvarians from ever entering worlds like Isodonia again."

"Can't you stay a little longer?" Darby's eyes turned downcast. It surprised Ambrielle a little to see the disappointment in her face.

"I've been gone too long already," Ambrielle said. "My dad will probably ground me until I'm thirty."

"I'm going to miss you and Gavian," Darby said. "But at least this time I'll know he's alive and doing well."

"I don't know for sure that Gavian will want to leave," said Ambrielle. "He's been wanting to come here ever since he got his memory back."

"Don't worry," Darby reassured her. "There is no chance he's going anywhere without you."

Ambrielle felt warmth spread through her cheeks. "I hope you are right."

"Right about what?" said Gavian, walking toward the garden.

"I was just telling Darby that I have to leave soon." Ambrielle stood with her arms crossed, taking in a deep breath while she waited for Gavian's response.

Gavian sat beside Darby on a large, flat stone, his hand resting on his knee as he spoke. "We both do; as much as I hate to leave again, there's more work to be done elsewhere." Ambrielle breathed a sigh of relief.

Darby leaned forward. "Where will you two be going?"

"To a place called Solsellion," Gavian said. "We might have stopped the Shadows here, but there are other worlds out there facing their destruction. We have to find some way to stop it from happening. If we don't, they will return to Isodonia and finish what they started."

Ambrielle could see the weight of responsibility in his eyes, but there was also hope in his voice. She nodded, her mind racing with the enormity of the task. "That brings up another problem." Ambrielle felt a pang of sadness. She had grown attached to Darby, Dexius, and all the people she had met here. "We have to close off the rift so the Shadows cannot return to Isodonia."

Darby's face paled. "Only the Shadows or does that mean you won't be able to come back either?"

Ambrielle kneeled next to Darby. "We don't know what will happen. I can't take the chance of being stuck here with no way to get home. I can't leave my dad and my little brother behind like that. But we have to close as many of these rifts as we can."

"I'll help you close it if I can." Darby nodded, her eyes brimming with tears. "You should both be together. We don't have to see each other to be a family. I'll always think of both of you no matter where you are." Darby stood and wrapped her arms around Gavian. Ambrielle could see the pain in his face as he hugged her back.

"If this is the right thing to do, why does it feel so bad?" said Gavian, clenching his eyes shut.

"Because sometimes the wrong choice is the right one." Darby released Gavian and hugged Ambrielle.

"We saved a world together," said Ambrielle, as she hugged Darby back. "We'll never forget you, or Dexius either."

Suddenly a huge furry animal bounded over to them and bumped against Gavian's leg. He reached down, petting Flumpy for a moment before she nearly jumped on Darby, forcing her to sit on the stone. Flumpy licked the side of her face, bringing back her smile.

Vilura and Dexius made their way over, and Darby recounted what they had been discussing.

"I will help," Dexius said, after he heard about Darby sealing the rift. "I hope this time we've seen the last of the Shadows."

"Maybe one day we'll be recorded in the tomes of Strakenbridge," Vilura said.

"They'll need more than a few tomes to write about me," Dexius joked.

"Now that the war is over," said Ambrielle, "what do you plan to do?"

"I plan on eating," Dexius said. "I have a lot of catching up to do."

"When did you ever stop?" Ambrielle laughed.

Dexius crossed his arms. "I mean some real food."

Darby chuckled. "I don't know what I will do yet. Everything is wide open now with the war over. I suppose it will be fun to figure out."

"Hilvan, Bradwyn, and I are heading to the Gulflands," Vilura said. "We need to spread the news that the war is over. Maybe many will return to these lands in time.

Bradwyn called Flumpy to his side. "All citizens and soldiers are gathering in the courtyard to eat. We're using the rations we have left to feed everyone until things get back to . . . well, until everything is working again. You may want to eat again before you leave. I'm afraid it won't be quite the same food, though, as we ate last night."

❧

Ambrielle watched as a group of Strakenbridge civilians carried tables and stacks of wooden bowls into the courtyard outside the barracks. Ambrielle and Gavian followed Dexius to a bench where many others gathered to eat. Wegin watched and listened to all the sights and sounds as he floated above Ambrielle. More of the soldiers filed in, and some of the civilians brought them a bowl of the same thick stuff they had been eating nearly every day.

"Did you see what they are serving Gav?" Ambrielle teased.

Gavian glanced at her. "No, what?"

"Your favorite," she replied.

He looked behind them while some of the servers carried bowls of gruel to the tables. "Not this again."

"Here you go," said a white-haired girl, as she set a bowl in front of Dexius. "Dex! I didn't realize that was you!" Lirah set another bowl in front of Gavian, skipping Darby and Ambrielle. "And Tav! I heard about all the great things you both have done to save Strakenbridge! I think Dexius boasts about you as much as he does himself!"

"I don't talk about him," muttered Dexius.

"It's okay Dex," Lirah said. "Nothing wrong with bragging on a friend."

"Who said he's my friend?" said Dexius.

Lirah placed her hand on Dexius's shoulder. "I guess you are more like brothers now." She turned to Gavian. "I'm sorry about your father, Tav. I didn't get a chance to say anything before." Lirah's positivity that Gavian had described seemed to have returned, despite all the sorrow.

"I'm sorry about your parents as well," Gavian said.

"Thank you. So, what do you guys plan to do now?" Lirah said. "It seems like the war is over."

"We're leaving soon," Gavian said. "There is more work to do elsewhere."

"Elsewhere?" Lirah's brow furrowed. "Tav, there's plenty to do here. You always wanted to fix things, building them better than they were before. Now you have a whole city that needs rebuilding. It's almost like fate led you to this, where you are needed most."

Ambrielle glanced at Gavian, waiting for his reaction.

"I feel like I'm being led on a certain path now. There are other things I need to help fix first," said Gavian. "The giants weren't acting on their own. We have to make sure this doesn't happen again."

"I know you'll do the right thing, whatever it may be," said Lirah, grabbing two more bowls from a man carrying a large platter filled with them. She set them in front of Darby and Ambrielle. "But I was right about one thing."

"What's that?" said Gavian, as he swallowed a mouthful of food.

"I told you that someday we would all be here together on Rootcore," said Lirah. "You, me, and Dexius."

Gavian smiled. "I guess you were right, but I didn't expect it to be anything like this."

"Nor I, I thought it would be quite different," said Lirah. She leaned over and kissed him on the back of the head. "You'll always be my best friend, Tav." Dexius turned around when she was about to kiss him, making her pause and redirect the kiss to his forehead. "Both of you will," she added.

Lirah gestured between Dexius and Darby. "Are you two . . . together?"

Dexius laughed. "No, Darby is—"

"He's like my big brother," Darby said, as she playfully punched his shoulder.

"Oh, that's sweet," Lirah said. "You couldn't find much better than Dex."

Ambrielle sat quietly eating the bowl of gruel, when Lirah turned to her.

"I saw the two of you dancing," Lirah said. "You looked perfect together."

Gavian looked at Ambrielle as he put his arm around her. "We are."

Lirah smiled. "I knew you would find the perfect girl."

As Lirah officially introduced herself, Ambrielle thought about the way Lirah had treated Gavian in the past. As much as she wanted to dislike her, Ambrielle couldn't help but find her polite and sweet. With the combination of charm and her unique natural beauty, Ambrielle could see why Gavian once had a crush on her. Even though it was in the past, it still made her a bit insecure.

Once they finished eating, Gavian took Ambrielle's hand and walked over to where his mother and Valea were sitting.

"Tav! Come on sit with us," his mother said when she saw him.

Gavian put his arm around her. "Mother, I would like you to officially meet Ambrielle."

"Oh," his mother said, glancing at Ambrielle. "This is one of the girls you met on Rootcore? Are you promised to each other yet?"

Gavian twisted his lips together. He seemed a bit embarrassed at the question. He peeked over at Ambrielle. She figured he probably didn't know how to answer with her standing there. He wouldn't want to answer too strongly in either direction. "Not exactly. We haven't known each other that long."

"Well, how long do you need?" his mother said. Ambrielle was quietly amused by the stress Gavian must've been feeling right now.

"There's been a lot going on," said Gavian. "We haven't talked about a lot of things yet."

"How long does it take to talk?" she said, turning to Ambrielle. "Do you like him?"

Gavian answered for her, "That's for us to talk about."

"Well, it seems you're getting nowhere on your own," his mother said.

Ambrielle wrapped her arm around his waist. "I think I do kinda like him."

His mother nodded her head. "I can tell by how red his face is getting that he likes *you*."

"Mom—" Gavian looked away for a moment before bringing his attention back. "I came to tell you, well with," he said. "Ambrielle and I are leaving for a while. I don't know when I'll be back."

His mother got up from the table and hugged him. "With everything that has happened since you left the mountain, I hope you find peace."

"I've already found everything I need." Gavian pulled Ambrielle closer. "But there are things that must be done. I don't even know how to explain it."

"Whatever it is, I'm sure you'll accomplish it," said his mother.

"Despite the fact that you used to wet yourself in the middle of the market," Valea joked, "I always knew you would find someone."

"That only happened once." Gavian turned between Ambrielle and Valea. "And only to embarrass you."

"Embarrass me?" Valea said. "I'm not the one who wet their pants."

Ambrielle couldn't help but giggle.

"Don't encourage her," quipped Gavian.

Stifling a laugh, Ambrielle turned and noticed Dexius saying goodbye to his mother and sister. He stood next to his mother, looking straight ahead, his arms crossed. They seemed more like acquaintances than family. Dexius gave his sister a quick hug and started toward them.

"Well be with you both," Gavian told them while Dexius walked up.

Before they turned to leave, Valea tugged at Gavian's shirt. "Don't blame yourself for father's death." Gavian's eyes dropped as she continued. "I only say this because I know that you will. You were protecting us, just as he was protecting you. It isn't your fault."

Gavian nodded, putting his arms around her in return.

⌘

Across the river and down the road, the jagstriders carried Ambrielle, Gavian, Darby, and Dexius toward the mountain with Wegin floating along in the air, the group stopping only at nightfall to rest. They made it to the waterfall the next evening.

Gavian waded through the shallow waters that trickled into the chasm, stepping onto a trail of rocks around the wall of the mountain. Darby and Dexius stared at the waterfall as it crashed over rocks on its way to the pool that fed into the lake.

"This is it." Gavian stood before the dark chasm, the pools of water pouring into it. "This is where we killed the Blight Whidge."

Dexius gazed up at the great falls cascading down the mountain. "Where you lost your memory?"

"Yes, the first time I went through," he said. "It didn't happen on the way back."

Ambrielle reached out to him. "I think it's because we had some of the substance of The Hollow on us by then, or mekkadium I guess is what it is."

"You believe me now?" Gavian said.

Dexius turned and walked toward the jagstrider. "Well, you proved there is a waterfall."

Ambrielle handed Darby one of the small round pieces of plastra. "You remember how to use it, right?"

"Place it on the ground outside the opening of the vault in the cave and tell it to repair," Darby said. "That sounds a bit crazy when I say it."

"There's a lot of crazy things beyond this world," said Ambrielle. She and Gavian gave Darby one last hug. Dexius extended his hand to Ambrielle, but instead of shaking it, she wrapped her arms around him. He gently squeezed her back in return. Dexius then stepped over to Gavian.

"I can't say I believe all this," Dexius said, as Gavian gave him a hesitant hug. "But it was good to see you again for a little while."

Gavian let go, straightening out his tunic. "It was good to see you too."

Ambrielle and Gavian waded into the water, climbing onto the stones around the plunge pool.

"Wegin, I'm going to have to put you in my bag again for a bit," Ambrielle said.

Reluctantly, he swooped into her satchel. Ambrielle turned and gave Darby and Dexius one last wave, and Gavian joined her. Stepping near the swirling mist, Ambrielle held out her hand to him. "We'll go together."

Taking her hand, Gavian walked forward with her as the water beat down on them. Everything went dark. Ambrielle held onto his hand tight with the world tumbling around them. In the dark space, a tunnel of water flowed around them, the roaring now muffled.

A familiar soul has entered our domain, the girl who swims between worlds, said a voice that seemed to echo into eternity. *Your flourishing gardens will wither and decay, and you shall have nowhere to run. As you waste time saving but one world, we effortlessly claim hundreds more. The moment is fast approaching when we shall open the initial pathway through the Everance, and you will be left behind in the eternal night. Alone and bereft, you shall ponder the worth of delaying the inevitable for but a fleeting moment amidst the expanse of eternity.*

As Gavian and Ambrielle crossed over the gulf of time and space, they emerged from the waterfall inside the Darterran caverns on Anatharia. Gavian launched the light rope toward the circle of fading light coming through the ceiling.

"Hold on tight," said Gavian. His silbrace retracted the rope, carrying them to the hole above. He helped Ambrielle push her way out into the darkening forest. Settled on her knees, she returned the favor by assisting Gavian as he climbed out.

Ambrielle let Wegin out of her satchel, and he returned to her shoulder. The moon Pathea glowed through the trees while they set off on their way out of the forest. They swished through the piled leaves, and a voice yelled out behind them.

Startled, Ambrielle and Gavian glanced at each other. There was nothing in the forest but branches swaying with the soft wind. They heard the voices again. Ambrielle grabbed Gavian's hand, ready to run.

"It sounds like someone in distress," Wegin informed them.

They cautiously stepped back toward the hole, and the voice became clearer. "Hey! It's dark in here! We can't see a thing!"

Gavian turned on his silbrace light, aiming it into the hole. Darby and Dexius stood at the bottom of the cave, waving their arms at them.

"What are you guys doing here?" Gavian said. "You said you would close the rift."

"We did," said Darby. "We decided to help you fight the Shadows!"

"Are you sure it closed all the way?" Ambrielle peered at them over Gavian's shoulder.

"I'm positive," said Darby. "It's all completely solid now."

Gavian looked back at Ambrielle. "So, the path through the waterfall still works, even with the rift sealed."

"I suppose the energy is still there," said Ambrielle. "If the Shadows come directly through the rift, it closes them off. Hopefully they can't come through the water."

"It would probably turn them into mekkadium if they tried to go through the waterfall or the spring," Gavian said.

"Are you going to get us out of here or what?" said Dexius impatiently.

"Stop shouting," Gavian advised. "The Darterrans will be waking up soon."

Gavian attached the light rope to a nearby tree, lowering himself into the cave. He took Darby up first and then Dexius.

"I suppose I have to believe you now." Dexius surveyed the new world. In the setting sun, leaves of blue, green, red, and gold clustered densely through the forest, with the mighty balcain trees towering over them.

"Welcome to Anatharia," Ambrielle said. "Do you still have your memory?"

"The Grundians, Rethia, yes it's all still there," Dexius said.

Darby held up one of her mekkadium arrows. "We had these with us."

They made their way out of the forest to the lake at the foot of Mekkinspire. Darby and Dexius stared up in awe at the mountain as they came to the basin where one of the waterfalls poured into the lake.

"Dive in with your whole body submerging as fast as possible," Ambrielle said.

Dexius furrowed his brow. "What are we doing now?"

"We're off to another world," Gavian said and jumped in, splashing into the lake.

Darby shifted her weight from one foot to the other as she glanced at Ambrielle, as if to ask if she should go ahead. Ambrielle nodded yes, and Darby leapt into the water. Ambrielle waited for the surface to settle and dove in. Taking in a deep breath when she broke the plane between water and air, Ambrielle swam toward the banks of the spring where Gavian and Darby attempted to squeeze dry their wet clothing.

The slow-moving sun of Solsellion neared the horizon, shining its red rays between the trees. Watching the ripples in the water fade, Gavian paced impatiently along the edge of the spring. "Do you think he changed his mind?"

"You never know with Dex," said Darby.

"He'll be here." Ambrielle stared at the blue glow from the cave at the bottom of the spring.

"Maybe we should go back," Gavian said. "Talk to him again."

Dexius splashed out of the water, coughing loudly. Once he climbed out, he leaned over, still coughing. Darby went to him, but he waved her off. After a moment, he straightened his back, walking to them. "Don't tell me there are more worlds to jump through."

"No." Ambrielle headed toward the red trees. "We're here."

"So, what now?" Dexius tried to shake the water out of his long hair.

Gavian waited at the edge of the forest. "Ambrielle's bladestaff is made of mekkadium. We have to get it to Avo'Doria," he said. "The sentinels can help us finish cleansing this world of Nulthereals."

Ambrielle led Darby and Dexius onto the synthetic road made of solid light, which carried them swiftly through the forest. The drones flying overhead left them gaping in disbelief. The path carried them through a wave-shaped archway where it ended, allowing them to step into a great hall inside the main complex. The floor contained tiles of many colors, creating intricate patterns that stretched out ahead of them. Each tile varied in size and shape but somehow fit together perfectly.

At the end of the hall, several figures stood in a circle, surrounding a projection of many spheres of light. "I'm afraid that is all the data we could find," said a voice from the group.

"If this was so important, why would they tell us so little?" another voice asked.

"Based on my analysis, the founders were cautious. They were likely concerned that widespread knowledge could lead to it falling into the wrong hands. More than anything, they did not want to risk being destroyed," a third voice added.

The four of them reached the end of the hall. The colored lights of the projection reflected on the faces of the six people standing around it. Ambrielle recognized Syra'Dosa among them.

"Ambrielle," said Syra'Dosa. "It is good to see you again."

"It's good to see you too." Ambrielle relaxed upon seeing someone familiar.

"We brought the black stone I was telling you about," Gavian said, as Ambrielle raised the bladestaff toward them.

"Excellent," said Syra'Dosa. "But it seems we were able to procure a portion already."

"What?" Gavian exclaimed "How?"

Syra'Dosa gestured toward two people behind the projection. "May I introduce—"

"Tavarian?" a woman said, stepping through the glowing light.

Gavian's eyes widened. "Malidora! What are you doing here?"

"So, this is why they brought me here," Dexius said and stepped forward. "If you wanted to see me this badly, you could have just asked."

Malidora tilted her head and looked at Gavian. "Of all the people in the universe, you brought *him*?" Her flame-colored hair sprung around her face as she straightened her stance. "Is that? Darby?"

Darby smiled and nodded her head. Her timidity seemed to have returned with these surroundings that were unfamiliar to her.

"It's hard to believe four years have passed for you. I think it's only been a year for me," said Malidora. "Syra'Dosa believes time is volatile between The Hollow and this universe."

"It seems we have a new objective," stated Syra'Dosa. "But we have little information to go on."

Malidora cocked her hip. "We need to find the awakener."

"The awakener?" Gavian queried, a mischievous grin playing on his lips. "That shouldn't be too hard."

Malidora looked at him, curiosity gleaming in her golden eyes. "You know where to find them?"

Gavian's touch on Ambrielle's shoulder was comforting, his gaze filled with assurance. "I already have."

Ambrielle's heart quickened as everyone in the room fixated on her. Though not always fond of being the center of attention, a sense of purpose surged within her. She had always been drawn to the unknown, but this time felt different, as if the universe was calling out to her. It felt good to be needed once again.

END

Bewilderness is a five book series and Book 5,
the final book, will be coming soon!

THANKS FOR READING!
I would love to know what you thought of Stormwaker.
Please don't forgot to leave a comment on Amazon!

JOIN MY NEWSLETTER AND GET A FREE BOOK!
Get my short story, Elyravess, free when
you sign up to my newsletter at https://authorkevincox.com
The newsletter will give you monthly
updates on upcoming books in the series,
behind the scenes, and artwork!

In ancient Elyravess, a young boy's chance encounter with the daughter
of a galactic archaeologist leads to a discovery that will alter the course of
their future and the fate of their worlds.

ACKNOWLEDGEMENTS

I would like to begin by expressing my gratitude to God for providing me with the strength, guidance, and inspiration to complete this book. Without His blessings, this accomplishment would not have been possible.

To my family, who have always been my pillars of support and encouragement throughout my life, thank you for standing by me every step of the way. Your belief in me has been a constant source of motivation and inspiration.

To my friends, thank you for your unwavering support, your kind words, and your valuable feedback. Your presence in my life has enriched me in ways I cannot express.

I would like to extend my deepest gratitude to Emily Katzenberger, my exceptionally talented and dedicated developmental editor. Her insightful feedback, keen editorial eye, and unwavering support transformed this manuscript into something special. Her commitment to refining the story, characters, and overall narrative structure played a pivotal role in bringing this book to life. I am immensely grateful for her expertise and guidance throughout this creative journey.

Once again, thank you to all those who have contributed to the creation of this book. Your support and encouragement have meant the world to me.

ABOUT THE AUTHOR

Author Kevin Cox has always been fascinated by the splendor of the universe and the mysteries it holds, using his imagination to fill in the vast unknown. Though he never planned to be a writer, he often had ideas for stories playing in his head. After deciding to write a single chapter to see if he could do it, he discovered a love for writing he never knew was there.

Much of his inspiration comes from growing up during the 80's, reading and watching all the fantasy and science fiction stories he could find. Ideas come to him during long drives or while listening to music. He often listens to music while writing, especially songs that match the mood he is trying to capture.

He believes that a good story needs great characters that each have struggles and desire to find ways to overcome them. Kevin hopes that his readers will see their own struggles in these characters and are inspired to find their own strengths and always be learning and improving to be the best version of themselves. Connection with friends and willingness to help others are central themes in his writing.

Kevin lives in southwest Georgia in a small town called Leesburg. When he isn't writing, he enjoys playing guitar and video games.

Please contact or follow on social media.

For the latest news and info on the next book in the series.

Email: authorkevincox@gmail.com
Instagram: @kevincoxauthor
Twitter: @authorkevincox

OTHER WORKS

KEVIN COX
BEWILDERNESS
BOOK ONE

KEVIN COX
SHADOWSPHERE
BEWILDERNESS
BOOK TWO

KEVIN COX
NEVERSCAPE
BEWILDERNESS
BOOK THREE

Bewilderness: Book One and Shadowsphere

Available on Amazon.com
https://www.amazon.com/dp/B09J3Z9J2F

Named one of the BEST BOOKS OF 2022 by Kirkus

"This meticulously crafted YA journey will challenge
readers' expectations until the last page."

— Kirkus Reviews (starred review)

When a young girl wakes up in an unknown world and encounters
dark forces that threaten the universe, only she can change its destiny.

*Accessing portals to other realms, Ambrielle journeys across multiple
worlds as she searches for answers to find her way home.*

Sixteen-year-old Ambrielle has no memory of her life. In fact, she doesn't
even know if her name is Ambrielle, the name her new alien friend gave
her when she woke up mysteriously stranded in a desolate world with
no humans. As she slowly cobbles together bits and pieces of her life,
Ambrielle tries to fit in with the many alien species she encounters and
settle their divisive conflicts, all while eluding shadowy entities from
a realm beyond the universe as she seeks a way to return to Earth.